Pries

finit due
nov. 10/61

The

TROUBLED
MIDNIGHT

The
TROUBLED
MIDNIGHT

A NOVEL BY
JOHN GUNTHER

HARPER & BROTHERS PUBLISHERS

New York and London

2-5

FIRST EDITION

M-T

To

Leonora Morris

CONTENTS

The

TROUBLED

MIDNIGHT

Leslie at Taksim's

I

SOMETIMES they toss a child under your car. Unpleasant, what!" He lit a cigarette, and blew the smoke out slowly.

Strangeways wondered what kind of young woman this was. You could never tell about Americans. He couldn't quite make her out. Of course this was the first time they had dined together. He looked closely at her strong, clear face, and thought that she seemed friendly, earnest, human. Yes, above all, human. She had certainly known the bite of sorrow, which might account for her quality of reserve. You might call her too crisp, but that was like the veil of gossamer ice covering a warm spring.

She certainly seemed to know her way about politically, for an American, even if she was a Government Official on a Mission Abroad.

At his words, Leslie hunched her shoulders up. She made a twisting grimace of distaste, and shook her head sharply, as if to say, "But people can't really do things like that!"

Not even Germans . . . She knew why she was reacting so violently; her mind froze on a recollected image of Berlin, an image which never left her, but which was usually dormant. She blinked to keep a long blackness from returning.

"Matter of fact, they don't kill much nowadays," Strangeways went on calmly. "Turkish police took a very dim view of it. Can't afford antagonize the local police, y'know."

He proceeded, "We lost a man . . . about six months ago. One of our best men, too. Poor chap." But his voice was

1

casual, almost light. "They kidnapped him, took him to their embassy, and got what they wanted, maybe. Then stuffed the corpse in a mail sack and shipped it to Sofia on the Lufthansa plane. Carried it as mail. Damned original, what!"

"If you like being original that way, well, I suppose you'd call it original," Leslie said. But she always took a very personal view of things and she began to wonder about the man in the mail sack. Had he been young, was he dark or fair, had someone loved him, did he have a family? She asked Strangeways, almost with resentment, "How did they happen to catch him? Why didn't they get you instead?"

"Ha!" His laugh had a quick ironic snap. The sound went upward. "Because they damn well couldn't lay their hands on me!"

Leslie made an effort to be more detached. "Do our people do things like that too—make away with people and so on?"

He looked at her fine, brilliant eyes, which were the color of strong coffee lifted out of the cup in a silver spoon. This was probably a girl capable of much, Strangeways thought. He was about to answer, "You know perfectly well we do," but instead, a shade guardedly, he replied, "What makes you wonder?"

She responded levelly: "Because war brings out the worst in everybody, doesn't it?" She was a woman, and, though wars might be necessary, they were an indignity to her kind.

Still, they had to be won. They might tear the soul loose from the roots, blast the beating heart out of the body, but it was better to win than lose them. Why was she here except to add her infinitesimal bit to winning?

"It brings out the best too. Never forget that."

"I wonder." She had read that in books, but she didn't necessarily believe it yet. "I don't understand about tossing babies under cars. What does that get them?"

"Oh . . . easy!" His voice was cold and facile. "Suppose you're driving along and you run over somebody. It's embarrassing. Ties you up. Probably you get arrested. Nuisance with police, publicity, and all that. Destroys usefulness. Or maybe you want to get out of the country in a hurry. You can't, if you're mixed up in a serious accident. And of course the chap who did the baby-tossing, nobody catches him, he gets away. The baby? Oh, they pick up any baby."

Again she shuddered. Strangeways ordered two vodka-vermouths, and she lifted her glass evenly. Behind her coolness, her reserve, there was something flashing, something that could burn out into the open any minute.

He offered her a cigarette.

"No thanks."

"Don't you smoke?"

"I used to."

"It dulls the appetite?"

She shook her head. "No. I gave up cigarettes when the Germans took Paris. I swore not to smoke again until they were driven out. Maybe it sounds silly . . . But I loved Paris. I felt . . ."

"You were doing a penance for all our sins? Self-punishment, what?"

She looked at him with the coffee-colored eyes. "Not quite. I haven't got much sense of sin. It was just a gesture."

"Do you show so much will power over everything?"

She gave a clear round laugh. "It depends on the circumstances."

"Damned good. Well, anyway, if things develop as we hope, you won't have long to wait." He drank his vodka, with a quick toss. "We'd better order dinner. Food quite tolerable here. I can recommend the shashlik." He resumed: "Of course they go to such artifices as shipping bodies out in mail sacks because you can't just toss stuff in the Bosphorus any more. Damned sticky, the Turkish police. Besides, a *corpus delicti* may show marks. Not professional. Not very neat." He looked around for a waiter. "Matter fact, all this espionage stuff is getting rather dull. Very cut and dried. Most of it paper work nowadays. Not much melodrama to it any more. Yet—"

Why was he talking to her this way, she wondered? Now he

was describing what the Gestapo did when they got someone, what they did with your fingernails and a lighted candle on the soles of your feet. Her face almost showed hatred that he was telling her things like this. Was he trying to test her, to see if she had guts? Yet she listened with horrified fascination; she could not keep from listening.

"Now, take the chrome."

"Yes, the chrome." She did not want to sound unfriendly, but she thought she might mimic him, this Englishman who almost seemed a parody of an Englishman. "The chrome, what."

"Eh? Well, it's a bloody nuisance, all the work we have to do on chrome. Important, though. Dull, but important. The Boche gets all his chromium from here. Needs it badly, too. Can't make armor-piercing shells without chrome. Well, you know, damned strange things happen out in the mines. Damned strange." He was looking at her with a special keenness, his eyes wrinkling. "When the Boche has to get his chrome out fast, there may be a sudden shortage of rail transport; no goods wagons at all, not a goods wagon in a hundred miles. Peculiar, eh?"

"You mean we have men out there? Sabotage?"

"Call it that if you like. A conveyor belt gets broken, say. Very strange, but if we're on the job, all the resources of your great country and mine won't be able to procure a substitute conveyor belt of exactly that type, for months and months. What do you think of that? Deuced peculiar, isn't it?"

"You mean our people are doing all right?"

His eyes shifted suddenly, and she thought that he was going to say No, that our people were not doing all right. But he retreated into an enigmatic look.

"Quite a show we get here," Strangeways changed the subject. "Glance at that table behind the pillar. That's the German press attaché. Poisonous little rat. Next to him is our councilor of Embassy. Look: how they avoid catching each other's eye. That table over there is Vichy French, and next to them are Jugoslavs. There's the Swedish minister

coming in; see how he bows, both to us and Axis. Damn
the blasted neutrals. Now: don't watch too conspicuously;
that's the Jap ambassador. We rather liked the little blighter
before the war. That blonde?—she's Viennese, name of Eva;
being kept by a Swiss."

"Do you know everybody, Mr. Strangeways?"

"Almost."

"Are you a member of the British secret service," she
smiled, "or is that an improper question?"

"My dear girl, *all* Englishmen are members of the British
secret service."

She laughed: "Are any other people in the world so sure
of themselves as the English, do you suppose?"

"Ah, André," Strangeways said. The waiter was a short
young man, very dark, with sloping shoulders. Strangeways
addressed him with a peculiar mixture of condescension,
familiarity, and respect. "André, we'll start with the pilaff,
shall we?" The waiter noted the order soberly. "And I'm hoping the shashlik will be particularly good tonight." André
turned his eyes on Leslie, and she was startled. She had
never seen such eyes. They were so darkly luminous you
could not see the pupils. They were both reproachful and
imploring, and they stared at her piercingly, almost accusingly.
They seemed to say, "Do not talk to me, unless you too have
known what suffering is. Do not take me into your community, because I know too much of the bitterness of death
and mortal burdens."

There was something threatening in his eyes too, and
Leslie felt vaguely frightened. The single glimpse she had
had of this waiter's eyes told her more of the tragedies and
bondages of this part of the world than anything Strangeways
had imparted. She thought, "I feel a pattern." Only once
or twice in her life had she had such a compelling intuition,
such a feeling of the imminence of charted but invisible events.
She felt almost as she had felt the evening she met Hal
Corcoran. "Why am I here?" she asked herself. She won-

dered what had brought her here, though she had thought she knew.

"What's wrong?" Strangeways said looking at her sharply, and she pulled her eyes toward him, with her lower lip trembling.

"That waiter . . ."

"André's all right. He's a Greek."

"It's silly . . . but somehow he frightened me."

"We'll take good care of you. I can promise you that."

"You mean I won't end up in a sack?"

II

Now Strangeways was telling her about Taksim's; everybody in Istanbul came here in the warm spring evenings. "Like Fouquet's in Paris or the Café Royal in London, don't you know." But it conveyed more than the mood and atmosphere of any western metropolis; it conveyed the Orient too, he pointed out. The Turks did not look very Oriental. They seemed western, hard-headed, and realistic. But only a generation separated them from the Turkey of the seraglio, of fat-hipped women with rippling bellies, of eunuchs in striped bloomers, of plangent chants to Allah from tall minarets, of the suppressions and cruelties of Abdul-Hamid. Here at Taksim's half a mile from the Bosphorus and Golden Horn, Europe merged into Asia, Asia merged into Europe, and the dividing line might be a silver fork on any table.

Leslie followed Strangeways' voice and gestures. The restaurant was set in a private grove; tables on broad terraces flanked three sides of an open-air dance floor, which projected like a drawbridge. At one end was a stage, and at the other a bank of trees, with nests in the lower boughs for spotlights, so that the whole effect was that of an amphitheater. But if it were chilly, one could dine inside, where the restaurant proper was decorated in maroon, ivory, and gilt. Upstairs was a small bar, with a series of loges opening on a terrace and overlooking the big dance floor beneath. Tonight it was warm, with a milky lopsided moon, and the moonlight sank slowly through the trees of the grove, flaking them with silver. Soon Florian and the other Hungarian entertainers would put on their show.

Strangeways kept on talking. Not only was Taksim's a bridge between Europe and Asia; it bridged Axis and Allies too. People pumped in from Sofia, from Bucharest, from Cracow, Prague, and Athens; they might be German army officers, Balkan *agents provocateurs*, or frightened neutrals; they came by Lufthansa plane straight from Berlin, or by bullock cart across secret frontiers. And from the other direction, from New York, from London, from Algiers and Cairo, came Britons, Americans, Fighting French, men of the Allies; three times a week they were gathered into the steel blue flanks of the Taurus Express at Ankara, and discharged in a close-mouthed, cryptic stream at Haydar Pasa. Almost everybody had either just arrived from somewhere, or was taking off somewhere in a day or two. And so, Strangeways explained, Istanbul had become a kind of neutral cosmopolis, the end of a journey, and the gate to everywhere. And of those who arrived to knock on this gate, a good proportion came every night to Taksim's. He smiled: "At least those who can afford it."

But despite the bland moonlight, the intermixture and intertwining of friend and enemy, the throaty purr of the downstairs orchestra which was now preparing its first number, despite the blonde Hungarians in their pretty dresses at a dozen tables, despite the tart bottles of Turkish wine and the French champagne at forty dollars a quart, Leslie saw that Taksim's gave a note of drabness and sobriety. People did not come here merely to play. They came to work. The effervescence, the gaiety, were all on the surface. Underneath was the hard unknown core of what tomorrow might bring, the tomorrow no one could exorcise beyond a night. There were very few women, except the Hungarians; Turks did not commonly show their womenfolk in night clubs. And the fact that almost all the men wore such bad clothes—worn, shabby suits years old—gave a peculiar added touch; it

reinforced the atmosphere of deadly earnestness and seriousness. There was something almost sinister about Taksim's.
Even when an occasional rich refugee spent money in a big
way, he spent it coldly as if it were buying nothing but tem-
porary surcease.

André brought Strangeways and Leslie their dinner; it
started with a pilaff of the superlative Turkish lobster. Later
would come the shashlik, stuffed peppers, and a bottle of
Kavaklidere wine.

A tall dark-blond youth with a crew haircut and a cheerful grin drifted in, looking lonely. Strangeways identified him;
he was a new arrival for the O.W.I. He joined three other
young Americans who were drinking at the downstairs bar;
they were newspaper men and they wore soft white shirts and
looked bored and casual. One of the Hungarian girls meandered toward the bar, hitching her skirt over her hips as she
walked, and Leslie saw the Americans greet her amiably and
buy her a drink. Hungary was an enemy state, of course. She
asked Strangeways, "Can we mix with Axis people?"

"We don't, as a rule. The Germans are encouraged to mix;
they think they can pick up stuff. But when you see an Englishman or an American with Axis, it usually means he has
specific orders to be with them."

"Even the Hungarian girls?"

For a second, Leslie thought that she saw emotion in his
face, as if he were worried about something. "Well, in some
cases—" he stopped short.

"You mean you have trouble resisting them?" she smiled
warmly.

Before he could reply, Mr. Poppa, one of the proprietors of
Taksim's, came up making his rounds. He was a very fat man,
shaped almost like a top, who giggled. Also Strangeways knew
Mr. Poppa to be one of the most interesting characters in
Istanbul. He greeted the Englishman with bursting cordiality,
looked at Leslie with appraisal, rubbed his fat hands together, and waited greedily for an introduction. Later he proceeded to say good evening to the German press attaché,

bowing and bubbling at his table with the same mannerisms. Mr. Poppa pretended to be a modern Turk, but he still maintained a mental harem, and an invisible fez was still perched on his moon-shaped head.

"Quite a chap, Poppa," Strangeways said. "I used to wonder what made him tick. Then I gave up wondering; he's simply a man who likes to enjoy himself. Everything is a game to him, a show, or a business, like his own Taksim's."

Leslie pointed to a table across the center aisle, between the marble pillars with their gilt flutings. The burly man sitting there had a shaven skull and two thick folds of fat behind his neck. "That must be a German," she guessed.

Strangeways laughed, "Matter fact he's a Scotsman. The assistant manager of the Ottoman Bank."

Strangeways was looking at Leslie carefully now, between his quick sentences. She certainly wore good clothes; she made most of the other women, except Florian, look like frights. He did not know the technical terminology very well, but mostly she was in black and a little white. Her black dress, pencil slim, was of fine sheer wool; the long sleeves ended in white lace cuffs, which fell lightly over her hands, flattering them; Louis XIV cuffs, Strangeways thought they were called. The neck was cut in a V, also lined with white lace, and her small black hat had three thin rows of starched white lace on the brim. She carried short white doeskin gloves. No jewelry to speak of, except a big clip in the shape of a ballet dancer, set with what looked to be rose diamonds. She had a smaller clip of similar design on a black doeskin bag.

Damned good-looking girl, Strangeways thought. More than that: unusual-looking, interesting-looking. He almost always observed people's hands first, and hers were strong and lovely, very slim but with vitality; you could see that they were made of flesh. Her wrists were small and finely turned, underneath the crisp lace cuffs, and the perfect ovals of her dusty-rose nails, especially the little finger nail, were like narrow, highly-polished, and beautifully pointed almonds.

He studied her face. It was a good face, vital and harmonious with a clear broad forehead and a sensible shrewd nose. Of course the eyes were remarkable, with the irises and pupils so brilliant and the whites so white. Her mouth was remarkable too: quite small and determined, a selfish mouth perhaps, but with very full, round, ripe lips. Like a small moist balloon, he thought. Or a moist scarlet tire; that is, if a tire could be beautiful.

The O.W.I. boy had been carefully watching their table, and he sauntered up. Strangeways introduced him, and after a drink he asked Leslie to dance; with Strangeways' permission she slipped from her chair and walked with him to the floor. She seemed completely at ease with herself, and therefore at ease with men. Yet she gave a note . . . how would he define it . . . something akin to sadness, of sadness and expectancy . . . of freedom too.

The Englishman lit a cigarette and watched her dancing; American women with those fabulous waistlines always looked so well on a dance floor and most of them danced so superbly. He even noticed her shoes: black pumps of perforated suede, with a double bow. And of course her legs were wonderful. Her body too was provocative, but with a sense of reserve. Her shoulders were slim and her breasts seemed small, firm, and high. Of course you could never tell how girls got themselves up underneath. Her hips were smoothly oval, full, and curving, even in that straight dress. You got a sense of everything concentrated there between the hips.

The O.W.I. boy deposited her back at the table, graceful and self-possessed. "Imagine!" she exclaimed. "If anybody had told me three months ago I'd be dancing under moonlight in Constantinople!" And for the first time this evening, she seemed happy.

III

After dinner and coffee she became more aware of what Strangeways looked like and what he was. Alexander Strangeways might have been a diamond merchant in Johannesburg. Or the editor of an old-established British newspaper in Bombay. Or a ne'er-do-well keeping up front on the China coast. Or a sportsman or civil servant in Wellington, Vancouver, Nairobi, or Pall Mall. The locale didn't matter, or even the profession. Strangeways would be the same anywhere. Probably he was about fifty-five, though he looked younger. He was tallish, leanish and graying. He had bright and rather protuberant blue eyes, and his cheeks were flat, red, and glazed. He wore a smudge of graying mustache, and his clothes seemed poured on him with an inch to spare; he had that look of always having kept himself perfectly fit, despite much casual living. Above all he gave the sense of being British; more than that, of being British by dedication. He conveyed the note of active fidelity to a British ideal. He might mock this ideal, jibe at it, laugh at it and himself; but it was always there. The only permanent reality in his life was the British Empire, which he served in his own fashion. He was British, he had never been anything but British, and he would be British to the end.

"Over there," Strangeways pointed, "is a new arrival among your compatriots. Been here a couple of weeks, and I'm afraid we'll have to get rid of him. Talks too much."

"It's a national trait. Most of us do."

"Yes. That's why Americans are seldom good at security work. I don't mean they blab secrets. Oh, not at all. But they can't resist boasting. Funny, eh? Take an Englishman. He'll come here with some big secret job, and do his work quietly under any old kind of tag. No conceit about it. Young American pops in, maybe he'll be called a third secretary. Bless me, he isn't that at all. But what does the silly blighter do? Tells everybody what he really is! Bloody silly, what. Vanity, thy name is U.S.A. Oh, sorry, no offense."

There is a peculiar quality about this man, Leslie thought. He's too clipped and glib, yes. But that's not it. Something seems to be gnawing at him, yes. But that's not it, either. He has a strange kind of coldness, heartlessness. Perhaps dedicated men always became somewhat inhuman, she reflected. Perhaps all men completely absorbed by an ideal or an idea, and serving it to the uttermost, became to some extent dehumanized. But there was more, she kept on thinking. There was a kind of hollowness about Strangeways, as if he were empty. Something sucked out of him. The sap and vitality mostly gone.

Crisply she picked up the thread of talk: "Aren't you being rather indiscreet in telling me all you've been telling?"

"My dear girl, I haven't told you anything that isn't gossip in every bazaar. Give anything away? My aunt! I'm British; we British never give anything away, you know."

She could not help laughing: his expression was so indignant. He went on sharply, "For all I know you may have been sent out here to check up on me. As a matter of fact you might even be a Nazi spy. Not that it's very likely."

"Well, I'm not."

"You can never tell in this business. That is, you ought to be able to tell if you're any good at it, but sometimes the best of us make mistakes. We're all human, aren't we?"

"Even if you toss babies under cars?"

"*We* don't do that. I say!"

"It is a strange kind of business. Why are you in it?"

"There's a war on. It's my job."

When Strangeways first met Leslie at the Embassy tea early in the week he asked her to dinner at once. You didn't see girls like this in Istanbul very often. He had been lonely for a long time now. His wife had borne him three children, but he had not been in love with her for years. He was conventional; but also like so many Englishmen of the upper class he was utterly beyond morals. This was, he sometimes reflected, not so much a symptom of decadence as of a growing sexlessness. Healthily sexed people took love seriously; love for a woman counted above anything; it meant life or death. It was the undersexed who, as a rule, were profligate, perverse, corrupt.

The minute he laid eyes on Leslie Strangeways thought, in the abstract, how pleasant it would be to make love to her. But now, after an hour or two, he knew that there was little likelihood that they would ever be anything but friends. She simply had no interest in him that way. Even as a potentiality it was impossible. You could always tell. You could tell in an hour. And he was too inert in heart, too scooped out by vicissitude, to undertake a long pursuit. Anyway, a pursuit would probably be useless. She gave the note of being completely virtuous, not given to promiscuous affairs. But, dash it all, no harm in being a little personal . . .

"I can see you don't want to flirt with me." He smiled; when he was young, women had liked his smile. "But you're going to be bowled over by all the youngsters in town, and I want to get full benefit of my innings, eh. Tell me something about yourself."

"I'm a little afraid to say anything after your talk about how Americans are indiscreet. My own life seems so dull, compared to all that's going on here."

He noticed another quality she seemed to have, neatness. Look at her shoulders in the black wool, which were immaculate. She was almost dainty. Not a speck of dust or a misplaced hair.

"I can give you a thumbnail sketch. But really, it isn't very exciting. I'm twenty-seven, I was born in upper New York State. After college I lived abroad for a while. The war came and I wanted to be useful, but I didn't think I'd be much good as a nurse or a Wac or a Wave. I know French and German fairly well and I got a job in Washington with the Lend Lease Administration. I worked there from Pearl Harbor till last winter. Then the Lend Lease office here was shorthanded and needed someone who knew languages, and I was asked if I'd come out for a while. So I came. That's all there is."

"I don't know much about American women. Are many of them like you? You've managed to tell me the story of your life without any mention of what's important, namely, love."

What business was it of his, she said to herself, inwardly shrugging. Still if he wanted to talk this way, why not? It was bound to happen at any dinner. Besides, she wanted to be polite. There was absolutely no spark between them; he gave out no emotion at all. But he was a man in an interesting position, who might be useful, and with whom it would be pleasant to dine once in a while. And like almost all Americans she wanted to be liked. And the easiest way to be liked was to like.

"Of course I left all that out. Purposely. My life that way has been rather . . . botched up."

"Everybody's is, in wartime. Are you in love with anybody now?" She's been badly knocked about, more so than she'll admit, he thought.

"As of tonight, April 6, 1944, at about ten in the evening, no. I can't answer for a month from now."

"So you're looking for a man I suppose."

She thought she would reply with the obvious remark that that was what all girls did, but she surprised herself by saying, earnestly and with complete candor, "No. Really. No. One might happen of course. But I'm certainly not looking for anybody. Good Lord, no. I'm trying to forget . . ."

He did not know how to reply for a second. Her seriousness put it all on a different plane, and he reached for something to match her mood. "What you say probably means you've had a good deal of a past."

"Not necessarily." She was drawing her lipstick from the doeskin bag; her eyes were averted slightly.

"People don't resent the past if it doesn't interfere with the present," Strangeways proffered, watching her.

So he's intelligent, Leslie thought. "That's right." She looked up. "And do you know why? Because people change . . . They become different persons."

This girl is quite bright, Strangeways thought. For the first time their eyes met closely. Their minds had made contact, and now they could be friends.

IV

Now the floor show was beginning, and Leslie squeezed closer into her chair with a quiver of anticipation. The orchestra tuned up, and a restless pause came over the

somber, glittering world of Taksim's. As the lights were
dimmed Mr. Poppa escorted a dark young man to a corner
booth a few yards from their table; as he passed them
closely she felt that he knew Strangeways, but he did not
nod or bow; she felt too that the dark young man, who
seemed to give out a note of something both attractive and
menacing, was looking her over swiftly, with a competent
masculine appraisal.

She felt Strangeways touch her arm. He whispered,
"There's a chap to watch. That's Hugo Reichenau."

"Who's he?"

"The enemy."

She glanced at her watch; it was midnight. A spotlight
roved through the terraces; it passed over their table and then
the booth where Reichenau was sitting. He appeared to be
fairly tall; his shoulders looked compact and graceful, and he
had strong bony hands. His head was big and his hair dark;
probably he was about thirty-two or thirty-three. He had a
straight nose, under brows which almost met—or perhaps it
was a V of hair between them—and a big hard mouth. She
could not see the color of his eyes. He looked fervid,
aggressive, and, she groped for a word, nocturnal. She could
feel an aura of intense magnetism spread from him.

"Hugo's quite a character," Strangeways murmured
guardedly. "And dangerous. He's their best man, all in all.
Does most of their fancy work especially in regard to British
and Americans. Been to the States. Knows English well. He
came here from Buenos Aires where he was their commercial
councilor. Or at least that's what they called it. Quite a
sportsman. Plays good tennis. And quite a ladies' man.
Hangs around here a lot, picking up pretty girls." Strangeways paused, and Leslie saw a compact grimness in his face;
the blue eyes were icy slits. "I'd like to get him. Break up
their organization. I will, some day."

Leslie reflected how remarkable it was that a woman
should be stimulated when she heard that someone was a
great ladies' man and dangerous. It was exciting; it put a

woman on her mettle. But she asked quietly, "How would you go about getting him?"

Strangeways grunted. "Oh, lots of ways."

"You measure him for a sack?" She smiled awarely.

"Tut, tut. No, the easiest way isn't so melodramatic. It's always easiest to buy them out. Every once in a while they want to give."

"Give?"

"Blab. Change sides. Sell out."

"How do you guard against their double-crossing you?"

"Oh, easy. Ship 'em out of the country. Promise 'em immunity, and intern 'em for the duration, say in Kenya or the Sudan. Quite safe, if you do it right!"

Leslie pondered. The unshakable superiority of these British . . . "Why should you assume he's less patriotic than you?" she asked.

"I don't necessarily assume it. He's tough and dangerous; he's a real fanatic—really believes in all the Nazi pap. Just the same, I have my doubts. Not the last ditch type. And like *all* Nazis he's on the make. Every Nazi has a breaking point. Hugo's been around; he's a cosmopolitan. He must see that the game is practically up, he must see the way the wind is blowing, what!"

Leslie felt suddenly that she might giggle. She felt a little groggy. This was all very serious, but she had an almost uncontrollable desire to laugh hysterically. Here she was in Istanbul sipping coffee under a Turkish moon, about to watch an entertainment that would doubtless be all foam and tinsel; yet beside her was a man who had life and death at his fingertips and who talked of tossing children under cars and what you could do to a man, with refinements, before he broke and the shattered spirit rushed screaming from the body. And sitting twenty feet away was the enemy. And the enemy, who did all these things, was a powerful-looking young man who, unless she was gravely mistaken, was covertly inspecting her as she was inspecting him.

"What would you pay for Reichenau?" she could not help asking. "What's he worth to you?"

"A lot."

"I don't understand just why." Her face was warm and earnest.

"Well, for one thing he could tell us about Nazi plans everywhere in this region. He might even bring the codes."

She wanted to say, but again she was afraid she might giggle, "May I offer you my services? Could I help you get him?" She felt gooseflesh up her trim arms.

He looked at her oddly, as if guessing her thoughts. "It's no game for nice girls. But I'd pay a lot."

CHAPTER II

Enter Florian and Gerald

I

THE orchestra blurted out a fanfare, and a girl in gypsy costume slipped out on the stage, descended to the floor, and danced a Spanish number. All the Hungarian and Viennese girls who had been dining and dancing with the guests were now ready for the show.

"Not worth watching," Strangeways commented. "Name of Lilli. Hungarian, about twenty. Been here two years, engaged to the hall porter at the Serapia Hotel."

"Do you know all the girls, every one?" But Leslie still half-watched Hugo Reichenau. He was giving an order to André, the Greek waiter.

"Oh yes. They come and go. Rather nice crop just now. Of course none of them can hold a candle to Florian."

"Who's Florian?"

"The star. The queen of Taksim's. The queen of Istanbul. Tell you about her when she comes on."

"Are they all party girls?" She made a slight grimace.

"Party girls? Don't understand."

"You know, professionals."

"Oh, tarts. N-no. Hardly. We call 'em house girls. *Animierdamen*, the German name is. Girls who animate you. Why, they come down here, with contracts as entertainers, they sit around, they get a cut on the drinks of course, and you tip them if you dance. Sometimes they sleep with you, but as a rule they don't."

Like most women she was curious and a little excited when

18

men talked about professionally loose women or inferred that someone who looked respectable was a prostitute.

"Only one of this batch is an outright whore. Name of Kathi, you'll see her later. Quite a nice girl. But she's strictly business. Trying to save up enough cash to go back to Budapest and buy a millinery shop."

A clown number came next, and then a girl who played an accordion, and then Kathi—a girl with dark red hair—sang a ballad about the Wienerwald. It was all very decorous. In contrast Leslie remembered some floor shows she had seen in Paris and New York. Gracious! Then she heard steps behind her, and a tall blond man was approaching. He pulled a chair back, leaned over, smiled, and held out his hand.

"Well . . . Gerald!" Strangeways rose.

"Hi, Alec. Thought I'd see you here. Mind if I sit down?" His smile was disarming and also mischievous, as if he knew he deserved a spanking but hoped to avoid it.

"Mrs. Corcoran, may I present Gerald Heath."

They shook hands; he held his hand high across his chest in the English manner.

"When did you get back?" Strangeways asked. His manner was intimate, even idle, but the tone was surprised and cold.

"An hour ago. Thought I'd pop into town for a bit."

"Well . . . How's everything up there?"

"Pretty good. I 'phoned down, but couldn't get through to you."

"How long do you propose to stay here?"

"Oh, couple of days."

"And meantime, who tends to the little things you're supposed to be tending to?"

"Oh, Neale's watching everything. It's all in good hands." Gerald glanced at the nearby table. "I see Hugo is with us. Where's Florian?"

"Haven't seen her tonight. She'll be on in a minute, I daresay."

Leslie felt that if she had not been there, the conversation would have been quite different. Gerald, in an easy way, took advantage of the fact that Strangeways could hardly make a scene with a lady present. He turned to Leslie accepting her with a friendly nod, "New arrival, Mrs. Corcoran?" His smile was direct and gay. "You're not a refugee? You don't look the type, I must say."

"I suppose I might be called a refugee from Washington," Leslie said.

"We're all refugees from something, aren't we?" Gerald said, watching her.

"Including job and duty?" Strangeways' voice was sharp.

"Oh, come off it, Alec."

Gerald Heath looked, Leslie thought, rather like a younger edition of Strangeways; he had the same loose dress and understated manner. He must be in his early thirties. They both had a lean, greyhoundish appearance; though whereas Strangeways was a fatigued but experienced thoroughbred, Heath gave a note of tentativeness, of uncertainty. He was younger, stronger, with many races still to run. His cheeks were rounder than those of Strangeways, and his blue eyes much warmer. He looked as if he might blush easily, and the curving line of his smile, up into his full cheeks, made him seem affectionate, humorous, and graceful.

"Just seems hard to keep away from this town," Gerald said as if to himself, but smiling at Leslie. "You'll like it too, I hope."

Strangeways eased off: "Irresponsible folk, these youngsters who mix pleasurable business with painful pleasure . . ."

André came up, and with a cheerful grin Gerald set out to order dinner. "Don't know what I want," he ruminated over the menu. "Let's see. Suppose I have a double vodka and then the roast chicken. Is the chicken all that it should be, André? Well . . . Perhaps I don't want chicken after all." The Greek waited patiently. "Suppose you make me a filet, André. Very underdone, just in and out of the fire, *saignant, Englisch*." He hesitated. "And before that, a plate

of hors d'oeuvres. No, I'd rather have some consommé.
Beastly food we get up in the hinterland." André took the
order, and left the table; then Gerald called him back. "I say,
André, just a moment. I'll have hors d'oeuvres and the roast
chicken after all."

"Make up your mind, boy," Strangeways said.

"*Kellner!* Waiter!" the voice came sharply, commandingly,
from Hugo Reichenau's table, stopping André as he walked.

Reichenau pointed to his plate, as if to indicate that something was wanting, and André slowly plodded toward the
German, his shoulders hunched.

"*Schafskopf!*" Hugo snapped at him, but with a certain
ease. "Idiot!"

André stood there. He opened his mouth but did not speak.
Leslie could see his neck stiffen.

"*Die Suppe ist eiskalt. Nehmen Sie's zurück.* The soup is
ice-cold. Take it back."

Slowly, dutifully, with hatred in every gesture, André
took the soup from Hugo's table.

"And hurry up with it," the German ordered with a kind
of confident insolence. "Are all Greeks idiots? Soup is to be
eaten hot."

Gerald was watching and listening too. "You know I
think André would do our friend Hugo in just for fun, any
day of the week."

Strangeways said to Leslie, "Greeks are something special. André had a family in Athens. His wife died of
starvation."

Leslie watched Hugo, whose fingers nervously tapped the
table; she had a feeling he may have made himself so con-
spicuous in order to attract her attention.

Gerald reconsidered. "No. André's not very personal. He's
too serious. It's simply that he hates *all* Germans."

Mr. Poppa came up to pay his respects, and Gerald spoke
to him rapidly in a heavy foreign tongue.

"Is that what Turkish sounds like?" Leslie asked.

"Yes. Gerald knows the lingo. That's what makes him in-

dispensable. You are indispensable, aren't you, Gerald?"
Strangeways' tone was bantering, but with tightness in it.
"You are my best man, aren't you, Gerald."

Again Gerald said, "Oh, come off it, Alec," and turned
to Leslie, still smiling. He was boyish and apparently delighted with himself if only because he was back in Istanbul.

A British colonel in mufti passed down the aisle. No
foreigners were allowed to wear uniform in Turkey at this
time.

"Ah, old bloody ass," Gerald murmured.

"Who? What?" Leslie was curious.

"That old duffer who just walked by."

"Matter fact, he's a distinguished citizen," Strangeways
pointed out. "Only officer I ever heard of who won a
D.S.O. in the last war and another one in this."

"Exactly," Gerald said. "That's why he's such an ass."

"Now, Gerald."

"Imagine the silliness of anybody wanting to win a big
decoration in two separate wars."

"Relax, old chap."

"Bloody silly old ass."

"Take it easy, Gerald."

"Silly ass. Valor, gallantry, all that bloody rot!"

"Take it easy."

"All of it—bloody silly rot."

Then the orchestra trumpeted a double fanfare, and
Florian came out.

II

Florian was a tall girl, with two shades of glistening blonde
hair; she wore it in a high, solid pompadour, where it was
honey-color; then it fell shoulder length in a curling bob, the
color of molasses. She wore a strapless evening gown of dusty
tangerine, and her shoulders and breasts were wonderful,
Leslie saw. The dress was something, too. It clung smoothly,
form-fitting to the hips; then the full skirt flared out, so that
bluish shadows made furrows in the swinging taffeta. An-

other skirt of matching tangerine chiffon, glittering with sequins, hung filmily over the taffeta, and she carried a light chiffon scarf of the same color, playing with it as she sang. It was over her shoulders, over her hair, and in her hands.

Gerald was watching her fascinated. All the self-doubt and self-division that Leslie had seemed to glimpse in him vanished. He watched her like a man totally in focus at last; not only in focus, but utterly absorbed, condemned, possessed.

The minute you saw Florian, you knew that nobody else in the show was anything; she was everything. She was the only person who counted at Taksim's. She looked like a strong healthy girl but there was something extraordinarily feline about her. Leslie thought of a tiger, and the phrase tiger-tawny came to her mind. She wondered what color Florian's eyes would be, and she felt that she knew without seeing; they would be yellow eyes, topaz eyes. Her lashes would be dark gold and heavy, and she would use sea-green shadow on her lids.

Florian moved into her act, and Leslie's curiosity increased. She had an electric magnetism, but she was giving little of it out; she looked almost as if she were searching for something, as if she had mislaid something. First she sang an American tune that had just drifted into Istanbul, "I've Got You Under My Skin," and then a Viennese ditty, *"Ich küss die Hand, Madame"*; she sang it with a hardening of her voice, almost as if she were a man. The voice was not good. But it had a piercing resonant quality. Nor did she sing particularly well. She sang as if she held in contempt those who were listening, as if she hated having to sing for them. There was no happiness in it, no pleasure in performance or accomplishment; no singing heart, no heart at all.

But the audience billowed with rapturous applause. No one cared about her heart. They cared about her looks. She was beauty. She was passion. She was the unattainable who might become attainable. Even the women in the crowd clapped hungrily. For Florian seemed to be showing them what they themselves could be, if they were bold and confident enough.

"Well . . ." Strangeways sighed. His eyes looked upward; they were regarding something distant. "There you have it." His tone was now abrupt. "Name of Florian. Twenty-four. Born in Szeged, father a tailor, left home at sixteen, waitress in a *Konditorei*, got to Budapest, engaged to her dance partner, made a couple of Balkan tours—"

"Shut up, Alec."

"Hungarian citizen. Axis. Enemy. There you have it. Goes out with Hugo Reichenau. Name of Florian. Good-looking in an animal sort of way. Best known girl in town. But Axis. Enemy. Sleeps with enemy, too."

"God blast your bloody chatter." But Gerald's voice was still amiable. "What business is it of yours, anyway?"

"I'm just giving Mrs. Corcoran the picture, don't y'know."

Leslie put in, "I must say it's a very enticing picture. Any man would be lucky."

"But there's the patriotic angle, don't y'know," Strangeways pointed out. "Man involved with enemy, what."

Leslie wanted to be helpful; it was unnerving to have two men quarrel before her about another woman. Besides, she wanted to take Gerald's side. She smiled, "Nothing like war and patriotism to give a bit of zest to falling in love, I suppose."

Gerald snorted, "Patriotism, balls. Your country right or wrong, and all that rot, balls! Bilge! Balls!"

"Gerald, old boy, lady is present."

"Oh, sorry, Mrs. Corcoran," Gerald said. "Not that it matters"—he was all charm now—"but, really, I am sorry."

"It's nothing," Leslie replied. "Just count me as an interested listener."

"Forgive me," he repeated. "Alec gets into one of his vicious sardonic moods"—but he looked at Strangeways with a grin of affection—"and I go off the deep end. Sorry."

Strangeways interrupted with, "I don't get into a vicious mood except when you behave like a blasted fool."

"Well, bugger it, lay off!" Gerald said.

"All right, bugger it then. Sorry, Mrs. Corcoran."

"Well, bugger it!" And Gerald's eyes were now fixed on the stage, waiting for Florian to reappear.

Leslie thought: he apologizes too quickly. He must want terribly to be liked. He *needs* someone.

III

They became conscious of movement at the nearby booth, and Leslie saw that another man had joined Hugo Reichenau. He was heavy but cadaverous; he wore pince-nez and his skull was bald. As he talked to Hugo he seemed to pant heavily, and a malignant grin creased his face. A glassy grin. He kept pressing his palms together, pressing and rotating them one against the other, as he panted. Then Leslie noticed his lips. They were extraordinary. They lifted over his teeth as he talked. They were big, pale pink, and serrated with what seemed to be tooth marks, notched in squares as if the teeth had bitten out cubes of live flesh. Leslie shivered; there was evil in this man's face.

"That," murmured Strangeways softly, "is the well-known Dr. Max Dortmund, the former dentist."

"Who's he?" She was still shivering.

"Chief of Gestapo here. Hugo's boss."

Hugo listened to Dortmund with strict and disciplined attention; unobtrusively Leslie watched, and she overheard Hugo say a respectful *"Jawohl, Herr Doktor."* But she would have been willing to swear that all was not smooth between these two Germans. Dortmund looked at Hugo with a derisive leer, and then half-gestured at their table; Hugo appeared to be despising Dortmund, underneath his attitude of deference. Then Hugo laughed suddenly, the peculiar overbearing laugh of a man with no sense of humor. Leslie noticed that he had big, strong, very white teeth.

The O.W.I. boy with whom she had danced earlier—his name was Randall—slouched up, very drunk, and uninvited he sat down; Strangeways nodded, and Leslie introduced him to Gerald. One of his elbows missed the edge of the table, and he began to mumble mournfully. She felt a little irritated, patriotically, that an American should hold his liquor badly before two Englishmen.

"Say, Mrs. Corcoran . . . Yes, I'm tight. I know I'm tight. I've been tight every night for a week." His tone was defiant; yet something in her melted. "And do you know why I'm tight? Because I miss my girl so God-damned much I can't stand it. She's in Des Moines. And I'm stuck out here in this Godforsaken hole. Aren't you homesick, Mrs. Corcoran?"

Strangeways looked rather cold, with the fastidiousness of one who drinks well before one who drinks badly, but Gerald said sympathetically, "Buck up, old chap."

Leslie said warmly, "I'm not homesick yet, because I've only been here a few days, but I know just how you feel."

"Thanks. Didn't mean to butt in. Guess I'd better go," Randall said, and with the unpredictable movements of someone young and drunk, he rose, slipped on one foot, lurched, and then moved off with super-steadiness, probably in the direction of the toilet.

Strangeways and Gerald talked to each other in a careful monotone, with concealed gestures toward the German table, and Leslie's mind retreated into itself, her mind went swiftly, fleetingly back, she was momentarily taking no part in this conversation, she became suffused with memories of America, the one quickly melting into another. The sky of New York at dusk, cobalt, mauve, and gray. The lights of the great hotels like rows of cards, where giants might play vertical solitaire. The mountains near Lake Placid, when they were a flat blue-gray backdrop, without perspective, against the sun. How she had loved Robin even for his bald spot, and how he laughed and talked, and how she had kissed him that last time.

Suddenly she caught Hugo staring at her. With a physical effort, she pulled her face away. Then Florian appeared for her second number.

IV

She danced this time, and a fixity came into Gerald's eyes; he watched her with concentrated bliss, his mouth tense in a proud smile. She danced a czardas, and Leslie felt a pulse of delight at the bursting color of her costume; it was a kind of dirndl, with a green velvet bodice laced with red, heart-shaped and cut very low. She danced better than she sang; one could not be bored or aimless in a czardas. Her plaid skirt ended just over the knees, and three small petticoats made a cascading foam of white ruffles as she kicked. There was something *gamine* about her now. And this time the savage magnetism and vitality poured out unchecked.

To Leslie, the realization that Gerald was so obviously fascinated by another woman, perhaps in love with another woman, was a morsel of challenge; it made her want to be attractive to him. She felt a close sympathy for him, and though she had only known him a few moments, a warmth and security seemed to bind them. Then she wondered, almost romantically, if he were one of those traditionally weak characters who, as the phrase went, could be "regenerated" by a strong woman. Emphatically she closed her mind to the possibility. She was all through with rendering gratuitous assistance to another. There was only one person she wanted to help now, and that was herself. She shook her head, a little angrily. No, no. You very seldom succeeded in helping yourself unless at the same time you were helping another person too.

Florian bowed swiftly, proudly, and left the stage; Gerald, after a breath, turned to Leslie. Then, out of tactful consideration for her, another woman, he was attempting to modify the pure, helpless enthusiasm he felt for Florian. "She really isn't too bad a dancer, you know," he remarked. What he wanted to say was that, indeed, she was wonderful beyond words, and he wanted Leslie to agree with him, to be enthusiastic too. But, out of an instinctive sensitiveness toward her, he talked of Florian almost deprecatingly. "She's quite an interesting girl, Mrs. Corcoran." And Leslie, understanding perfectly, was impressed by his good taste and manners.

"Now, Gerald, come off it," Strangeways said sharply. "Ought to get that damned girl out of your system."

Gerald's reaction was surprising. He laughed easily, and then addressed Leslie, and she was astonished, because he said, "Maybe you might help, Mrs. Corcoran. I wonder if you'd dine with me tomorrow evening?"

She reflected quickly on what to answer, and glanced at the elder Englishman as if asking his permission, though it was not his to give. Strangeways looked torn. He wanted to get Gerald out of town and back to work. But—

"Why, thanks," Leslie said. "I'll lend-lease you my company for the evening." And she found herself very pleased.

v

Covertly she watched the German table, and Hugo was still carefully watching her, she knew. She would have known him to be a German anywhere, she decided, though he had none of the more obvious stigmata. He carried no saber marks, and he was certainly not a blond, nor was he stiffly self-conscious in public like so many Germans; indeed, his manner was insinuating and relaxed. Yet she was sure she could have identified him for what he was, by something in the way his tweed coat didn't hang exactly right, by something unhumorous and precise in the smile with the big white teeth. He was certainly a handsome, virile-appearing brute. He looked too as if he knew a good deal about women, and was therefore successful with them. Probably he was very conceited, Leslie thought. And she continued to glance at him intermittently with fascination and repugnance curiously combined.

Hugo bent to Dortmund with a whisper and then put on a pair of dark glasses. There was a bold, sly smile on his face. That too was German-typical, Leslie thought. He must think that, with dark glasses, he could observe her while making it more difficult for her to observe him. Like an ostrich. How silly.

Leslie shivered in distaste. These were Germans who had run knowingly amok in a dozen countries, who had muddied and sullied the decency of man; these were Germans who had burned the books, almost their most heinous crime, and tortured innocent old men and starved babies and asphyxiated Jews; these were Germans who uttered every word as if it were a bark and wept sentimental tears when women with fat behinds made bad jokes in a music hall. It seemed an indecency that she could be sitting quietly a dozen yards from people who did these things. She thought of Berlin, and again a dark look filled her face.

Gerald caught her watching him. It was hard to keep her eyes away. Then his own features hardened; they changed entirely, and she saw him stare at Hugo coldly.

He asked her suddenly: "Do you hate your enemies?"

"Why, I suppose so. In some cases—"

"I don't at all. I may hate individual Germans, but not Germans as a whole."

"Gerald's too bloody tolerant," Strangeways said.

Leslie considered: "Well, there are a couple of hundred thousand anti-Nazi Germans in concentration camps. They're on our side. So I don't hate them."

"There are plenty of good Germans. We're not making war on Thomas Mann," Gerald said.

"Only good Germans are dead Germans," Strangeways said.

"What do you believe in most?" Gerald asked Leslie, ignoring him.

"The United States of America."

"Hear, hear," Strangeways said.

"You really love your country?"

"Yes, quite a lot."

"Would you die for your country?"

"Yes. If I knew why it was necessary."

"To die is the biggest thing," Strangeways put in.

"No. To live, surely," Leslie said.

Gerald looked at her sharply, though he was not one of those men naïve enough to think it startling when a pretty woman was intelligent.

"Can't laugh nationalism off, you know," said Strangeways, "whether or not you're going to live or die. Look at all these people in this room. Poles, Japs, Swedes, French, Jugoslavs, all the little countries. One thing dominates them all—nationalism."

"I think nationalism's bunk," Gerald declared.

"Well," Leslie put in, "whether it's bunk or not, or whether you can laugh it off or not, you can be discriminating about it, surely. I love the United States, but I recognize its defects. I wouldn't change it for any country in the world, but there are plenty of things about it I don't like."

She went on to Gerald earnestly: "How can you say nationalism is bunk? What are you fighting for, anyway? Aren't you fighting for the survival of your own nation, England?"

"Ah, we're fighting for much more than that," Gerald said.

"Yes, but if you got beaten, and England went down, would any of the rest be left?" She turned to Strangeways. "As to all the little countries, well, I admit, it's easy to get bored with them. Their worry about frontiers, all their discordances and petty quarrels. But if I say I love my country more than anything on earth, I don't see how I can deny the right of other people to feel the same thing."

"Even the Germans?" Gerald smiled.

"Well—"

Gerald interrupted decisively: "Nationalism's just outmoded hocus-pocus. I don't give a damn for England. Shut up, Alec. But I do give a damn for what England stands for. Nations don't count. What counts are ideals and ideas. Ideals and ideas overrun any national boundary. Americans aren't Chinese. But plenty of Americans fought for China before Pearl Harbor."

"It was to our own national interest," Leslie said.

"Take Spain. Thousands of Frenchmen and Italians and Jugoslavs and Americans and even Germans, the right kind of Germans, fought for Spain. But they weren't Spaniards. Love of country doesn't count a damn. What counts is love of causes."

She tried a new tack.

"What about Freedom? Don't you concede the right of small nations to get rid of oppressors, to form their own states? What about all the folks who belonged to the Turks, right here, or the Austrians before the last war? What about the Czechs and Poles? Don't you have to admit that their kind of nationalism is authentic and legitimate?"

"Yes, but let's have it in some kind of broader framework. Look at your own country. No one wants nationalism for Texas. You fought a great civil war to preserve the principle of union. Nations ought to be like your states, more or less. Let them have their local insignia, their local prides and patriotisms, but merge it all into something bigger, something federal."

Leslie thought this over. Of course he was right in a way. But she concluded stubbornly, "Anyway, I care more for the United States than anything there is."

VI

Now the Hungarian girls, the *Animierdamen*, had finished their show and they were coming from backstage, wandering from table to table among the guests and clustering against the bar. The dance music recommenced, and Florian, with her head high, walked slowly across the floor, in the tangerine dress again. Gerald was trying to signal her silently. But she paid no attention; ignoring him, she approached a table near the center aisle. She looked radiant; she really did look like the queen of Taksim's now. She sat down with a bald man who had a short, inch-wide belt of black mustache below his long nose.

"Polish chap," Strangeways explained. "Coal owner from Silesia. Been dining with him past few nights."

Was this why Gerald had asked *her* to dinner, Leslie wondered. Had he asked her only because Florian was tied up with the Pole? She hoped that this was not wholly so. As if reading her thoughts, Gerald smiled at her confidentially, reassuringly.

After ten minutes Florian rose, shrugged her beautiful shoulders, left the Pole stranded, and walked in their direction. Gerald half rose. Now his face was that of a man anguished and tormented by uncertainty, but alive with hope and waiting for deliverance. Florian waved to him casually, nodded to Strangeways, swept Leslie's face with a quick look, and passed within a yard of them without speaking. She reached Hugo Reichenau's table, where she comfortably sat down.

"The enemy, don't y'know," Strangeways said quietly.

"Dash it all, no one takes Hungarian girls seriously as enemies," said Gerald.

And Leslie had a strong feeling of resentment against Florian, not because she was beautiful or glamorous but because she was treating a man badly, and treating him badly in front of others.

As Gerald talked now his eyes shifted like those of an actor; he flipped his eyes back and forth, though his head hardly moved; he continued to address Leslie with apparent interest and attention, but his eyes constantly flashed and re-flashed toward Florian; there was a quality of madness in the way he physically could not keep his eyes away from her, for more than a second at a time.

"Well," Strangeways decided to change the scene. "Time to go upstairs for a nightcap. Must show Mrs. Corcoran the upper bar."

They passed the German table, and Florian made a small gesture, just lifting her hand with a bend of the wrist, as Gerald bowed; of course they could not speak since she was with Germans. Hugo carefully lifted his dark glasses while Leslie went by. He stared at her, and she stared back. She could outstare anybody. She would not be outstared by any German. There was a jumping current between them; then Hugo dropped his eyes, rotated his head, and turned to Florian with a whisper. Then Leslie felt his eyes on her back.

The upstairs bar was charming; they sat in a horseshoe-shaped loge, looking over the crowded, animated tables far below. Here the orchestra was intimate: a cembalo player, a violinist, and a Hungarian who sang. A soft breeze made the moss-green branches rustle in the moonlight, and a mile or so away they could just see the sliding silver of the Bosphorus.

Leslie was dancing with Gerald, when they looked down and saw Dortmund and Reichenau prepare to go. The two Germans paid their bill, kissed Florian's hand, and walked swiftly and with precision down the aisle; then Florian drifted toward the bar, alone. She looked like a beautiful vagrant now. She looked lonely now. Gerald finished his dance dutifully, and then circled Leslie back toward their loge. He said without explanation that he had to go. Strangeways' face was blank.

"Well, cheer-ho," Gerald said. His voice was full of charm, but a shade defiant. He turned to Leslie, smiling. "Don't forget, we're dining tomorrow. I'll pick you up at eight o'clock."

To Strangeways he said, "We ought to be having a talk, you know." He acted as if he were blaming Strangeways for his departure in order to conceal his own embarrassment at going.

"Tomorrow quite good enough, old chap."

Ten minutes later André, the Greek boy, came up to the balcony, hovered near their loge until no other waiter could overhear, and then said briefly in bad French, "Your friend and the Mademoiselle Florian, they have go now." Leslie felt a vibrating thrill. So André, the Greek, was one of Strangeways' men.

CHAPTER III

"I'd Have You Shot"

I

LESLIE did not know much about the British. She had
visited London briefly, but she had never lived there
long enough to appreciate the flavor of the most subtle city
in the world, nor had she ever known anyone English really
well. If she had been asked to define the concept "Englishman" she would have envisaged someone haughty and stuffy,
rather snobbish, tepid, and dull. She would have thought of
novels by Compton Mackenzie and Hugh Walpole, which
she loved in school; of immaculately groomed lawns, superior
servants, and ugly cathedrals; of jokes in *Punch* which it
took her an extra fraction of a second to understand; of
men with walrus mustaches, Sherlock Holmes, watery vege-
tables, insularity, and rain. In other words she knew extremely little of what the English are really like.

Strangeways she could grasp, in outline; because she had
read books by Maugham and had seen many movies in which
the Englishman was cynical on the surface but principled at
bottom, in which he was at once casual, arrogant, and incorruptible. She might even have guessed, though without
knowing quite why, that the thing Strangeways loved most
in life, next to England, was gardening.

But for Gerald Leslie was quite unprepared. She did not
realize that he had asked her to dinner the next evening
mostly because, like so many Englishmen of his type, he was
kind. Nor did it occur to her that the impression he gave of
seeming indecision was a peculiar British amalgam composed

of deference, the shyness of careful manners, and unwillingness to impose his personal problems on another. Nor did
she have much conception of what a young Englishman
brought up on W. H. Auden rather than on Rupert Brooke,
on T. S. Eliot rather than Thomas Hardy, thought about.

II

Strangeways dropped Leslie at her hotel at about two in
the morning, and returned to his apartment. When Gerald
was in town he always stayed there. He did not think Gerald
would get in till quite late, but he decided to wait up for him.
He poured himself a Scotch, and started to read a detective
story.

"Well, well. You up?" Gerald smiled as he came in at half-
past four.

"Didn't feel like sleeping, boy. Besides, things to talk about.
Maybe better not to postpone."

"Wait till I go to the can," said Gerald walking through
the room. He called over his shoulder: "Alec, trying to make
that American?"

"Interesting-looking girl, isn't she?"

"She's attractive."

"Damned *chic*, too."

"She has pretty legs." Gerald returned, lit a cigarette
which hung from his lip, and sat down. Strangeways said
easily, "Now let's hear all about it. You could have knocked
me over with a duster. Why did you come back?"

Gerald shrugged. "Felt like it. Just a short week-end here.
Nothing to bother about, old man."

"I'm not so sure of that. When do you propose to return?"

"Monday or Tuesday."

"It's too late to argue now. But you ought damn well to be
back on the job Tuesday morning, and you know it. How's
Florian?"

"All right."

"Goes badly, does it?"

"I didn't say that."

"How's Hugo?"

"Oh, to hell with Hugo."

"I think you ought to drop it, Gerald. Let's have this out once and for all."

"You know her pretty well," Gerald said. "You know what she is."

"Yes, but I think you'd better drop it now, especially if you've lost it."

"I tell her nothing."

"Yes, old chap, I know that."

Gerald had an odd look. "I might even pick up things from her. Those things work both ways."

"Doubt if you'd behave that way. Anyway, drop it. Call it off."

"Is that an order?"

"Not quite. Persuasion always so much neater, don't y'know."

"Even if it is an order, I refuse to drop it," he stood up defiantly.

Strangeways thought a moment, and then murmured, "You mean you won't give her up because you *can't* give her up?"

"That's about it."

"You are a weakling and a coward."

Gerald flushed. Strangeways rose, sighed, and let his hands fall loosely. There was resignation, not supplication, in the gesture. "Well, time to turn in, I suppose. Good night, lad; we'll talk about the chrome tomorrow. Get some sleep."

III

Gerald, it was notorious among his friends, had a fabulously powerful imagination. He had loved to day-dream as a child, and his fantasies were often as real to him as actual circumstances. Even now, he could walk down the street, Atatûrk Boulevard in Ankara, say, and five seconds after a thought struck him, he would be lost in clouds. He could construct a whole existence out of a suddenly conceived image; he could remember a person whom he had not met for twenty years, and immediately build up a complete projection of his life; or he could propel himself twenty years forward and enact imaginary scenes with the utmost realism. But then his modesty and sense of humor would rescue him and, realizing that none of this was in any way important, even to himself, he would brush it all away, laugh, and forget until the next fantasy came.

Tonight as Strangeways left the room he slipped into the long gray shadows of a reverie. Sitting there he closed his eyes, and instantly he was dreaming, though he hardly knew if he were asleep or awake. What was real? What was not real? Here he was, almost thirty-two years old, the tormented victim of an obsession. Did he love Florian? He was not at all sure he loved her. Could this agonizing frenzy be called love? All he knew was that he was obsessed by her, that she was never out of his consciousness one second. Cloudily, but with sharp images in the clouds, his mind shot both back and forward. They were together that first time and it was like a dream. She had been passive at first, and then incredibly proficient, and all the time, emotionally, almost bored. What was the name of the special hell for people like that, who could be taken without emotion, or worse, to whom it was almost a matter of indifference if you took them or not? But Gerald had possessed her once, briefly, very briefly, and he knew what she was, and therefore could not forget her.

Two hours before they had been sitting in her small flat up a flight of stairs near the Galata tunnel. She was drowsy and aimless and again, almost bored.

"Florian," he had said almost roughly, "for the last time, I beg you, I implore you, to get out of here."

"Why?" she asked, as she had asked more than once before. "You talk not with reason. I have my life here."

"What kind of life is it?" He came behind her, as she sat in the big chair, and put his hands smoothly over her cool forehead, then softly upward on the high glossy pompadour.

"You're not getting any younger, you know. And you know what will happen?" His voice was more strident, he seemed to have lost his charm, and he paced angrily back and forth across the room. "You'll not be queen of Taksim's always. People will get tired of you and you'll grow stale. And you need money all the time. You can't live on what Taksim's pays you. You know that. And the Turks are damned well suspicious of you already and they'll get more suspicious as time goes on. Then one fine evening our friend Mr. Poppa will tell you that the minister of the interior will pay one hundred pounds for the privilege of your company for the evening. And what will you say? You can't refuse Poppa or you'll lose your job. And you can't possibly afford to affront the minister of the interior."

"Where would I go?" Her voice was petulant and even surly, but tired.

"Budapest. Go back home."

"And in Budapest what do I do?—starve."

"Nonsense, you'll pick up a job."

"All I would do there would be exactly as here, but worse."

"You could live with your family. Wait till the war is over, then I'll come and get you."

She appeared to be considering, "I am compromised with the Bulgarians because of the time I spent there. I do not think I could receive a visa."

"I'll get you a visa."

"You? An Englishman? From the Bulgarians?"

"There are ways," Gerald said stubbornly.

"Well, I think about it."

"To think about it isn't enough!" he cried. "You've been thinking about it for a month!"

And he suddenly remembered something she had said to him that first evening they had met. She had not said it too seriously, but to shock him a little and for melodramatic effect. "I like it to have men crazy about me and drive them crazy!" Then later she tried to express clearly what she thought about herself. She was hard and almost bitter. "Now I forget all nonsense. Now I trust no one and become rich and famous. Now I live for myself and make use of men."

Gerald resumed, "There's another possibility, Florian." He paused for emphasis. "Will you come back to the mines with me?"

"The mines? What would I do there?" She was astonished.

"We could live together. I'll marry you if you want. That's why I came back. To ask you that if everything else failed."

A secret look came into her face. What kind of a man was this, who would first beg her to leave him, for her own sake, beg her to go away so that he might not see her again for months or years, and who now shifted his course abruptly, asked her to run off with him to a muddy village in Anatolia and be his wife? It was bizarre, but sweet. It was quixotic, but appealing. And when he implored her to go away, to return to Budapest, he was considering her above himself, he was obeying the first law of love, which is to think of the other first.

Florian shook her head.

"Is it because of Hugo?"

"No."

"For the last time, are you in love with him?"

"He amuses me."

"Why not marry me, then?"

"Because I am not interested in you that way."

IV

Tired and depressed Gerald walked into his room and undressed. "God damn it," he muttered to himself. He could not sleep, and at about six in the morning he went into the other bedroom and watched Strangeways sleeping there.

All his life, it seemed, Gerald Heath had known Alexander Strangeways; they had met first when he was a child in Cairo, and Strangeways was a secretary in the diplomatic service. Now Gerald watched him as he lay sleeping quietly and his thoughts took a distant, almost forgotten turn. Throughout Gerald's youth he was intermittently in England, and his comfortable big house near Middleoaks, where his own sons were growing up, became a kind of home to Gerald . . . What a good career Alec had had . . . First the Foreign Office . . . He had reached the rank of councilor. Then a partnership in a London bank . . . Now, for the duration, he was head of Bureau X for the whole Middle East . . . Gerald kept on watching him. He thought briefly of his own remote youth.

Gerald had been born in Aleppo; his father, Sir Reginald A. F. Heath, was the British consul general there. He was considerably older than his wife, Gerald's mother. His years in the flinty desert and hot Levantine ports had, as it were, dried and concentrated him; when he walked through the house, one could almost hear him shake and rattle, like a pod full of dry peas. He was one of the kindest and most considerate men who ever lived. Also he was inordinately shy. He was so shy that he would ask his wife's permission to sit down at the breakfast table. She was not pretty but she had a nice figure and a kind of boyish recklessness. People wondered how Christian missionaries in Aleppo, severe and angular folk, could have produced a daughter so given to lonely rides in the moonlight, and sudden excursions into the desert where the sheiks were all her friends. She married Sir Reginald quite suddenly. He was an excellent match, and the only eligible white man for a hundred miles around. She died the next year giving Gerald birth . . .

Sir Reginald and his infant son had to leave Aleppo when Turkey entered the First World War, and Gerald lived in Egypt till he was eight; then in England he went to a minor public school. He wanted to be a musician. It seemed that he had considerable talent. He went to Oxford having won a scholarship in music. He became interested in politics too, as one necessarily becomes interested in a pervasive irritant, and he was one of that considerable number of young Oxonians who, thoroughly disillusioned, voted never to fight for King and Country. Gerald was ten when the British and French bickered viciously over the Ruhr, nineteen when Britain went off the gold standard (which was more shocking than a disavowal of the Trinity), twenty-two when the concert of powers sold out Ethiopia to Mussolini, and twenty-six when Chamberlain murdered Czechoslovakia at Munich.

It was Strangeways who, in 1939, persuaded Gerald to take a more realistic view of the war. Gerald could not believe in the quality of the men who were running England at that time. Contemptuously he would refer to Chamberlain as that umbrella-toting duffer . . .

"Believe in the people," Strangeways urged him.

"The government would have been tossed out of office if it had not declared war!" exclaimed Gerald.

"Exactly! Yet you complain that the war isn't popular!"

"I don't think that those old fools in the government have any conception of what they're fighting for."

"Maybe not. But don't disbelieve in Chamberlain because he wanted peace. You wanted peace too."

"The government wanted the wrong kind of peace."

"You can't have it both ways, my lad. What you're saying in effect is that you oppose the war, yet you blame the government for not fighting it with sufficient integrity and spirit. Why, Gerald, you surprise me by your bloodthirstiness."

Gerald enlisted, became a lieutenant, and served in France during the Sitzkrieg. He hated every minute of it, except once or twice when the stimulus of physical danger blotted out any other emotion. Then it became known that he spoke Turkish and Greek perfectly as well as several other languages. Obviously he was being wasted watching an ammunition dump near Soissons. So Strangeways pulled strings at the War Office and he was transferred to the Levant and after a brief time in Cairo and Jerusalem he found himself in Turkey, with the elder Englishman as his chief.

He tapped Strangeways on the shoulder and woke him abruptly.

"What? Hello, boy. What's up?"

"Let's talk about the chrome now."

"Right." He slung his legs out of the bed. "Other stuff than chrome on my mind, too." He lit a cigarette. He determined not to talk of Florian again. The thing to do was keep Gerald away somewhere, or contrive to squeeze Florian herself out of the country. Also another idea was teasing him.

"Having certain amount of trouble smuggling our chaps into you-know-where. You know the language, maybe you'll have to take a hand. Also there's this operation coming in the Aegean. Can't tell you where, just yet. But it's coming up quite soon. May send you there, old chap. Right up your street, I should think. Be bloody dangerous. But—"

Gerald was about to say something, and then stopped. Strangeways was not looking at his face, or he would have noticed.

"Now as to the chrome, things aren't going as well as they should at the mines, are they?"

Gerald controlled himself. "No."

"The Germans got two big shipments last week that should certainly have been stopped. Eh?"

"Wasn't my fault."

"I know, old man." Then the elder man's tone sharpened. "You bloody well make it your responsibility that it doesn't happen again!"

"The Boche is damned active there. They've bribed a lot of engineers. They've got the plant manager in their pocket."

"Well, outbribe them, you fool."

They wrangled for an hour, until their Armenian servant woke up and started to make breakfast.

"You've had no sleep, old chap," Strangeways said. "Better turn in now, don't you think?"

"I'll have some coffee first." Gerald was looking at him as a man might look at a combination of Satan and a priest.

"Alec, you know what's troubling me. It's at the root of all this difficulty. I'm tired of this job, Alec. That's what the trouble is."

"What? Gerald, go to bed. Sleep it off."

"I want to quit, Alec. I'm fed up with everything out here. Give me something else, or let me quit."

Strangeways looked at him. "My dear boy, there's a war on, and you are talking unmitigated rot."

"I don't want to do this work any more, Alec. I want to quit!"

Strangeways said calmly, but measuring him, "If I took you seriously, I'd have you shot. Now calm down, and go to bed."

CHAPTER IV

Morning Near the Golden Horn

I

THE next day was Friday, and Leslie had left an early call. Today she was moving from the massive old hotel overlooking the Golden Horn, and she had to pack. She was leaving the hotel after a week for several reasons; for one thing it was too expensive. She couldn't easily afford it; and the Ambassador's tiny canary-bird of a wife had found her a pleasant room with a Turkish family. She thought it would be good to know some Turks, and besides to live with a family was a kind of protection.

The telephone woke her, and the operator said in thick French, *"Huit heures et demie, madame."* She lay in bed a moment, sleepy, and her first thought was of the night before; the images of Strangeways and Gerald Heath floated in her mind. Then, as if someone were showing her a playing card, or a series of cards falling sideways, she saw Hugo Reichenau's dark face. Frowning, she shook her head. Strangeways, Gerald, Hugo, slipped crosswise through her thoughts, and she got out of bed.

She seldom slept with anything on, and shaking her hair loose she put on the only robe she had with her, the one in green and white, and slid toward the window and lifted the Venetian blinds. The view was breath-taking. She would not have this same view after she moved, and she would miss it; she tried to absorb every atom of it, to memorize it. Surely it was one of the most remarkable sights on earth, the white ships with slanting masts and puffed-out sails, the white

44

buildings looking stiff and starched, and those unbelievable minarets like tall chessmen and the golden domes, across the sky-colored water stretched like silk and rippling.

The view gave her reassurance, it seemed to give her something to grasp in this exotic world. But it seemed very remote from the war which she was trying to help fight. Then she felt lonely. "Oh, dear . . ." she sighed. And again, the dark nocturnal face of Hugo Reichenau, with the heavy white teeth and the brows almost meeting, flashed in her mind. She closed her eyes to shut his face out, and there it still was, now small like a postage stamp, imprinted on her lids. She frowned again, walked into the bathroom, and drew a bath . . . Then she thought of Gerald, and wondered what the coming evening with him would be like.

How wonderful to be in Europe again, Leslie thought. This was certainly Europe in that the bathroom had a *bidet*, but you had to ask for soap. She looked at herself in the mirror—her skin was a glow of creamy beige—and sought to put thoughts of last night behind her. How different a morning bath was from an evening bath. Morning was the time for good resolutions. In the evening you thought about all the things that had happened and that hadn't happened, and in the morning you had to face the uncertainties and decisions of a new day, you had to plan, you ought to look forward instead of reminiscing. Yet, as a rule, she found it difficult to think consecutively in the morning, at least till after breakfast; waking up was a little like crawling out of the womb.

She washed her face in soap and water, dried it, and doused it with a light floral lotion. She picked up her stockings which she had washed out carefully the night before and slung over the shower curtain, and put on shoes and stockings, panties and a bra. She peeked into the closet, deciding what to wear, so that dressing would be largely automatic after she had done her make-up. She saw the dress she had worn last night, hung up neatly and with the buttons buttoned. She took out the suit she would wear today, a pearly gabardine with a collarless single-breasted jacket and a good sharp waistline.

Taking her home Strangeways had been punctiliously correct and courteous. Not a pass. She was relieved, but she hoped that he would call her and take her out to dinner soon again. As an older man he had been very cautious that she should make the first move, if any. He was a very complex character, she decided, much more complex than she had first thought. Then she telephoned for breakfast.

II

Now to pack. It would not be much of an ordeal, since she had only been allowed forty-four pounds of luggage which meant two medium-sized suitcases. She was above all a realist, and she had organized her wardrobe realistically for this trip. She had to have clothes of basic and lasting design, because it wasn't going to be easy to replace things; she had had to choose clothes that would last, that would wear emotionally as well as physically.

One by one she laid her immaculate dresses on the twin bed she hadn't slept in. First the black wool. Then another party dress, also black, of silk with a low round neck and a gathered lace apron, but with short sleeves. With it she liked to wear black lace gloves. Where were they? She fished in a drawer. Then a print dress; the color was a dark lilac with small green leaves and stems. Then a beige spectator sports dress, a good classic model with big pearl buttons and long sleeves. Then an ice-blue dinner dress, cut low with a lovely full skirt. Then she had a washable white pique, like a dirndl, and a second suit, of muted brown Glenurquhart plaid.

The dresses almost filled one suitcase, and she began to pack the other. She had a bed jacket in shocking pink, and seven pairs of nylons. At the last moment in New York she had thrown in one pair of pajamas, that matched her robe, and one white satin nightgown. You could never tell. She emptied the drawers of the commode. There were several cashmere sweaters, a couple of snoods, a pair of pale green roses which she sometimes wore with her hair down, half a dozen shirts including the orchid one she would wear today and one in pale blue she was crazy about, a pair of navy blue slacks, two gay printed scarves, and a short wool coat of smoky red.

"Oh Lord," Leslie murmured. "Now to get the shoes in."

She loved good shoes, and she had brought six pairs, which she assumed would be the minimum necessary: the Delman pumps she had worn last night; the brown spectator pumps she was wearing now, her basic walking shoes; a pair of patent leather pumps; a pair of silver evening slippers; wedge-sole doeskin play shoes, of chamois-colored suede; and multi-colored sandals with ankle straps. She wondered if all this were excessive. She had no exaggerated worship of clothes, but she liked to be well-dressed.

Prodding through the room she picked up her make-up case and her jewels, especially Robin's pearls that she often wore with the black wool. She had been reading the Modern Library edition of *Swann's Way*, and in Cairo she had picked up an old copy of Walter Lippmann's *The Good Society*. These would have to go in somewhere, and also the big Koret bag and one small silver evening bag. Then she had to pack an address book, aspirin, bicarbonate, two gold bracelets, sunglasses, comb and brush, a box of Kleenex, some stationery, six extra lipsticks she would die for rather than give up, a notebook, a mechanical pencil in which the lead was jammed, a leather-bound alarm clock, a flashlight (everybody had told her a flashlight was an essential, but she had never used it once), a bottle of vitamin pills, a tiny vial of Patou's Moment Supreme, some Ciro toilet water, some Blue Grass eau de cologne, an identification bracelet which she was not wearing now that the flight was over, a gold locket with a picture of Robin inside, a pair of tweezers, needle and thread, a studded leather belt from Henry à la Pensée, some baby oil, tissue paper, ankle socks, a pair of pink scuffies, a lucite clothes brush, an eye cup, two lipstick brushes and an extra one for the Dark Fire by Germaine Monteil which she used on occasion, a black half-slip, silk panties to go with slacks, dental floss, a razor, nail-polish remover, a bottle of shampoo, nose drops, a jabot, a suede brush, a handful of bobby pins, and a couple of grip-tooth combs.

Leslie picked up the rose-diamond brooch in the form of a ballet dancer she had worn last night. For some reason she had a special fondness for this spirited bauble; she wrapped it carefully in a bit of Kleenex and stuck it in a corner.

She closed the bags, with effort. Then she did her face smoothly and sparingly; she didn't use rouge, and she didn't need an eyebrow pencil. She combed her fine, dark, shoulder-length hair, which had the color and patina of old walnut furniture, and put it up. She slipped on her blouse and suit, surveyed herself, and put a little of the Blue Grass on a white handkerchief. It was too hot and damp in Istanbul for any strong perfume which clung.

III

There came a knock on the door, and a bellboy brought a telegram. Like telegrams in France, it was pasted up on the obverse side of the envelope; she tore it open impatiently, ripping the message. She had wired her family that she had arrived safely, and this was the reply. Just like her father to make bad puns at 75 cents a word. The message read, DELGHTED DARLING JST TALK TÜRKIYA TO TURKS LOVE, and it was signed with her father's and mother's full names. She smiled affectionately at the cumbersome signature made necessary by wartime censorship, and the mistakes in spelling.

Leslie sat down on the narrow bed, and thought vividly of home. She pressed her elbows into her sides, hugging herself, as if squeezing and concentrating the emotion she felt; her head, with the chin up, vibrated in a series of tiny movements from side to side, as if to say, "No, no, I could never love anybody more."

Her mother was one of the most competent women she had ever known. She cooked well; she ran a household well; she made speeches well; she led committees well; and she was a considerable power in her community. Her mother was white-haired now, a trifle stout, and occasionally acidulous. She was a fighting liberal. What she believed in most was integrity. What she admired most was a man or woman who put character above money or ambition; she thought that what the world needed most was people who thought of success in terms of integrity, rather than of wealth or fame. Leslie's father was a tall man with brown eyes like a spaniel's behind steel-framed spectacles. He was a lawyer, and the friendliest man in town. He had never made a great deal of money, because he wasn't competitive enough. What he loved most was sweeping the lawn in autumn and raking up the leaves and burning them. In the late afternoon, with a violet haze rolling down from the Adirondacks, he would stand and rake the leaves, and watch them burn, silent and contemplative, enraptured by some secret community he felt with the mellowing of the year, the dying of the day.

Leslie thought, "Oh . . . God." She could close her eyes now, and feel that she was a little child again, and her father was blowing soft kisses on the back of her neck . . . Then she had a quick memory of Fleming, her younger brother: how it got dark early when winter began, how she and Fleming would run into town, whistle at the cold, and rub with their thick mittens on the frosted window of the bakery shop, with its wonderful warm smell inside . . .

Leslie wondered what her mother and father would think of Constantinople. She could physically hear, right here in this hotel room, her mother's ejaculation of astonishment at the beauty of the view, but then she would take it all in her stride. It would neither impress nor excite her overmuch, and she would be critical of the unkempt streets and unsanitary restaurants. Her father would roam in the bazaars and go over St. Sophia and the Blue Mosque carefully with a guidebook, enjoy the café life, and wonder why the Roman Empire should, of all places, have perished in Byzantium.

And Fleming, her kid brother? Fleming was a handsome and adventurous young man who, of all things, had got a job in the movies, and had then quit to take up flying and join the navy. He was out in the Pacific somewhere now; she hadn't heard from him for months. For Fleming Leslie had a feeling like none she had ever possessed for anybody. What would Fleming say about Istanbul? "Hell, sis, this is a knockout of a place but we've been here a week and I'm restless and what the hell, let's push on somewhere else."

She could be impatient with Fleming and even angry with him—at his reckless vitality and the lack of direction that went with it, his commanding romanticism about every girl he met. But there had never been anyone like him and she loved him.

IV

Leslie was full of nostalgia now, though this was an odd time of day to be nostalgic. And she must hurry, because she was lunching at the Embassy.

She walked to the window. She felt that she might cry suddenly. A fleet silvery yacht was cutting through the silken harbor, ripping it and leaving foamy tissue behind. She leaned against the wall, her strong hand against the plaster. She said aloud, "Robin . . . Robin . . . "

She stopped short, blew her nose, and remonstrated with herself angrily. She hadn't said that name aloud for months and months . . . Of course Robin wasn't his name. But she had called him that, because his head was round and compact like a robin's, and he had a sharp nose straight out of his face and robin-colored hair, soft gray and red.

Her face became suffused with an extreme tenderness. Her emotion was compounded at once of yearning, wistfulness, abandon, a determination to have no regrets, and—yes— pride. Pride because she was a woman who really knew what it meant to have profound emotion, who understood what it meant to love, who knew her power to accept and bequeath happiness.

What did a woman want in a man? Health, confidence that he had confidence, courage, tenderness. A good and permanent relationship was possible if, first, a man was madly in love with you, or, second, if he gave you a sense of complete security. But you had to have the one or the other. Sometimes you got both. If you had neither, everything went to pieces.

Yet basically when a woman lost a man, it was her own fault. That was the most terrible thing about it. She had lost him because of some failure in *her*. In the last bitter analysis, it must have been something *she* lacked, or he would not have left her. In spite of his crazy selfishness.

Her mind leapt forward; she felt a sharp image of Gerald again, and then of Hugo Reichenau. Then urgently, almost despairingly, as if she were calling for help in a supreme moment, she grasped the memory of Robin. How people could sleep together like two spoons. How two people could love one another *for* their defects. How, even when she knew exactly what he was going to say, she wanted to hear him say it, and say it again, and love him for saying it.

She thought, "But that's all over. Finished. Done with." She plucked her coat out of the closet, blew her nose again, and tried to feel resolute. Please God, she thought, the next time I fall in love, let it be right. Don't let me fall in love with a baby or anybody spoiled or anybody complicated by too much ambition or, please God, a married man. She rang for the bell-boy to take down her bags, and standing there sought to make a pledge to herself. She so profoundly wanted it to be safe and secure next time. She swore to herself that never again would she fall in love with the wrong man.

Leslie took another quick look at herself in the mirror. She paid her bill downstairs, and no one who saw a beauti-fully-dressed young woman with a lovely figure walk briskly through the lobby would have thought that this was a Government Servant on a Mission Abroad, whose heart was badly broken. She was not one to wear her heart, or anything else, on a sleeve.

V

The taxi propelled her to the traffic circle near Taksim's, and then down the Grande Rue de Pera. The street cars plunged in close file, and the automobiles honked and hooted angrily. She passed some cheap restaurants, two or three dingy pharmacies, and a jewelry shop which, behind its exterior, contained some of the most precious art objects in the eastern world. She saw two theaters, each showing ancient American movies, with the names of the stars outlandishly transliterated into modern Turkish, Klark Geybl, Jinja Rojuz, and Surli Templ. She tried to think what this part of Istanbul was like. Not like Cairo, certainly, because here everybody wore western dress. But not like a European city either. This could not conceivably be the main street of Zurich, Hamburg, or Milan. It was in transition between the caliphs and a brusque modernity. It was mongrel, it was Balkan. In contrast Leslie thought suddenly of what an American city was like, and she remembered the streets of her own home town.

The taxi swept up broad boulevards and through parks to a cluster of new apartment buildings with the shining water just beyond. Here the city resembled Vienna, except that Vienna did not have the Bosphorus to look at. The box-like modern buildings were made of stucco and painted a mild buff; they had French style elevators, that carried passengers up but not down; they had plenty of windows, modest balconies, and tolerable plumbing. Leslie paid her driver, and he helped her in with her two bags. There was no doorman, and she searched along the row of bells and rang for Mrs. Atif Musifer.

So this was where she was going to live. Apparently none of the Musifers was at home, and a maid led her to her room. It was medium-sized with a divan bed, so that by day it looked like a sitting room. She had a bath of her own, and a

shallow terrace. She had the emotion of one who has trav-
eled far reaching a haven at last, without quite knowing
whether she would like it. Her face seemed to say, "Well,
for better or worse, here I am."

Leslie wrenched open the French windows and put foot
on the terrace. This wasn't the Ahmedie and the Golden
Horn any longer. This was a different view, toward Kadikoy
and the Asia shore. But it was just as thrilling, if not so
beautiful. She watched the water where squat ferries and
skiffs with triangular sails beat against the current visible
in the water as if it were being raked.

VI

She had met the Musifers the other day, through a note
from the yellow-haired Ambassadress. The family had once
been well-to-do, but now Mrs. Musifer seemed pleased at
the money her rent would bring. Dr. Musifer was a journalist,
and like many Turkish intellectuals she was to meet, he had
been educated abroad, and had once briefly visited the
United States. He was in his late thirties. He was the foreign
editor of the great Istanbul newspaper *Crescent*. Leslie had
met several American newspaper men in the days she lived
in Paris and Berlin, but Dr. Musifer was quite a different type
of journalist. He did not drink. He did not sit around cafés.
He did not flirt or gamble. He was deadly serious. He was
passionately interested in politics, with an insatiable curiosity
about political affairs. And like all Turks he was an ardent,
a fanatic nationalist. His wife, whose father had been a
leading Ankara gynecologist, educated in Vienna, was a
plump woman who would grow plumper, who had a slight
mustache, and who viewed her husband with obedient and
respectful awe. For Mrs. Musifer, an Oriental, a man, a
husband, had an extreme and unique value. Also she was
raptly convinced that Dr. Musifer would have a great political
career. In this part of Europe, all journalists were politicians,

had been politicians, or would become politicians sooner
or later.

The day Leslie called she herself had been somewhat over-
whelmed by Dr. Musifer. He had no small talk whatever.
Straight out he began to ask her questions about America.
He spoke English quite well, though his wife knew little.

What was a sharecropper?

Just why was the Middle West more isolationist than the
rest of the country?

Why was the American labor movement traditionally conservative rather than radical?

Why were comparative nonentities so often nominated as
presidential candidates?

Inasmuch as the United States was approximately ten
per cent a Negro nation, what about the racial future of
the country?

What exactly was the difference between Republicans and
Democrats?

Was it difficult to find school teachers for American rural
districts?

Were policemen and such minor functionaries customarily
underpaid and corrupt?

Leslie gaped. She began to talk, but it was hard to put
concrete answers into words. She was not ignorant, but she
was out of practice. For a second she wondered if life with
the Musifers might not be a severe trial, if this were a trust-
worthy sample of their tea-table talk. But she felt a challenge.
She felt that she had a responsibility as an American to do
her utmost to be intelligent and informed and she determined
to find answers and more answers to everything Dr. Musifer
asked. It shocked her, as it had often shocked her in Europe
before, that by and large Americans were so much more
self-conscious about serious conversation than Europeans,
so much less familiar with the niceties of argument and
discussion, so incurious, complacent, and imprecise. Suppose
a Turkish politician should turn up as a week-end guest in
Westchester, would his American hosts have the equipment

to ask analogous questions so blunt and penetrating? Leslie thought she might carry on the talk by turning the tables and asking Dr. Musifer about Turkey. She asked him about many of the things she had already discussed at the Lend Lease office. By and large she had found most of the Americans in Istanbul rather fed up with the Turks, irritated, and almost hostile. She wanted to know how Dr. Musifer would talk about his own country, and particularly its neutrality.

That any nation should choose to remain neutral with the whole future of the world at stake seemed to Leslie inconceivable . . .

VII

Now she was unpacking, opening a closet with her back to the door, when she felt rather than heard that someone had come into the room. On the threshold stood the most beautiful child she had ever seen.

The child stood there, appealing, curious, and mute. She held one hand akimbo, and then with the other on her chin, shyly, she walked forward. She had thick curly hair almost jet black, and skin so white, so lustrous, so gardenia-like that it seemed unhealthy; her green eyes were the color and shape of olives and almost as big, and her hands were exquisitely long and slim. Leslie took breath. The child opened her mouth: it was a shock that she had braces on her teeth.

This must be the daughter of the Musifers, and she was about five, Leslie judged. She half-knelt down, and put her hands around her back, under the delicate shoulders, along the straight small back. "Why, hello, hello!" she exclaimed. The little girl had a knuckle in her mouth. She didn't reply.

"Do you speak English?" Leslie asked. "No? French? German?" The child stood transfixed as she was addressed, her fingers across her lips, and a wild secret look in her eyes. "Only Turkish?" The child remained mute. "I'm afraid I don't know any Turkish."

Leslie continued. *"Tu parles français? Sprichst-du Deutsch?* No? Well, well, you'll have to teach me Turkish, then!" She picked a pencil from her bag. "Pencil. *Crayon, le crayon. Bleistift, der Bleistift.*"

It would soon be time for lunch, and Leslie had to go on with her unpacking. The little girl, as if awestruck, watched. In her face was all the wonderful envy of a child for the adult's world. Leslie pulled out a black dress and then the lilac-green print, and searched the closet for some hangers. Then the little girl was stroking her clothes, touching them with wondering, admiring fingers. She made a leap, pushed a chair in the closet, and stood on it. She wanted to help. She wanted to share. Now her face was rapt. As Leslie handed her things, she hung them up.

"Why, thanks, little girl."

Everything was finished now except the jewels and small odds and ends. The little girl surveyed the bottles, and she kept making small appreciative sounds, cooing and bubbling. Leslie unwrapped the rose-diamond ballet dancer. The child stared at it, held out her hand, and then touched it with a finger. She uttered a happy shriek, grasped the ballet dancer firmly in both hands, and burst out with a stream of excited words. Then still holding it tight she rushed wildly from the room.

Leslie stared after her. And the stab of an intense emotion tore into her heart. Her own little girl would have been just about this age.

CHAPTER V

The Spauldings Have a Lunch . . .

I

LESLIE picked up a taxi and got to the stately, old-fashioned American Embassy at 1:12. She had been asked for 1:15. She was always prompt. She had never been late for anything in her life.

The American Ambassador to Turkey, the Honorable Arnold Travis Spaulding, was a man nearing sixty, tall and stooped, with brown eyes touched with olive, gentle hands, and a comfortable slow voice. His face was gaunt and creased in deep folds. He belonged to one of the great American families, like the Adamses or Roosevelts, and he had been a career diplomat all his life. He had been a vice consul in Stockholm, a second secretary in Teheran, a first secretary in Berne, a consul general in Madrid, a councilor of Embassy in Tokyo, minister to Finland, and Ambassador to Chile, before becoming Ambassador to Turkey.

People said that he was too tolerant. They knew also that he was incorruptible. People said that his humor, his humanity, made him lazy; also they knew that he was completely devoid of ambition, and had never pulled a string in his life. He was the most selfless man anybody had ever met. Not merely did he never think about himself; he was unconscious of himself. There was a cliché about Mr. Spaulding in Istanbul: that he was Lincolnian. And, indeed, he was. The first time Leslie met him, he reminded her of a gnarled oak, but with soft branches; of the American frontier, camp fires, and wood smoke at dusk; of smoothly worn coins, buffaloes, and a weathered granite crag; of empty roads, milestones, books under a reading lamp; of Oyster Bay, Green Mountain, Ticonderoga, Boulder Dam, and Lake Placid; in a word, of home.

Of course the capital of Turkey was Ankara, but the Spauldings maintained two official residences, and they came to Constantinople, called Istanbul by the Turks, half a dozen times a year.

The Ambassador, when in Istanbul, both lived and worked in the crimson-walled Embassy, where the ceilings were higher than the rooms were broad; when Leslie entered the foyer, she saw him behind the glass partition of his office. He rose at once, in shirt sleeves and broad suspenders, and walked out to greet her. If he had been in a bathing suit, it would not have detracted from his dignity, his projection of a courteous good will no one could take advantage of; if he had been dressed in pirate's costume, you would have known he was the American Ambassador. He gave an intense aroma of the best of the United States. He made you proud you were an American.

"Well . . . Mrs. Corcoran. You're part of our family now. That's what I like to think of us here, a family, a fellowship. Yvonne isn't down yet? Well, she'll be along. Vassily!" he called a servant. "Let's have a cocktail. Cigarette? Oh, of course, I remember, you don't smoke . . . Have you got settled nicely? . . . Well . . . "

II

The Ambassador slipped on a jacket, Mrs. Spaulding came in, and the other guests assembled. The Ambassador's wife was a tiny creature with a pert nose and canary-colored hair; she had borne her husband four stalwart children, and still had the figure of a young girl; for years, she had been famous as the most *chic* woman in every capital they lived in; some people feared her caustic tongue, and some disliked her; she was ruthlessly intelligent in a slightly insane way;

it was an experience to watch her and the Ambassador together.

Mrs. Spaulding was a Frenchwoman. She was Parisienne. Her milieu there was the Etoile and the Avenue George V, not the Faubourg St. Germain; she was a modern French-woman. Sometimes Mr. Spaulding said that his greatest triumph in life had been to make her an American, to which she replied impudently and not quite meaning it, "I love the United States only because I love my husband."

The Spauldings had been married for thirty-two years, and had scarcely been a day apart. Leslie remembered how Mrs. Spaulding had said to her early in the week, when she first called and they talked of the Embassy routine, "But it is my first job to keep my husband fit!" This struck her sharply—how marvelous for a woman to express herself in such terms!—and a look of admiration mixed with slight envy crossed her face. She, too, would like it as a first job to keep a husband fit! Mrs. Spaulding caught this, made an instantaneous transition, and snapped at her, "You have to work at happiness." An obvious truism, but something that unhappy people often forget. Then she quoted a proverb in quick French, *"Le secret du bonheur est le pouvoir de le saisir.* The secret of good fortune is the power to grasp it."

Mrs. Spaulding was indeed what the gossips called a character. She was impertinent, she cared little for social con-vention, she always spoke her mind.

But Leslie would speak her mind too.

"It's not always easy. Everybody these days seems so adrift, so anchorless . . . Everybody in a kind of transition between one set of ideas and another . . . or between a first marriage and a second . . . or between one faith and the next . . ."

"The world itself is adrift. Everybody yearns for stability, for a kind of form," Mrs. Spaulding said.

Leslie thought aloud: "But we are adults, are we not? To drift is so childish, so undignified."

"I do not press the analogy. But without peace in the world, it is difficult to have peace in the heart."

Leslie knew as they walked toward the drawing room that the Spauldings represented something which, through no fault of hers, she could never reach—a towering tradition, a fixed series of family relationships, wealth, and public service. She did not resent it that Yvonne Spaulding loved her husband, and had three grown-up sons and a daughter at Vassar; what she felt was a sense of regret that her own family did not have such adhesive roots in so thickly studded an American past. Leslie thought fleetingly of Robin. Compared to Mr. Spaulding, Robin was only superficially American . . . What was America? A community, a fellowship, like this Embassy. Sternly Leslie put Robin out of her thoughts . . . She was entering a new world now, and she would make the most of it . . . She chatted with the other guests, glad that it was a small party.

The Ambassador's private secretary, Mr. Rummel, was a hunched, small, buzzing, abstracted bachelor who had been with the Spauldings twenty years, and who played superb poker and an efficient game of bridge.

Leslie's boss in the Lend Lease office, Dave Urquardt, was a serious youngster with prematurely gray hair who had been a teacher at Robert College and who knew Turkey well.

Mrs. Meredith O'Dowd, the wife of the Standard Oil man, had the finest garden in Istanbul. She was determined, narrow, and a little silly. She had divorced two husbands before marrying the Standard Oil man, who loved her and was afraid of her.

George E. Saxton, the veteran correspondent of a London paper—a veteran at thirty-eight—had had one country after another shot under him, like horses: Austria, Czechoslovakia, Poland, Jugoslavia, Greece. A liberal, his political life had been a series of bitter disillusions. Before Hitler, he had been very pro-German. Before the Russo-German pact, he had been very pro-Russian. Now he didn't know what he was.

The wife of the Embassy councilor, Mrs. McBride, was a snob, who lived so closely in a limited world of her own that she had no room for outsiders, unless they were also snobs.

She was an ugly woman, hence she wore exceptionally lovely clothes.

Strangeways came in, alert and smooth, looking tired. "Ah," he addressed himself to Leslie. She was glad to see him, but she hoped he wouldn't be proprietary; it would be nice if he pretended to know her well, but she wanted to be free to circulate.

They moved into lunch, and Leslie found herself next to the Ambassador, with Strangeways on the other side. She was thrilled. She wanted to be at her best. She had never been to an intimate lunch in a great Embassy before.

III

The long room was pleasantly proportioned, and great oblong windows hung with buff curtains looked out toward the water. The table seemed to be old Spanish or Italian, of massive walnut, and the thonged leather chairs were deep. The candlesticks, the small plates for bonbons, the ashtrays, were of Turkish silver, and a great bowl of fuschia-colored flowers shone warmly as a centerpiece. One servant in ultramarine livery was serving a mousse of shrimp, and another stood silently by the paneled door.

"My cook . . . *Varliked* to the tune of five hundred Turkish pounds . . . I'll have to pay it, or she'll be deported. It's an outrage, if you ask me." This was Mrs. O'Dowd's voice from the other end of the table.

Everybody always talked about *Varlik* first; everybody always had a new *Varlik* story. *Varlik* was the confiscatory wealth tax, which the Turkish government used as an instrument for liquidating the minorities, the Greeks, the Armenians, the Jews.

Leslie wanted to listen, but Strangeways was whispering to her in a private undertone. He told her that she was looking well, and then directly spoke of Gerald.

"Glad you're dining with my young man tonight. Do him good. He's in a bad mood. Tricky mood."

"I should think that girl would put anybody in a mood if you weren't sure of her."

"Florian? Yes. But other things on Gerald's mind too."

"That's the worst of all possible fates, isn't it," Leslie meditated. "To be in love with someone you're not sure of."

"I'm not sure he's really in love. Just a crazy infatuation . . . Mrs. Corcoran . . ." He appeared to be hesitating, as if wondering whether to take her into his confidence. Something in his eyes told her that she could be a gift to him. But all he said was, "He is a good boy, you know."

"I'm sure." She found it pleasant to be talking about Gerald Heath. "Have you known him long?"

"Dear me, yes . . . Maybe he seems mixed up a bit. And dreamy. Does wild things occasionally. Needs control. Like so many of our youngsters nowadays . . ."

"Why is he so bitter about the war and patriotism and all that?" She was curious.

"Ah! Don't you understand? Didn't it hit you in your country the same way? Gerald's a perfect product of modern disillusions. Spent his whole youth in being debunked. Lost faith after faith. Lost all belief in belief."

"I like people to have convictions." But she nodded. She knew plenty of American boys like that, though Americans were more resilient somehow.

"One thing about him—he's one of the few genuinely modest men I've ever met. And in this age of exploding egos!"

Leslie was thinking of what to reply when she overheard a swift sentence from Mrs. Spaulding: "But the real reason the French collapsed was that they hated war more than they hated Hitler!"

IV

The Ambassador was speaking now. "What you say about *Varlik* . . . Very unpleasant, yes, of course . . . But . . ."

Mr. Spaulding's basic philosophy of life was that it *was* worth living. His own happiness contributed to this philosophy, which in turn led to his mellowness, his tolerance.

Because he thought instinctively that everything was, some-how, going to be for the best, he found it hard to take sides with deep conviction. Also he had been trained in a profession where the qualities of fairness, balance, objectivity, were held to be paramount. Since his days as a second secretary he had been taught to see both sides; he had been brought up to be disinterested. And he still thought that one of the most valuable things in the world was an expert with no ax to grind, an expert who was non-partisan.

Leslie noticed that Mr. Spaulding had had a stiff drink of vodka at the luncheon table, following two cocktails, and that he was now helping himself to wine rather liberally. Did he drink a lot? Was this his defect, if he had one? She remembered Berlin again. She hated people who drank too much . . .

Mr. Spaulding was of the old school and he did not alto-gether appreciate this new world of short wave radio, micro-phones, and diplomacy by long distance calls to Washington. He did not admire some of the things that folk like Strange-ways did. War was war, but . . . There were some phases of the work of his own Embassy that the Ambassador didn't like. That upper garret, for instance, which had been the servants' linen room. What had those technical people from the navy installed up there? He did not know precisely. There were some things that, considering the necessity of proper relations with the Turkish government, it was better for him not to know. Then he would never have to lie . . . There were even things about which he actively did not want to know . . .

"You talk of *Varlik*." A couple of sentences at the other end of the table were snapped off, because this was the Ambassador addressing everybody. "I met Madame Kurban's doctor the other day. I hadn't seen him for quite some time."

A grimace of pain crossed Mrs. Spaulding's sensitive, restless face. "That story . . . "

"You know about Madame Kurban?" The Ambassador turned to Leslie. "Her story is one of many stories. She is the wife of a Czechoslovak lawyer, and she was herself a history teacher. Once they lived near Kosice. They were intellectuals. They were the leading intellectuals of their community. When the Germans came, she was caught, though he escaped. She was made to work as a laundress as the German army advanced. She was a woman of much refinement . . . "

"Arnold, do not tell that story . . ."

But Mr. Spaulding proceeded: "She and her sister were among a dozen Czech women who were forced to accompany that segment of the German army as it advanced into Russia. They were given a hut to live in on the outskirts of some Ukrainian town. Each day, they had a certain amount of laundry to do. The clothes were filthy—greasy, eaten with lice, bloodstained, stiff with dirt. At the beginning they were given enough laundry so that if they worked steadily, without any pause or interruption, from seven in the morning till seven at night, they could just finish it, but only just. Then, systematically, they were given a little more each day, so that they did not finish till eight, or nine, or ten . . . They survived the first winter and then Mrs. Kurban's sister became ill. Madame Kurban was then forced to do the sister's laundry too until she physically collapsed . . . Two of the women in the camp had children. One died of typhus; another had a sharp attack of dysentery. The mother appealed to be let off the laundry long enough to take care of the sick child; whereupon a German sergeant said, 'There's an easy way to settle that.' He picked up the child by the leg and bashed out its brains against a tree stump. Mrs. Kurban's sister died. Still the piles of laundry came in every day. Mrs. Kurban had been a stout woman; she became skin and bones. The Germans advanced further into Russia, taking what women survived with them. They reached a place near Kursk. Mrs. Kurban slipped and fell, cutting her arm badly. The German doctor refused to treat her and infection set in. The arm had to be amputated at the shoulder. Thereafter she could not work in the laundry. She became a maid in a house of prosti-

tution for German privates. The fate of some of the other
women was quite interesting. One lost her mind and killed
herself. Another seized a German officer and bit him in the
throat one day. She was horsewhipped in the public square,
and then hanged. Mrs. Kurban's arm did not heal properly,
because of exposure and privation, and the Germans, bored
with her, drove her out of town. She managed to walk and
crawl some miles until she found refuge with a Russian
peasant's family. Then the Soviet counter-offensive began,
and the district was retaken by the Red army. Mrs. Kurban
got out, and joined her husband here. When he saw her and
heard what had happened he went insane. He's in the hospital here, a raving lunatic. Mrs. Kurban is recovering."

Leslie felt sick; she could not touch her food. Her face
wanted to pucker out in angry gasps. Some things were so
horrible that the reflex made you want to laugh in a gnarled,
twisted way.

But Mrs. Spaulding was impatient. "I dislike that story
because it puts things in false perspective . . . Those poor
creatures . . . But it is war itself that is the ultimate horror—
war itself. The isolated atrocities, they are tragic, but they
should be minimized, they are incidental. War *itself* is the
atrocity."

Now the Ambassador was relaxed and tolerant again.
"Yes . . . Of course. But we were talking about *Varlik* . . .
The Turks aren't so bad, really . . . There are degrees in
outrages . . ."

v

Strangeways was trying to regain Leslie's attention, and he
thought how difficult it was to place an American girl. Now
if she had been British, he would have known in five minutes
what part of the country she came from, who her parents
were, where she had gone to school; he would have automat-
ically known her social and financial status, her basic asso-
ciations, tendencies, ideas. But you could never tell with an

American. He couldn't visualize what Leslie had sprung out of.

Now she said something that astonished him. "I've a little something on my conscience, Mr. Strangeways. I told you a fib last night. I'm twenty-nine, not twenty-seven."

VI

Then of course they were all talking about the war, about the masterful Soviet offensives and when the Anglo-American invasion, the second front, would come in France. They were all curious and impatient. The Ambassador thought there was a good chance of victory before the year was out. Somebody mentioned the future intentions of the Russians, and the table exploded in disagreement—as it always did in Turkey at this time—until Mr. Spaulding set out to clarify a point:

"You can't have it both ways, can you? Here you say on the one hand, the Russians will stop on their own frontiers and that will be a catastrophe. Then you say on the other hand, the Russians will advance further into Europe and that will be a catastrophe. Make up your minds which you fear most."

"Russians or no Russians, anything that helps bring peace is what I want," said Mrs. Spaulding. "Permanent peace. A good peace. After all this war is being fought so that our children's children won't have to fight another. Or so at least I hope." She added grimly, "No more war, ever." Leslie felt sharp exhilarated agreement; all the horror women had ever had of war was expressed in Mrs. Spaulding's taut voice.

"With peace in sight what do you think our plan for post-war Europe ought to be, Mr. Ambassador?" asked Dave Urquardt.

Mr. Spaulding chuckled. "I don't know. All I know is my own personal peace aim which is to live on the Riviera for three months and bask in sunshine."

"Arnold, do not be frivolous." Leslie admired the way Mrs. Spaulding said this. Her voice was both sharp and affectionate. Leslie looked at her golden curls, and then at her tiny, curving hands; Leslie felt that just as she could curl a strand of that canary hair with her little finger, so could she curl the whole person of the gaunt, seasoned Ambassador. He was regarding her now with a kind of amused tenderness. Why did men worry so much about being dominated, Leslie wondered. If you really loved, there was no question of domination. What was love for if not to give, to serve?

Leslie thought of her brother Fleming, and leaning up the table she mentioned the Pacific. But Mrs. Spaulding was wholly uninterested in the Pacific war; she considered it a total bore. She had never been able to take the Japanese seriously, possibly because she and her husband had once lived in Tokyo. Anything to do with the Pacific was a nuisance because it distracted attention from the continent of Europe, which was all that mattered.

"I don't see why we objected to the Japanese taking the Philippines. After all, we were going to give them up!"

This was the kind of feminine outrageousness for which Mrs. Spaulding was well known. The table gasped. And Leslie saw the Ambassador pucker his lips, then look at his wife as one might look at a brilliant but distorted child. Also, he knew that she would never have made a remark like that if there had been anybody but Americans and Britons in the room.

VII

They left the luncheon table, and had coffee in the heavily-curtained drawing room. This was the nicest part of a lunch, always; people were relaxed, and you could cross your legs and talk to the people you really wanted to talk to. Then the Ambassador was leading Leslie into his office. She stood against his desk, creasing her skirt against it; he paced slowly back and forth.

"You're a newcomer. I don't go in for what they call pep talks, but I always like to have a word with new arrivals . . .

As I said before, we are a small community here. And you are now part of it. Stay with it. I don't need to tell you to be discreet . . . And since we all have to live together here, with the Turks, I find it's rather a good rule, try to get along with them. You'll be popular. I want you to know . . . Yvonne and myself . . . anything we can do for you . . . we'll be most pleased to do it."

"Tell me something about the Turks."

"Most of the Turks I know hope to stay out of the war as long as possible. Probably they'll come in at the very end." Now an ironic smile furrowed his cheeks. "Some Turks hope the war itself will last as long as possible. They make money. They take from both sides, you know." He began to sketch the details . . .

The talk last night, with Strangeways and Gerald Heath, had been exciting and provocative. But this was different. This was more mature; it was on a more elevated plane. The Ambassador was not preoccupied with chrome, espionage, or counter-intelligence; he was dealing with something much more basic and complex; the broad flow of international ideas, the elusive and durable realities that underlay the Turkish problem.

Macedonia . . . the Dardanelles . . . What Churchill said at Adana . . . How the Russians might react.

"I can tell you what Turkish foreign policy is in one sentence." Again the aware, tolerant smile. "To play everybody against everybody, but to hope most from us."

It was time to go, and the Spauldings walked with their guests to the door, saying good-by and making everybody feel comfortable. Yvonne stood with her hand just inside the Ambassador's arm; the touch was confident, admiring, and proprietary. Then his arm was going around her as if she were a little girl. Leslie was filled with excitement and delight. This was one of the rarest things in life, a really happy marriage. Yvonne said something cryptic, and Mr. Spaulding patted her on the head. Leslie watched her, and thought that if the Spauldings had ever been poor or ill, this woman would have sold her body to buy her husband warmth.

Strangeways offered Leslie a lift. He did not know that the emotion now making her radiant was intense delight in the happiness of the Spauldings, and vibrant hope that they would like her as she liked them; also, because she had been so moved by seeing a marriage that was a practicable affair, that really *worked*.

"Stop with me and have a spot of drink?"

"Thanks, not just now." They drove a block.

Again Strangeways reflected on her coffee-colored eyes and the soft red balloon of a mouth; again he noticed the slim shoulders, then the very sharp waistline and the oval curving hips.

"What did you think of the Ambassador?"

Leslie laughed: "He made me feel all stirred and smoky inside."

Strangeways' gray-blond eyebrows danced upward on his forehead. A virtuous woman? He began to wonder.

VIII

"Look." He made a gesture to his chauffeur, and stopped the car. She turned to him puzzled. "Do you mind if we walk a block?"

They were quite near her office. Evidently he didn't want to be overheard by the chauffeur. They stepped out to the cobbled street.

"Mrs. Corcoran . . ." For a second he paused. "You wouldn't care to do me a great favor, would you?"

"Of course. I'd like to help you in any way I can."

"Listen to Gerald with sympathy tonight. Be kind to him. Make him like you. Make him like you quite a lot!"

A peculiar and subtle expression crossed Leslie's face: "Is that all?"

"Make him aware that there are other women in the world."

The expression deepened. It wasn't often that one man asked you to contrive that another should fall in love with you.

She laughed: "You don't want me to seduce him, do you?"
But she was pleased.

He grimaced. "I didn't say that."

"Not quite, but that's what you really meant." Her eyes
were very clear, alert and alive.

"I simply expressed the hope that you would like him, and
that he'd like you, and that you might have a pleasant time
together."

They crowded their way along the narrow sidewalk. His
car—a very heavy car—was parked ahead. Leslie murmured,
"I'll do my best. That is, I'll try to be the way I would be
normally, without reference to this conversation."

"Thanks."

"Let come what may," Leslie said.

They reached her office. He eased off gracefully, almost as
if he were talking to someone else, "Don't you think it's a fact,
impersonally, that any woman, given the proper circumstances, can take any man from any other woman?"

She laughed. But her face was earnest.

His voice was deadly serious again. "You could do us all
a favor."

"All right. I'll try."

CHAPTER VI

Gerald, Leslie, and Something Else

I

SELDOM in her whole life had Leslie felt stirred to such a point of awareness and vitality. Not only did she live now in a totally new environment; she felt that she was becoming an actual participant in unpredictable events. The pressure of an atmosphere like none she had ever known stimulated and excited her. And she felt the strong exhilarating pull of contrary impulses and ideas.

Coupled with her excitement was an incredulity. She felt a momentary emotion of superiority and disdain that adults, men like Strangeways, should be forced to spend time and energy worrying about such . . . such a basically extraneous business as a love affair. Of course most of these men in Istanbul had been womanless for years, separated from people they loved at home for barren years and years. Everybody in Istanbul was hungry; everybody yearned. The whole town was choked with yearning.

They drove to a small restaurant on the Grand Rue called Abdulla's, which Gerald assured her was, despite its modest appearance, the best eating place left in Europe. He was fresh, fluent, cordial. They planned to go on to Taksim's after dinner.

What kind of a girl, what kind of a human being, was this he was talking to, Gerald wondered. In her present mood, rather cool, a bit too crisp, with her direct single sentences and perceptive manner. But he thought this must be a sort of defensive pose, that she was probably quite different underneath, if you knew her well. My God, women are the devil, he thought, but cheerfully.

Then he blushed; actually, he blushed. "I say, Strangeways gave you a little sketch of Florian last night. He made her sound like a whore." He stammered. Really this was the most delightful and *good* young man, Leslie thought. "As a matter of fact, she isn't. Hasn't had more than half a dozen men all her life, I should judge."

Leslie wondered if this could possibly be true. She asked herself with a quick internal smile what it was that gave a full life to a woman.

"People tell the weirdest stories!" he exclaimed. "How she goes out with anybody, Allies or Axis or neutral, worms secrets out of them, sleeps with them to get information, and all that rot. It simply isn't true."

"What about Hugo Reichenau? Isn't she Hugo's girl?"

Gerald's face fell. "Yes," he conceded. "Off and on. It doesn't matter much to either of them. Anyway, what the hell."

And though Gerald's preoccupation with Florian was so pervasive, he was thinking with a submerged part of his mind, as he had thought the night before, Why cannot I forget this stifling insanity, why must I remain the slave of a harrowing obsession? He looked at Leslie closely. She was wearing a short-sleeved black dress, and she had the smoothest, creamiest skin. It was a long time since he had met anyone so attractive. There was no down at all on her forearms, and the hollows of her throat, under the determined chin, shone softly. And her attitude of lively composure, if you could call it that, remained a challenge.

Yet, several times when he looked straight at her, with a youthful and romantic kind of tentative appeal, he wasn't really seeing her. In the middle of a sentence, his eyes would suddenly snap off; it was as if she, Leslie, were not there any more, and he was seeing only Florian, Leslie thought abruptly: Let's get this out into the open.

"Why don't you tell me more about her?"

He hesitated. "Actually, there isn't so much to tell. She's been here in Istanbul the past couple of years. An Englishman brought her down, then she ditched him."

"She certainly seems to have a fatal attraction for the English," Leslie smiled.

"Yes." Gerald grinned, but not wrily. "Then there was a Hungarian boy who used to come here for week-ends, all the way from Budapest, two days on a train, for a couple of hours holding her hand. Sounds weird, doesn't it?"

"It sounds as if she must have been worth it." And she felt a flicker of admiration for what Florian must be.

Now he was leaning forward with modest eagerness. "There's one strange thing about her. I don't think she's ever been in love." He paused. "I know it sounds inconceivable. I've never met anyone else in my whole life who hasn't been hit at least once. But I'd be willing to swear that she's never really loved *any*body."

That, if true, could only mean something ugly and twisted in her childhood, Leslie thought. She asked, "When did you meet her first?"

"Oh, couple of months ago."

"Is Hugo in love with her?"

"I doubt it. He just uses her."

"It's rather a mess, isn't it," she said, suddenly depressed.

"Yes."

And Leslie felt a new kind of distaste for Hugo, not merely that of an American for a Nazi, of a free citizen of the world for a representative of the vicious Gestapo, but of a woman for a man who was frustrating the happiness of another human being. But when she thought about him he kept pulling on her somehow.

Gerald ordered dinner and they ate lamb skewered into crisp cubes and a pungent salad. Enough of Florian, he seemed to say; let's get onto something else. It was always such fun to dine with someone attractive and sympathetic for the very first time. At first you fished around for experiences in common; you talked about movies, politics, books, music. You hoped this would flash into something mutually understood, mutually felt. Then suddenly you got more personal. Then—

"I say," Gerald laughed gaily. "Let's make a compact, you and I. Let's be real friends. You tell me all your troubles, and I'll tell you mine."

II

Gradually she became more conscious of him physically; he slipped into focus, as it were. Wavy blond hair, rather longish; good blue eyes and lashes which practically swept the round, rosy cheeks; a mouth on the small side, and perhaps a bit irresolute and indeterminate; full well-carved lips and fine small teeth; a nice stance to his shoulders and a pleasant bearing as he gestured; well-cared-for hands, the fingers rather short. He was good-looking certainly. But more than that—he had a comfortable kind of warmth that made her feel comfortable too, comfortable and relaxed.

"You've never been to America?" They were having coffee. Her brilliant eyes looked into his steadily. "How odd. I don't know if you can picture what youth in America is like. There was nothing abnormal or wrong about the way we lived, but it was profoundly un-European, *non*-European. I suppose what characterized it most was a striking kind of freedom— freedom . . ."

It rather amazed her that she had started to talk this way. But urgently she wanted to reach this young Englishman somehow. All this around her was slavery, she thought impatiently. Strangeways' slavery to an impersonal ideal, Florian's slavery to vanity and her own beauty, Gerald's slavery to a girl who was an enemy, Hugo's slavery to distortion, to an utterly false conception of the life of mankind. She wanted to convey to Gerald what free Americans were like.

"My first friend," Leslie smiled seriously, "was the popcorn man. His name was Tony; he was Italian, what we called a Wop. When I was about twelve, I'd take my brother, and we'd run down on Sundays to where Tony was. He had a big nose and a greasy hat and sad, marble-colored eyes . . . And we'd eat bags and bags of sticky popcorn. The point is: even if Tony was a Wop, a popcorn man from the shanties on the other side of the tracks, he was one of us, one of our friends.

"We ran in gangs. But the gangs were inclusive, not exclusive. It was always a great event when you brought someone new into a gang. We'd meet in the afternoons at Zelinski's ice cream parlor, and the soda jerker there—he was a Polish boy—gave my brother his first job, selling crackerjack and licorice sticks and all-day suckers. There was a salted nut machine, with lights inside."

Gerald seemed slightly puzzled. Crackerjack? Soda jerkers? A salted nut machine with lights inside? He knitted his blond brows.

"About the town." Leslie pondered. "I suppose the main thing to say is that it was like a community. Like Mr. Spaulding's Embassy here . . . But it wasn't much like an English or French or German community. It wasn't stratified. It wasn't built in tiers. The whole town was like a family. That's what so many Europeans find it hard to understand. Every street was my front yard.

"On Thursday nights there was a band concert in the courthouse square, near the stone lions and the triangular pile of cannon balls . . . Once a boy named Joe Swenson dared me to climb out on the portable stand while the band was playing, and I slipped and cut myself on a tin sign advertising Cherry Pop. Joe was the son of the barber and he smelt of every tonic in the shop, but he was the best dancer in town . . . They took me to the doctor and he stitched me up. The doctor always hung around on Thursday nights. His office was above a grocery run by Italians that later became a supermarket. The dentist had an office there too. I always had a hot fudge sundae before climbing up to see the dentist . . ."

"It sounds infinitely more exotic than Istanbul," Gerald declared. "It all sounds like nothing I've ever heard of."

"You know, it was! And in a way, just as foreign!" She thought about it. "The shoe-repair shop was run by Greeks, of course, and the stationery shop was Polish. There were lots of Germans, like Heinrich Romeier, the Town Clerk, and the Hartmann family, they ran the biggest filling station. The best druggist was a Dane. And one of the first boys I ever went out with was named Sverdlka, I suppose he was a Czech. The haberdashery was Jewish, run by three brothers, Harry, Gideon, and Albert Mintz. Once at Christmas they gave me a sweatshirt in the high school colors." She mused. "You know, I don't believe that half the people of Juneville were Americans even fifty years ago! But they all *became* Americans! Isn't it remarkable? I know it sounds trite, but our melting pot certainly did melt a lot of people down, and kept them nicely melted!"

"Of course the melting pot is a basic source of American isolationism, too."

Leslie looked puzzled. "How so?"

"Because so many of your people *did* come from Europe. And they grew to dislike Europe in retrospect, after America gave them greater opportunities. So they and their children resist any kind of politics that pulls them back to what they fled from."

"That's interesting." She considered. "My family name is Matthews. My father's family lived in New York State for generations, but his descent was Scotch, Basque, and Irish. My mother's name was Gertner. Her family came from Germany after their revolution in 1848. So I'm partly German."

"Have you any Jewish blood?"

"Not a drop so far as I know. But I was always interested in Jews. Once I liked a Jewish boy very much, but I stopped going with him because his Jewishness was so disconcerting.

I hated myself for dropping him. But I did. I was ashamed.
It worried me terribly." She gave a peculiar little laugh. "My
term paper in college was on the Jewish question, how we in
America were losing our tolerance, how anti-Semitism was
spreading everywhere."

"Term paper?" Gerald was still bewildered by some words
she used. Why shouldn't he be, she reflected. What a difficult
thing it was to transpose idioms. In her own country one
generation could hardly understand the next.

"I was always on the serious side," Leslie continued.
"And from the very beginning, my parents thought that I
ought to earn a little money. I majored in sociology. I had
all sorts of jobs. I don't suppose Europeans can understand
that either. That a girl of good middle-class family, the
daughter of a lawyer, should have to work, or *want* to work.
I worked in a filling station for a while. I peddled magazine
subscriptions. I learned typing."

She had a flashing memory. During high school she had
wanted to earn a little money so badly, even a couple of
dollars, money that would be her very own. She got a job
selling hats at Mrs. Holden's millinery shop, for three dollars
every Saturday. Then during the Fall Fair when the streets
were filled with small concessionnaires, fortune tellers, dime
photographers, and merchants of pink taffy made while you
watched, her father would walk past the shop slowly and
catch a glimpse of her selling hats through the window. But
he never told her that he watched her, and she didn't know
about it until years later . . .

"You make me feel an awful wastrel," Gerald said easily.
"I've never done a stroke of honest work in my life."

She digested this, somewhat shocked.

"But about your music?" Because he had told her earlier
that he was a composer and musician.

"Never mind that now. You go on."

"One memory is teasing me. Every April, when spring
came, we wanted so badly to take off our heavy skirts and
wool dresses and the sweaters we'd worn all winter. So

early in April I'd go to the department store and try on a new cotton dress and have it sent home. Then I'd wear it walking to school and shiver and almost freeze, because I couldn't resist changing from wool a week or so too soon . . ."

She laughed. "I suppose I must have been in love, and I wanted to look springlike and pretty before winter ended."

III

"When did you first get interested in boys?"

Leslie pondered. "That's another thing Europeans never seem to understand. All of us, boys and girls, grew up together. We played games in our back yard, where we had something called the Cave, built out of boxes; we'd all get in there, boys and girls together . . . We had beaux from the time we were twelve or so. There was nothing surreptitious about it; it was the accepted thing. It was just healthy normal growth . . . European children whom I met years later, they seemed very different, much more self-conscious about sexual things . . .

"I was never the most popular girl. Where other girls had dozens of beaux I had a few. When I was about fifteen there was a boy with curly red hair and big blue saucer eyes. He had an ancient Model T. I'd walk down the lane from school, and he'd be waiting. So everybody thought I was his girl. But I wasn't." She chuckled. "He was crazy about a friend of mine named Alice, who was a year older, and he only went out with me between spats with her . . .

"It was still a kind of gang-life right through high school. We'd take sleigh rides in winter, and go to hear name bands in the towns." (Name bands? Again he looked puzzled.) "And we'd follow the basketball teams around, and drive thirty miles for a dance. In summer we'd get a lakeside cottage, four or five of us, four or five girls I mean. I'd talk their mothers into it, just as I talked my own family into letting me go out on the long drives. Those cottages were

such fun . . . the passionate innocence . . . the flaming
excitement . . . the long drowsy nights and all those
boys . . ."

"You make it sound like something out of an anthropology
textbook," Gerald exclaimed. "The social habits of the South
Seas seem tame by comparison." He wanted very much to
ask a question, but he didn't quite dare.

"I don't think any European will ever know quite what an
American co-educational university is like. The casualness
. . . the freedom . . . I don't think it can be like that in
any other country. I made a good sorority." (Sorority? But
Gerald guessed what it meant.) "I studied hard and read a
lot. I belonged to a peace movement, and I helped organize
student committees and so on. You belonged to a peace
movement too? Well!" Leslie smiled.

"Two or three people were quite fond of me. That Jewish
boy I mentioned, and then a lad who got killed later in the
Eagle Squadron. I went to most of the proms and the big
games. There were special deliveries and telegrams at all
hours of the day and night, and people would be 'phoning
long distance until my parents went crazy. One friend of
mine had his own plane, and he'd fly in for week-ends, from
Detroit or Hot Springs or Miami."

"Were you in love with all these boys?"

"No, not really. I'd have a crush for a time. Or maybe I
was. Anyway—"

He prodded her with a smile. For at least ten minutes he had
forgotten Florian.

"After college I went to New York and got a job. I worked
in a broker's office. First I was what we call a receptionist,
and then lo and behold, I became a secretary.

"Then I married Hal Corcoran. I was only twenty-one
but most of my friends were married by that time, and I
wanted badly to marry someone. I was so tired—. Do you
mean, had I had affairs first? No. That's the strange thing
about the way we carried on. Most of the girls petted and
necked, of course, but they didn't have actual affairs. It was

the way we were brought up. One day there was a party at the Plaza, and my best girl friend, Esther Mavroudi, said that an old beau of hers was coming in. As she said it I had the strangest, most intense feeling that something important was going to happen. He arrived after a while; he was a little tight, and he took me out to dinner. Five minutes after I met him, I knew I was going to marry him. I wasn't at all sure that we'd be happy permanently, but in five minutes, I knew absolutely that we'd get married."

"What made you feel that way?"

"I don't quite know. He was tremendously good-looking and attractive."

"Was he in love with you?"

"Oh, yes!" She breathed. Then her eyes clouded.

"Were you in love with him?"

"Well, of course. At the beginning." What did he think?

"What happened?"

"It went to pieces after a while."

"You're separated now?"

"Yes. We got divorced."

"Where is he now?"

Her eyes looked sad. "He's a major in the army somewhere. I hope he's all right."

"Why did you leave him?"

"Well," Leslie said evenly, "I suppose what kills love is when you lose respect for persons as persons. For one thing he drank too much. But it was something more important than that." She hesitated. "Hal was an economist for one of the big New York banks. They sent him abroad and we lived in Berlin for a year or two." Now her face assumed a totally different look, a kind of protective hardness. "Well, life in Berlin cast a sort of shadow over everything. And we had a baby. A little girl. She died there. If she hadn't died, we'd probably never have broken up.

"After that, I was unhappy a long time and everything went wrong. Well, and then I *really* fell in love." Her mouth seemed to tremble. "And after a while, it seemed to me that

Hal was either too intolerably stupid, if he hadn't guessed, or that he knew all about it but was afraid to speak for fear of losing me. In other words he was either a fool or a coward. So I left him."

My God, these American women, Gerald thought.

IV

Gerald's turn. She asked him about what Strangeways had said at lunch. And he was explaining how he had grown up in the period when religion, history, ethics, even science, were subjected to the pitiless scrutiny of the emancipated. How he learned that hero-worship was an insult to the intelligence, that Mr. Gladstone was a hypocrite and Queen Victoria a prig. How he came to maturity in the era when a slip of the tongue, or a casual witticism, meant that you were in love with your grandmother, and when it was revealed that parallel lines did, alas, meet.

"But you're not a cynic, surely?"

"No. I hate cynicism. Call me a disappointed idealist." He added, "Maybe my marriage had something to do with it. Oh yes, I've been married too . . . Her name was Rose. My God! . . . It all happened a hundred years ago."

For some reason this came as a sharp shock to Leslie. He had seemed, in spite of Florian, the freest person . . .

Rose Marshall-Fox was a year or two older than Gerald when he married her, a big handsome girl, vigorous and possessive. He was in his early twenties, and they moved to Vienna. He was studying harmony and counterpoint.

"I had just enough money to live on without working. My father's estate . . . That is, it had been enough for me to live on. But even though we lived quite simply, it wasn't enough to run a marriage on . . . I wanted so badly to have two years of close, hard study . . . I wanted to write good music . . ."

"Did she help you?"

Gerald grunted. They had gone to the Wörthersee for a

winter holiday. Rose met an insolent, totally inarticulate and unimaginative Guards officer, a blasé athlete and sportsman whose cheeks always looked blue no matter how closely he shaved; also he was rich. She fell in love with him, broke off with Gerald, and ran away to St. Moritz. Later she married him . . .

Gerald gave up serious music for a time. Also he had a short nervous breakdown. A wise old Vienna doctor cured him. The doctor said one day, "Every person is a riddle. *Ja*, every person is two persons. In every human being, there is a player and a counter-player. In every human being, there are both religious and skeptical impulses; both pedestrian and artistic impulses; both libidinous and continent impulses; both solitary and gregarious impulses; both conservative and liberal impulses."

Gerald thought this over: "Does that mean," he asked, "that man is his own worst enemy?"

He then became convinced that his tendency to self-doubt, self-division, was not his own responsibility; he was not the only man in the world cursed with this trait. He felt himself as one of a great mass of victims of modern dislocations and disharmonies; he became aware that his material disbeliefs were the natural outcroppings of his environment. When he savagely doubted the sincerity of, say, the aims of the Atlantic Charter, he was simply giving expression to the realities of an inner personal conflict. When he mocked God or something much more serious, the British Empire, this merely meant that he was dissatisfied with his own private life.

He reverted to his marriage, "Of course it was a stupid and silly marriage. I didn't know my own mind; it was simply a mistake. I got over it years ago."

Rose . . . He talked about her more. And Leslie was deeply surprised: the emotion she could not help feeling was jealousy. When he had discussed Florian she had not been in the least jealous; but toward this former wife, this unknown woman who had shared some years of his actual life, she felt a sharp resentment, a sharp antipathy.

This is perfectly ridiculous, Leslie thought. Only this

morning I was telling myself not to get entangled. Only this morning I swore to myself not to fall in love again, unless I was absolutely sure. I thought I was dead in the heart and here I am, getting full of emotions about a man—a man tied up with someone else.

Gerald stretched his hand across the table, and gently, with the lightest gesture, let the balls of his fingers just touch her nails.

"One thing I've learned . . . I think I've learned. Tragedies happen to people, yes. But mostly they are, or should be, avoidable. Mostly they derive from bad thinking, from taking the wrong decision. Because there's something in life itself that wants to help. If you *choose* right, life carries you along."

She was impressed and a little startled. Lots of people made intelligent remarks, but few were wise. *If you make the right choice, life helps.* That was something wise.

v

Now Gerald was all gaiety and charm. He held her warm, smooth arm just above the elbow, where her dress ended, squeezing it a little as he directed her. But she thought back and wondered if he had been repelled by her talk about her own marriage, whether he thought her harsh or brutal. She, like Rose, had left a husband. Of course she had foreshortened it a lot, she had left out all the things not her fault. Nor had she mentioned Robin. That was an intimacy she could not give away.

In Taksim's lobby Gerald bumped into a tall man with confident eyes, three lateral wrinkles across a sunburned brow, and a positive intelligent mouth. Gerald was about to introduce them but the tall man was busy talking to a friend. Leslie watched him. He had a wonderful air of appearing to know exactly what he wanted, and was on the road to get it. He did not show any internal stresses, and he gave the sense of a person who would not swerve from a fixed objective.

And he seemed one of the healthiest people she had ever seen.

"Who's that?" she asked.

"Russian consul general," Gerald answered.

VI

The cabaret had just concluded, and they went upstairs to the little bar. After half an hour Florian came out, in street clothes—a russet suit with a pencil stripe, and wide lapels where the stripes went the other way—and sauntered to a nearby table where some other Hungarian girls were sitting.

"Want to meet her?"

"Of course. I'd love to."

Leslie remembered how precipitously he had joined Florian the night before, and she said, "Gerald, if you'd like me to slip away now, or if you want to take me home and then come back here, why, it's all right with me. I don't want to be in the way."

"No, this is my evening with you. But if you'd like to have Florian come over, we can probably arrange it."

He scribbled a note and sent it to her by Mr. Poppa. Then they saw Hugo Reichenau arrive. He saw Leslie and stared at her boldly for a second. He did not join Florian, but looked around slowly—almost warily—and walked to the bar alone.

Gerald was regarding him. Then he asked Leslie abruptly, "Do you know why the Germans are going to lose the war?"

"No. Why?"

"Because they're so gullible."

He still glanced at Hugo, whom Leslie would not have thought to be a very gullible person.

"Perhaps Hugo's an exception. But the rank and file of Germans are the most gullible people I've ever met. They're cruel, full of inferiority, efficient, wonderfully good philosophers and musicians, but above all they're sentimental, they're gullible. The gullibility derives from the sentimentality, I suppose. That is, the Germans want things to be the way they'd like them to be. Who but Germans would have fallen for anybody like Hitler? And who but Hitler would ever have fallen for an oaf like Ribbentrop? Or who but Nazis would really think the Poles and Jugoslavs and French would willingly play their game? The New Order and all that rot. They're gullible as children. They believe *anything*. Perhaps they're so gullible because they lack intuition; then they try to over-balance their lack of intuition by being so incredibly system-atic. They plan everything. They never improvise. And what does it mean if a man or a nation is overly addicted to planning? It means that he or it is compensating for some inferiority, for some lack of security. You only have an exaggerated disposition to plan when you're afraid things left to themselves won't come out the right way. And behind all this, always, is the gullibility. The Germans are never sure of themselves; so they can always be taken in."

VII

"Two whisky-sodas, André," Gerald ordered.

"What kind whisky, Mr. Heath?"

"Scotch whisky."

"Only Turkish Scotch whisky tonight, Mr. Heath."

The Greek waiter hovered by their table for an instant. Last night he had frightened Leslie; now she wanted to overcome this apprehension, she wanted him to be friendly.

"I'd like so much to visit Greece sometime," she volun-teered. "After the war . . . when it's free again. It must be such a lovely country."

The great black eyes looked guarded. "*Oui, madame.*" He seemed to be deciding whether to give her an opening or not.

Her voice was almost timid: "Perhaps when the war is over we'll all meet there . . . perhaps we'll all find worth-while things again . . ."

"Nothing will ever be as it was, madame," the eyes were stony now. "No country, no people, will ever be the same."

"Oh, come off it, cheer up, André," Gerald said. Yet he looked as if he agreed.

"There has been too much of death and shadow," the Greek continued stubbornly. "Nothing will ever be the same again."

"Lots of us have suffered, André," Leslie put in gently. "Nobody has a monopoly on pain."

"*Oui, madame.*"

"After all, things *might* come out all right. No matter how irreparable a loss may seem."

He was inflexible: "*Non, madame.*"

He went to get their whiskies. Gerald said, "It just dawned on me. I suppose you realize what André is."

"What?"

"The burden of our past."

CHAPTER VII

The Beginnings of Encounter

I

GERALD talked so earnestly, and she was listening so intently, that they did not see Florian approach. Then she was standing next to their table and he rose quickly. She certainly is gorgeous, Leslie thought.

Her eyes were, as she had guessed, a luminous golden-topaz color, flashing with pin-pricks of brown; the irises were very large, set in the whites like unmounted jewels in a satin box. Her coiffure was different tonight, with the pale honey hair fluffed up around the top of the head, where it was thickly smooth and amber-colored. Then Leslie noticed that she had ugly hands. They were broad, with blunt fingers, peasant's hands. And Leslie reflected that when anybody very beautiful unaccountably lacked complete perfection, or had one blemish which though minor was outstanding, it made her seem more human, it almost served to make her beauty greater. She remembered how Florian had played with the bit of chiffon in the cabaret the night before; she must have subconsciously adopted a technique for hiding those strange, ugly hands.

Florian lit a cigarette, animated but a trifle defensive. She began to talk about a friend, a girl named Sophie who had not been able to dance for several evenings because of illness. She had been visiting Sophie that afternoon. She seemed to be helplessly fascinated because her friend was suffering from what a Turkish doctor diagnosed as food poisoning; like so many people who live bizarre lives, she was abnormally capable of being impressed by simple, homely events.

She was speaking fluently: "*Mein Gott*, to think that such pain and disorder could come from one drink of bad tomato juice. Sophie drank the tomato juice at the bar of the Serapia, and I told her, 'Sophie, the tomato juice is thin and yellow at the top, it looks not as tomato juice should look.' But she drank it anyway. It is the fault of the Serapia. *Mein Gott*, how poor Sophie has suffered. I have told her she should bring action against the Serapia, she should make a law suit for the amount of her lost time and the doctor's bill."

Then her eyes narrowed. "Of course it is not rare that people become poisoned here, but Sophie is entirely non-political, there would be nobody who would wish to poison her."

The suspicious look remained. And Leslie reflected that among Europeans she had known, suspiciousness was often a characteristic of those who had had a hard, acrid youth.

Now for the first time she addressed Leslie; she uttered a shriek of admiration at the dusty-rose color of her nails. "*Gnädige Frau*, you cannot know how difficult it is to procure proper accompaniments for the costumes." Leslie felt a quick remembrance of Berlin at being called Gracious Lady. "*Gnädige Frau*, you have only recently come to Istanbul, you cannot comprehend the difficulties of our existence here."

Leslie was considering. There was nothing cheap about this girl. Obviously she was a bit nervous because Leslie was a lady, and because she was good-looking too. She talked inconsequentialities because she must be wondering why Gerald wanted them to meet; she talked as if she did not expect anyone to take with much seriousness what she said. Yet she was not trivial. It was as if everything really important was locked inside, a secret. Leslie thought she would try to put her more at ease:

"When the war is over you ought to come to the United States, Mademoiselle Florian. You'd be a great success on Broadway or in Hollywood."

For a second Florian was suspicious; perhaps this competent-seeming young American was pulling her leg. But she saw the discriminating sincerity in her face.

"I do not know if I have the talent necessary, and my English is not yet adequate."

Gerald interrupted with an easy smile, "Of course I'm going to kidnap Mademoiselle Florian one of these days, and it might be a good idea to take her to America."

Leslie was shocked. Florian had treated her own remark with seriousness and respect, but when Gerald chimed in to carry on the idea, she turned on him with bitter coldness. "If I go to America it will be to make a great career, not to elope with you."

"Come, Florian." Leslie could see the hurt in Gerald's eyes. "We're just making conversation, don't you know."

"Make your conversation on another subject."

Leslie felt a twinge. This was one of the most heart-breaking situations possible. Obviously this girl cared nothing for Gerald. He meant nothing to her at all. She was not even interested in keeping him dangling. And this made it inevitable that he would always be at his worst with her. He was condemned to beg. He could never be easy, affable, humorous, as he had been at dinner.

Now Florian was contrite at her rudeness. She put a hand on Gerald's tweed sleeve, wriggled closer in her chair, and smiled at him brilliantly.

"Darling, do not worry about what I say tonight. I am worried about Sophie and her sickness with the tomato juice. Also the Pole has made me an offer."

Downstairs they could see the Pole who had been dining with Florian the past few nights. He was alone, but standing near Reichenau at the bar. A confident look came into Florian's eyes.

"What kind of offer?"

"He says will I come to Cairo with him where he will establish me."

Gerald's face looked as if it were being trampled on.

"Is the Pole rich?" Leslie asked for want of anything else to say.

"Of course."

Leslie thought, "This is too painful," and her mind leapt

back to Strangeways. She would like to be of service to Strangeways and to Gerald too, though she would never under any circumstances deliberately make trouble between any man and another woman. She had been delighted to meet Florian and she knew that Gerald hoped that his appearance with her might incite Florian to jealousy; also she knew that Gerald, in a way, was rather excited at being with them together. But now she knew that it was hopeless. It was worse than that; it was humiliating. What Strangeways wanted was impossible. Gerald really must show more strength, more manliness, and get out of this affair—but he had to get out of it alone.

Something flamed in Leslie suddenly; what she had been thinking came out in her skin, her face, her eyes. All the reserve was released for the first time; she flashed into the open. Gerald had not looked at her directly, except in an impersonal way to help the conversation along, since Florian arrived. Now he was swinging in his chair, to say something to Leslie to ease his embarrassment with Florian, and unexpectedly, with a sharp impact, their eyes met. And for the first time, Gerald really saw her, saw her intimately for what she was.

He stared. For a second, he could not believe his eyes. By Jove! What an astonishingly *lovely* girl! He had of course known all along that she was attractive, but, now, it was as if she had changed utterly, by some mysterious alchemy, or that blinds had been abruptly snatched from his surprised eyes. She made Florian seem obvious, she made Florian seem almost blatant. Florian's beauty was extreme, but it was all on the surface somehow; Leslie's was infinitely more subtle, more profound, quieter, more delicate, almost secret. Feature by feature, Gerald saw her: the fine dark hair, the extraordinary eyes so white-and-brown, the soft round lips and the perfect arches of her teeth, the level forthright chin, the long full throat. And the quality of unexpressed emotion behind it all . . . emotion awaiting call.

"Leslie," he heard himself say. His voice sounded choked. He hadn't called her by her name before.

Florian broke in. Like almost all Hungarians she was crazy about the United States. She kept her hand on Gerald's arm, but otherwise ignored him. She addressed Leslie, with her own glorious eyes steady:

"Always I have wanted exceedingly to visit your country. Not just because of Broadway and Hollywood but because of stronger things. When I was a baby I would have starved but for the Americans. The United States sent a food mission to Hungary, and the food administrator in Szeged, where I was born, was a doctor who wore a funny crinkly suit in gray and white stripes" (seersucker? Leslie wondered) "and a red bow tie that was always slipping sideways. Everybody loved this doctor, but not just because he made away with epidemics and gave us soap and food and sometimes things to play with when it was our birthday. The doctor was good. You know, *good*. *Ein anständiger Mensch*. And when I was a girl growing up we saw the American movies, all with the big spaces and the very fast cars, the gangsters and the slapstick. In Budapest one café got the Sunday papers from America. I would sit there with my *Weissen Ohne* and look at the pictures printed on smooth paper with brown ink; I would count the number of stories in the skyscrapers and think that if we had that many stories on a building in Budapest, we would be a great city too, and filled with kind Americans like the Szeged doctor."

Why couldn't Istanbul get along like Juneville? Leslie thought abruptly. *Why couldn't Europe get along like New York State?* It was all so simple really. Get a melting pot started over here and give it a couple of generations and it might work.

"Then another thing," Florian went on. "Plays translated from the American would come to Budapest, and sometimes novels, and *feuilletons* in our newspapers. Always it was made that American love was only romantic. Always the Americans seemed clumsy when love got serious, and they were never mature about such a thing as marriage. Why do Americans marry so quickly and with so many divorces? Why is there such an immature attitude toward what a proper marriage should be?"

Leslie answered, "I suppose because we think a love affair and marriage should be the same thing. We want it springtime and a honeymoon all the time."

Gerald had a torn look, Leslie thought; he kept shifting his eyes between them. And she thought with amused grimness that she could give Florian a run for her money if she wanted to. And if Florian was, at this moment, having an affair with Hugo while leading Gerald on, though not caring for him, why, it was outrageous! Now Florian was being very close to Gerald, much closer than before. She hadn't taken her hand from his forearm, and she was laughing, whispering, flirting with abrupt softness. What did Florian think of *her*, Leslie wondered. As a much older woman? There was not more than a few years' difference between them, but in a decade when years counted a great deal; anybody in the early twenties thought that anybody nearing thirty was pretty old.

"*Du!*" Florian said to Gerald. "It is perhaps strange, but I find you *reizend* and *süss* tonight."

The small upstairs orchestra played "The Things I Love" softly, and then Leslie felt a sensitive compunction. After all Gerald was in love with Florian. She must not interfere in any way; perhaps they wanted to be alone a moment. She asked to be excused, and walked toward the powder room. She had a sudden intuition that Florian might, if he asked her, marry Gerald; she did not love him in the least but she might very well marry him; and Leslie thought, good lord, it shouldn't happen. Let them have any kind of affair together, but Gerald ought not marry her. There was nothing at all wrong with this girl, but most distinctly he shouldn't marry her. Yet—that melting pot idea! Gerald and Florian might produce good European children!

She waited a moment in the powder room. She felt confused. A look of helplessness came over her clear, honest face.

She opened the door and started for the terrace. Then she stopped rigid with shock. Waiting for her there and barring her way was Hugo Reichenau.

II

"Ah, good evening, *gnädige Frau*—"

She tried to circle past.

"Forgive me, but I have a great desire that we should meet." His voice had both strength and softness.

"*Nein!*" said Leslie, uttering the sharp negative in German. "Please. It's impossible."

"But, *meine Gnädigste*, a little moment sometime—"

This was not a beautiful blond Hungarian. This was the Gestapo enemy. "*Ausgeschlossen*," Leslie said. "Impossible."

"Why?" His big head, with the smiling teeth, leaned closer.

She twisted free. She must not let him talk to her. She heard him whisper, "Let us at least be civilized . . ."

She was furious. "*Ausgeschlossen*," she repeated. "Please." And she slipped past him.

III

Slowly, adjusting herself, composing herself, she walked to her table. Would Gerald notice anything? She didn't want to tell him what had happened. After a moment Florian left, wandered over to the bar to have a drink with the Pole, and then disappeared. Hugo sat alone, his back turned.

Gerald took her home. He was regarding her acutely. In the taxi he said, "You seem rather troubled; has anything upset you?" She hated to have people mixed up in her private affairs; her pride couldn't bear it if anybody were solicitous. "No," she replied, a bit stiffly.

"You're certainly excited about something," Gerald suggested, still watching her.

"Well, it's been rather an exciting evening." Now she wanted to get home quickly.

"I say . . . About Florian . . ."

"I thought she was marvelous," Leslie said.

"I don't know what's got into me. I don't want you to think I'm an awful bounder. I don't chase women much. But—"

He was holding her hand; she felt an expanding warmth; in a second he would try to kiss her.

"No!" Leslie said decisively.

"Please . . ."

"Don't!" she protested.

To hell with what Strangeways wanted. To hell with all of this. She wasn't going to be any momentary substitute for Florian or for anybody.

"Forgive me . . . I'm so sorry." She had never heard a voice more contrite.

"I'm sorry too."

Of course her anger at Hugo had something to do with this. If Hugo had not accosted her this might be different. She was tense and shivering.

"Well, good night," Gerald said, as the taxi stopped.

She smiled now, twisting her face. "Good night."

"Why, you're trembling . . ." Then he became rather formal and polite. "Look, when I get back to town, I hope we'll have another evening."

"Of course, Gerald."

"Really, I can't quite explain, I want so very much to be seeing you again."

"How nice."

"Well, good night."

"Good night."

They shook hands firmly at her door.

CHAPTER VIII

Shadow

I

LESLIE got down to the Lend Lease office, on the Istiklal near Tokatlyan's, in the building where many foreign firms were housed, like Vagonli-Kuk and Foksfilm Korporeysen. Dave Urquardt was a skillful boss. He was telling her that they had just had new instructions from Washington, and that some American shipments of *matériel* were being curtailed. The Turks had asked for a fabulous lot, but they weren't going to get all they requested, not by a good deal. Apparently we used Lend Lease as a kind of weapon. Quite right, too. When the Turks behaved, they got most of what they wanted. When they flirted too much with the Germans, we cut them down.

Urquardt ordered, "Now you go to work on these B-File reports; I'd like an analysis by tomorrow, if you can manage it."

This was work which necessitated great precision in detail, and Leslie bent over her desk. But she was finding it difficult to concentrate. The B-File reports. Stacks and stacks of them —about army boots, canteens, flashlights, jeeps, radio installations, marmalade, artificial legs, aircraft. She worked steadily an hour, but in between the typewritten lines there floated Gerald's jovial, restless smile and the dark face of Hugo Reichenau.

She got up, intertwined her hands, left her desk, returned to it stubbornly, and then walked to the window, sighing. She looked out over the crowded traffic winding through the cobblestones of narrow streets. She felt a helpless resentment that people were grabbing at her, when all she wanted was to work well at her job and sleep peacefully at night. She felt like kicking something.

Urquardt drifted in.

"Letter from my wife today. Took just five weeks to get here. She says people are all steamed up over the strikes, and that our eight-year-old girl has tonsillitis, and that she's sending me a book called A Bell for Something, and that everybody's crazy to know when the invasion will begin, and that the Dodgers are having a lot of trouble."

"It all seems remote, doesn't it," Leslie said.

"Yet the world is one." He said this lightly, not sententiously.

She finished work at about twelve-thirty and left the office. She thought she would take a street car back to the Musifers' because taxis were so outlandishly expensive; she had promised to have lunch with them, since it was Saturday and she had the afternoon off. Urquardt told her where to pick up the street car, and she waited at the corner.

The crowded car bounced and screeched, and her impatience, her ill temper, mounted. She watched for a landmark in her neighborhood, and got off near a big café called the Waytaus, White House. From here, she had two blocks to walk, down one of the steep streets leading to the water. She had only gone a few steps when she saw that a small green automobile had left the curb, and was following her.

Her first impulse was to walk faster. Then she stopped short, abruptly, and the automobile, just abreast, stopped too.

"*Gnädige Frau*—"

Hugo leaned from the wheel, and had the door half open.

"Mrs. Corcoran—"

She stood there squarely. No one was in sight, except a *hamal,* porter, bent like a jackknife under a trunk he was carrying.

"I was prepared to wait by the café all day. I knew at some time you would come."

Levelly she said, "Please don't bother me any more."

"I wish only to have a few words with you. Then we will see."

Impudence! She started to walk off. "I don't want to talk to you. Now, go away."

She cut across a grass plot, through debris and broken stones, where the car could not follow. She felt weak and shaky. She reached her door, and slipped quickly inside. Hugo was rooted by the car. She could hear its motor purring.

II

Germans . . . Germans . . . In fact she knew quite a lot about the Germans. She had locked into herself for a long time most of her memories of Berlin; now, one by one, they emerged as she succumbed to the biting luxury of reminiscence. What could you do with a people like the Germans? Incorrigible, incomprehensible . . . Had they been purely evil, there would be no issue. A wholesale blight, a pestilence: such contingencies present no problem; you eradicate, you cleanse. But what about Herr Richter, who had been their *Portier*, concierge; grave, upright, a Social Democrat to the marrow of the clean bone; what about Frau Hofmeister, their cook, with her inordinate neatness, industriousness, and sanitary efficiency; what about the talkative seamstress who came in on Friday afternoons and the plump young *Dozent* who gave Hal the German lessons and the cool-handed, winking barman at the Bristol? Good people. Simple-minded, maybe; but good, honest. Of course by this time the Nazis had probably killed them all . . . Of course too they could not be acquitted of responsibility; one and all, witlessly, they had let the Nazis in, let the Nazis lead them . . .

Leslie's mouth bent around and tightened in a hard ring of contempt; the loathing her lips and eyes expressed was so deep, so gripping, that it reflected and concentrated the vision of something not merely evil, but nasty, sick-making. She had been taking a stroll in the park near the Brückenallee, on one of her first evenings in Berlin; a fine, revealing introduction to the folkways of the Reich! In the green twilight a heavy man, in a respectable black suit—he might have been a *Geheimrat*, a professor—darted suddenly out of the bushes near the gravel path, exposed. If he had been a sweating lout in overalls or a peasant in leather pants it would have not been so shocking. But a man no longer young, belonging to the better fabric of society, wearing pince-nez, a man of obvious standing and position, leering and gesturing at her as he stood by the bushes—exposed . . . She paused a second, dumb with shock and disgust, and then turned and walked swiftly off. The man called something; she couldn't understand. She thought she would find a policeman, but no policeman was in sight. Then a kind of hatred filled her. When she reached home her teeth were chattering with hatred, loathing, and contempt.

She and Hal lived on the upper floor of a three story stone building on one of the leafy streets near the Tiergarten. There was no elevator and the stone steps were narrow and slippery. But it was a soundly made apartment, well-heated in winter and with a comfortable modern bath. She and Hal thought they would be very happy when they moved in. They had an income quite large by European standards; they rapidly made friends in the American colony; they set out, a modern young couple, to lead healthy, serious-minded, constructive lives— that is, insofar as Berlin in the late thirties could possibly permit healthy and constructive lives to be led. Hal, she discovered with uneasy prescience, was going to like these people much better than she did. He was somewhat timid, cautious like most young bankers, very conservative, and still trying to give Germany and Germans a chance.

What distorted, frustrated, frightening people they really were! . . . Their association of the principle of duty with pleasure, which destroyed pleasure; their consequent fear and hatred of the innocent, the decorative, the spontaneous. She stared inwardly at herself, and recalled that small episode in the subway. My God! She had picked up an American magazine at the Adlon bookstand, and was riding home in the *Stadtbahn*. It was Frau Hofmeister's night out and she and Hal were going to have a gay night out too, dining on the Kurfürstendamm and then visiting a beerhall or two and maybe ending up at one of the small, rather *chic* supper clubs, like the Koenigen. She was happy. She was as happy as she had ever been. She was pregnant, and it was the most wonderful thing in the world that she was going to have a baby. Now she knew at last what life was for. She had been thinking of names for it all day, and making the most elaborate and secretly delightful plans. Luckily their apartment would be big enough, if they converted Hal's study into a bedroom. They would get a nurse from the country somewhere. Leslie was brimming with warmth, with assured delight that she was a woman, above all, with happy pride. Late that afternoon she had her hair done—it had never been so highlighted with color, so fine and lustrous, and it seemed to be growing now by inches overnight—and the manicurist did her nails a shining, brilliant scarlet. *"Die gnädige Frau sieht glänzend aus,"* the manicurist congratulated her.

Suddenly across from her on one of the straw seats of the *Stadtbahn* an unkempt bumpkin in S.A. uniform, who looked as if he had just arrived from some remote farm, snapped at her in a cold, hostile voice:

"Diese roten Nägel sind unausstehlich. Ekelhaft! Those red nails are not to be endured. It's disgusting!"

Leslie dropped her magazine in astonishment. She spoke slowly: *"Sprechen Sie zu mir?* Are you speaking to me?"

"Ja." Even the monosyllable sounded hysterical.

She thought a second, and said icily, *"Wenn Sie diese roten Nägel nicht ausstehen können, dann nehmen Sie rückwärts Platz.* If you can't endure my red nails, then sit down at the other end of the car."

The young Storm Trooper turned pale and stared at her, gaping. Finally he cried, "If you were not a woman, I would knock you down. *Wenn Sie keine Frau wären, würde ich Ihnen eine 'runterhauen!"*

Scornful, with her eyes now blazing, Leslie shot at him a single word, the worst of all words to a German, *"Unverschämt!"*

The Storm Trooper hissed at her, struggled with himself, and finally walked to the rear of the car, his shoulders twitching with rage. After he left the train at the next station, three other passengers clustered around Leslie, grasping her hand, commending her and saying *"Sie hatten recht, gnädige Frau.* You were right."

Then there was her doctor. In reminiscence her eyes were sober, earnest. Dr. Zehden. What had happened to Dr. Zehden? A bespectacled, gray-haired man of fifty, with long precise fingers, strangely shaped, so that the tips seemed broader than the roots. His favorite word was *Ordnung,* and he assured her that it was inconceivable that anything could go wrong, because even in medicine nowadays everything was predestined to be ordered well. But did she perceive a faint tinge of irony in his voice? She had never talked to Dr. Zehden about politics. She had no idea what his politics were. She didn't want to know, because though the idea was horrible, it was just possible that this superb machine of a doctor might be a Nazi, and that she couldn't have borne; she would have had to leave him, and conscientious doctors who would take foreign patients were getting increasingly scarce in Berlin.

She was undressing neatly in his examination room. She lay down on the narrow metal table.

"And what does a pretty young American, who is little more than a school girl but who has great confidence, think of our Third Reich?" he asked her.

Our Third Reich? But again the objectivity of the scientist seemed peppered with a light, almost imperceptible irony. Leslie, however, would not equivocate. She said flatly, as she lay there, waiting, "I'm against it."

"Why?" He began his examination.

"Because I believe in freedom." She squirmed a little.

"A cliché," he dismissed her remark. Then, searching her,

patiently probing her, he grunted with satisfaction. "*Ja . . .
Alles gut. Alles ganz normal . . .*" He looked at her face,
"Freedom for what?" Still he probed, delicately, searchingly,
as if his fingers had eyes.

She couldn't help it; she began to laugh. Really it was too
wildly incongruous. Lying there on his white table, while an
examination of this kind was proceeding . . . Talking about
the Third Reich, liberty, and the rights of man, while he
calmly inspected the position of her unborn child . . .

Also it was so terribly German. He took off his rubber
glove, tossed it in a container, and told her to sit up.

Then Dr. Zehden began to chuckle too. But when she was
dressed and he was giving her instructions on diet and exercise
and the like, he looked deadly serious.

"Nations are like children . . . They need care. A nation
that lacks trust, lacks confidence; it needs care, control, education. Like a child. Because it must be educated in security;
it must be educated to forget fear.

"I am a doctor. I should be examining the wombs of pretty
women . . . while there is a raging sickness in the heart of
Europe.

"This Germany of ours . . . it is sick too . . . Sick with
primitive, explosive, relentless forces . . .

"But a country must find its own way out. Nothing can
be imposed on a people, from above, from outside, that will
endure . . ."

Utterly to her surprise, Leslie found herself weeping. He
looked at her with a kind of calm, frigid benevolence.

"*Ach!* You are healthy woman. But in pregnancy, no
woman knows why she does what she does. *Sie sind nicht
Herrin ihres eigenen Willens . . .*"

Of course it had to happen that her little girl should be
born the day of *Anschluss*. She timed the pains for half an
hour and then called Hal at the bank; he said it would be
quicker if he met her at the hospital. Then Dr. Zehden's voice
was steady. "Take a taxi to the *Klinik* at once. I will be
there when I have concluded my work in the office, at six

o'clock." What a relief it was that it was happening at last! What happiness that these weary, dedicated months should now come to fruition and produce life! She walked heavily downstairs. She would pick up a taxi at the usual corner. But there was no taxi there! The streets were thick, riotous, with marching crowds, with dourly celebrating men and women. Panic struck her, and she walked slowly, panting, toward Lessingstrasse. Not a taxi was in sight. But every other kind of vehicle swarmed through the streets. She thought she'd go back home and telephone. A taxi veered at last from the park, and she seized it. But the driver didn't want to take her; he was finishing work for the day. She insisted, snapping, "I'm about to have a child, you fool!" Then they couldn't get through the parade lines on the Unter den Linden. The streets were blocked solid, and there was no way to detour. For an hour they were held up, as armored cars, tanks, artillery wagons, crunched heavily by. When she finally got to the clinic, not so much frightened as angrily impatient, Hal looked the picture of death, and even Dr. Zehden was alarmed. She had her little girl very easily and promptly then. Her first words were to Dr. Zehden, "Well! And you talk of *Ordnung*!"

They named the baby Sally, which seemed to give a pleasant note of both their names . . . She was a compact, pretty child, with Leslie's dark hair and Hal's slate-colored eyes. Like a doll at first. A vivid, breathing doll.

. . . Leslie thought of the happy plans she had for Sally as she grew, how she would learn to walk and talk, what her first words would be . . . And later, all the pretty dresses she would have, and tiny shoes that had to be bigger year by year, and when she'd first braid her hair. She was fascinated too by Sally's early groping signs of recognition; it was marvelous to observe how she knew *her*; she was passionately happy, and she thought that soon she'd start another child.

Hal had of course wanted a boy. But in the mysterious manner of fathers he was notoriously in love with Sally by the time she was a month old . . . Hal was behaving quite well these days. Though he did drink a bit too much and once or twice she had caught him drinking secretly.

Late that summer Fleming came to Berlin. He had just finished Amherst and he and a classmate crossed the Atlantic by freighter to have a holiday abroad. They picked up a fantastically decrepit red jalopy; they had fine adventures in Rouen, in Liege, in Aix, in Cologne. Now they were proceeding to South Germany and perhaps Czechoslovakia, and they would return to America *via* Paris and Marseilles. One morning Fleming, who had always been fascinated by the movies, drove out to the Ufa studios; he hung around a few days and then picked up a kind of job as an extra. He did not quite understand what the film was about, but he didn't much care. Everything was an adventure; everything was the satisfaction of insatiable vitalities and curiosities.

"Gee, Les, that's quite a joint they have out there. Of course, nothing to what California must be. Aren't these crazy Germans the limit, though. I ran into a procession, and some kid in a black uniform asked me why I didn't salute when their cockeyed flag went by . . . I just laughed at him. Say, Sis, any place in Berlin you can get a coke?"

She realized with some apprehension that Hal and Fleming didn't get along too well. Fleming made Hal uncomfortable— his healthy rawness, his irresponsibility, his brash sense of fun. And more and more she became bothered by political differences between herself and Hal, by a series of distinctions in basic attitude. Hal could never be a Nazi. Of course not. He was not that kind. But his work threw him constantly closer to the small but incisive and influential group of rich foreign business men in Germany who played a pro-Nazi game. The American manager of the bank's Berlin office was out-and-out for Hitler; he hated Jews, communists, and what he called "disorder." The bank had God-knows-what in German investments. It wanted to protect them. It was part of Hal's own job to protect them. And Hal temporized. Once at a party Leslie overheard him say of a friend, a newspaper correspondent, "But of course remember he's a Jew . . ."

And he took to half-defending the regime. He would say things like "Well, let's not generalize too much from one particular."

Fleming came back from the Ufa studio one evening in a blast of excitement. Somewhere on the lot they were making a propaganda short, and Fleming noticed some actors made up as Jews; they were having a grisly time, being kicked and pushed about and tormented, pulled around by their beards and stepped on and laughed at. It all seemed horrible. And very real. Too real. He grew curious, and asked the director, who told him with a contemptuous shrug that the actors were *real* Jews, who had been dragged out of their shops and made to work, made to portray in a film the actual ignominy they were suffering.

Leslie saw something in her brother's face. "What happened?" she asked alertly.

"Well, Sis, guess my days as an extra there are over."

"You didn't have a row, did you?" Hal said, anxiously. He took a drink.

"Well, I got into a kind of argument with that director, and it seems I slugged him."

Hal was horrified. This kind of thing might get them, him, into trouble. And though the word hadn't become fashionable yet, Leslie knew suddenly what her husband was: an appeaser.

Once, just once, Leslie saw Hitler plain . . . It was their nurse's afternoon off, and she had taken Sally out for a sunning in the Tiergarten. She was pushing the carriage along the Charlottenburger Chaussee, when two motorcycles bent fast around the Grosse Stern. Then came a long black car filled with men with guns. Leslie put her hand on Sally's shoulder inside the baby carriage, as if protectively, and watched, waiting. A closed automobile, smaller, careened just behind the bigger car. On the back seat, she could see, Hitler sat. She caught a fast glimpse of the warped, flaccid figure, leaning against the upholstery, the pasty vacuous face, and the dash of mustache. His eyes were open, but he seemed asleep.

Some things you never got over. Even years after . . . In her room at the Musifers' Leslie's eyes filled slowly with tears, and she felt she was in that Tiergarten flat again. The essence of tragedy was irrecoverability; also incomprehension that anything so meaningful could have happened meaninglessly. This was today; that had been almost six long years ago. What was time? what was fate? Her lashes twisted in the hot tears. Was there any compensation? What had Sally been spared? Would she have had a happy life? What might have happened to her later? Where was she now? . . .

Their nurse, Annie, was a Bohemian, a thin nervous girl with blond braids from a village near Prague, competent enough and pleased with her job. Of course it all happened at the exploding height of the Munich crisis, the day after Hitler's ultimatum at Godesberg. Annie had been violently distraught and preoccupied. No wonder. They all were. They were thinking of how to get out, if war came. They listened hour by hour to the radio and its indescribably vicious, vulgar, and provocative stream of threats and slander. Hal was contrite now at the line he had taken the year before. He kept calling the Nazis "bastards . . . bastards." And Annie said to Leslie at breakfast, "I cannot help it, *gnädige Frau*, but my wits are at their end, I am *ganz nervös*."

Over and over again Annie tried helplessly to explain what happened. After lunch Leslie joined Hal at the bank where they could hear late bulletins. Annie, with the radio on at home, heard the news of Chamberlain's departure and the full extent of the Nazi terms. She told Leslie how she had thought blindly of the way the cobbles glistened near the river in the thin Prague sunshine; the taste of the gray wurstels at the railway station at Karlovy Vary; the red embroidered skirts of the country women, like her mother, and the walks in the moist woods near Masaryk's castle . . . Going down the steep stairs, with the baby in her arms, she tripped. She tried to right herself by grasping the balustrade, but Sally fell out of her arms, and slipped head-first down the long stone stairs.

Purely and simply an accident. The most villainous kind of luckless and fortuitous accident. Their baby doctor, Dr. Parisius, was at a patriotic mass meeting, and the child was dead, with a cracked forehead, by the time he came.

III

That evening, just before she was going out to dinner with Urquardt and two or three friends from the Embassy, the 'phone rang. The Musifers had only one 'phone, and Leslie walked down the corridor, papered with grayish water lilies, to reach it. She knew before she answered that it would be Hugo Reichenau.

"No," she said into the 'phone, and bumped the receiver down. Enough was enough.

Instantly it rang again. "But I must see · you. It is *notwendig*, really important, necessary," Hugo said.

"You must understand I cannot," Leslie said.

"It is not just what you think. Why are you so afraid of me?"

"I'm not afraid." She got angrier.

"Have you no faith in yourself? Do you fear to meet a man with faith?" His voice was smooth and smiling now.

Faith? A Nazi to talk of faith?

"I simply can't talk to you, and that's all there's to it." But suddenly she had an idea.

"You know nothing of me and my kind," Hugo said.

"I know plenty. I know all I want to know."

"Everybody you meet here . . ." his voice held a kind of imperturbable scorn. "Everybody so respectable. So respectable and reasonable and meek. Should you not like to have conversation with somebody *un*reasonable for a change?"

Back in her room she began to wonder. Why was he pursuing her—*why*? Could this behavior mean something more than it seemed to mean? She thought of what Strangeways had said. "Don't be a blithering ass," she told herself.

Dinner was fun. It was good to be with a group this way,

to become part of the gang. They did not go to Taksim's, where they might have run into Hugo. She did not know whether to be sorry or relieved.

IV

Strangeways dropped in for tea the next day.

"Got Gerald off to the mines last night, finally. Good thing too. Didn't mention our talk about him, of course. So I'm curious to know: how did you make out?"

"Did he seem much changed?"

"No, can't say he did. Still, a bit more relaxed, maybe."

She avoided his eyes. "Well, I didn't do the dance of the seven veils for him, but I was just as nice as I could be. I hope he liked me. I liked him, very much."

"Damned fool asked that girl to marry him."

Leslie had always prided herself on the way she could stay dead-pan, but she had to fight a second to keep her face from dropping. Then Strangeways went on, "She turned him down, luckily." Again she had to struggle to keep her expression static. She said, "She's quite a girl."

"Not one who's good for a man, though."

"Why not?" Her voice concealed a quiver.

"A man like Gerald, anyway. He needs somebody stronger."

"It isn't usually strength a man looks for in a woman."

"Or somebody who'd be more affectionate. Strange, how that boy craves affection."

"Don't we all?"

Strangeways was ruminating. "Well, anyway, thanks." He lit a cigarette. "Now, tell me all you've been doing."

Leslie described how Hugo had been pursuing her.

"Hugo? I'm damned. Hmm. Humph."

"What do you think I ought to do?" she asked.

"Do? What can you do? Do what you're doing."

"Yes, but it might be interesting to see him and have a talk."
For some reason she didn't want to explain further.

"Nonsense." He looked at her sharply. "Wouldn't advise it, if I were you."

"Why not?"

"Why not? Because it might be damned dangerous."

"What do you suppose he's after?"

"You."

The idea she had had seemed fantastic, far too fantastic to mention to this Englishman; still, it teased her.

"Dine with me tonight?"

"Thanks, no. I'm going to read a bit, and go to bed early."

"Hmm." His mind flashed back. The more he thought about Hugo the less he liked it. You could never tell about American girls. It might appeal to something crazy in her, though she was certainly not the crazy type.

"Had an interesting afternoon today. A bit on the gruesome side, but interesting. You know we have folks scattered in the Balkans. Drop 'em in by parachute. No, no, it's not much of a secret. Everybody knows it. Otherwise I'd not be telling you."

"Would you ever tell me anything that actually was a secret?" Leslie smiled.

"Depends. Some things, yes. If I hadn't trusted you, I wouldn't have asked you to help me out with Gerald."

"What if I should have lunch with Hugo Reichenau? Would you trust me less?"

"Let me finish what I was saying. One of our chaps got back here from the Balkans early today. No, not an Englishman. Just one of our chaps. Look at this."

He took a photograph on shiny paper from his wallet and showed it to her.

Leslie felt sick.

"New trick the Boche has. Nice, what?"

She handed it back.

"That's what they do when they think they're through with them. But, as I say, this chap managed to get away. And he carries evidence of where he was right with him, one might say." Strangeways grunted.

The photograph showed a man's back; between the shoulder blades he was branded. Two initials: then an identification number.

"If they catch someone they think is a Jew, they add two more letters. J. S. *Jüdisches Schwein*. Big letters. Probably takes off a foot of flesh. Nice to carry around with you all your life, eh?" He added almost lightly, "They brand women too. When they catch them. On the breasts."

"Stop it!" Leslie was angry. "Stop trying to frighten me!" She was furious. "If you're telling me all this just for fun, it isn't fun, and stop it, please. If you're hinting at how dangerous Hugo is, and warning me not to see him, don't! I'm not sure I really want to see him. But if I do, I'll take care of myself all right!" She felt that she might cry.

"Come, come. Let's not have a scene. You asked my advice. I was giving it."

"Sorry," Leslie said. "Let's have some tea, shall we?"

Strangeways was silent. He narrowed his eyes and intently thought, I wonder if she *could* get away with it. I wonder if she could make him fall in love with her. I wonder if she's got enough. I wonder if she's big enough.

The Musifers' little girl, Etta, crept shyly into the room. Every afternoon now Etta waited for Leslie and breathlessly tried to talk to her and loved her with all her child's soul and clung to her when she left. She still had the rose-diamond ballet dancer.

"Pretty child," Strangeways said.

"She's wonderful," Leslie said.

v

She was undressing when a note came by messenger. She looked at the handwriting on the envelope, and thought she knew whence it came.

Madame:

A party of us will tomorrow swim and have *Jause* at the Klub Lido. We would be so happy if you can join and amuse with us. At 5:30. Please to forgive my *Englisch*.

Florian

She knew who would be there. Everything she had been thinking all day made her decide to accept, to take a chance. And confusedly, almost perversely, another thought came to her mind. She remembered what Gerald had said that first night at Taksim's. "We're not making war on Thomas Mann."

CHAPTER IX

American Girls Are Pushovers

I

WHILE Leslie was having tea with Strangeways the German agent Hugo Reichenau sat with Florian in the Konditorei of the Park Otel. The Park was, of course, the best hotel in Istanbul, and full of Germans; its Konditorei looked like something out of Vienna. Parasols in striped blue and red; a fragile old lady in a lace cap behind the pastry counter; white garden chairs and wooden tables and coarse gravel underfoot; the headwaiter who positively would not accept the responsibility for delivering billets-doux to the Hungarian girls, who always came to the Park in pairs, except for a really substantial tip.

Hugo looked rather strained, Florian thought. Yet he still gave the impression of superiority, toughness, and conviction. But why did he talk this way? Normally when he mentioned other women he was half-contemptuous or amused.

"You sent the letter?" Hugo asked. She nodded. "You are an angel." He added anxiously, "Do you think she'll come?"

She responded with a question, "Why is it you are so excited over this American?"

"I do not know. From the first moment I saw her, she has meant something important to me . . . mysterious and most important."

Florian looked skeptical; she knew her Hugo. When he 'phoned asking her to write Leslie, she had first felt mischievously amused. What did it matter? What did anything matter? She giggled writing her note, with her little finger

111

in her mouth, mischievously. Hugo was fond of her and she was fond of him, and it pleased her to do him a favor; if she could assist him in a small flirtation, that was not unamusing. Also she had admired Leslie intensely the other evening. That American girl knew her way about. And Hugo would not get away with anything, cheap. He might get badly fooled.

"*Du bist ein Schlimmer!* You are a naughty boy."

"No. No." Hugo disclaimed the compliment. "It's much more than that."

Now she was rather surprised. And then very moved. And then a shade angry and a little jealous. For Hugo was saying flatly, unapologetically, "I feel it beyond my control. I have never felt this way before."

First she wanted to say, "Not since last week." But she saw from his eyes that he meant it. He actually seemed to be suffering. And she responded to something romantic in the situation.

"You're really crazy about her, Hugo?" She did not want him to look at her too closely. Even if it had not been very much, always it was a little of death when it ended.

"Yes."

"What about me?"

He had to ride over a certain moment; after that they could joke about it. "*Schatzi*, you are busy with the Pole. Even, you dine with him tonight, when I am lonely. Besides we are good enough friends to understand one another."

"What has she got that I haven't got?" Florian asked.

His voice, though he softened it, had the peculiar brutality of any masculine voice that tells one woman he loves another. "Just look at her."

"You mean I can't hope to compete?"

"*Schatzi!* You know I'm not in love with you. You know you're not in love with me. We've had fun, that's all. Now I ask you to help me in something serious. Do not behave like a child."

"I do not think it is just her looks. And it cannot be her

mind, because you have never even talked to her. I think it must be that you are excited because she is American."

"*Vielleicht*. Perhaps."

Her eyes, which had been distant, focused below his.

"You are wearing a new necktie," she pointed out.

"English," he said. "It is very *chic*."

"You are always imitating the English."

His dark face flushed.

"The great misery of your life is that you are not an Englishman."

"What for nonsense," he laughed, but his voice had an edge.

"You wish it more than anything."

"What for nonsense."

Nobody had ever accused her of not being a good sport, Florian thought. And if Hugo were really in love with the American she would certainly not stand in the way. "I do for you what I can," Florian said.

His face opened. His relief was great but he did not even thank her. It was safe now. He muttered, "Something pulls me out of myself, out of myself by the roots . . . No longer have I contentment here. *Schatzi,* you have been good to me, sweet to me. But I feel a necessity to change wholly the circumstances of my existence . . . It is like a revolution in my soul, a grasping toward . . . toward . . . "

When Germans got introspective and talked about themselves in sentimental terms they certainly used big language. Florian thought.

"You may not find the American too easy," she kept on smiling. "You may find her something you do not anticipate."

There were two sides to Hugo, Florian knew. He was like a medallion which unaccountably had worn differently. Half the time he was bright, literal, precise; then he would become irritable and violently moody. For some days now he had been in this insecure and troubled state.

Her middle finger explored her upper lip. It was good-by.

"We will have a coffee now, and then never a coffee again," Florian said.

He knew exactly what was in her mind; he replied, "Nonsense, *Schatzi*." But he was thinking that she was a girl without much will and that he could pick it up again any time if he wanted to.

"I have been very fond of you, Hugo darling."

"You are an angel. *Du!*"

II

"There is something else." Half of it finished, Hugo thought; now for the rest. Impersonally he admired her glistening hair, set in the solid, swelling pompadour. "For a week or ten days, you are to go out to the mines and stay close to the young Heath."

She stared at him. She couldn't believe what he said. It sounded like some complex and silly joke. "So you will be free to make sport with the American?"

"*Nein, nein*, this is politics, this is business."

He explained. Notoriously, Gerald was madly in love with her. Notoriously, she could twist him around a finger. Notoriously, he had been careless about his work. Well, the next few weeks were going to be critical in regard to the chrome. Let Florian go out there, let her stay constantly in Gerald's company, let her completely occupy and saturate his mind, with the lovely essence, the perfume, of her being . . .

"I do not ask you to compromise or ruin him, to steal secrets. Just be with him for a week."

"I do not like it much," Florian stated. She was not a very intelligent girl, but she had no delusions about herself and not the faintest ambition to be a Mata Hari. "I cannot do such a thing."

All of this: Dortmund's idea at lunch today. That asthmatic *Schwein*, Hugo thought. That panting cadaver. Hugo loathed his boss, Dr. Dortmund. Of course they had to work together for the Führer and the German state, but Hugo loathed him.

All the time at lunch he had been loathing him, while saying with hypocritical alacrity, *"Jawohl, Herr Doktor!* A most engaging plan, *Herr Doktor!"*

"Baby, orders are orders, and you know I have no choice but to insist."

"I have never done this kind of thing before. I do not like it," she repeated stubbornly.

There was a kind of primal indecency to this, that Hugo, who had been her lover off and on for months, should ask her to journey to the remote hinterland of Anatolia, and there make love to someone who loved her but whom she did not love . . . But she knew that she had little power to resist him.

"There is the matter of your eventual return to Hungary," remarked Hugo coldly.

No matter what Gerald had told her the other evening, Hugo was the only person who could get her out of Turkey quickly and en route back to Budapest if she had to go.

She looked frightened and angry, and his tone softened. *"Du,* if any intimacy is distasteful, you do not have need to be intimate. Just occupy the young Heath. Take his time, keep him preoccupied. Take his thoughts and energy."

"And meantime you and the American . . . " Now her voice was edged again.

He croaked with mock-serious delight. "You are jealous. Splendid. At last."

But she thought of something quite different suddenly.

"When would I have to go?"

"Soon. I will arrange all the transportation, and you will have a comfortable *wagon-lit* with many Turkish officers to flirt with."

"How could I leave Taksim's for ten whole days?"

"That is all being fixed and paid for with Mr. Poppa."

"I do a lot for you, Hugo," Florian said.

His mind shot back to Dortmund. How respectful and attentive he had been while inwardly hating him. What contempt he had for Dortmund with his narrowness and vulgarity, his lack of grace and élan.

He called for their bill, and his voice was gentle now. "Perhaps it may be amusing for you. Who can tell, that village in the mines may hold great surprises."

She had not told Hugo that Gerald had asked her to marry him. Well, if she went, and did marry him, that would certainly be a surprise to Hugo, that would surprise him all right.

III

Hugo drove Florian home, joked with her, and kissed her lightly as he said *auf Wiedersehen.* He had a free evening, and he wondered what to do; he could go to one of the Turkish cafés, or hang around Taksim's. He drove past a movie, parked his car, and looked around to see if he were observed. He had a consuming passion for American movies, but this was something he could not publicly admit. Dr. Dortmund would not be likely to approve. The poster said Rozlund Rusl and Spensr Treci. He slipped within.

Hugo Reichenau, *alias* Hugo von Seidlitz, *alias* Hugo Bötzmann, had begun scratching for a living when he was ten. Now he was quite well-salaried, and he had a big expense allowance. Hugo grew up in Fröbelstein, a mountain village bright with tent-shaped pines and snow on naked rock near Munich. His mother, a stout woman with golden hair, hated his father, and so tried to make Hugo as different from him as possible. Often she said, "You must be a success. You must be ambitious. You must get on in the world. *Gott sei Dank,* you are not a stupid child." His father was the village baker.

When Hugo was four, Hindenburg won the battle of the Masurian Lakes and Von Kluck lost the battle of the Marne. When Hugo was eight, he had not seen an egg or a glass of milk for a year, and Germany lost the first round of the twentieth century sequence of giant wars. When Hugo was twelve, he had a job as a busboy in a Munich hotel and a postage stamp cost forty million marks. When Hugo was sixteen his mother died, he left Fröbelstein forever, and the Weimar Republic began to totter. When Hugo was twenty he was earning a precarious living as a tennis teacher and he became a Nazi not merely out of desperate frustration and bitterness but because it was the thing to do; he became a Nazi as naturally and inevitably—for a German—as a boy becomes a man.

He was good at sports, though not superlatively good, and he did what hundreds of Bavarian and Austrian boys did, taught tennis in the summer and skiing and ice-skating in the winter. He drifted from Bad Reichenhall to Kitzbühl to Zoppot and beaches on the Baltic. So he began to know the English and later the Americans and all the fashionable people who came to Europe every year. Later when he had no need to earn a living by sport he would sometimes play in amateur tournaments in summer resorts and when he won, there was no need to tell people he had once been a professional.

Hugo's ideology, his conviction and perfervid faith, came from a double set of stimuli. As a child he felt that he had been cheated out of nourishment, both of the body and the soul. So all his life thereafter, he would seek to reap from existence more than normal dividends; all his life, he would be on the make. The Nazi system made this possible. And there was something yearning and confused in him that, at the same time, made him long for discipline, which might account for the hold that Dortmund—or any boss—had on him today.

He made his way almost like a marauder through the torn chaos that was Europe in the 1930's. He learned English well, and French almost perfectly; he acquired a useful sophistication in the arts and manners. Through some of his summer-resort friends he got a job with a German automobile company; five years later he was an assistant export manager. All the time, as the war came closer, he got deeper into government and party work. And with his connections he was useful. He went to Italy, the United States, and the

Argentine for the Auslands-Amt; and from that it was just a step to what he was doing now.

When he was a youngster Hugo had had great jealousy of the rich, and a deep grudge against life. He got over this when he became moderately rich himself and found out how generally people were attracted to him and liked him. Especially women. Practically he made a career of women. Women for years told him how they found in him an irresistible combination of the fanatic and the tender. He had a great love for sex but not so much for human beings, except himself. All he had really cared about—for years—was the Nazi party and the German Reich.

Hugo waited for the newsreel at the end of the feature, and left the theater. He disliked having dinner alone, and he was not particularly hungry. He looked carefully around him, on the street, and saw nobody he knew. But when he turned the corner to pick up his car he felt the itch at the back of his neck which told him he was probably being followed. But it hardly mattered since he wasn't doing any business. Where to go now? This was a dull town, this Istanbul, despite its brilliant coloring. He had been here too long now. He would like a change. And with the way the war was going . . . He shook his head dubiously. *"Ach, Gott!"*

He might go and see Yfet. But Yfet bored him now. She was a Turkish girl from the south, near Adana, who sang that belly-dance music in the cafés. She didn't know a word of any language but Turkish, but Hugo had picked up enough to be able to talk to her, primitively. When he met her in a bar she was excited and exciting; he grimaced slightly, at the way she might lean over and bite the butt of his palm till he cried out. Then at home: timid, with her hands demurely, protectively, folded; crying as a rule afterwards, and asking in a bleating voice if he loved her. Bah, Hugo thought.

He slipped into the bar at Tokatlyan's to have a sandwich and a *kahve*. Usually he found friends here but tonight the place was deserted, except for a couple of American newspaper men whom he envied and avoided. He wondered where Leslie was. He must get over this feeling of staleness somehow, this atmosphere of being deflated. He wanted to meet someone who would give him a chance to express himself, who would stimulate his ego; above all, someone fresh, someone new . . . The way to get them was to be appealing at first. To be gentle, imploring, almost humble. To put himself, and all his potentialities, in their hands, so to speak, without a word. Then at the proper moment to be masculine and demanding.

Hugo left Tokatlyan's, and wondered whether to stay the night in town—he kept a small suite at the Park—or to drive out to his villa in the country. He asked himself what Leslie would be doing now. "I can do anything I like to a woman," he thought. American girls were pushovers.

CHAPTER X

Scared Money Never Wins

I

LESLIE did not tell anybody where she was going. Her coffee eyes had a look of determination, of excitement, of expectancy. Dave Urquardt waved good-by to her, "Well, be seeing you tomorrow." He wondered why she seemed so dressed up today, in a lilac dress instead of the suit she usually wore.

The Klub Lido was on the Bosphorus, twenty minutes out of town on the narrow, tram-ridden Serapia road. Leslie paid off her taxi, and walked briskly to the white turnstile. A few cars were scattered around, and she thought she recognized the small green coupe in which Hugo had followed her.

She passed close to it, and looked it over. The green leather seat was crunched down where the driver had been sitting. She had a sudden wild desire to open the door and sit down there, on the crunched leather behind the wheel. Then she thought as she had thought the day before, "But really this is awful."

Within the Club enclosure, she glanced around and then went toward the pool. There was no sign of Hugo; he was nowhere in sight. Of course it was too public here. Yet that was certainly his car outside. She wondered how it was going to be arranged. Then she saw Florian. In a white bathing suit she detached herself from a group under an awning, and came up and shook hands warmly and said hello.

Florian said almost primly, "I'm very *very* happy you could come." She thought, "This is almost what is called being a procuress, but Hugo will pay for anything he gets."

Leslie said, "I'm so glad you asked me." In a second, it was understood between them. But she thought, "I wonder if I've made a mistake or not."

Florian led her forward. "But let me introduce you to my friends. *Darf ich vorstellen . . .*" There was another girl, apparently the Sophie who had been poisoned by the tomato juice, a young man now climbing out of the swimming pool, in clinging trunks, and the rich Pole. They were all talking in the sand.

Florian murmured briefly in English, "We will dine together later, perhaps? My friend, who lent me his car, is hoping we will join him in the country." This was a little more than Leslie had bargained for. The Master Race, what? Making her come to him. Still, it was the discreet way to do it, and discretion was as important to her as him. But this business of being led like a lamb to slaughter . . . However, having come this far, she would go on.

Leslie had not brought a bathing suit; it made the others seem more naked. She sat down neatly. The young man in clinging trunks devoted himself to her, when he discovered that she spoke German; it seemed he was the saxophonist in the Taksim's orchestra. Florian was stretched on a *Liegestuhl*; how stunning she really was, Leslie saw. The shoulders were glorious, and her breasts stood out like lovely canteloupe-halves. She had long, thin, muscular legs, and very lean hips. She rose restlessly and bent to pick up a handful of sand. But if she were a man she would like a woman whose thighs just touched, Leslie thought.

With a kind of humorous contempt Florian turned toward the rich Pole, with his short belt of broad mustache, who so far had not said a word. Then she remarked to Leslie in German, as idly as if she was discussing the weather, "Herr Zelikowski is very angry with me. Very cross, very *böse*. Aren't you, Herr Zelikowski?"

The Pole made an irritated gesture.

Florian switched to English, which the Pole apparently did not understand. She began cheerfully to discuss his various defects and failings, and it gave Leslie a bewildered sensation to hear him thus thoroughly taken apart in his own presence.

Florian concluded, "So I tell him that all he is good for is to buy champagne and that now I am bored with too much champagne which gives me butterflies in the stomach the next day and so now I have declared to him that I cannot dine with him any more."

Sophie remarked, also in English, while Herr Zelikowski looked glum, "The Pole is a collaborationist." And the young man in swimming trunks, who was Tyrolese, added, "So even most of the *Reichsdeutsche* despise him."

Leslie thought that someone ought to be courteous to the Pole no matter what he was, and she turned to him. But he snapped something at her, "*Nicht sprechen,*" and hunched himself away from everybody in the sand.

"You see what delightful manners he has," Florian said. "You buy us a sandwich now, Herr Zelikowski."

"I will take caviar sandwich," Sophie said, in German.

"For me, also," declared the saxophonist. "Two sandwiches."

The Pole looked surly, ordered the sandwiches, wrapped himself in a beach robe, and walked off toward the cabins.

Florian made and unmade pictures in the sand, her head bent low, secretly. What is it Leslie has, she kept wondering. What could she do to be like Leslie, she whispered to herself. So poised and fastidious, so *chic* and creamy-smooth. How she would have liked to be born with Leslie's advantages, her opportunities . . . Then she had a sudden sharp desire to show off before her.

But Leslie had momentarily turned away. A few paces beyond them she saw André, the Greek waiter. He was lying flat in a deckchair, as if every ounce of energy had fled his body; he lay inert, sucking in the declining sun; his eyes were closed. Leslie felt a spasm of alarm. What would André think at seeing her with Florian?

The Greek stirred in his deck chair, and Leslie made a

quick decision; she walked over beside him. "Hello," she said friendlily. He was startled; he wriggled to his feet, saying "Ah, *oui, madame.*" To him, everything was an intrusion.

"Don't get up, please," Leslie said. Then Florian saw him too and waved cheerfully, asking him to join them. *"Merci, non,"* André said. But she pulled him over and for a few moments he joined their party. "Enjoy yourself now," Florian said.

Still the Greek's eyes were stony, guarded; but he talked amiably enough to Florian. And Leslie felt a curious certainty that André, a Greek, was closer to this Hungarian girl, an enemy, than to herself, an American, an ally. She felt that she was an outsider in his eyes. She was not a European, so she did not count.

Leslie drifted back to Florian, who now seemed spoiled and moody. "I am not happy in my life. I will make the high dive just once, *ich glaube.* When I make it I will say to myself, 'Good-by, Florian!' "

"It is too high to dive from," Sophie protested.

"I was in an automobile wreck once," Florian said. "And when the big car hit us and we went smash, and we turned over and all went black and I thought I was dead, what I said to myself was 'Good-by, Florian.' " She laughed. "And I wanted to cry, I was so sorry I was dead, I was so sorry that nobody would ever see beautiful Florian again."

The saxophonist saw the Pole walk back from the cabin, still looking glum. "Let's go to Prinkipo and swim tomorrow," he suggested. "Without the Pole."

"Nein. I cannot. I leave Istanbul for some days," Florian declared.

Sophie shrieked in surprise. Then Florian put her finger on her lips, as if she had uttered something that should not be told, and enjoining secrecy.

"Where, *du*?"

"Nowhere."

"Tell me where."

"Anywhere."

"Florian leaves Istanbul, it is a catastrophe!" exclaimed Sophie to Herr Zelikowski.

"*Ja*," the Pole said, coldly.

"Good-by, Florian," Florian said. "Good-by, beautiful, beautiful Florian. Good-by forever."

"A catastrophe," the saxophonist said.

Florian . . . proud, generous, defiant, Leslie thought. Like the beautiful body of Europe, helpless, crushed, defiant . . . she smiled at herself for being so fanciful. Florian was Europe. That was it. No. André rose from his *Liegestuhl,* stretched his thin arms, made his muscles tense, and looked as if he were seeing something a hundred miles away. No. Gerald had said what André was. But he was something else besides. It was *he* who was Europe, the Europe that had truly suffered, that was grim with black patience, that would not forgive.

Florian jumped up and walked to the ping-pong table with the saxophonist. He was quite good, but she beat him easily. She sliced and chopped balls all around him, and then drove with long, lean strokes. Sophie said, "The Florian, she was once table-tennis champion in our *Bezirk* in Buda-pest."

II

Florian tucked her amber-colored hair inside a white bathing cap, and Leslie walked with her to the edge of the water. The Bosphorus slopped back and forth, sliding with a purple sheen over mossy boulders. Above, a stairway of rock mounted thirty feet. Florian beckoned to the swimming teacher, a young man in a purple bathing suit. He came over, joined them, looked doubtful, shrugged, climbed the rock, and made the dive, very carefully. His head popped up, and he nodded. Then, while swimming against the strong current to the shore, he pointed toward the spot which Florian must try to hit. She climbed the stairway, crouching, with her hands flat on the hard thin thighs, straightened, and without pause, made the long, dangerous dive into the heavily sliding water. Her body swerved half-way down, and she hit the water sideways. Then she swam slowly toward the bank, with a half-crawl, and dragged herself up.

"Did you hurt yourself?" Leslie asked anxiously.

"No." But she pressed her hand hard against her side where the water had smacked her.

"I'm afraid you must have."

"I did not do it very right. I will try again."

"My goodness, don't!" Leslie protested.

"It is nothing."

"Please! You *will* hurt yourself!"

She grinned, and the swimming instructor looked even more doubtful than before; again she tramped up the steep stairway, and this time, while crouching, waited. Leslie looked straight up thirty feet. "Don't do it," she called. She kept shaking her head vigorously. "Please don't."

Florian gave her a reassuring wave.

Leslie pled with her, her head still shaking.

Florian straightened, joggled on her toes, felt her side, dove again, and this time hit the water true.

They walked back to the cabins together. Florian dressed and they had drinks in the small alcove bar. The Pole paid.

III

Florian looked at her watch after a while, took Leslie's arm warmly, and said, without haste, "Shall we go now?"

They slashed along the slaty road toward the Black Sea at dusk; they passed swiftly through the outskirts of Istanbul, and soon were in the remote suburbs, on the lonely shore road where isolated villas perched like watchtowers. Soon it would be completely dark, and they would be in open country. Florian turned the small car into a side road, and they overtook a plaster farmhouse. It was well over a mile before they saw another.

Leslie could feel her heart begin to thump. Really this was a somewhat foolish and perhaps dangerous thing she was doing.

She had had no idea they would be taking such an expedition; she had envisaged nothing more than a quiet talk in some out-of-the-way metropolitan coffee house.

Yet, she trusted Florian. She could not believe that she would wantonly lead her into any serious predicament. *And the bizarre idea she had seemed to justify all that she was doing*. It would justify almost anything if it worked out that way!

"This is turning out to be quite a ride, isn't it?" she murmured nevertheless. "You might tell me where we're going."

"Hugo has a small country house beyond Togli Point. A little place." No explanations, no apologies.

Florian remembered Leslie's face when she dove the second time, she had seen her earnest appeal not to risk hurting herself again. And she was glad that Leslie had been concerned, since it must mean that she liked her. With her eyes on the road she said suddenly, "I lead you into a difficulty, perhaps. You are not fearing to compromise yourself?"

"No." Leslie's lips were round and firm.

"I admire so much Americans."

But Leslie began to think, *could* she reasonably trust Florian, after all? To be blunt, Florian was an enemy whom she had met only twice in her life. Really this was a most peculiar kind of chance she was taking. It was fully dark now, and the scent of extreme loneliness hung thinly on the countryside. They must be well beyond Yenikoÿ or the town above by this time. Nobody knew where she was. Nobody could reach her. If she were being duped, if this whole business was a trap, the arrangements were certainly ideal.

"Do you think I am too *sportif*?" Florian asked abruptly.

Leslie didn't understand. "You mean too athletic?"

"No, no. Too *sportif* with men." She laughed with an ironic triumphant expression. "That Pole, now. Men are so strange. The Pole is furious. He wrote me a letter yesterday, a savage letter. He called me a bitch. But what he meant was, that I was not a bitch. The Pole has taken me to dinner six or seven nights. He has spent for champagne every night, and

French brandy, real brandy. He has hired a car; he sends flowers and trinkets. Probably he has spent on me at least two thousand Turkish pounds." She shrugged contemptuously. "And I have given him nothing. *Gar nichts!*"

Her face looked bitter now. "Early today, before you came, he denounced me for a fool—a fool!—for not agreeing to accompany him to Cairo. That that Pole should call *me* a fool!"

But Leslie was not thinking now of Florian and the *vie sportive*. She wanted to make herself absolutely alert. She wanted to be on guard with every sense and instinct.

"That Pole shouted at me, 'I'll have you if it's the last thing I do in life!'" Florian's voice was hard and furled in a kind of immaculate contempt. He would, would he! She snorted with an exquisite superiority, "Men! . . . *Lieber Gott!* What men think they are!"

The car slowed down, and then slid bumpily over jagged cobbles; they were in a village. Most of the houses were shuttered, but they showed dim streaks of light, and from a café came the whine of music. Florian parked near a wharf, where the water looked solid and sleepy, but bobbing with reflections from the street lamps. She touched Leslie's shoulder, and talked in a confidential whisper. "Come. We walk a little now." Their heels crunched in gravel down a dark lane.

Leslie controlled herself. This was no time to give way to fear, to panic. Her heart was pounding harder, and her mouth was dry. She was an American, she was about to meet with and have a talk with the "specialist" on Americans of the Gestapo. And America and Germany were at war. War makes its own rules. What could happen? Well, anything could happen. She sought to reason with herself, to give herself assurance. But Hugo knew that she had a government job, that she dined with people like Heath and Strangeways, that she must have access to confidential information. Nonsense. She must stop thinking in such scary melodramatic terms. Such things didn't really happen. All she had to do was reach for a 'phone. But suppose there wasn't any 'phone . . .

All these fears were childish and silly. But she remembered that talk the first evening of shipping bodies out in mail sacks.

Florian stopped, with a big hand on her arm. Then she whistled softly. A few doors away, in the darkness of the lane, a window shade lifted quickly, and the flat light of the window flashed.

"He's there," Florian said. "It's all right."

IV

"Well!" Hugo was at the threshold. "How very nice of you to come." He led them in. "But I am ex-*haust*-ed. This afternoon, six sets of tennis, and then some swimming. *Ja, ja!*" He laughed. "Florian, *Schatzi,* I love you. *Gnädigste*, Mrs. Corcoran, enter now, and inspect my small abode."

Leslie looked at him. The figure very lithe and graceful, the head very big, almost too big, with the heavy white teeth. And those dark brows almost meeting. This was the first real chance she had had to see him; she saw that his eyes, like Hal's, were a deep slate-blue. She felt a twinge. But otherwise he did not remind her of Hal at all.

"Alas, it is one of my most peculiar peculiarities"—he grinned—"I do not drink. But let me pour you a little vermouth. I know how Americans are. They enter a house, whish, they reach for a chair, whish, then they must have a drink, *sofort*! Is it not?"

"Not all Americans," Leslie smiled. "It depends on the circumstances . . . and atmosphere."

"You mean you like to drink with friends?"

"Yes, I suppose that's it."

"I am not a friend yet. But will you have a drink?"

"Of course."

Florian was watching them with aware curiosity, missing nothing. Leslie slipped off her gloves, and without letting her eyes give her away she looked about warily. The windows, small, shuttered, were too high to jump through. No telephone in sight. Hugo, easy and sophisticated, was bending toward the bar. He held out her drink. She stopped with it half-way to her lips. Now, really, she must control herself and not give way to these absurd fears. But what a perfect arrangement all this was! If Hugo meant harm to her and if Florian were a sinister accomplice, she could disappear, and not a soul in the world for hours, for days, could possibly know what had become of her. Suppose that drink were drugged. Oh, really, nonsense. Still, Hugo wasn't drinking. Would Florian? Leslie waited a second, and now both of them watched her steadily.

"*Prosit*," Hugo said.

She and Florian drank.

"*Schatzi*, make ready with our *Nachtmahl*, I beg you." Dutifully, swinging her skirt, with an airy I-don't-give-a-damn smile, Florian went out into the kitchen.

"At last, *endlich*, after all these days, we meet!" Hugo exclaimed. "Ah, but you are exquisite, you are most lovely. Much have I been in your United States, always have I so appreciated the American women."

Leslie didn't want any misunderstanding. Get it straight right away.

"What is it you want of me?" she demanded, poised, steady.

"Need you ask?"

So he was as sure of himself as all that. But his smile was so direct that the impudence glanced off. There were many things she might have countered with. She said simply, "If it's just to talk a little, why, all right."

"It is much more than that."

"Then we ought to stop right now."

Look at him. In white, of course—white shoes, white socks with an elegant clock, white tennis slacks, even a white belt, and a conspicuously monogrammed white silk shirt. Open at the neck, of course. Oh, but she knew all about him. He got that thin, country-like scent from a toilet water put up by Knize's, and he spent hours every summer getting just the proper tan on his shoulders, and she would bet a million that he wore a hair net at night.

My God, he was attractive, though.

Then she decided she could not simply dismiss him as a type she had several times encountered. She thought he might turn out to be like that Jugoslav fencing champion she had met at the Esplanade in Berlin, or the young radio executive from Geneva who, even though Hal was with her, pertinaciously and defiantly flirted all of a long holiday at Mürren.

But this Hugo Reichenau was much better stuff than those two. Perhaps at the very bottom, if you knew him well, he would turn out to be unsure of himself and, like Hal, given to self-pity. But as he stood before her now, he *had* something. He most certainly had. Also his manners were quite good, for a German, and he had good taste. Her eyes took in his house as he talked. There were books in French and English; she saw novels by Hemingway and Steinbeck. The furniture was bland, blond, and modern, the rugs soft and of solid pastel colors. On the mantle was an enormous picture of Florian in a sleek silver frame.

"Now it is my turn to ask you something. Why did you accept my invitation?"

"Two reasons. One was simple curiosity."

"I know the other, too," Hugo said.

"I don't think you do," Leslie said.

He congratulated her on her knowledge of German and then said that, for all its magnificence as a vehicle for philosophical or political thought, it was totally inadequate as a medium for flirtation. "How could you possibly say *je t'adore* or *ta beauté adorable* in my ungainly tongue?" he grinned. Now he was paying her another compliment, that she seemed *geistreich*. And that was a word you could only say in German! He was extremely attentive. His eyes were on her every second, smiling. She could not move an inch or change an expression by a shiver, but what he followed, swift as a fly.

Leslie felt that she was fascinated by him and couldn't help it. He was talking seriously now and she sensed that he must have a fanatic devotion to whatever work he did. Then suddenly, with quick intensity, she thought of Robin. Robin too had that wonderful passionate fixation on his job, or jobs. All at once she missed Robin so much that she felt sick inside. Why wasn't Robin here? She turned to jelly missing him.

Then astonishingly Hugo said without explanation:

"I can see it that you have loved a man. But I hope you are not one of those women with only a single heart."

He looked at her searchingly. And she felt oddly, sharply frightened.

Now he smiled again: "I will tell you about your character. You are clear-eyed. Too clear-eyed perhaps. There is no mystery about you. No mystery or mist."

Florian came out of the kitchen; in an apron she looked entrancing. She wanted to know where the paprika was.

"Do you not love my Florian?" Hugo bantered. "I love my Florian. Do you love me, Florian?"

"*Yok*," said Florian, which was Turkish for No. "Do I find the paprika now? *Yok!*" And they laughed at what a funny word *yok* was.

v

Dinner was ham and melon and salami and then a splendid goulash and some pastry. With coffee they talked about the war. Leslie hated herself for listening. This man was presumably engaged in the most dangerous and sinister kind of espionage against her country. Yet he made the most extreme effort to appear detached and even nonpartisan. This must be just a game he was playing, a role he was assuming, Leslie thought; this must be a ruse to take her in. His tone when he mentioned the recent German defeats and setbacks was of grave concern, of considered and deliberate sorrow. That his country was not having a period of success was a matter to him of mortal sadness, not of acrimony. Or so he sought to pretend.

"You wish to know how broadminded I am? Well, then, let us listen to the B.B.C. instead of to a German station!"

But the radio, grasping through static, brought nothing but liquid bubbles, like strident canaries singing.

"Tomorrow we can talk of politics all day. Tonight, let us not think of the ugly, painful world!"

Tomorrow? He saw Leslie's face, so appraising. But he was certain that he had made a powerful impression on her already.

VI

They tidied up the dinner table, and Florian went out into the kitchen to wash the dishes. Instantly Hugo darted close to Leslie; she shook her head, avoided him sharply, and followed Florian from the room. She put on an apron too, and they stood together by the sink.

More and more she liked this girl. Not for anything would she do her any kind of injury. And she must get Hugo out of her mind at once, if only because he was so capable of attracting her. She touched her arm, smiling. "Are we going back to town pretty soon?"

"Yes . . . whenever you want. Perhaps Hugo will drive us in."

Florian felt very close too. Her eyes were tentative. She had a sense of what Leslie was going to say.

"Look. It's none of my business . . . But I gather, I rather understood, you and Hugo are close friends—"

"He is naughty man. I have seen how he pursues you. With his eyes he devours you."

"That's what's bothering me," Leslie said. But she knew that anybody could have taken Hugo from Florian, since he didn't love her. "It's what I wanted to talk about."

Bluntly Florian asked, "Do you want him?"

"On the contrary. No! And I wanted to tell you I didn't want to interfere."

Florian considered. "Thanks. I am through with him."

"Well, I just wanted to get it clear." They finished the dishes. "Don't you have to get back to Taksim's?"

"No. I have two weeks' absence, starting tonight." Florian

had utterly no sense of political discretion. Or perhaps she
was being mischievous. Or perhaps she remembered how
Gerald had looked at Leslie a few evenings before. "I go to
the mines to be with Gerald."

"What?" Leslie was dumfounded. This made a new picture
altogether. She felt a flash of pique. This girl, with *both*
these men . . . She had followed Florian into the kitchen to
give something back to her, so to speak. Now she felt that
something else had been rudely snatched away.

Hugo walked into the kitchen; his voice was bold and his
eyes gleaming. "I know all what you girls talk about. You
talk about how desirable it is that every young lady should
have a man. Every man should have a young lady, too!"

They all talked together, but Florian now had a rather
guilty look, and Leslie felt constrained.

VII

They squeezed into the little green car, and drove swiftly
back to town; Leslie remembered how the leather seat had
been squashed earlier in the day. Now Hugo was at the
wheel, and Florian sat between them. She was glad that it
was arranged this way. She wondered how Hugo would bring
up the matter of whom he would drop first. He was certainly
tough enough to leave her off at the Musifers' and drive on
with Florian alone; but if he thought this would anger her
or make her jealous, he was much mistaken about her character. They slowed down entering Istanbul; Hugo circled near
Taksim's and the Grand Rue, and slid to a stop at what must
be Florian's apartment.

"Good night, Florian."

"Good night, Leslie. I have enjoyed so much."

"Me too. Thanks a lot."

"Good night, *Schatzi.*"

"Good night, Hugo darling."

"Good night," Hugo repeated.

"Good-by, too."

They drove off. The streets were dark. Now Leslie would be alone with him for the first time. Either she must stay pushed against the far edge of the car where she had been sitting, or take the difficult initiative of sliding closer, since he was driving. Carefully, she moved into the exact middle of her half of the green seat.

Suddenly his voice was harsh. "Why are you so frightened? Are you a child, to have fear of a man alone in a car?"

"I'm not afraid. It's much more complex than that," Leslie said.

"It is because I am German?"

"Of course. Naturally."

"Do you hate me because I am German?"

"No. But because you're a Nazi."

"I wish it were not so. You are not stupid. All Germans are not bad."

She thought a second. "I don't say that all Germans are bad. I do say that all Germans are responsible."

He stopped the car at her building, and she got out.

"Would you fall in love with me if I were not a German?" He had followed her to the door.

"Perhaps." She saw his dark face shine. It was the easiest thing to say.

"Confess—you would not leave me tonight, if I were something else than German."

She didn't like sentences beginning with Confess. "I can't tell you how wrong you are."

"Then why did you consent to come?"

"I've answered that before."

Suddenly good humor came back to his voice. He sounded almost gay. "Would you kiss me good night if I were a Swede? Or a Swiss?"

He laughed. While he watched her eyes with a caress, she said good night and unlocked the door.

CHAPTER XI

Two Is Company, More or Less

I

TWO minutes later he telephoned from the corner café, and bullied her into promising to lunch with him next day. They met at a small restaurant called the Emerald, spelled Emruld, which was run by White Russians and where he said they were not likely to be seen. "Today, who can tell, you will perhaps find out what kind of person I am!" he said arrogantly, but smiling.

"I ought not to be seeing him," Leslie said to herself sharply. "This is definitely unwise. We really ought *not* to be seen together. I must be crazy." Then that something she could not suppress, no matter how outrageously ridiculous it might seem, burst from her. "Maybe I can make him sell out!" She felt excitement, a sense of guilt, and an inexplicable confidence. She had the feeling that as an American with American largeness and vitality she could do anything.

They ordered hors d'oeuvres, spelled Or Duvr. She was wearing a beige sports dress, and she had a bright new manicure. Hugo watched her eyes. They reached for the salt together, and their hands touched; Leslie felt it like a shock. She withdrew instantly. Never had she known anything like the purely physical pressure he seemed able to exert at will.

But that was what Nazis were! That was what they had been everywhere in Europe—a tremendous physical impact!

"You have been for a time in Berlin. Let me ask you what you disliked most about my country."

Good Lord! What had she disliked most? Really! Murder;

135

extinction of the human spirit; baseness and cruelty; tawdry boasting by little men; hysteria and hypocrisy; obliteration of every civilized value. But she thought she'd begin gradually, that she might start on something simple.

"The uniformity of everything."

Persuasive, agile, Hugo leaned across the table. "You, an American, talk of uniformity! When your own country is the most uniform thing I have ever seen. Everywhere, the same blue plate lunch. Everywhere, the same cartoon strips, the same columns in the newspapers. Everywhere, the neon lights and the filling stations and the place to dine in the shape of a train! And such imitators as are the Americans, that no one has ever known before! An actress in the movies, she does her hair a certain way; presto, *sofort*, like a wave from one end of the country to another, all young women do the same!"

Leslie was amused. "But, you see, we're uniform out of free will. You're uniform because you get shot if you're not."

He brushed this aside. "That was one of the first things in America I noted. The very first, perhaps."

"What else impressed you?" She much preferred that he should talk about her country than vice versa.

"The dreadful manner of your waste. I was appalled. We, who had to preserve every scrap of paper, every bit of string . . . The way one could walk down the streets of New York, and see waste flow! The trivial, inconsequential things that Americans used brass and copper for! The hundreds and thousands of signs, all in metal—real metal! Arrows on the streets, and inscriptions telling where to walk dogs! . . . And the way packages are wrapped. *Mein Gott*, that cellophane! On everything, that so-irritating wrapping, that one had to tear and gnaw at! Cellophane! That might be made useful for explosives." He caught himself. "*Mein Gott!*"

She laughed. "Exactly. You won't find much wasted cellophane now. Maybe we start slowly, but we learn fast. And as to what you say about waste, well, I concede some of that, but in a way it was a healthy symptom; it showed our enor-

mous overflow of wealth and power. We could afford to
waste. You couldn't. And so you envied us."

"Then," Hugo went on, "there were some smaller things
which struck me first. For instance the worship of the name.
In the hotel, the name of the clerk. And engraved on metal! In
the banks, the name of each teller by his window. In the fashionable bars, the nickname of the bartender, embroidered on
the white jacket. I found it a childishness, a childish seeking
for the expression of an unformed individuality; also something suggesting an inner desire for regimentation, that you
accuse us of!"

"I must say it comes oddly from a German to worry about
the worship of a name, when your whole nation is forced to
worship one man, Hitler!"

"Let me go on. You are not annoyed? I make a small
index. Then I dismiss from myself all the things I did not
like." He smiled. "Well, there was the vulgar commercial-
ization on the radio programs. Really, something to make the
grown person blush." Leslie thought quickly, Yes, but we
can choose among programs, which is something you can't
do. "And then, perhaps it is part of the same herd instinct,
the same vulgarity, the *behavior* of people—in the parks, on
the bathing beaches. And, again, the way Americans drink!
It is like nothing ever seen in Europe. Especially the way
the women drink. I could not endure it how almost all young
American women drank so much. It was to me a kind of
personal affront." He paused, and added quite seriously, "It is
a sign of decadence. That and the collapse of your sexual
morals."

Leslie thought fleetingly of the man in the Berlin Tiergarten and the S.A. boy on the *Stadtbahn*. "There's nothing
decadent about the way we're building a hundred thousand
airplanes a year. Or about the way the Marines fought at
Tarawa. Or the way we cleaned up your U-boats. And we're
just getting started; don't ever forget that. As to alcohol and
sexual morals, some of us do drink badly, that I admit, but
there's nothing in America half so decadent as Berlin."

"Your country will be like mine, some day," his voice was assured and confident. "There is much basic similarity. If you should ever have a great catastrophe, like the inflation . . ."

This was an idea Leslie didn't like, though—strangely!—it brought them closer. But for the moment she wanted to listen, not to argue. She asked, "When did you visit America? Have you been there often?"

"Three times. First, when I was a boy of twenty-two. I crossed as a steward on the *Europa.*" He grinned. "It was working your way, like what the young Americans do. And I stayed some months; I taught skiing in Colorado and then Quebec. Second was in 1938. I was business man, I worked for Opel, the automobiles affiliated with General Motors; I lived six months in Chicago and Detroit. The third time was in the following year."

"For the Gestapo?" Leslie guessed.

"Certainly! Why not?"

His frankness startled her. "Well, it's not the purest or most innocent type of organization known to man, is it?"

"Who is talking about the pure and innocent?"

"Well—"

"I will try to explain. We Nazis see life straight. We know, we understand, we accept, that all political existence is a struggle. You must know that also. But we do not practise self-deceit as you do. There is plenty of cruelty in your country too. But we, *we* face facts frankly. What does it matter if a whole generation is exterminated, obliterated, sacrificed, if it is for the future good of mankind!"

"Not our kind of mankind." She must get it further into the open. "You work for the Gestapo. Does that mean you take part in . . . in actual atrocities, and so on?" She shivered. "Do you do that sort of thing, yourself?"

"Of course not!" He laughed.

"Even so—"

"*Bitte,* the Gestapo is an immense organization, with tens of thousands, hundreds of thousands, of officials, employees. As in everything very widespread, there is much not known to others. I do only organizational work. Paper work, *ver-standen?*"

That was just what Strangeways had said about what *he* did. These folk were pretty much alike, it seemed.

Hugo grunted. "I have nothing whatever to do with what you call atrocities. *Mein Gott,* what should you think? That is for underlings." He thought of Dortmund, though Dortmund was not an underling, and his nose wrinkled in distaste.

"But about America." He pulled the conversation back. "Your culture—"

He was certainly a German. He couldn't let anything alone.

"Now," Leslie resumed more easily, "that's one thing we're not going to talk about, our culture. I don't care what you say, but last night I saw some of your books, and so I know you have knowledge and taste, that is, if you've ever read them. You know that we have plenty of culture, and that we disseminate it more broadly, more democratically, than any other country known to man. Besides, I won't hear a word on the subject of culture from anybody who took part in the Burning of the Books."

"I deplored that," Hugo replied. "But mostly the authors were Jewish authors, and—"

"Another thing," she declared, "and we might as well get it straight right now. Not one word about the Jews. We may, or may not, ever see each other again. But if we do, don't say anything against the Jews, or I'll leave the table."

He paused. "I found much to admire in your country."

"For instance?" Her voice was cold.

He laughed. "The great automobile roads leading out of New York. And in the Music Hall theater, what are known as the Rockettes." He lit a cigarette. "Very well, I will be more serious. Politically I found you underdeveloped and immature. And monstrous with hypocrisy."

"What kind of hypocrisy?"

"For instance that presidential candidates so seldom admit that they are candidates."

"I'm not sure what you mean by immaturity and hypocrisy. We're a country where the rank and file of the people can vote for the president they want to have!"

"Tell me other things you have high opinion of."

"I like America because it's a country where you can say 'Hello, Joe!' to the corner cop!"

"The cop will probably be fat, lazy, and corrupt!"

"It's the country where you can find real variety of opinion in newspapers, in spite of what you said about our uniformity. It's the country where soap-opera commercials are pretty distressing, yes, but also you can hear Norman Corwin and Raymond Gram Swing and Town Hall of the Air! It's the country where institutions like the Rockefeller Foundation have grasped what is the proper function of great wealth. It's the country where the bootlegger's daughters grow up to become honor students at Vassar. It's a country made largely by people who *wanted* to make it. So it's unique. In a sense every American is an American not because he happened to be born one, but out of choice."

"I have a feeling the United States has never genuinely suffered as a nation. Have you had true hardships? Do you know the experience of national dismay?"

"My dear child, until you folks broke loose in 1914, our civil war was the bloodiest war in history."

But Hugo was tenaciously, with great literalness, holding onto his own ideas. He said abruptly, "The one thing I found most disturbing was your freight cars."

II

Leslie didn't know if she had heard him right. "Our what?"

"Your freight cars."

"I don't understand."

"I saw them everywhere. In the barns near Columbus, Ohio, and out on the tracks for mile after mile in Chicago. In Kansas City, Memphis, Baltimore. When you went from New York to Detroit, always they passed you, tremendous

long heavy trains of freight cars. And as a rule, not too fast,
so you could read the lettering as they swept by. I remember
all those names, all the inscriptions like tattoo-marks of
savages. Monograms. Symbols. Chicago & Northwestern,
Pennsylvania, Marquette, Delaware & Ohio, Fruit Express,
Santa Fe, Chesapeake, Milwaukee & St. Paul, New York
Central. Of one, the name I have forgotten, the symbol was
a polar bear with a red cross. Another was the profile of an
Indian on a big black shield. I would watch these cars, as
they swept past, fascinated and bewildered. I would count
how many different kinds I saw. And I could scarcely sleep
at night, for the horror they instilled into me. *Because they
were all on the same train!*"

She looked at him wondering if he, or she, had gone mad.

"But you must understand, it seemed to me an outrage
against reason. The lack of organization, the disorder. All
those cars belonging to different systems, different companies,
strung together behind the same locomotive, on the same
track. It always seemed to me, those cars should have been
neatly sorted out! There was no excuse for Chesapeake to
be on the same track with St. Paul! This all indicated a
failure of mentality somewhere. It was not *right* that cars
should be so mixed up, that they should have to be disen-
tangled at the end of the line. Why should not cars belonging
to one system stay with one system? It was irregular. It was
as if indecent. What *right* had the Indian head to be next
to the polar bear? Why, even cars from the West coast,
Southern Pacific, were in line with Albany & Boston! It
seemed to me a complete symbol of your mixed-upness! It
had no *order!*"

"Oh, Hugo!" For the first time she used his name. "Oh,
Hugo, Hugo . . . " Now she was sorry for him.

He was stubborn. "But if you are so economically immature as to have different companies, instead of a single
state system, then why not keep all the cars properly separated, as we would do?"

Always these pathetic, overriding Germans wanted to

make order! They turned the whole world into a blazing cauldron, a spitting holocaust, in the name of that bogus shibboleth, order! And this must be because of their own insecurity, their own hideous lack of inner glue, their own inability to achieve harmony and cohesion.

A single state system? Leslie had a thought, "Why didn't you sit tight after Munich? Why did you try to take everything else too?"

"Because it was ours by right of our strength and we wanted it." He added coldly, "What business was it of yours? Why did *you* want to fight in Europe?"

"Now really!"

"What are you fighting *for*, anyway?"

"For lots of things. Mainly because the kind of world you'd make isn't the kind we want our children to grow up into. Most of us would rather die than have it that kind of world. It's like Lincoln carried on a bit. Internationally. The world can't exist half slave, half free."

"I do not agree at all. Americans have no conception of European ideologies. When I see your movies about Hitler, it is on the level of gangster films. You treat great and serious issues on the identical plane as adventure stories."

In a way this was true, and she was nettled. "It seems to me the gangster symbolism is quite appropriate."

"Why do you hate us so?"

"When I lived in Germany I didn't hate you. I felt sorry for you, but I didn't hate you."

"That's much worse."

She shook her head at the interruption. "I didn't like your government, I certainly didn't *like* it, but if you wanted it that way, well, that was up to you, that was your hard luck. I'd never have wanted it for myself, but I don't believe in interference. But this brings up the precise point. It was because *you* began to interfere with everybody else that the whole decent civilized world rose against you. What you did with your own country was no great concern of mine. But when you started to attack other countries, then it was. When you started to make war, it became everybody's concern."

She looked at him closely: "Another thing. Another reason why we're fighting, if you're really interested, is to liberate you Germans. We're not only liberating Europe, we're liberating Germany too. Though why on earth we should be bothering with you, I don't know." She answered her own question. *"Because we'll have to deal with you after the war just as much as now!"*

"Germany is Europe."

"No, it isn't."

"One must pay attention to the laws of historical development," Hugo said. "One of your own writers talks about the Wave of the Future."

"Now that makes me rather angry," Leslie replied. "What have past or future got to do with it? On our side, we have a certain moral point of view; we don't think just in terms of past or future but of right and wrong. It's not only a choice between past and future; it's a choice between good and evil. You've got your dimensions all confused. You, who believe in clarity and order! But—if you really must talk about the future—we can talk about it too. To us the future means progress, development, not retrogression!"

. . . Never as long as she lived would she forget Hugo and the freight cars. It gave her an idea.

"I myself am partly German. That is, two of my great-grandparents were. From way back. I'm the product of English and Germans, melted together. We're a mixed-up lot, you know. Like the freight cars you talk about! But we're all Americans. Just as those freight cars were all American. Getting somewhere, too. And getting there, *right*, in spite of what seemed a confused spectacle to you. You believe in the superiority of race. I don't. I'm a mongrel. Well, let's see who comes out ahead. You talk about the future. Well, I'm quite confident about that future. You are representative of the master race. Have you the same confidence as I?"

"Certainly! I will explain!" But now for the first time he didn't look confident.

Leslie smiled. "Do you know something? I've just thought what the difference between us is."

"What?"

"I concede our failings. I understand all about the frailties, the defects, in our way of life. In many countries, democracy is a sham, a fraud. Even in mine, I sometimes think it won't last twenty years more, unless we really *work* for it. But in my world—for all its faults—I'm not in league myself with organized suppression . . . with suppression and persecution as institutions. Our system doesn't force me into . . . into active collusion with cruelty and evil. I can at least oppose things I don't like. I can criticize. But you can't. I'm free. You're not. I can absolve myself from guilt. But you're *part* of all the evil."

"Freedom?" Hugo had that superior look again. "You do not understand that we of the *élite* are above such conceptions."

"I live in a world of truth," Leslie said. "I can tell you *any-thing*. But you cannot talk truthfully to me." She ignored an interruption. "My love of country doesn't get in the way of my love for mankind. Yours does. I'm a free person. You're a slave."

They finished lunch; she glanced at her watch. "My good-ness, I have to get back to work." She laughed, openly, warmly.

He was annoyed by the validity of much that she said. How was he going to dominate a woman who talked like this? He did not want her to have the advantage. "Your work!" His voice suddenly became contemptuous. "What kind of work can it be that they give to beautiful women to do?"

Her brows lifted. "Europeans can't ever understand women working, can they?"

"Suppose you would describe to me, *wie soll ich sagen*, what duties you perform."

Leslie considered. "As a matter of fact I think I will. Not that I'll tell you anything I shouldn't tell. I'm new at it, and just getting shaken down to my routine. It's quite fascinating. This morning I was going over figures and checking inven-tories and calculating surpluses, mostly in the realm of cotton

uniforms, jeeps, and aviation gasoline. I can tell you this
because I've seen the reports as to what the Turks have told
you about what they want. So I'm not giving away any
secrets. Now." She paused decisively. "Can you tell me as
frankly what *you* did this morning?"

He flushed. He must make her submit. He called the
waiter, argued with him momentarily over the bill, and paid.
Then:

"You bring up large issues. Meet me here again at six."

She hesitated. "I don't think I can, really."

"You have other engagement, with some handsome young
man?"

"No."

"Then why not? Only now have we really begun to have
good talk. Also, you have challenged me, as it were; surely
it is only fair that I should have the right to reply."

She thought it over; her eyes became amused. "If I come,
will you tell me what you did this morning?"

"No. But I can tell you now what I shall do all the long
afternoon."

"What?" She felt that aura.

"Think of how remarkable a young woman you are." He
was making love to her with a gesture of his lips. "Please
come."

"But not just because you're flattering me."

"Please."

"All right," Leslie said.

III

She got back to the office. Then on her desk she found an
Ekspres letter with a Turkish postmark. What a pleasant
handwriting, she thought: everything perfectly spaced, and
all the letters so legible, so neatly formed.

Dear Leslie:

I find I'm thinking of you rather often. I remember our
dinner very warmly. I'm sorry I didn't have a chance to
ring you up the next day, but I was badly tied up.

It's strange, isn't it: two people meet for the first time; they talk, they laugh, they dine; most of what they have to give to each other is submerged; yet they manage to establish friendly contact.

I've never thought I was very vain; though to pretend to have no vanity would, of course, be the supreme vanity of all. But somehow I feel a necessity to add a little to what I said that evening, so that if you are interested you may understand better some of the things I was driving at.

Do you know a wonderful poem of T. S. Eliot's which has these lines?

"Sometimes these cogitations still amaze
The troubled midnight and the noon's repose."

The whole thing rather exactly describes my present mood.

I have a feeling that you thought I was something of an idler. But am I wrong in assuming that almost all Americans think a bit too much of work and money as the criteria of a good life? Actually I have worked quite hard at music. I would love to be alone in a room with you and a piano sometime. (Sounds vaguely indecent, doesn't it?) And always I have been interested in what were the true values of a good life. I would describe what I think these values are but I fear I should be presuming too much on a slender thread of association . . . What happened was that the years slipped by with disconcerting speed. Then the war came and all the past five years have, of course, been lost. Five years! It is a large slice out of life.

I do not think I gave you a very accurate picture of my marriage. And you were so frank with me that I feel I must be the same. Actually I must have been very much in love with Rose. And the breakup hit me harder than I gave you to understand. However it is a very long time ago and I know now how lucky I am to be out of it. Because it was a bad marriage from the outset. What happened to me was one of the grimmest things that can happen to mortal man: I fell in love with a woman I didn't actually "like." I couldn't endure her vanity for one thing. She was good-looking but not even Helen of Troy would have had the right to be so morbidly vain. Then again we never had *fun* together, the kind of wild fun young people should have, maybe because I was so much in love with her and always fearful of offending her. She was abnormally sensitive. Always *looking* to be affronted.

However that's enough about that. We talked about cynicism and so on. Actually I'm rather an optimist. That is, I don't know if things will or will not come out right for me, but I do feel they will come out right, eventually and by and large, for the *world*. And somehow I am an infinitesimal part of that world.

I'm being very busy. And liking my work for a change. It's raw out here, but, my God, how exciting!

Americans don't write letters much, do they? I have always imagined you as just telegraphing and telephoning. Whereas most Englishmen take a curious pleasure in expressing their thoughts on paper. Whenever one of my compatriots wants to get away from something he writes a letter, or "attends to his correspondence" as they say.

I hope you're having a happy and productive time in Istanbul. If you'd write me a line, I'd be pleased. I do want to tell you that I liked so much meeting you, and let's keep in touch. Of course I'll hope to see you the next time I'm in Istanbul.

I hope you'll forgive me if this letter is far too personal. My best to Alec if you see him. He's an odd cove, but very sound.

Sincerely yours,
Gerald Heath.

P.S. Once I heard a definition of falling in love that pleased me greatly, and seemed to me the best one-line description of that complicated process I ever heard. "Falling in love is finding yourself in another."

Leslie skimmed through it rapidly, and then read it again; her face had a curious perceptive look. She stuffed it in her bag and then in a few minutes took it out. That postscript seemed of different texture from the rest; even the handwriting was slightly different, as if he had refilled his pen or used more ink . . . She folded the letter carefully, and then stuck it in her passport for safer keeping . . .

Here she was . . . bumping around with unhappiness all this time . . . Almost a year now since she had been with Robin . . . And here a man she really *liked*. There is a unity among people who have suffered, Leslie thought. But Florian must be at the mines by now; she and the letter must have crossed. So there wasn't any use . . . She might as well forget it.

Then the letter made her think of Hugo, and suddenly she began to grasp it. She understood now why he fascinated her, the physical attraction quite aside. He was a kind of monster out of the unknown. All her life she had been taught to be, above everything, reasonable. But Hugo had a demonic quality that was beyond reason, beyond anything she had been educated to believe in, or believed in of herself. He symbolized everything in the world that she did not understand.

IV

He was awaiting her. He had changed his suit and shirt. He looked almost violently fresh, as if scrubbed and burnished. The aura spread out from him again. He kissed her hand.

"I don't think we ought to be seen," Leslie said.

"No one comes here. Not at this hour."

"Even so . . . " she thought aloud.

"We could go to my place. My apartment in the Park."

She considered. She wasn't afraid, but she didn't quite like it. "No," she said.

"But why not?" His eyes glittered, but he added, "I will behave."

"I certainly won't give you a chance to do otherwise."

"Come along, then."

She hated coy women. "All right." They started off down the street.

At the corner where Hugo's car was parked they walked into Mr. Poppa. He stared at them, as if hardly believing what he saw; then he smirked and giggled. They could not walk around him; he was too fat. Hugo bowed coldly, and Mr.

Poppa murmured, "Ah, good-day to you!" Mr. Poppa spent a second making up his mind whether it would be more tactful to pretend not to recognize Leslie or not. "*Madame, enchanté,*" he said finally. Then they got past him.

In Hugo's car Leslie asked good-humoredly, "Will he tell everybody in town he's seen us, or just almost everybody?"

"It is of no importance." But he didn't like it much.

She looked around in his apartment, and he ordered tea. She sat back comfortably in a gray sofa; he straddled a straight chair half-way across the room. She liked it that his manner was almost impersonal, so that she would feel at ease. But when she tried to pick up the talk from where they left it at noon, he shook his head. "No. No arguments now. I beg."

"Does that mean I won it? The argument I mean?" But her voice held no trace of vainglory. Any time she ever chanced to best anybody, she felt deep sympathy.

"One thing I grant you. Our ignorance. That I concede to you. When first I went to the United States, I was afraid to mention the name Woodrow Wilson aloud. Why? Because I had been taught that all Americans hated him so intensely that if you so much as mentioned his name, you were struck down on the streets . . . *Herr Gott!*"

She thought back to Gerald and remembered how he had said that all Germans were so gullible. Hugo walked up and down, and began to talk about his youth.

"But I had no youth." His voice sharpened. "They stuck a wooden musket in my hand when I was nine . . . " His mouth showed disgust. "When I was a child of nine . . . "

He went on: "What does it mean to have no youth? It means that all your life you are . . . romantic."

Leslie looked up. Yes, that was true.

"To have no youth . . . it means other things. We children were forced at the earliest age to assume the responsibilities of adults. It meant that we had no freedom of choice as to career; events fastened themselves on us, imposed on us what to do."

She thought of her own wonderfully happy childhood.

"And during all our youth, our early maturity too, we lived in a black cloud of fear. All our lives were dominated, utterly dominated, by one consideration—fear."

He grunted. "Then also the desperation. *Ach!* Those months, those years, when the Republic was gasping its last breath. There came from Brüning one *Notverordnung* after another; like a man trying to stop a flood with a piece of paper. People groaned; they held their heads in their hands, they were desperate and starving, there was no hope, they exclaimed, 'But what *good* will this do?' All was like an insane illness, spreading like an epidemic; a disease of disillusion, desperation, fear."

Leslie said evenly. "You wouldn't have been desperate and starving if you hadn't spent all your money on armaments . . ."

"But after the last war . . .

"And you wouldn't have had to spend so much money on armaments, if you hadn't made the last war."

He was sharp. "That is a deliberate misreading of history. We alone did not make that war."

"Perhaps."

Then the implications of his sudden change of mood staggered her. They stood together gazing from his terrace toward the glorious, silken view; if he moved an inch closer, their shoulders would touch. Perhaps he was not a strong man with faith—after all! Perhaps he was not, after all, a person who subordinated everything to a cause; perhaps—she thought sharply—she really *could* get him, if she were willing enough to live dangerously for a while.

She saw that he wanted to take her in his arms, but the wall between them was still very high. She looked along a small bookcase and felt a peculiar relaxed shock. There in a corner was a leather-bound copy of Heinrich Heine.

He saw her see it. He shrugged, then grinned, a little sheepish. "*Ach!* About some things I am broadminded . . ."

So Hugo too had intoned *Ich Weiss Nicht Was Soll Es Bedeuten* in darkling moonlight when he was a boy. So Hugo too must have walked down sad-sunny paths whispering to a pretty girl, *Auf Meiner Herzliebsten Äugelein.* He too, like any non-Nazi boy, must have memorized *Du Bist Wie Eine Blume*; perhaps even now he knew the words of *Die Welt Ist Dumm, Die Welt Ist Blind.*

It would have been so easy to laugh chidingly, "So, Hugo, you keep in your apartment a well-worn copy of a Jewish poet!" But she resisted the temptation. Distantly, once more, her thoughts went back to Berlin. Life in Berlin had made her responsible, just as Paris—and Robin—had taught her what the values of a good life could be . . . Hugo must have been a quite normal youth; then like a million others he had been sucked and shocked into conformity, dragged and gagged into a march of slaves until a whole continent became a shambles . . . But these inexplicable Germans *were* human beings, in spite of everything; they were, like everybody else, all mixed up between good and bad, only more so. Her feeling for humanity overcame her hatred of his Germanness.

Good Lord! She stopped. She had thought she could influence Hugo. But were the tables being turned? Was it *he* who was now influencing *her*? She shivered. That was what the powerful physical impact of Nazis did. Or did it?

The 'phone buzzed abruptly, and she heard Hugo answering. "*Jawohl, Herr Doktor. Nein. Heute Abend, nicht möglich.* (Tonight, not possible.) *Ja? Wirklich? Jawohl, Herr Doktor.* At the first moment possible, *Herr Doktor*!"

Hugo listening to his master. Hugo being sucked in again. She felt rescued; she felt relieved.

He walked up to her, though he must have known the mood was broken, and his eyes looked bruised. He put a hand on her back, then her shoulder, and tried to turn her around. "No," she said sadly. She slipped away and walked toward the window. She kept her back to him, and stared outside.

"I will for always think how wonderful you are."

She whispered as if to herself. "A fine young animal . . . With the conscience in abeyance . . . lost."

"What?"

"Nothing."

What had Strangeways said? "Break up their organization, don't you know." With Hugo would come priceless information. With him might come any kind of vital document. Secret plans about the whole Middle East. Even the codes.

No. She *did* have a conscience. She *was* a decent human being. She could not set out on any enterprise so dubious, so mean and sordid. Yet—!

"Your skin is so maddeningly beautiful . . ."

He had both arms around her, and was holding her with bent shoulders trying to kiss her. Dear God, it was a hundred years since she had kissed anybody. But she pushed herself away, sharply, panting. He followed her, his face hot and alive and she felt his big mouth smudge against her chin. She punched him, hard, not a slap, but a punch, from the flexed elbow, hard.

Weakly, she sat down.

Then with his eyes tight closed his head fell in her lap and he started to cry.

Jesus Christ, Leslie thought. She waited a moment, and then said briefly, "Let's get out of here and have some dinner." Her knuckles stung from where she had hit him.

v

Mr. Poppa felt very good. He was chuckling to himself. He drifted down the Istiklal and wandered toward the somber façade of the English Club. Almost always Strangeways could be found there at this time; it was an invariable habit of the Englishman. And Strangeways would receive him, Mr. Poppa knew. Then he would still have time to cross town and drop into the German building where Dortmund had his offices. Dr. Dortmund often worked quite late. There would be ample time for both; even—Mr. Poppa giggled— time later for a new Hungarian girl who had just arrived. Mr. Poppa tried them all out. He had never missed one, except Florian.

CHAPTER XII

Double Judas

I

WHAT was real? What was not real? Gerald ruminated. He was tramping in the hot dust toward the railway station, where the buffet, spelled Bufe, was the focus of life in the town. . . . At about this time he'd be finishing an hour or so at the piano. The cottage would be in Essex or Kent, a cottage surrounded by hedges and low brick walls, with squat chimneys and vines running along the eaves. Outside on a hilltop would be his wife, wearing a light sweater and with a ribbon in her hair. He'd call; she'd hallo back. Perhaps there might be a light spring rain, which would make the rhododendrons glisten with special brightness. Then they would have tea with piles of soft sandwiches on crustless bread, or cocktails from the shaker Strangeways had given them as a wedding present. Then there would be just time for half an hour with the children, in a nursery painted blue and white, before dinner . . . Gerald's imagination raced. He could see the titles of the books in the dark-oak cases, read the notes of the music on the piano, and hear precisely what he and his wife would talk about.

He returned to earth. "Wonder why I idealize women so ridiculously. Why I overvalue them. Maybe it's because I've been lonely for so long. Perhaps it has something to do with the fact I never knew my mother."

He thought of Leslie. He was glad he had been impelled to write that long letter, and he wondered what she would think about it, and whether she would answer soon. Intellectually, in the manner of emancipated Englishmen, he sought to analyze her. That was a good girl, Leslie . . . Several things about her puzzled him: the crisp brevity of most of her sentences, together with a contrary note of indecision, and the sense she gave of holding to a secret. "But I scarcely know her," he murmured to himself. Yet he was getting more vividly interested in her all the time. "I know her well enough."

In his pocket were detailed orders from Strangeways about the forthcoming Aegean operation. First he must finish up with the chrome; then in a few weeks he would be on the wing again, somewhere near Rhodes.

He talked to himself:

"That'll be quite a job. Softening folk up down there. Do you really want to take it on?"

"Yes. Might be an interesting show."

"You'll have to drop in by parachute. Then hide in the villages until we're ready."

"Okay. Luckily I know the language."

What was real? what unreal? By God, this mining town near Ankara was real enough. He rubbed the sweat and dust off his hands. He reached the station, and slipped into the Bufe for a quick shot of *raki*. This town was real, all right. This was Asia, as remote from Istanbul as if it were on another planet. This was the edge of some inner segment of the non-western earth; yet, at the mines, Westerners clawed metal out. This was the Asia where children looked perpetually fatigued, and walked the streets silently, never running; it was the Asia of filthy tablecloths, and sores on the eyes of women crouched in shawls; of peasants with dark sagging faces, and starving dogs that howled all night; of flies, bad teeth, and old men with water pipes clutching amber beads.

A train had just pulled in. It was jammed with troops, brown-uniformed, unshaved and filthy, sticking their arms and heads like monkeys out of the boxcar windows. The train seemed to be panting, shimmering, in the heat. It was like a metal animal, exhausted by its journey; it shivered on the tracks, while trainmen clattered along the line, peering underneath the trucks, rapping the wheels and axle boxes, as vendors in dirty shirts sold *kouskous* and *yo'ourt* to the soldiers shouting and leaning down.

But this was only a minor train. The great tri-weekly express with its shining cars came in from Istanbul later, after sundown. Gerald turned his attention to the Bufe. There, at one table, was Aschentoller, the Nazi who was his *vis-à-vis*, and who was never far away. Gerald had a habit of winking or smiling at him, which made Aschentoller nervous. There was the rich pasha who owned the garden-restaurant near the river; there the assistant manager of the mines; there the youthful, energetic schoolmaster; and there riffraff from the town. Out of the window he saw villagers and peasants, waiting for some other train, squat in the cindery gravel; they would eat and sleep along the gutters, or stretched out on the hot pavement, tangled and crowded like beasts, sipping sweet drinks and spitting, groaning, for hour after hour, until the swarming, crawling train came in.

. . . After dinner, with a long drink of Scotch, they would listen to the B.B.C. news, take a stroll near the white trellis which was the entrance to their garden; later glance at the *New Yorker* which had just arrived in the post from America, and talk vitally, earnestly, about the Fourth Conference of the United Nations then assembling in Copenhagen . . .

Gerald sauntered down the platform and watched some freight being unloaded. There seemed to be a lot of commotion; a series of heavy boxes looked a bit unusual. Stuff for the mines, of course. And it was one of Gerald's minor jobs to note everything that went to the mines. He reached over, casually, to see the consignment markings, and a Turkish gendarme sharply waved him aside, muttering the word for "Danger!" A box slipped, cracked open at the end, and poured out some brownish dust. Someone yelled "Look out!"

but Gerald leaned down, scooped up a handful, and walked away. Nothing unusual, after all. The T.N.T. in his hand was the exact color and consistency of maple sugar; it stuck to his fingers moistly. They used it in the mines all the time. But—? He almost ran into Aschentoller rushing up the platform. Smiling, Gerald held out his palm, and let him see the T.N.T. slipping through his fingers. Aschentoller walked past furious.

After dinner in the garden-restaurant Gerald's assistant, Neale, joined him for coffee. "Our friends do the damnedest things, sir. Got in 'alf a ton of T.N.T. today. After all that other stuff we checked on last week."

Gerald was puzzled. He had assumed the explosive to be part of the routine supply of the mine. However, it was nothing to worry about, since above all the Germans wanted to keep the mines working, not the contrary. No motive for destruction. "Hmmm," he thought.

It was pleasant in the garden and he decided not to go back to the station to see the express come in. He had a brandy, and listened to the fat Turkish girls bellow and chant from the stage a hundred feet away. You could see them, but the sound seemed to come from the opposite direction, from behind, since the loudspeakers were placed that way. Cockeyed. Like so much here.

Suddenly he was bored and he took a droshky back to the hotel. There at the reception desk he saw Florian registering.

II

They were sitting in her bedroom. She had kicked off her shoes; she sat Turkish fashion on the bed. Her smile was wan.

"Well!" Gerald couldn't get over his surprise. "Really, I never dreamed you'd come. Bit of a lark, isn't it!" But he was puzzled as well as pleased.

"*Ach*, that train. It bumped and seemed to go backward

and forward all night, and there were bedbugs so-o-o long."
She demonstrated how long with thumb and finger.

"It isn't so bad here. If you'll stay a while, it won't be so
bad." The hell with anything he had been thinking.

"I do not know."

He leaned to kiss her; she avoided his lips, and held
up her cheek. But he felt a slight self-division.

"Well, the main thing is, you're here. We've lots of
time!"

He put his arm around her; she held his wrist hard, but
averted her face.

"You need a drink. I'll pop off to my room and get a
bottle." This was what he had so long and ardently hoped
for. But in the oddest way he felt that he was being untrue
to Leslie, a girl he had never had.

"Gerald, *Liebling*, I am tired tonight."

"Tired?" He hesitated. "You won't be tired in a little
while."

Florian sat there blankly. Her eyes had an unnatural look,
as if they were haunted.

Only once in her life had she ever done it for money;
that had been years ago, she suddenly reflected. Her mouth
grimaced in a bitter-sweet, recollected smile, then the lips
separated with affection for all that she had been. She was
a kid of seventeen, out on her first dancing tour, and
stranded, utterly stranded, in Bucharest. Her boss, that
filthy Rumanian Georgiu, said he had gone broke, and without warning suspended their contracts. The show closed, and
Florian hung around the cafés. There was a place where she
could get some money dancing naked, above the waist, and
Georgiu had often tried to pat her on the breasts, grinning,
and saying that was a way she could always earn a living.
She remembered the night that Georgiu had said he'd fire
her if she didn't sleep with him. But she had managed to get
around that somehow. Men! You could twist them around
a finger. Yet, often, they got back at you. "I won't become
a whore, I won't become a whore, I won't become a whore!"

she had whispered passionately to herself, waiting day after day in the cafés. All the essential femaleness of her nature protested; she would not debase the act of love, even if she starved. She sold her costumes and the few pathetic jewels. The American was a writer, a newspaper correspondent he said. He too was hanging around the cafés. He was young, though older than he looked; he wore heavy glasses, he had indeterminate blond hair, he was plump. He smoked a pipe incessantly, and his name was John. When he picked her up she hadn't had a thing to eat all day. And she would be turned out of that tawdry hotel room, no matter how much the stocky mustached hall porter tried to protect her, by the end of the week. The American didn't seem terribly interested in her. But he suggested dinner. She hardly knew a word of English then; the youthful American knew practically no German. The way he tried to pretend, with single short sentences, that he could talk the language, was comical and rather touching; whenever she talked fast, he could not understand a word. He knew French, but she didn't. They struggled. Then Florian had a laughing fit and began to cry. "Why, you poor kid, you're hungry! That's the trouble, isn't it!" he tried to say. They made some kind of talk over the menu by pointing. She met him the next afternoon, after he had sent what he called a "story" to a newspaper in Tchicago. He seemed to have plenty of money, an amiable disposition, and very little curiosity. They took a walk and then a ride. That evening he asked her to go to bed with him as casually as if he were talking about the weather. She refused and the next day he asked her quite impersonally, without a trace of emotion, how much money did she want. She had managed to tell him most of her story by this time, with waiters in various cafés interpreting. "Why, you poor kid," he said amiably, "come along with me, now, and I'll buy your *wagon-lit* fare back to Budapest, and give you fifty dollars." They bought the tickets and they had a long dinner, and she felt poignant and heartbroken, but curious and excited also, and then they walked slowly back to her miserable hotel. She remembered going up to her room, and waiting there, alone, waiting there, trembling, for minutes that seemed hours; he was downstairs in the lobby and would take her to his place, which was better. She waited, and waited, and still waited. She thought he would go away. She waited for a full hour and a half. She could not budge. Her heart was beating as if struck by hammers. She thought, "I must take a toothbrush with me, and some make-up." When finally she got downstairs he was still there, reading a newspaper placidly. "Well," he said, "come along."

Her first lover. So!—

Now Gerald had returned to the small room, looking anticipatory, surprised still, and rather shy.

"You're in what they used to call a 'brown study,'" he laughed. "What on earth have you been thinking about?"

"Something in Rumania once."

"Well I hope it was nice."

In a way what she was going to do now was much worse than that affair in Bucharest, she thought confusedly. When Hugo first suggested that she run down here she had considered it as half a joke. Also she had been much bruised, and the impulse to bruise others sometimes arose spontaneously, without ugliness; one became tempted to ignore the normal responsibilities, through a search for forgetfulness, for gaiety. Also Gerald was, in fact, an enemy, an enemy of her nation. She was doing Hungary a patriotic service in performing Hugo's mission. Oh, *Quatsch*! she muttered. She never thought about politics at all and the idea that England was an enemy was ridiculous.

The trouble was, Gerald was so nice, so decent. If he had been like Strangeways, say, or that other Englishman, it might have been good sport to play games with him, to deceive him, to laugh at him for a fool.

That was why she hadn't broken off with Gerald; after all it would have been perfectly easy to get rid of him. She had tried being moderately selfish and even mean, but this had little effect, since Gerald simply refused to accept the genuineness of these attitudes; he knew they were artificial, and he would not deal with her in that guise. She knew that, as a last resort, there was one infallible way of getting rid of a man: she could insult his sexual pride. But there was nothing to insult in Gerald that way and besides, she couldn't do it; he was too pleasant to be with, too generous, too kind.

He was pouring her a drink. Somehow, now that she was here, she did not think she could go through with it.

"Gerald, darling, I think I go to bed now. I am tired from the so-long trip."

"Oh, please, Florian." He knew that it was not just because she was tired.

"Darling, we discuss everything tomorrow."

"I know you're not in love with me," Gerald said. "But even so, while you're here, we might as well be pals."

"I cannot talk about it."

In a curious way he felt relieved. But he went on, "Now you're behaving just as you did the last time at Taksim's. Please, Florian. I should think you'd be tired of being just a flirt."

"I am not just a flirt. Sometimes I do not understand myself."

"What I don't understand is why you should have come!"

She wondered what to say. "I am fonder of you than I have ever been."

"All right," Gerald said, "the hell with it."

"Tomorrow," Florian said, "maybe." They talked a while. He waited at the door. "Well, cheer-ho."

III

They were sipping hot tea in glasses in the Yeni lounge the next afternoon. She wore a green blouse the color of a dark ping-pong table, which flowed loosely over her shoulders and breast.

"I think I'm going to drop it, Florian," he said calmly.

"Go on back to Istanbul. I don't want to see you any more. I don't see any point in your being here. Blast it all, why did you want to come?" And he was continuing to himself, "After all, enough is enough." Then he reflected vividly on Leslie and how much he'd like to be seeing *her*. How wonderful Leslie would be here at the mines, he thought.

"I cannot make love without love."

"That's a nice idea. But what about Hugo?"

She shrugged disdainfully, her nose perked up. "Oh, Hugo. He is just a kind of a machine."

"What's he been doing lately, incidentally?"

"He is after that American, Mrs. Corcoran."

"What!" Gerald jumped as if pricked by a burr. "He is? Why, the son of a bitch!"

Florian gave him an expurgated account of their meeting, the drive out into the country, their dinner.

"Whether she will see much of him or not I do not know."

"The son of a bitch." Gerald had snapped to his feet, and was scowling as he paced. "By Christ, I'll put a stop to that. I'll call Strangeways; he'll warn her off. By Jesus, I won't have that Nazi son of a bitch monkeying with an American!"

"I think Mrs. Corcoran is very well capable of taking care of herself."

They walked toward the Bufe. From the kitchen came a wonderful smell of sage, of thyme, of marjoram, sharp peppers, of cucumber, of young lamb grilling. That dolt, Aschentoller, was in the bar. He stared at Florian. His eyes popped open staring. Gerald grinned at him broadly. It always made Aschentoller twitch irritably when he grinned. Nazi twirp.

IV

"I think I follow that old advice," Florian said aimlessly. "I will leave Turkey and try to get back to Budapest."

They were strolling in the gardens near the sleek, slow-flowing river. Good Lord, Gerald thought, I haven't done a stroke of work all day; Florian had knocked a lot out of his mind, and now, this talk of Leslie with Hugo Reichenau . . .

She slapped her wrist sharply; there were mosquitoes. "You must take that atabrine," he said absently. "I forgot, after dinner. This place full of malaria."

Something was gripping Florian now. She had to tell him. She must tell him now. Why, she did not know. But she had reached the conclusion that the whole manner of her life must change. She would go back to Istanbul, and then Budapest. She felt a surge of tenderness for Gerald. She felt an acute dissatisfaction with all that she was, all that she had been. Perhaps her meetings with Leslie had something to do with this. That American, now there was a girl who played things straight . . .

Florian, who was a sentimentalist, became overwhelmed with contrition, with remorse. Especially in view of what Gerald was saying:

"I wish I could tell you something about my work here. I was terribly fed up, as you know. I even wanted to throw my hand in, and quit. But, dash it all, we all have to do something, don't we, and this seems to be my stint . . . Matter of fact, I slipped up on some things I should have done today. Been too busy with you." He smiled. "Now about us. Listen, Florian . . ." In his voice was that wealth of charm, and the kind of innocence on which charm often depends.

She did not know that she would say it. Her throat was choked with something. She stopped. "Hugo sent me here."

He halted. "Mind that mosquito. What?"

"I did not come because you asked me. Hugo contrived that I should descend on you, take your time and spoil your work."

"Well. Really. Well!" His voice did not sound angry, only shocked. "Well, I'm glad you told me."

"Let us go from this place. The mosquitoes."

"Our friend is certainly full of tricks, isn't he," Gerald said, warming up to it.

She didn't say anything. She felt forlorn. She felt very lonely, and forlorn.

"I'll get that bastard if I have to wait a hundred years," Gerald said. The shock was passing.

Florian was crying. "Now I am a Judas. A double Judas."

Gerald was thinking hard, but he said, "Never mind that. Matter of fact, Judas was quite a useful citizen."

"That is blasphemy," Florian said.

"Not at all. Judas made Christ a God."

"How can you say such things?"

"Without Judas, Jesus might never have become Christ."

"You have the strangest thoughts." Now her hand was on his arm.

"Besides, there's a bit of Judas in everyone, don't you think?"

They reached the entrance to the gardens. The river moved slowly, a swollen green.

"Now I don't know what to do," she wailed.

She rubbed a mosquito from her forehead.

"It's the south wind. They come with the south wind."

"What?"

"The mosquitoes. Well," he turned to her. "This really does end it, doesn't it? This really bitches it between us, doesn't it?"

Still, he hadn't reproached her. Apparently it never entered his mind to reproach her. Oh, Gerald was good, she thought.

For the first time, she wanted him.

v

That evening they lay together quietly in her dimly curtained room. She seemed drowsy and content, but an inner pain made her ache, because though his fingers were touching her, his eyes and heart were not. He was lying there with his head thrown back, his blond hair tossed on his scalp and moist, and the adam's apple jutting out sharply from the arched throat. He seemed to be groping for something with his eyes, searching for something he would soon find.

"Sweet . . . You're sweet," she said.

"No."

"What you think of now, sweet?"

All the past had fled from him now, he felt. All the past was gone, he knew.

Florian did not say it aloud, but a drastic and terrible thought had seized her. It was that love could survive anything except distrust. Probably Gerald was such an extraordinarily decent person that it had not once occurred to him that she might be a triple as well as a double Judas, that she had now made love to him and let him make love to her as a further execution of her original design. This, the impulse to betray him newly, had not once, not to the extent of one iota, entered her mind; all she had felt was tenderness for him, delight in his company, and an urgent longing to have him comfort her. But that he, obviously, had not once considered that she might still be tricking him; that, that was extraordinary. Yet, from the remoteness in his eyes, the way he lay there almost silently, pondering, from the very way his fingers touched her skin, she knew that everything was over just as it had re-begun.

"Darling . . ." he turned over. His voice was gentle and curiously wistful. "Let's always be good to each other, darling."

She had nipples strangely, beautifully shaped like little checkers; they rose from the breast with straight edges, like small red checkers.

Quietly, strongly, he was kissing her, but with a purely physical desire; the inner love, the passion, was almost spent.

The second most important thing in Gerald's life had happened. He fell out of love with Florian, and would never be in love with her again.

CHAPTER XIII

Black and White

I

LESLIE sat perturbed in her room with her chin pushing down on her bent knuckles. She didn't know quite what to do. Mechanically, methodically, she thought that she must have a quick bath in a moment and then change into the ice-blue dress, because this was a formal party at the Embassy she was going to . . .

It was now several days since they had dined. He was pursuing her incessantly; he sent flowers, letters, telegrams. That evening, after his burst of weeping, he had run through the whole pattern, the full circle. First masculine and would-be-masterful; then cold, detached, what-a-fool-you-are-I-don't-give-a-damn; then almost violently tender; then calm, masculine again. What a European he was, Leslie thought. So much so that she wasn't sure how much of his behavior was acting, and how much not.

Not conceivably could she ever love a German. It was beyond the realm of the possible; it was overwhelmingly, utterly, *im*possible. "I can't change the way I'm made," she muttered to herself, "I can't make myself over!" She felt that she must not see him any more. No matter what, no matter how urgently he pursued her, she ought not see him. But—if she could be of real service to Strangeways, to the Spauldings, to her own people? And she could not get away from the tremendous magnetic attraction he had for her.

There came the usual shy knock on the door.

"Hi," Leslie said.

Etta peered in. Every afternoon now the little girl waited

for her; sometimes they took brief walks together, sometimes they played together in her nursery; always, if she were going out in the evening, Leslie stood by her bed and kissed her good night. She adored her, as one can adore an exquisitely beautiful cameo or piece of porcelain; but she was a shade embarrassed by Etta's limitless, rapt devotion.

She had taught her a few words of French but conversation was primitive and difficult.

Etta pointed to the dress on the bed and Leslie nodded and the little girl gestured toward the window.

"Where am I going? To a dinner party, and then probably we'll dance at Taksim's."

"Taksim's," the child repeated. "*Oui*. Taksim's."

With her enormous green eyes set like olives in the gardenia skin, Etta watched her silently, and then fled the room.

Leslie slipped off her clothes. Dear God, she thought, how I would like to have a baby. Here she was, almost thirty; she looked at her creamy shoulders and the warm slope of belly; here she was and she would be thirty in a few months. Time was flying; life was fleeing. She and Hugo might have a baby, she thought suddenly. Have I gone out of my mind, she asked herself.

She slid out of the tub, put on her stockings, and did her make-up.

. . . Once when she was a growing girl, she came in from school and met her mother on their front porch. The rocking chair squeaked, and the stone wall on which she half sat, half leaned, was moistish . . . She could even remember what she wore: a navy blue dress with a white collar, a blue felt sailor hat with streamers down the back, and red kid gloves with a purse to match. Involuntarily she looked at herself now . . .

What was it her mother said, one of the rare times she ever talked that way? "*If you love a man, be willing to follow him to the ends of the earth. But know that you must pay the cost of your pleasure.*"

"Won't I ever be able to tell things to a little girl of my own?" she brooded mournfully thinking of Sally first, then of Etta.

That first evening at Taksim's, she had said to Strangeways that she had very little sense of sin. A sense of sin was so vulgar, so cramping and debilitating. But sometimes in fatigued moments she felt that Sally's death must have been a punishment for something. She didn't know what. But for something. Perhaps punishment for her life with Hal. Not for having left him later, but for having married him. Because, in a romantic world, marriage without love was the worst of all crimes, since it meant living a lie every minute.

But—she must be fair to herself—she had certainly been in love with Hal and at the beginning they had certainly been happy. All the curiosities teased and extinguished and the urgently novel and challenging experience of living with somebody, anybody, side by side, day by day; the intellectual and moral problems constantly posed—the necessity to concede, to face reality, to compromise, to stand firm, to make adjustment. But—happiness? Well, that wasn't quite the word, perhaps; Hal himself had little capacity for happiness; he couldn't help it, but nobody can give what he hasn't got.

Etta rushed out of the dining room, a napkin around her neck, as Leslie walked through the hall, and she nipped her on the forehead with a kiss.

"Good-by now, Etta darling. Good night, Mrs. Musifer."

What was in this radiant child's mind? Leslie could only guess. With her eyes round and shining, she gazed at Leslie in the ice-blue dress, her slim bare shoulders and the sloping throat; she gazed at her as if she were a vision, an enchantress, from another universe. But at the same time what she saw was her own future, her own mysterious, beautiful, and unexploited life when she should be a woman.

"Good night, Etta."

"Taksim's," Etta giggled.

Leslie laughed. The child clung to her.

II

Hugo was prodding excitedly through his apartment at the Park. Mostly he was astounded at himself. That this should happen, of all things, to him, of all men—he who had always considered himself immune to the shock, the stir, of genuine emotion! He had thought of women as playthings, as amiable companions. But to become a slave to a woman—that was what happened to weaklings, not to healthy and superior Europeans! To become not merely absorbed, but possessed —that converted a man from the hunter, the enjoyer, to the suppliant. To become humble, to become abject—that was no role for Hugo Reichenau!

She had been maddeningly calm over the 'phone.

"Could we not meet for half an hour late this evening?" he implored her.

"Tonight? Oh no, Hugo."

"At least will you telephone me the very instant you get home, and we can talk together," he commanded.

"I don't think that would be wise, do you?"

"Leslie, I am out of my mind for not having seen you for some days."

The laughter was light, sweet, and controlled: "How nice. But I'm sure you're exaggerating."

"You don't know how it is with a man."

"My experience is that they differ greatly."

"*Liebling*, you fence with me. Can we not meet tomorrow?"

"I don't know, Hugo."

"But wouldn't it be *nice* to meet tomorrow?"

"It might be." Her eyes were shut.

"You make always the same difficulties."

"But Hugo," she said earnestly now, "you know what the difficulties are. We can't just ignore them and push them away, can we?"

"*Ich liebe dich*." She had used the word "we."

"Now, Hugo." But he could hear a tremor in her voice.

"Tomorrow at the Konditorei at five. I beg, I implore."

"I don't know. I'll have to let you know."

"You drive me crazy."

Then she said good-by and he dropped the 'phone on the hook, and for an hour her voice was still warm and close in his ear; for an hour, he could literally taste her warm voice, and his mouth and tongue lingered on it, tasting it.

American girls were pushovers. Oh yes. He could have any woman. Oh yes. He remembered that girl in Detroit, the student who worked as a model in the afternoons, the girl named Paula with elusive eyes, who gave him absolutely everything—except the ultimate. American girls were push-overs. Not all, though. He remembered that girl in Pitts-burgh, who had picked him up in the hotel lobby, the girl with the pageboy bob and the wonderful legs and the vanity, who just laughed at him. He could have any woman. Could he, though. But all this was quite different now; it was utterly different now. This was like nothing that had ever happened. "*Herr Gott*," he said to himself in indignant desperation, "I'm in love!"

He gritted his teeth as he looked from his window to the water. There he saw sloops, barges, ferries, and the ships with slanting masts and ocher sails. Also he saw two German tankers, flying the swastika, and a German merchantman that had been hit by a submarine in the Black Sea; half its bow was blown off. Near the German ships was a British motorboat, its flag flapping. The British motorboat was pert and agile; it darted through the harbor as if packed with neat curiosity . . . Hugo felt very dark and sad. He thought about the war. It made him feel irritated and resentful.

"I'm in love! And with an *Amerikanerin* . . . !"

That should have given spice, pepper, wickedness, to it; but it didn't.

Why did he love her so, Hugo wondered—why? He could not quite face what he felt to be the truth. It was not merely that she seemed to him unutterably desirable. She fascinated him if only because she was so completely unlike German women. Those fantastic and amazing people the Americans

. . . But more than that, Leslie was the first *free* person he had met since the war, in five whole years. He had completely forgotten what free, unpossessed people were like. She was the first person in years who made him think!

Hugo became acutely worried. Leslie lived in a world of tolerance and truth. And why was she impregnable, unattainable? Because she *was* free! So free—so armored by truth—that she even dared to see *him,* an agent of the Gestapo! How could he conquer her? It dawned on him apocalyptically—he could reach her, conquer her, only by being free himself. He had to become free too . . .

The 'phone rang. Instantly Hugo composed himself.

"*Jawohl, Herr Doktor.* The usual place? *Gleich, sofort,* at once, *Herr Doktor!*"

III

When Leslie was with Mr. Spaulding, always she felt at her best; when with Mrs. Spaulding, always she wanted to be better than she was. They were talking after dinner in fluid groups. Leslie balanced a coffee cup on the silken blue knee, and with the other hand held a glass of benedictine on the table.

"We are all human beings on this planet together." Yvonne Spaulding's voice. "Every *good* person ought to be on the same side, no matter what his nationality. All of us should work together to create a kind of world republic of good people, and make more people good."

That was like something Gerald had told her once, Leslie recollected. Gerald?

"There is also the point that exaggerated nationalism, patriotism if you like, leads to the kind of villainy that now rules Germany. If you carry nationalism too far, you become a totalitarian, you become a Fascist, which, *mes amis,* is what we would all seek to avoid."

This was in talk to an aggressively nationalist group of Turks. Then Leslie found a chance to be with Mrs. Spaulding alone.

"I was so interested in what you were saying," she began. Yvonne twisted her back slightly so that no one else would join them for a moment. "You don't value love of country above *every*thing?"

"Certainly not," Yvonne Spaulding snapped.

"You wouldn't do absolutely *any*thing for your country?"

"The question of a child. Of course not." She saw that Leslie's eyes were puzzled and appealing. "It is only human relationships that count. I am a Frenchwoman. But if France and the United States should ever go to war, I would unhesitatingly stand by my husband, who is an American."

"Suppose you were an American woman, married to a German?"

Yvonne's sharp nose twitched. "A dreadful thought. *Quelle horreur*. But in a thousand years, a thousand years from now, there will be no Germans, no Americans. We will all be one."

"Sometimes I feel a kind of vicarious patriotism for everybody," Leslie reflected. "I feel sympathy for people defending their own soil. It's like a feeling for a family. That's a rather feminine point of view, I suppose."

"There's nothing wrong about having a feminine point of view." Yvonne was ironic swiftly. "Even if one is a woman."

Leslie went on: "You don't think that patriotic instincts, wanting to do something for your country, would ever justify a person in doing something that was . . . well, a bit ignoble."

Mrs. Spaulding gave her an odd, penetrating look.

"No. I do not."

She rose.

"Human nature is enough debased by war. Let us save what we can."

Over her taut shoulder she continued, "And if I've ever learned anything from experience of life, it's that anything done with an unworthy purpose always gets you into trouble."

But it wasn't her purpose that was unworthy, Leslie thought. She drifted toward the group of men at the other end of the room. She saw that Mr. Spaulding was out on the terrace, talking persuasively with head bent to the Turkish foreign minister. There was a cabinet crisis in the offing, someone told her; politicians were shuttling down to Ankara and back. Mr. Spaulding looked adamant, and the foreign minister, a small glossy man, seemed to be expostulating.

An Embassy *kavass* approached her. "Madame Corcoran? *Quelqu'un vous demande au telephone. Un monsieur.*"

She was surprised. At this hour? At the Embassy? "Please ask who it is."

The *kavass* returned. "Monsieur Blank."

She went to the 'phone, trying to make herself inconspicuous. Hugo never drank, but he sounded as if he were slightly drunk. She was a trifle annoyed and a trifle thrilled. That he should call her here . . . !

"Leslie, I have now my mind made up."

"Yes?"

"Every hour, on the hour, I shall telephone you no matter where you are, from this time on. Like your trains. Every hour. On the hour."

She looked at her watch; it was exactly midnight.

"I shall make you miserable before all your friends, and none of the Musifers shall ever get sleep, even that little girl you are so fond of."

"Hugo, don't be an idiot."

He could tell that she was half-pleased. "Until you consent to meet with me again."

They talked a minute. He seemed both arrogant and appealing. This was Thursday. Finally she agreed to go out to the country with him Sunday morning.

"So I win a small victory."

"I wouldn't put it that way if I were you."

"I will never take advantage of it."

He rang off. Returning to the salon she passed a mirror; her face was flushed. Dave Urquardt had been next to her when the *kavass* came up. "Who and what is Mr. Blank?" he asked with mild curiosity.

"I'm not sure I really know."

IV

He picked her up Sunday in the small green car and they drove along the beaches until they reached a resort beyond Bakirköy called Ittaki. There were rows of casual-seeming hotels with creaking floorboards jutting out over the water, and lobster pools superintended by small boys with inquisitive eyes; women guests in white dresses sat listless with the spring heat, and radios squeaked inside latticed kitchens. They found a table on the veranda, picked out a lobster, and had lunch.

Hugo looked at her: the brisk, smooth Glenurquhart plaid and a blue silk blouse; her brown-and-white eyes so aware and vivid; her strong lovely hands with the rosy nails, and the dark hair richly combed and neat.

"I think I tell you what I think," he grinned. "You, Mrs. Corcoran, are probably the most attractive woman I have ever met. To others, you may not be so. But to me, you are. So let us make fun of all the others. Or shall we just be sorry for them, yes?"

Leslie bantered. "You, Mr. Reichenau, speak romantic English quite well but if you keep on paying me extravagant compliments I'll begin to believe them, and that wouldn't do at all."

His tone changed. The eyebrows were close. "You evade."

"Of course." But she was smiling.

"It is an odd thing," Hugo said, "but when you evade, I do not think it has altogether to do with me. *Wie sagt man,* you certainly are troubled because I am not of your country and cause, but I feel that something beyond that locks you up too."

"That's probably right, Hugo." She mustn't give herself away.

"Perhaps you unlock yourself for me?" His tone was just casual enough so that if she said no decisively, he could pretend that he had not been serious.

"I'll try, but maybe I won't be able to." She was exploring a lobster claw. They bent to their food.

"I have a feeling that you are in love but not with me." He looked at her with a kind of sharp tenderness.

"Falling in love is a kind of illness, isn't it? An infection, rather. Very pleasant and exciting, but . . ." she sought to wave the idea aside.

"I am in love with you from the first moment."

His big, heavy, well-proportioned head; the dark troubled look; yet when he smiled, boyishness; when he moved, agility and grace. He continued: "But I did not know so at first."

"Hugo, it's the one thing in the world you do know about, if it really happens," she said warmly.

He paused a moment, seriously considering. "*Nein*. I do not think so. It is the most wonderful thing in the world to love and then *fall* in love later. It is perhaps the reversal of the normal, but sometimes it happens, and it makes for wonderful delight. In several marriages of my friends, I have known it to happen."

She wanted so much to keep it all on an abstract plane. "Yes, I can see that. All the fire and passion coming *after* a good, solid, friendly relationship is established, so that the fire and passion have something permanent to feed on."

"*Ja. Ja.* But—" Now he looked confused and a little guilty. They finished the lobster and had figs stuffed with cocoanut for dessert.

"I've thought quite a lot about love," she went on. "In the abstract, you know. Impersonally. Its structure and function, so to speak."

"You are afraid to become truly personal with me."

"If this isn't a personal conversation, I don't know what is," Leslie smiled. But he was right.

"Very well." His voice was dogged. "You may describe to me what you think about love, its structure and function, so to speak."

"Oh, Hugo." She caught him with a fork half-way to his mouth. "Hugo, we can't make talk this way. It's like a parody. None of it sounds real."

He looked at her.

"None of this is any good. You know that as well as I. I think it would be wonderful if we could be close." Her voice was direct but low. "But truly, it's no good. Hugo, we ought to call this off right now. I don't think we ought to see one another any more."

The figs and cocoanut were forgotten. "Why not?" sharply.

"You know just as well as I."

"Because I am Nazi."

"Of course."

"I am good German," he said proudly. "To see you is as difficult and embarrassing for me as for you!"

"I don't quite believe that, Hugo. I try so hard to be realistic, to be . . . honest," her eyes were clouded. "I try to think things *through.* I'm not much good at being a flirt, because love seems to me a very serious matter. I think we ought to stop seeing each other, because, frankly, it's too great a *problem.* Not simply because of the war. The war will end some day. But because I could never live in sympathy with a German, I could never be a German woman."

"I am not asking you to become a German woman . . ."

"That's what it might amount to." Her look was distant.

"*Nein.* Can it not occur to you that I could become American?"

She searched him quickly. "Could you, Hugo?"

He called for their bill, looked at it carefully, and paid. "Let us leave this place. It is spoiled by my unhappiness."

v

But now she was more confused than ever. They walked along the beach, beyond the fringe of bright umbrellas like gay mushrooms on stilts. She didn't know whether she was saying good-by to him or not, and he was letting her make the decision . . .

The beach was a long swathe of peach-colored tape, laid for mile after mile on the sharp edge of the sea, hemming it. The water was pale blue and calm, but occasionally a lazy breaker curled into white and broke into foam near the shore. They could see a great distance in either direction, up and down the beach, so that when they looked out to the sea, and then turned their eyes toward the peach-colored sand, the water seemed evenly cut in a giant semicircle. The horizon was circular, like half a plate.

Silence held them; the beach, the sea, were fixed in space, translucent. "I don't suppose I've ever seen before that the world is really round," Leslie murmured.

"But it's hard to believe we stand now on a spinning globe, is it not?"

"Are we?" her voice was dreamy.

"So says the word of modern science and who shall it be among poor human beings to impugn that word."

High white clouds blew by, imperceptibly swift.

. . . Then perhaps oddly what was foremost in her mind was a book. But perhaps not oddly, because that book contained some of the most beautiful descriptions of nature ever written. She loved to read; the printed word was an essential part of her existence. Not like Robin, who had been a restless, impatient reader; he broke open a book almost defiantly, as if to say, "Well, what have you got to teach *me*?" and then skimmed it, working backwards from the end. She herself read books slowly, lingering over them, brooding sometimes, seeping them up, absorbing them. Books were as important as life sometimes. It was often hard to tell the source of what conditioned or influenced a person, hard to tell from which you got the most, the texture of experience itself, or the vicarious pages of a book. The derivative could often be more real than the real.

She thought of one of those long, tightly lapidary, fire-white paragraphs in *Black Lamb and Grey Falcon*, one of those single luminous paragraphs in which the whole discordant experience of a lifetime was distilled, harmonized, and held up for inspection like a shining bubble. It could not be paraphrased; the meaning was too sensitively and complexly dependent on each single word. But its gist was that whereas in older days people could be friends no matter what their political convictions, this was no longer possible. Whereas in pre-war society, people met and loved for purely personal qualities, no matter how diverse, nowadays life and love were circumscribed and walled off by nonpersonal affiliations. Black was black and white was white and you couldn't mix them any longer.

But—?

Leslie thought dreamily of happy moments she had known, happy people she had loved. They plodded slowly through the sand, and her mind kept opening backwards. What made happiness? . . . Her brother Fleming, bursting around the corner of the porch, dressed in a white sheet for a charade and tooting a long striped horn . . . And then Robin, with that delightful nose straight out of his face like a beak, Robin in Paris, after all that blackness in Berlin, that interminable moaning of the soul . . . What a savior Robin had been. And what a revelation! He was twenty years older than Hal and not half so good-looking. But what a *revelation* . . .

"You are far away now," Hugo said.

"But I'm rather happy," Leslie said.

"You come back to me soon?"

"Yes." A tumult grew in him.

The veranda of the teahouse where they sat late in the afternoon was screened, and at dusk, through the screen, the world which had been so flatly extended, so flatly horizontal, became suddenly a sheer vertical world. Sea melted into sky; sky melted into sea; the color was of huckleberries; and there was no horizon. They looked through the screen and into the dusk and the world was a vertical huckleberry wall. No one could tell where sea ended, where sky began. Sea and sky were one, indistinguishable in the blue glowing wall outside their window.

They had tea.

"I confess to you something now," Hugo said.

"Tell me."

Her voice was quiet, but she no longer felt reserved.

"When I first saw you, and chased after you like a conceited boy, all I had thought for was this, 'The American will be something new. She will distract me from my boredom; she will relieve me from my discontents. I will deceive her, I will push her over, I will make love to her, she will be fine company for a while, then I will drop her, as I have dropped many women.'"

In her, something began to stir.

"But all the time I was in love with you, from the very first moment, even if I did not know it. I am now in love with you, I am in love with you as never before with a woman, and I do not know what to do."

He had to say it over again.

"I thought you would be a pleasant object to conquer, to amuse with in bed, to canvass between a pair of sheets, as your Shakespeare says, and that was all I had desire for. And I thought you would be—easy."

He was going to say it once more. She stopped him:

"Oh, Hugo, I'm glad you said all that." Yes. Yes. Now she could say something too. "I've got something to confess too, Hugo. When we first met I had . . . false motives too. I thought I'd let you play around with me for a while and I felt I could make you sell out, I felt that I could work on you and influence you somehow, as an agent, as a . . . spy . . . I thought I could make you come over to our side."

Now she really did know how much her conscience had been troubling her; tears were in her eyes.

Hugo thought a moment soberly. Then he declared, "Now that it is cleared up on both sides, we have the basis for a relationship."

She shook the tears loose. "I'm not sure. But I'm glad we've both said what we said."

They walked back to the place where he had left the car. "We have dinner in town," said Hugo.

She clung now to his arm. She was grateful to him because she had told the truth. Now they could be friends—in spite of everything.

CHAPTER XIV

Interlude

I

WORK was serious. Work was important. That was why she was here. On the dot of nine, she arrived at her office, in the building like a vast marble barn that had once been the town house of a Syrian millionaire. A wheezy lift rose naked and exposed in the pillared lobby; Leslie tripped over a ragged bit of carpet, where the parquet floor had worn through. The Lend Lease offices were makeshift and dilapidated; they were filled with clacking typewriters, Armenian messengers, half-completed wooden partitions, posters and news-sheets, and filing cases jutting every which way from ancient, mottled alcoves.

. . . Hugo had suddenly had to go to Ankara for a few days, on Dr. Dortmund's orders. In a way she was glad he was gone. It would be a relief not to have to think about personal problems for a while. She was quite content that she had no engagements at all for a day or two.

She saw Urquardt come in; he was always prompt too, and they had a little game, which neither had ever mentioned; each liked to get to the office first. They got along very well. At the beginning, Leslie knew, he had felt a faint uncertainty, almost a resentment, that Washington should have sent a woman, instead of some bright young man, as his assistant. So many men feared women in a well-ordered office. Therefore she had sought to behave exactly like a man. Now he accepted her completely. She watched him through the glass; his gestures as he arrived never varied. He peeled off his jacket, and in one fluid motion hung it on a rack; he lit a pipe and turning to his desk scratched his youthful gray hair, on a spot an inch behind the left ear.

Today was quite an important day, because for the first time he was taking her to the big committee meeting, where final decisions on Lend Lease were made. The committee was Anglo-American; its chairman was a Bank of England man, Sir Harold Loomis. But Urquardt had almost as much to say. First the Turks prepared the lists of what they wanted; these, if not particularly controversial, were passed on locally. But if they brought up questions of major priority they had to be referred both to London and to the Munitions Assignment Board in Washington. Then word would come back. Weeks late, sometimes. Finally the Istanbul committee would meet and put whatever orders were necessary into effect.

There arose a million complex and dovetailing subordinate details. Suppose the Turks wanted machinery of such-and-such a category. Well, it might be easier to procure it in England than in America, in which case London had to be consulted; or it might be lying around in one of the great supply dumps near Cairo. Or suppose shipping was temporarily jammed up in the Mediterranean. They might have to calculate on other routes. Or suppose some urgently needed hospital equipment happened to get stalled at Port Said. Could they get planes to fly it to the frontier? All these problems, under Urquardt's strict and discriminating control, Leslie had become familiar with.

Then there was the moot question of what the Turks might, or might not, do with the stuff they got. Perpetual rumors came that they hoarded it deep in Anatolia not for their own legitimate defensive needs, but as a cache for future use against the Russians. So the Lend Lease organization worked closely with Secret Service.

"I'm sending Paul to Erzerum tonight. I don't like what I've heard out there," Urquardt said.

"Is he going black?"

"No, we'll risk it white."

Black meant when you sent people on missions clandestinely, without official knowledge or permission.

Often Urquardt talked eloquently about the larger implications of Lend Lease. By profession he was a teacher; he had a nice messianic touch. Of course Lend Lease was turning out to be a prodigious boon, a windfall, not merely to Turkey but to the whole Middle East; we were giving all these Levant countries an enormous amount of new plant—for nothing; they were literally being recreated. New harbors, new airfields, new railway lines; new roads, docks, and radio networks; machine shops, telephone lines, printing presses. Fields were being sown with our wheat; children were going to new schools we built.

"Of course there's a lot of scrounging," Dave Urquardt explained. "Even our gallant allies aren't above using some of our stuff for their own political purposes. But we watch everything damned carefully. And I think it's all quite magnificent as well as being absolutely necessary from a military point of view. What we're doing is to raise the standard of living everywhere. Which means helping to keep it raised at home."

"Besides, there's the humanitarian aspect," Leslie echoed. She felt very proud to be part of this work.

"It's for the one thing in the world that counts—people."

II

After the committee meeting she picked up with her routine. She read the Turkish papers in western languages with their hodgepodge of O.W.I. handouts, Axis propaganda, ancient *feuilletons*, occasional pieces by well-known Americans that seemed like lightning out of the dark but weirdly dated, and turbulent discussion as to when the Second Front would come. Also she read carefully every day a summary in English of the vernacular press, and a mimeographed bulletin short-waved from Washington, with official news from

America, that the Embassy distributed once or twice a week.

Glancing at this she saw Robin's name. She had often seen it in print in the United States but this was the first time she had ever come across it in Turkey. She started a little, and put the bulletin rather carefully at the side of her blotter.

It was right and good for a woman to have a man. So declared the heart within her heart. But—

Something prompted her to think about Robin's defects, his limitations. Of course there was his single-trackedness, his intense demanding selfishness. But till recently she hadn't thought much of something else: that Robin had not been very much interested in people, that is, people in the mass, people in the abstract. He was certainly "human" enough, God knew. But oddly he had very little preoccupation with people as a whole; he was quite opaque to broad social impulses; he had little understanding of the love that is *above* love of country, love for humanity.

What has been making *me* think so much in this direction, she reflected. Hugo? Gerald Heath? Yvonne Spaulding? The nature of her daily work?

Of course it was part of the delight of this job that she was helping to distribute some of the things that *he,* Robin, produced in such illimitable streams . . .

The next morning Urquardt took her with him to the office of another American agency in Istanbul, the ultra-hush-hush agency that acted as a watchtower over the Balkans. Here too, in a quiet way, Lend Lease played a role. And here Leslie met Bulgars, Rumanians, Greeks, Cypriots, Wallachians, Moldavians, Cretans, Bessarabians, Albanians, Ruthenians, Macedonians, Bosnians, Serbs, Slovenes, and Croats, besides the British and Americans who shepherded these charges into interlocked spheres of influence and function.

Urquardt said at lunch: "It may sound confusing, but the common denominator is as simple as apple pie. It's the same everywhere—the *people* who stayed at home and suffered—the *people* who took it on the chin while refugee governments sat outside—are damned well going to demand a share in

power later, they are going to demand the right to rule.
And most of the people who sat inside and suffered and
waited are peasants, little men in the towns, the poor folk,
the underpossessed. So the people's governments that will
spring up everywhere are almost certain to be on the Leftist
side. The question is whether or not we and the British will
be willing to support them. If they *are* genuinely rooted in
the people, as they should be, it would be madness not to.
Because of course if we play with reaction and old-time
forces, if we still think we can turn back to 1939, why, we'll
inevitably help to produce exactly that which we say we want
to prevent, that is, revolution."

Leslie thought this over; it was getting into rather a new
field. It would be a field fascinating to explore. She looked
for some kind of personal rock. "Does the Ambassador
understand all this?"

"Ah, the Ambassador understands *every*thing."

There were two girls in the Lend Lease office she was
interested in. One was the secretary she shared with Dave;
he had about five-sixths of her, she had the rest. Her name
was Miss Hanun, pronounced Ha-noon. Miss Hanun came
from somewhere in the Caucasus; she had been educated at
Robert College where Urquardt had been one of her instruc-
tors. She was heavy with a bad complexion but she had
magnificent black eyes; she hated Leslie at first because
Leslie was slim, *chic*, and good-looking. One day when they
were friends she said casually, "When I was three weeks old,
during the massacres near Kars, the missionaries managed
to get my mother out; my mother walked with me for four
hundred miles." Leslie gasped. There were always new
horizons. The other girl was a tough, gay, flashy youngster of
about seventeen, from Alexandretta; her name was Gen-
eviève, but everybody called her Giji. Until Leslie arrived
the whole focus of her life had been what she would do
someday in Paris; now it was what she would do in New
York. She was utterly fascinated by the mode of life and
social custom Leslie represented. She hung around her desk

by the hour, asking her every possible question from whether it was true that such-and-such a movie star had false teeth to what kind of dress an American girl of seventeen would wear to dinner at the Waldorf with a boy she was meeting for the first time.

Leslie liked both these girls. They both had what she prized above all, character. And she wanted very much to know them better . . .

It was about five. She was clearing up her desk. She looked at the tangled brown telephone cord—why *couldn't* some bright man do something useful and invent a kind of cord that wouldn't twist up this way?—and with a peculiar intuitive flash she felt that the 'phone was about to ring. She could almost see the wires vibrate and the mouthpiece quiver with a message bursting to be released. As it rang the switchboard girl called in French *"Inter! Inter!"* It took Leslie a second to remember this was short for *interurban*. The girl repeated *"Inter!"* All her life Leslie had been thrilled by long distance calls. She could never quite overcome a silly feeling that they might be from Robin.

Gerald's voice, faint and distorted.

"Hello? Mrs. Corcoran? Leslie?"

"You're through," a fainter voice said in English.

"I know I'm through. Thanks," Gerald said.

"But we're not through!" Leslie exclaimed. "We've just started to talk."

"You're through," the faint voice said again.

"That's English for we're connected," Gerald laughed. "It's my telephonist here. Well, how *are* you?"

"I'm fine. How are *you*, Gerald?"

There was an exhilaration in the way he talked. And a glow spread through her that he was 'phoning.

"Did you get my letter?"

"Yes. I'm sorry I haven't answered yet. I've been planning to. But I've been rather busy."

"I'm afraid it may have sounded rather forward."

She could not help thinking of Florian: "Are you having a good time?"

"Why, yes." She could hear him hesitate. What a nice voice he had. "But . . . it's not important—"

A confused burr on the line. Then an exploding noise and silence, and a French voice said, "*La ligne est coupée!*"

More burrs and buzzes. One operator kept saying, "*Allo! Allo!*" apparently to the central operator. Then a voice addressed Leslie:

"*Ne quittez pas, madame.*"

"*Oui, j'écoute.*"

She heard Gerald calling, but when she talked he couldn't hear her.

A voice shrieked, "*La communication est encore coupée,*" and then Gerald's telephonist said again, "You're through."

Leslie couldn't help laughing: "Maybe we are through," but Gerald cried, "*Mademoiselle, je vous en prie,* restore the connection, it is most urgently necessary that the connection be restored."

The central operator started to talk in Turkish and switched to German, "*Alle Gespräche auf fünf Minuten beschränkt.* All calls limited to five minutes."

Gerald shouted in German, "This is an urgent call!"

Leslie called, "Hello. Can you hear me now?"

"Yes. At last." They both laughed. Gerald called, "Is my memory still green?"

"Of course. When do you think you'll be back in Istanbul?"

"Don't know yet. I've still got a job to clean up here. Listen. Maybe it's none of my business, but Leslie, listen, I heard you were seeing a man, I wish you wouldn't; you know who I mean, but it's difficult to talk over this blasted 'phone. I say—"

Buzzes and burrs again. The voice of the French operator, screaming, "*La ligne est maintenant libre, monsieur.*"

"I know! Let me talk!"

He certainly sounded full of energy and brisk good humor . . . And amazingly confident and happy. But he went on:

"Please do let me say it again; I really wish you'd be prudent; and as a matter of fact I think it *is* my business in a way . . ."

The sounds coming now were like those on a radio improperly tuned, a faint singing just off beat. Gerald's voice began to ululate, swooping up and down like a swallow in flight.

Leslie shouted: "Gerald, thanks; I'm all right. Don't worry, please!"

Silence.

The first operator: "*C'est encore coupée! C'est dommage.* It is the fault of the other operator. She's a *mauvais type.*"

The other operator shouted: "*Qu'est-ce que vous faites? Répondez-moi, chameau!* Reply, you camel!"

"*Espèce de sauvage.* You kind of savage."

"*Espèce de chameau.*"

Leslie broke in: "*Bitte. S'il vous plaît.* Can you get through again?" She didn't know what language she was speaking. Then she heard the end of a sentence of which Gerald must assume she had heard the beginning: ". . . strongly about it, I hope you don't mind."

"*¿Estoy hablando con el agregado militar de la embajada alemana?*" My God, Spanish! "I await the military attaché of the German Embassy."

"Get off the line," Gerald shouted. "*Retirez-vous!*"

Leslie burst out laughing.

"Can you still hear me?"

"Yes. So can everybody else."

He started to laugh too.

"We'd better give it up. But I have one more thing to say. Maybe you'll think it's odd, my saying it. But I feel so very strongly about you—I want to see you—"

"*Sie haben schon über fünf Minuten gesprochen.* You have spoken for more than five minutes. *Schluss!*"

She hung on a moment. But the line was dead for good. She put the receiver down gently, and she felt strangely formal. Then she was very sober. Something in Gerald's voice moved her. Hearing it made her know that she couldn't be in love with Hugo.

CHAPTER XV

Strangeways Watching

I

STRANGEWAYS wrote her a note, and they met for dinner at Taksim's. He had called several times, and she had rather avoided making an appointment. But now she was glad to be seeing him. André, the Greek waiter, showed them to a table, and Leslie looked around, while Strangeways ordered. They started with some Turkish black olives, ink-colored olives with a purple luster and crinkled skin.

She had not seen André since the afternoon at the Lido. He did not respond much to her smile. It was always the same with that Greek. Living each night in a sharp haze of brightness, under all the glowing lights; and yet never emerging from his own dark thoughts. Seeing men and women, women and men, constantly coming together, making couples, making love; he who would never see his wife again.

Leslie felt conscious that she, or they, were being closely watched; this made her act a little. With subconscious volition, because Mr. Poppa was hovering near their table, she gave an edge to each gesture as she talked and listened, a note of sharpness, of deliberation, to the picture she and Strangeways made.

Imperturbably and without introduction he asked her, "Well, and how are you getting on with Hugo?"

"All right," she answered cautiously. She didn't know how much she ought to tell.

"You drove out to Ittaki starting from the Café Waytaus at 11:20 A.M. Sunday," Strangeways announced easily. "You had lunch, the bill for which was 42 Turkish pounds, at the Hotel Grand-Miramar, and then spent the afternoon on the beach. You started back to Istanbul at 6:42 P.M., having had tea at a place called the Eskisehir; you dined in town at a small restaurant called the Flotte, near the bridge, and Hugo deposited you at your doorstep at 12:17. That was Sunday. You haven't seen him since, inasmuch as he went to Ankara Monday night on the Anatolia Express."

He watched her. Her brows and lids had gone up so the whites of her eyes shone all around the irises. "Here's the bill for your lunch at the Grand-Miramar." He passed it over.

"You certainly are a professional, aren't you?" Leslie breathed. She hoped it didn't show in her face, her *ex post facto* relief that she and Hugo had not, in spite of his urgent plea, gone that evening to his apartment at the Park.

"It's damned well my business to be a professional," Strangeways said.

The only thing to do was to take the bull, so to speak, by what horns she could put hand to: "You don't mistrust me, do you?"

"I think you are being unwise."

Look at her, Strangeways thought. She had a sheen tonight, a luster, as if something vital in her, some essential inner health, had burned out to the surface, and was irradiating her.

"But," he continued, "don't think it's any concern of mine if you make a fool of yourself."

"I won't make a fool of myself," Leslie said slowly.

"I don't take it very seriously. You can't be in love with him: he has no sense of humor."

That was right, Leslie thought. But she was a shade annoyed at him for saying so.

His voice, which had had an edge, was now dry as salt. "I certainly know what Hugo wants. Like all Germans he wants the unattainable."

Leslie thought briefly. "Thanks," she said.

But she wanted somehow to change the equilibrium with

Strangeways, to reduce him from the obvious superiority and satisfaction he was now enjoying. What was the most outrageous thing she could say?

"I'm a woman living alone and why shouldn't I go out with an attractive young man? Don't you realize that I'm almost a nymphomaniac?"

But except for that one smudge of big lips against her cheek, Hugo had never even kissed her.

II

Then they talked as they had talked that first evening. She felt that he was rather tense.

"Enemy very nervous and upset these days. Funny, every once in a while they get these fits of nerves."

"Who wouldn't, with you chasing them? Besides, they must realize they're going to be beaten everywhere."

He smiled. "Maybe so. Pre-invasion jitters. Anyway, smallest thing touches 'em off. Anything makes 'em jump."

"That's good news."

"I'm not so sure. We're taking strict precautions, of course. Changed our locks on everything the other day. And for the first time in months, ordered all my men to carry arms."

He must be telling her this for a reason. He never did anything without a purpose, she knew now.

"We've worked out a new little trick," the Englishman grimly laughed. "American boat comes into Iskanderun, say; we tell the Turks it can only wait in harbor twenty-four hours. The Turks have to deflect all their rolling stock down there, to get their Lend Lease stuff off quick. Keeps the Germans from making any use of the trains, for material of their own. Then we fool 'em and keep the boat there as long as we like."

Everybody in this business was certainly full of tricks. She thought of Hugo. Was it conceivable, *could* it be possible, that Hugo might in some way be tricking her?

Now Strangeways was talking with a half-resentful admiration of the enormous pressure the United States was exerting in military and industrial fields everywhere, how the Americans were getting to be top-dog in everything.

And again he looked as if something were gnawing him, as if he were scooped out. What was it, Leslie wondered. Maybe because he took it so hard that his country was no longer the most powerful in the world.

III

They were relaxed now and secure with pleasure in each other's company and they danced once or twice, and Strangeways marveled at the way American girls danced as if you weren't even holding them. The floor show began and Leslie looked it over with the casual eye of an habitué. Kathi and Lilli and Sophie came out, and the saxophonist she had met at the Lido waved to her. But the show, indeed the whole establishment, seemed to have lost much of its luster with Florian not there.

"When's Florian coming back?" Leslie inquired.

"Soon."

"I want very much to see her."

"I feel a bit of an ass. Odd thing. Asked you to do something about Gerald, and it seems that Florian did it."

"Well, that's good."

"But I have a feeling that he's just about through with her."

What? She felt a tingle. "Why?" she asked.

"Don't know. Gerald's such an idealist; maybe he realizes she doesn't love him."

"Men are funny, aren't they?" Her lips parted gently.

"Some of them, quite nice."

"Very nice."

"Gerald's very exercised over you, incidentally. Because you've been seeing Hugo."

"I know." Her voice was warm. "He called me yesterday."

"I know too. I talked to him tonight."

Leslie laughed. "I hope you had a better connection than we did."

"Eh? Well, anyway, the lad is splendid. Doing the best work he's ever done."

"I'm glad." Her lips were smiling.

"I'm going to pull him out of there pretty soon. Plan to send him on another job."

Leslie knew better than to ask where or what.

He looked at her rather pointedly. "He'll be here some days en route, I daresay. Then a week or so in Egypt. Learning how to jump."

"What?"

"I'm dropping him in a place by parachute."

"Oh."

"It'll be bloody dangerous. If they catch him, we'll never even find the pieces."

She found herself agitated and anxious. She hated to think of his being exposed to danger.

"Does Gerald want to go?" she asked foolishly.

"Keen as mustard for it."

Even if Florian were not at Taksim's tonight, everybody else certainly was. Waving to them from one corner were Urquardt, two blasé and contented-seeming American newspaper men, and Randall, the O.W.I. boy. In one nearby booth sat one of the Vichy attachés, a man with pince-nez and sunken, closely-shaved cheeks, about whose habits in bed there was much talk; in another, one of the pro-German Finns, who, so far as was known, had no habits in bed at all. Along the bar, they saw the Egyptian commercial attaché who hated the British more than anything on earth and who mimicked them in everything, and the leader of the refugee Montenegrins, an expansive mountaineer the pupils of whose dark eyes looked encircled with a thin line of milk, and who loved to exclaim, "I am from the Balkans, so I could steal God from heaven!" Entering now, one after another, came the little Chinese journalist, who could speak no western language, whose every word was an indecipherable laugh, and who often wore a button, "I am not Japanese"; the cautious Swede whom none was ever sure of, but who said he represented a porcelain company; an icily beautiful Netherlands girl, reputed to be a *Jungfrau*, with her escort, the Portuguese councilor with fat hands, both of whom looked strained and tense and uneasily in love; and, inconspicuously, someone who outranked everybody in the room but whom no one ever seemed to notice—the British Ambassador, known universally as Puffin, who was so shy that sometimes strangers didn't think he spoke English.

There was a stir behind them, and Leslie saw that Herr Doktor Max Dortmund was also being shown a place, not twenty feet away, by the humorous, efficient Mr. Poppa.

Then standing in the upper loge she caught a glimpse of the blond, Viking-tall, powerful Russian consul general. Calmly, he was looking at the scene below, and irony cut the corners of his mouth. She thought of all the wearisome nonsense she had heard about Russians . . . Dostoevsky, the knout, tea in a garret, Siberia, introspection, wolves in the snow . . . This Russian didn't look like that at all. He looked like a man with an absolutely modern mind; a man who was an absolute realist in the modern world.

And not only did he seem satisfied and confident tonight, Leslie reflected; he had a rather different look; he looked proprietary.

IV

Randall paused by their table for a second, and then since the first show was over, joined Kathi, the only girl in Taksim's who was an outright prostitute. He was always with her now. He looked ragged and the crew haircut was growing out.

Leslie thought it was rather disgusting, but she asked Strangeways humorously, "Do you suppose the O.W.I. knows it's helping to finance a future millinery shop in Budapest?"

Strangeways shrugged. He did not look at Kathi closely. He remembered her cold whore's tongue, like a pickle.

V

Sophie sat in a booth not far off with a Turkish officer, a full colonel. He had heavy gold teeth. An Englishman, who had had two or three drinks, sat down with them. He was a youngster with a monocle, someone in Economic Warfare, who had to do with preclusive purchasing. Evidently the Turk thought that he intended to do some purchasing out of bounds. First Leslie heard a guttural voice sharply raised. Then there was a scuffle and a fight. The Turkish officer reached forward, tipped the Englishman's chin up, and then slammed him in the cheek. The monocle fell off.

Mr. Poppa had them all out in thirty seconds, as the table crashed. But you could hear him screaming at Sophie a hundred yards away. The Englishman wiped blood from his eye. André started to pick up the broken dishes, his face sullen with contempt.

VI

"Ah, André," Strangeways murmured later. "Two French brandies please. The old Bisquit Dubouché, if you still have it."

"None left, I am sorry."

"Well then, whatever tolerable brandy you've got."

André dutifully walked toward the bar. He was thinking:

It's just about three years now. I am sitting in Athens café getting shoes shined. Italian war, who cares about Italian war. Ha, we clean up lousy Italians right into ocean. Germans, they attack Belgrade. Germans, different matter. Very different. War comes close. Germans attack *us*. First raid, very noisy, we scared to death, not much damage though. Helen scared. Very scared. Next days, home guard, out in suburbs, drilling, I can never hold gun straight. More raids, they come like hell. We get to Corinth, everybody scared, angry now, fighting. I lose Helen, my sister takes her, I get to islands, must keep on fighting. I have bad sickness there, I crawl back to Athens, must see Helen, she gone. Germans take towns, take food, little kids swollen on streets, starving, dead. Helen in Sparta, then Germans take her. What to do now? I am not fighting man, but must keep on fighting. I get out, *kayak*, two days, small islands. Hungry, no papers. And in Athens, they die like animals, lie side by side without coffins on streets. Sister writes, I get word. I try to return, no food, no papers. Helen not strong girl, she dies fairly soon. I get here. Now almost three years now.

André picked up the brandies at the service bar—they cost $4.00 each—and served them. "Thanks," Strangeways said.

VII

Leslie had an uncomfortable sense now that Dortmund and Poppa were talking about her. She could feel that Poppa was pointing to her, nodding covertly, then rubbing his hands, while his eyes held an amiable conspiratorial smile. Dortmund was leaning toward him, a hand cupping an ear, and the ugly chopped-up lips extended.

Oh nonsense, Leslie thought. They're probably gossiping about the Ankara races or the weather.

Her eyes swerved toward the broad center aisle, and at first she could not believe what she saw. The man, in a mustard-colored open shirt, and with his cap apologetically in hand, looked about grinning with bewilderment. Searching the establishment with him was Etta Musifer. Etta saw Leslie at the moment that Leslie saw her; she gave a gleeful screech, and darted down the aisle.

Good Lord, Leslie thought.

Dr. and Mrs. Musifer, she knew, were dining that evening at the Foreign Office. Etta must have waited till their servant was asleep, then dressed and picked up one of the taxis at the Waytaus. Leslie rose and clasped her in her arms. "Why, what are you doing here?" she exclaimed. "You naughty little girl!"

Thrilled, burning with excited happiness, her olive eyes

almost popping from her face, Etta burbled. The taxi driver stood there, embarrassed, and Strangeways paid him off.

Leslie could not understand what Etta was telling her. Strangeways did not know Turkish; Mr. Poppa grasped the situation, rose from Dortmund's table, and joined them to interpret.

"I think we ought to get out of here," Leslie said.

The child showed no trace of fear; only excitement and delight. Mr. Poppa listened to her and then explained that she had heard Leslie talk about Taksim's and tonight decided to follow her. The music was pounding over the great downstairs floor; the lights were dimmed, and the second half of the show began. Etta pointed to the dancers, mute with happiness. She rocked back and forth with bliss.

Mr. Poppa said to Leslie. "Ah, madame, allow the *petite* to remain a small moment." Then he ogled her.

They sat there till the show was over. Leslie held Etta's hand. Dr. Dortmund was certainly watching them now. Leslie remembered with a shudder that talk the first evening about tossing children under cars.

CHAPTER XVI

Hugo to Leslie to Hugo

I

"COULD it be? *Could* it be?" Hugo looked violently suspicious, as if meditating a dire secret revenge. His voice was harsh and troubled. "Are we being deceived again, betrayed again? I am honest German. Could it be possible that, once more, we are merely dupes, slaves? I told you about my innocence, my naïveté, concerning Wilson. Is my whole generation being sold a stupid lie again?"

"It certainly could be," Leslie agreed succinctly. They had been talking for hours now; or so it seemed. She was nervous and uncomfortable, and he twitched with strain. Since Strangeways apparently had them watched, they could not meet except secretly. Hugo had picked out an inconspicuous café near Galata as a rendezvous. Afterwards they would cross into Stamboul and go sightseeing. It was not taking much of a chance since they would never be seen by anybody they knew in that part of town.

Hugo had just returned from Ankara. He had not had a very happy time there. For one thing their Ambassador had been too busy to receive him. From the point of view of rank he had no real right to be received; yet how much better one felt when that distinguished, crooked, strangely fascinating man asked you over, and suavely gave you tea, while he drank a Scotch highball by the fireplace. Real Scotch. And American cigarettes. The British and Americans only seldom had these, their own luxuries; but the Germans almost always had them. I am a snob, Hugo thought with self-disgust. But, really, it would have been so nice, so *gemütlich*, so proper even if improper, to have been received. He had performed Dortmund's mission perfunctorily but well enough. Every few months they had the same things to rearrange. What Turkish editors got how much. What Turkish officials in various bureaus got how much. What would be the new budget for the local German news services, and what particular expansion under what new directives would be required.

"The bad news in Russia," Hugo went on seriously, "is, we are told, the result of miscalculation. But whose? Surely not that of the Führer . . . The British fight us only because of the influence of the plutocrats, the capitalists, and the Jews. But it was puzzling, that I freely concede, their unwillingness to accede to a separate peace."

"Hugo, I cannot bear it when you talk like a fool. You're being either stupid or dishonest."

He went on grimly: "As to the Americans, your country is of course completely dominated by strikes, you have no real interest in the war, *wie soll ich sagen*, you have no martial tradition or ideology—"

"We went into that once before—"

"Yet the reports that I have access to, they make it clear that the American soldier is very well equipped, and is a good though inexperienced fighting man." He shook his head dubiously. "It is, of course, highly doubtful that there ever will be an invasion, and if it comes, it will be smashed into the sea, *sofort*. We have been promised that—unequivocally! But I have access to much documentary material, very secret, material from foreign sources, and I must say I am not content!"

Leslie thought a moment. "I'd like to ask you just one question."

"*Ja?*"

"What are you going to do when you *are* really beaten?" And she repeated something Mr. Spaulding had said a day before; the Ambassador quoted it from an American magazine that had just come in.

"You can't go on arguing that the world belongs to you because you're strong, when it's demonstrated everywhere that you're not strong, but weak. You can't argue that you're a master race and all that nonsense *after* you've been licked; you can't continue to talk about how democracy is decadent when, in fact, the war proves just the opposite. So what's going to happen to all your precious theories, Hugo? What are you going to believe in, *after* you've been beaten?"

He argued that the Germans were by no means beaten yet.

"But they will be, Hugo."

"If we go down we take a lot with us," he said grimly.

"What a charming thought," she replied, also grim.

"You wait and see."

II

"So now we go to the churches and bazaars," Hugo declared, after they had wrangled more. He tried to make his voice light. "For the rest of today, no talk of politics! Now, we have pleasure with ourselves. Business and pleasure should never be mixed. Is that not right?"

What a cliché, Leslie thought. And how frightfully "German" it was to think you could cut life into segments, separate the segments neatly, compartmentalize and isolate them . . .

He added, "There is much I know that I cannot say. There is much I cannot tell you." His voice was dark again.

Quickly her mind ran back to Strangeways. There was a lot she couldn't tell Hugo, she thought with a kind of detached uneasiness. That Englishman was smart!

They crossed the bridge into Stamboul, over the Golden Horn, and made for St. Sophia and the Seraglio.

"I show you now new sides of me," he said with serious self-satisfaction. "There are sides of me, Hugo Reichenau, of which you know nothing."

Indeed he turned out to be a competent and conscientious guide. He took her through the water-bound, bluish glory of the Ahmedie, with its six minarets; he told her how St. Sophia had been erected by Justinian in 532 A.D. and dedicated in 538; he showed her where the Byzantine mosaics had been covered after 1453, and how the patient work of scholars was now revealing them. He explained how Constantinople, as the focus of Greek civilization in the dying days of the Roman Empire, had produced Byzantine art, how no other city in the world, except possibly Rome, had so cardinally affected the whole course of history. He walked her through the threadbare park of the Seraglio, under the furled cypresses like umbrellas, and they inspected the marble pillars and cloisters so miraculously delicate, ornate, and pure. This was now the Turkey of the Turks and did she know that as recently as the 1880's a crazy Sultan had strangled with impunity his grand vizier? And finally they came to the great bronze statue of Kemal Atatürk in a dinner jacket dominating Seraglio Point; they had reached the Turkey of today.

They passed a mosque again, and seemed to hear a muezzin cry, *La ilaha illa 'llah wa muhammad urrasul u'llah*. The Turkey of today?

Leslie was impressed, not so much by Hugo's teutonically pedantic knowledge, but by his soberness, by the dutiful respect he paid these antique monuments—which meant rather little to her except aesthetically—and what they represented of the past.

Toward six they reached an antique shop in the bazaars. The rays of the late afternoon sun, interrupted by the patched and slanting roofs, penetrated the dark, sodden bazaars like searchlights crossing, searchlights glittering with dust.

"Gentleman and lady, I give it to you then for hundred forty *lire*! A bargain! One hundred forty *lire*!"

What a curious and charming ornament, Leslie thought. It was Damascene, so the shopkeeper said; it was a brooch, a disk of old gold two inches in diameter, bound by small cracked rubies and with a big, bruised, glowing cabochon, also possibly a ruby, in the center. Hugo shook his head. Before they knew it, the ritual of purchase had begun. One shop assistant flung himself out of the curtained door, and returned in a second with tiny cups of thick coffee; another was offering cigarettes and obsequiously placing chairs; small brown-eyed boys stood at the side of the showcase, watching tensely and respectfully; trays were produced of filagree boxes, Anatolian towels spotted by virgin's blood, Persian miniatures, and chunks of amber.

"One hundred thirty *lire*!"

That was quite a lot of money, one hundred thirty Turkish pounds. She fingered the brooch, and the shopkeeper volubly poured out its history.

"It is ancient, antique, I give the certificate of antiquity, of ancient origin, worn once by a Turkish princess, once an ornament of the *hareem*!"

"It's lovely," Leslie said.

"Shall I buy it for you?" Hugo asked.

"Oh, no, please." But she felt a warm pleasure in its color, its picturesqueness.

"One hundred thirty *lire*!"

"You are a robber," Hugo said.

Leslie winced at his tone. He noticed and said to her quickly, "But it is the only way to bargain. Just observe me. I know how to handle such affairs."

"One hundred twenty *lire*. I sell at a loss, I need cash today."

"I offer you sixty," Hugo said.

"Is that really enough?" Leslie asked out of consideration for the shopkeeper.

"You are a filthy old robber," Hugo went on coldly.

"One hundred fifteen."

"Robber."

"One hundred fifteen."

"Hugo, stop it." She felt embarrassed.

"Sixty-five," said Hugo. "You robber."

"One hundred ten."

"Sixty-five."

"Genuine rubies, the center stone four carats. Once worn by a Turkish princess. Antique and genuine."

"You had it made in Izmir last week," Hugo sneered.

"Gentleman! Gentleman!"

"Seventy," Hugo said.

To Leslie's astonishment the shopkeeper shouted, groaned, gurgled, cocked his head this way and that, thrust out his hands in appeal, grunted deeply again, gestured violently with the ornament, and finally burst out, "Very well! Sold!"

Hugo looked astonished too. Now he had it. And the fact that the shopkeeper had been willing to let it go at this price meant, of course, that it really *had* been made in Izmir last week, and probably wasn't worth half of what he paid. Hugo looked disgruntled and humiliated. "I change my mind. I do not wish it after all," he exclaimed in a pained voice.

"No, you can't do that, Hugo," cried Leslie promptly.

"We are being swindled!"

"You made him an offer and he accepted it."

"The brooch must be fraudulent to go at that price."

She laughed at the dismay on his face. "Hugo, don't be a goose. You asked for it. Now you have it."

He held it in his hand dubiously. "But it is really not worth the money, since it cannot be genuine."

Hugo paid over the seventy Turkish pounds, and the shopkeeper gazed at them benevolently. "But I have been cheated," Hugo expostulated. "I have been fooled!"

"Never mind, Hugo." She was still laughing.

He put the brooch in his pocket; then he laughed too, ruefully. They had dinner in an Armenian restaurant near the edge of the bazaar. He kept pulling out the ornament and inspecting it. "You will wear it as a present from me," he said. "A *Geschenk*. In memory." But he did not pass it over.

"You have never seen me at sport," he volunteered suddenly, as if wishing to efface an unfortunate impression. "That is still altogether another side. You have not seen me play tennis!"

III

It was an outright struggle between them now. If he had not gone to Ankara, almost anything might have happened.

That kind of accident occurred so often among people with complicated lives. A brief unexpected absence. A sentence off-center, or a sudden 'phone call. It could take weeks or months to recapture a broken mood. And sometimes you never recaptured it.

That evening after they had walked along the beach, if he had so much as kissed her, she might have been lost. But in a strange way, Hugo that night had seemingly wanted to keep it all on a friendship basis, as if respecting her discovery that they *could* be friends. And he kept prodding her about what he called her lost love, her past . . .

They finished coffee. There was a long tense silence. His gestures, his talk and mannerisms, were no longer stimulating; in a way, they irritated her. And he still threw her off by continuing persistently to pepper her with questions about her life before she came to Istanbul. She who was a very private person, who hated aggressive curiosities . . .

The more she thought about it, the more she felt that they must, in fact, call it off. Or at least she must have a *real* justification for seeing him, quite aside from personal emotion. The old idea came back with renewed strength. Otherwise she could not go on.

"Hugo, why don't you give up all you're doing? Why don't you come over to our side?" Her voice thrilled coming alive; she looked straight at him, appealing. Could she not win him by *reason,* that most sublime of weapons?

It was all right to ask this now. It was all above-board now; it was all right if she could convert him. Not try to make spurious use of his desire for her. No crass trickery or temptation. But simply ask him outright.

It was as if they were trains on parallel tracks going in opposite directions; they whizzed past one another. He dismissed her question; that was something they could discuss later. What *he* wanted was something else. He burst out abruptly, "This man in your life. Who is he? I've got to know!"

He went on angrily, "Your heart is closed. Before we can talk about me, you must open it."

"You know I'm so reticent about all that . . ."

"Where is he?" His voice was still hard and pressing. "Is it still going on?" He must make her give in to him, submit to him.

"No."

"What happened?"

Very well. This was fair enough. If she had to express it in a series of single sentences, what would she say?

"It's nothing unusual. I fell in love with a man, and he fell in love with me. He was married of course. A quite important person all mixed up in aircraft production and a new technique for making plastics and up to his neck in politics. We broke up about a year ago, and he went back to his wife. And I didn't want to go on having just half of him. The point came where I had to decide whether I had character or not."

But this was language far too simple to describe something that in reality had been profoundly complicated.

"Go on."

Then Leslie felt that she could not go on. Her face closed abruptly. She thought of all that Hugo was. Perhaps it was some defect in her, but somehow she could *not* tell Hugo, an enemy, this story, she could not disclose to him this secret. She put both hands on her face; it was physically impossible for her to go on. No matter what, he could not have her private soul. It was not his to have.

"I'm sorry, Hugo," she said stoutly. "Maybe I'm a fool, but that's all I want to say."

IV

A day or two later. He dropped in late in the afternoon. She didn't particularly like to have him in her room; still, Strangeways had had tea with her there, and it was the safest, most convenient place. She had a headache, like a light cobweb drawn across the brain, an invisible net.

"I who am German . . . who am proud of being German . . . I find myself, *wie soll ich sagen*, miserable and tormented."

"I'm rather miserable and tormented myself."

"Ja?"

"So let's cheer up."

She was tilted on the pillows of the day bed; he sat across the room. She wondered if he would notice that she was almost shivering. She saw those slate-blue eyes, so much like Hal's, which gave her a double memory: a faint tinge of distaste, yet something which linked him to her past, that is, herself. If he touched her, gooseflesh would spot her throat and climb along her slim arms, where the skin was so neatly, firmly, tucked around the flesh, the bone.

"Leslie . . . *Liebling* . . ."

"No, no!"

She pushed him away.

"Liebling . . ."

This time he would kiss her, and, deliberately, she made her mouth hard and pursed and pointed.

"No, no, Hugo."

"Don't you want to?"

"Well, perhaps. But I thought we threshed all that out the other night."

He muttered something gloomily.

"I can't help it, Hugo. I've told you. It's the way I was brought up, I suppose."

"It is more than that."

"Yes."

"It is still in the main because I am German."

"Of course." She was angry: "How can you expect me to pop into bed with an enemy?"

"But you do *want* to?" he asked stupidly.

No, she decided to herself. No. It wasn't just because he was an enemy.

He saw it was no good, and stopped trying.

If only she would not feel so inadequate, so miserably sorry and contrite, when men looked so sad.

V

She had room for nothing now but her own thoughts.

. . . Living alone. Good Lord, it was the worst thing in life for a woman! The very worst. She had never really been alone before. She felt so wasted. So terribly *wasted*. She had thought the change, the excitement, the new horizons of Istanbul, would stop the loneliness. She must never be alone again. Connecticut. Yes, or upper Westchester, near the Croton lakes. No, Connecticut. There was that road, Route 33 she thought, leading from Wilton toward Ridgefield and then cutting into Number 7 on the way to Danbury. There was a house near Wilton she remembered. You could just see the water of the Sound, over a diminishing bank of trees that looked like tall dancing women in green wigs. A creamy house, the underparts built of Connecticut stone, set low, very low, against the hill. Two children. Boy and girl. That was best. A living room with a dark floor and a pale oyster ceiling; blond furniture, with enormous off-white sofas. Lamps modern, but not too much glint; curtains with a pattern of magnolia, and Georgian silver. A stout well-mannered cook who would arrange fruit on the sideboard, grapes and plums and oranges, to look like something by Cézanne. What fun, shopping in the village. The A & P, the butcher shop, the dairyman; all in white smocks, all her friends. Roaming up and down and choosing boxes of salted crackers and opulent tins of juice and small exotic fish, things for hors d'oeuvres. And celery! American celery! Milk! American milk! Then the railway station, in the spring evenings around five; her fine new station wagon ribbed with dark wood, and marked with her initials. All the cars, the Ford convertibles and a lazy sleek Cadillac with too many headlights, a brace of big Buicks and a jalopy or two, circling in the gravel, almost sniffing it, like animals, waiting for the train. Then a shaking roar and a wheezing puff and the train would screech in and there he'd be. Tall, straw hat. Easily muscled. Light foulard tie.

It didn't seem quite like Gerald. And it certainly would

not be Hugo. She flung herself down on the daybed, sobbing bitterly.

Then she had another disconcerting thought. Even if she were comfortably married and living in her own house in Connecticut, would she be happy? Could she be happy? After the war, would it be possible any more for a person to be at home *any*where? After all the moral and physical displacements and trans-valuations. Would not everybody have outgrown their separate countries? What was home going to be?

Everybody in transition . . . everybody yearning for the establishment of some kind of fixity . . . Leslie recalled what Yvonne Spaulding had said. "The secret of good fortune is the power to grasp it." But how? Where?

The hell with all this gloom, she muttered to herself. She got up and made herself a pot of tea.

VI

They drove in his car from Yeniköy, where they had dined in a remote, inconspicuous café. Again they had talked for hours. He wanted to go to his country place, but she said no.

"So you ask me now to betray my country to you," Hugo said. His face had a somber look.

"I didn't put it quite that way."

"It is a very large thing to ask of a man that he give up that."

"Let's be calm and adult, Hugo. I think you'd be happier on our side."

"That is quite possible. But, *wirklich*, I am not a traitor."

They neared home.

Hugo thought: "*Ach!* Next year there will be death and ruin everywhere. Next year, what is now left of Berlin and Munich will be gone, and the Russians will be in Danzig. Next year, I could be working hard in the Argentine or skiing in Salzkammergut. If the war were over. If I am not killed in all the death and ruin. I could be sitting in Antibes perhaps and playing tennis and making love to Leslie. If the war were over. If I could make myself safe now. *When the war is over!"*

They reached the Musifers'.

She suddenly became terrified that he would say it, that he would overtly suggest that he would, indeed, sell out and come over to her side, *if* she would promise to go to bed with him.

She knew finally that it was not, in essence, because he was German that they could not make love. He was not merely the wrong kind of nationality; he was the wrong kind of human being. He had a violent attraction for her, she could not help or deny that; but he was the wrong kind of *person*, though she could not explain exactly why. The question of love of country, of patriotism, had nothing whatever to do with it. If she loved him she would have slept with him if he had been a Hottentot. It went far deeper. All his sophistication only on the surface. His lack of antennæ, his grotesque literalness, his conceit. The way he had been crestfallen over that brooch in the bazaar. The wide grin that concealed an utter lack of humor. The hint of basic dishonesty, and the toughness that had not been so tough after all . . .

The only thing to do was to say it as tactfully as possible. "Hugo, darling, I'm sorry, I don't know quite how things will turn out. It's so difficult to promise anything. You know how terribly confused I've been. And I'm glad we're such good friends. We'll have to wait and see . . ."

Her voice sounded lame. But he knew that she was that rarest thing on earth, a completely honest woman.

Strangely, he rescued her. "I know. The way you were brought up."

"Oh, Hugo!"

"I do not ask of a woman promises." And now he had great dignity.

"Oh, if only everything were different!"

He kissed her gently, and said good night.

CHAPTER XVII

No Lady?

I

GERALD waited for Florian in the bar. What a marvelous girl she was. It had all been most delightful, there was no gainsaying that; he would always remember her as something spectacular, almost magnificent, but short-lived; and short-lived because, in the long run, she had nothing to offer beyond her looks. At least so far as he was concerned. He felt deep affection for her, and he would be grateful to her always, and it would be fun to run into her again sometime, but, to be blunt, he didn't want to be with her any more. He was over it. And that was that.

All he wanted was to get back to Istanbul and see Leslie Corcoran. Nothing in the world mattered but that he should get back to Istanbul and see Leslie Corcoran again.

He had a drink with Florian and they talked a while and tramped through the gardens. Back in his room, she kicked off her shoes; he reached over, and friendlily held and patted her heel and instep with his palm. She felt the strength and warmth through the cool nylons. But then he was pacing back and forth, looking impatient and determined. She watched him, her chin low.

"Well, I go now." Her voice was pensive.

"The train isn't till evening."

"It takes me always hours to pack."

"You've been an angel, Florian. Hasn't it all been fun?" And he felt a welling glow of comradeship.

She was looking at the wall, following something invisible with her eyes. So this was over now.

"I can't tell you how wonderful you've been. I'm so glad you came. It's all been so very good."

"Yes, *Liebling* . . ." A man came, a man went . . . Her voice was lost and sad. "When do you return to Istanbul?"

"Fairly soon, I think."

He was not even thinking about her now, she knew. With a man it was so easily over. "Perhaps I will be there no longer when you arrive," Florian said.

"Listen, sweet. If Dortmund or Reichenau make any trouble for you on account of what's happened here, go straight to Strangeways. He'll help you out. Or take care of you, if necessary." He had another idea he wanted to express.

Her voice was disdainful. "I am not afraid."

"You seem a little low," Gerald said. "Very low, in fact."

She flirted: "And why not, since I am leaving you?"

"You're a darling. I adore you, Florian. But you'll have a good time back in Istanbul."

She sat chin in hand. She was inspecting her future. What would happen to her next? Had Gerald already forgotten the way he used to talk? But he couldn't help it. It was not anybody's fault.

"Listen." There was a different tone in his voice, and he watched her face.

"What, Gerald, *Herzchen*?"

"I have a sort of vague feeling you've become a little too fond of me." He looked straight into her eyes, direct and smiling.

"*Nein!*" She flushed, guessing what he meant.

What an irony, Gerald thought. Maybe she was going to develop intense emotion about him just as he lost all emotion about her. But any two people who had ever been in bed had a certain responsibility to each other. He must be honest at all costs.

"Listen. You must remember, though we haven't mentioned it again. In Istanbul I asked you to marry me. Do you remember? Do you want to?"

"Oh . . . But you did not seriously mean it in Istanbul!"

She was helping him but she could not conceal a frown. What a darling she was, he thought.

"I meant it seriously enough, God knows. And I don't want you to think I'm a backslider."

"Why should you have to speak about such things? You no longer want to marry me."

"But—"

"I must pack now," Florian said hastily. She rose. "Never have I wanted to marry you. So what is there to talk about?"

"Well—"

"Well what?"

He bent to look at her; she jerked her head away. He saw that her eyes were blinking.

"Florian . . ."

"Leave me alone."

He grabbed her and they wrestled and kissed and then both started to laugh, through her tears.

"I must pack now." She left the room.

"And do not concern yourself about me," she called from the corridor. "Even if I am no lady, I am a gentleman."

II

He picked her up to take her to the train. Her suit was extravagantly cut and she wore the dark green blouse. He saw the way her wonderful breasts stood out; he had never seen anything like them. But he was glad again that she was going.

They rang for the lift.

"In secret you think all the time about the American," said Florian, but without bitterness.

"Yes," Gerald admitted, startled.

"You are in love with her. A woman knows."

The lift came and they went down. "Perhaps I am," Gerald said.

Florian said, "If you want her, why don't you go after her?"

He scowled. "What do you mean?" He hauled her bag across the lobby.

"Return to Istanbul and declare yourself."

Gerald stopped rigid. "How can I?" But everything at the mines was well in hand and going smoothly.

"How can you risk losing her? If you are in love with her you should go back to her."

"There's my job . . ." He called a droshky.

"Of what importance is a job compared to a woman you love? When you have lost her you will say to yourself, 'Oh yes, I had a job!'"

He stood there. Could he risk slipping back to Istanbul for a day?

"If I were in love with a girl I would not stay away and let her consort with Hugo Reichenau."

Gerald raced upstairs, threw some things in a bag, and rejoined Florian. They took the night express together.

III

Gerald saw Florian into a taxi, dropped his bag at the Park, and called Leslie up.

"Hello. This is Gerald. I'm here just for tonight. Will you dine with me?"

He could hear how startled her voice was. "Why—"

"Not a soul knows I'm in town, except Florian. I haven't even told Alec yet. Please let me pick you up and let's dine."

"I'd have to break a date," Leslie said.

"Break it."

"I've never broken one in my life."

"I've got to go back on the midnight."

"Well—"

What could she tell Hugo? What would Hugo say? This

was the night when they were to have decided everything.

Suddenly Leslie felt sharp relief.

All her bad conscience, the lurking hatred she had of herself for being so fascinated by Hugo, burst loose.

She said into the 'phone briefly, "All right. Pick me up at seven."

IV

Hugo swallowed his disappointment. But he was not bitter or really angry. After all he would see her very soon, probably tomorrow. She had told him that someone she could only see tonight had popped unexpectedly into town. Then the 'phone rang again and it was Florian; promptly, he asked her to dinner. He found his car outside the Park and thought that someone in a tweed jacket, just getting into a taxi ahead, looked vaguely familiar. But he had no more than a quick glimpse of his back and he paid no attention. He was deep in obsessive thoughts. He drove across town and reached Florian's flat. "Hello!" she greeted him.

Hugo had had some bitter days. He felt that he was on a ship that minute by minute was wallowing deeper in angry waves; yet what was *terra firma*? He felt that he must grasp something, cling to something; but what if Leslie would not give in to him? Florian watched him, puzzled. He seemed nervously tired, but at the same time exhilarated; he looked worn out by suspense, and, she thought in surprise, almost frightened. And she remembered some of the things Hugo was: chaotic and impetuous, envious and weak. Maybe he was still those things. But somehow this was not the old Hugo any more . . .

"Well, *Schatzi* . . ."

"I couldn't help it, Hugo."

She outlined briefly most of what had happened.

"Dortmund makes much trouble for me as a result," was all he said.

"It was his idea. That *Schwein*! How have you managed with the American?"

She was watching him carefully, to try to catch him if
he lied.

"I have managed nothing. *Gar nichts.*"

"So," Florian said.

Just for the fun of it, for the amusing gossip it was, she
had intended to reveal to Hugo that Gerald was in town.
But something made her hesitate. He saw a confusion in
her face.

"What is with you, *Schatzi*?"

"Nothing," Florian said.

"I can read from your eyes. You have a secret."

"No." Better not to tell him after all, she thought; grop-
ingly, she felt that she must protect Gerald and Leslie; she
was responsible for them in a way. Of course Hugo could
twist and worm it out of her, if he tried. But luckily he was
holding to his own fixed channel of thoughts.

"Tell me all, Hugo, darling."

He talked, attempting to describe his relationship with
Leslie without giving too much away.

"Remember," he snapped the words out roughly, "some
little time ago . . . when first we talked about that *Amerikanerin* . . . I told you in big language how I felt mysteri-
ously carried out of myself . . . as if in a strange pursuit
of something . . . something I could not define."

"Yes, Hugo." What was he driving at? She felt worried
about him.

"I do not know how to describe. But I became conscious
somehow that I was only a *little* man. I had been very self-
proud as Hugo Reichenau but I realized all at once how
very *little* I was . . . I cared for nothing beyond my faith.
. . . Now . . . Now I find myself being reborn . . ."

He was staring at her but not really seeing her, his eyes
almost glassy.

"What *is* a German?" he asked abruptly.

"I do not follow you."

"*Ach!* Never mind!"

Had Hugo at last grown up? she asked herself. Was this the way maturity came to a man?

"What is your trouble?"

"It may be very serious trouble." No longer will I be a little man, Hugo thought. I am reborn, he thought.

"Always we will be friends, Hugo."

"*Ja. Du.*"

She had a sense that he was desperately wanting her, without knowing it. His whole being was elsewhere, but he craved her with a helpless energy. He cared nothing for her as a person, but a suppressed and concentrated passion was bursting out. Uneasy, she slipped across the room. She fished for a new subject:

"Tomorrow I resume at Taksim's. But I have decided to tell Mr. Poppa I will not stay long."

"Why not, *Schatzi*?" He was not listening.

"I think I find a new life somewhere."

"You too? *Ach!*"

"Hugo, what *is* the matter?"

He followed her into a corner, put an arm around her shoulder, and let his chin rest hard on her high, glossy hair. Their cheeks touched; he could feel her nipples harden; he held her closely, rocking. This is one thing that is *not* going to start again, she decided grimly. Both these men . . . in love with Leslie. Both these men . . . lost to her, gone. She patted his cheek, kissed him briefly, and moved away. He did not pursue her. Then she saw that what he wanted was to be comforted. All he wanted was to have someone hold him close, very close, and comfort him . . .

They had dinner around the corner and Hugo had a quick change of mood and was brittle and gay.

"*Schatzi,* tell me now about your Gerald."

For the first time in his life, he saw Florian blush. "I tell you nothing about such private things."

A few minutes later they decided to take in a Turkish café and then go on to Taksim's; Florian could watch the show, like someone on a busman's holiday. They stayed till about eleven, and then she yawned broadly and said it was time to go . . . So Hugo blotted an evening out. He dropped her at her flat, and meandered back to the hotel.

From the beginning, he had not given her any serious inkling of what griped and troubled him.

Herr Gott, Hugo said to himself. Perhaps Leslie is right. Perhaps they, not we, *are* the wave of the future.

Could he escape? Could he get out from under?

When Florian said good night she thought again that he looked frightened.

And Hugo had been brought up on fear.

CHAPTER XVIII

Leslie . . . Robin . . . Gerald

I

THEY dined at Abdulla's, where they had met a month or so before. The movie next door was showing Miryum Opkins and Gheri Kupr, with an old Saplin short.

"Well," Gerald said.

First he was glad that she looked just as he remembered her; then, at once, he felt a quick flashing hope that she would be all the things he had read into her.

"Well . . ." Leslie said.

She had been tremulous the first moment, because she hoped she would still like him as much as that night at Taksim's.

For a second, excited, they both talked at once.

Then he asked her about Hugo. He told her frankly how bothered he had been . . . The whole escapade with Hugo, if one could call it an escapade; it was puzzling, damned puzzling . . . Why had she wanted to run such risks? Why had she seemingly compromised herself . . .

She told him about it briefly, her eyes clear. Then she was anxious. "You do understand, don't you?"

"Quite."

Urgently, she wanted him to understand.

He shrugged Hugo off. But still, it was puzzling.

In five minutes, she knew that he was no longer in love with Florian. This was a new Gerald; he was like another man. "Why, he really is over it!" she exclaimed to herself before he told her.

216

They had a couple of rakis, and then some beer, together
with a chateaubriand. She remembered how Hugo never
drank; there was something inhuman in the way he avoided
alcohol. What a relief to be with a man who drank nicely,
but not too much.

He reached over, and just touched the tips of her fingers;
it gave her an acute thrill to watch his hands. The fan of
strong bones, the way the fingers splayed and separated; the
way, on the webbing between the fingers, there was a small V
of white, not sunburned like the rest.

"Tell me about Florian . . ."

Gerald felt warmly his immense debt to Florian. And
something made Leslie know that she was *her* friend, too.

"Why, she's the most wonderfully amusing girl. I was
crazy about her, yes. But—"

This man was practically warm from another woman's
bed. She had no right to object. But it bothered her. Then
she was deeply moved. Now that he was free of Florian,
something intense and satisfying, something vital, was released
in her.

Gerald said, "Maybe you'll think I'm mad. But I've come
back to Constantinople for just one reason. To tell you that
I love you."

II

Then began one of the strangest evenings of her life. It
was as if they were continuing, with scarcely any interruption, the conversation of a month before, and as if she were
telling Gerald everything that she had not told Hugo. She did
not understand the mechanics of it, but Gerald was now the
beneficiary of Hugo's violent questioning after the visit to
the bazaars.

Gerald went about it much more quietly.

"You told me a good deal about yourself a month ago.
I wish you'd tell me a little more. You give me such a sense
of being a prisoner, of having some obscure loyalty to a
shadow in your past."

"Not a shadow, really," Leslie mused.

"I love you." His eyes were steady. "I haven't said that to a woman in years and years. Someday when we know each other better I'd like to ask you to marry me. But I can't very well go on hoping, building up a life in my imagination, unless I know more of what you are."

"I'm so . . . so tied up," Leslie said.

"Of course. That's why I wish you'd tell me."

Only twice in her life had she met this man; one letter, and one long-distance call. She knew nothing about him really. What made her want to be good to him?

Now he was free of Florian and—perhaps—she was free of Hugo. And actively she discovered that she wanted to tell him everything . . .

III

That lucent evening in spring in Paris . . . the evening she met Robin first. She met him at a party. Of course. That was how you always met people, that was what parties were for. She was having a brief holiday in Paris, the spring after Sally's death; Hal was staying in Berlin. One of the lads in the bank's Paris office dutifully said he'd take her to the party; a rich American woman was giving it, in an opulent apartment near the Étoile. She had bought a new dress that day, beautiful and dramatic, and she wore it proudly: of glossy black silk with a high neck and turnover collar, and two black streamers tied at the throat in a flowing bow.

She and her escort had drinks at the Deux Magots, near the small hotel where she was staying. They drove in light rain toward the river and crossed it. That was the loveliest thing in Paris, the graceful rain putting a sheen on the broad boulevards, and the way the gray stones of the Louvre and all the statues in the Tuileries were tinted pink at night, a haunted pink beckoning through the light, opalescent rain.

What a funny, proud thing a woman could be! When

she had first told Gerald about Hal, her pride, her guarded-
ness, made her take all the blame; even years later, she
couldn't bear to confess the private shames, the secret
humiliations. Pride! Hal began to disintegrate after Sally's
death. That she should have been married to anyone who
behaved so badly . . . ! He drank frightfully. For days and
days, a stupid opacity of drinks and hangover. A whisky
bottle next to the bed at night. Ugh! Then he became
morbidly secretive, morbidly jealous. And she hadn't looked
at another man, not once, in four long years . . . Not even in
thought. Then Hal had a short, ugly affair with the wife of
a British newspaper correspondent; she discovered it in the
most ridiculously banal way, through a letter stupidly mis-
forwarded . . .

"Who's that?" Leslie said at the Paris party.

"Who? Oh. Culpepper. Big shot," her escort said.

She and Culpepper danced later, and stood at the buffet
together, and she knew just from looking at him that it
would be more right between them than anything that ever
was. He snapped along with them when Hal's friend took
her home, and both men said good night. Ten minutes later
he was telephoning. She came down and met him in the
lobby. Their eyes met and held together as if each were
projecting the same powerful ray. They drove down to Mont-
parnasse, and then up to Montmartre, and for the first time
in months and months, she was happy; she thought nothing
of yesterday, and little of tomorrow. And she was more
excited than she had ever been in her life.

She could savor it now like something living. She could
touch him, feel his touch, as if it were today. She was lying
there, in his apartment in the hotel so small, expensive, and
exclusive that she had never heard of it. Her beautiful new
dress was folded on the back of a chair where he, not she,
had hung it briskly; she could not believe that anything of
this was real, that this was really she. How had this
happened? Why? How? But years later every detail remained absolutely clear. "I'm the most surprised woman who

ever lived," she said breathlessly. He was smoking, and she lit a cigarette. She touched his soft, reddish gray hair, where it was getting bald, shyly. She looked at his nose straight out of the face. "I'm going to call you Robin," Leslie said. There was a long close silence. She added a sentence part of which was the truth: "I'm not a promiscuous woman, strange as it may seem, and I love my husband."

"But you're not in love with him."

She was startled. So brief, so categoric. "Why do you say that?"

Lightly, tenderly, but with a curious possessive touch, he was stroking the veins along her forearm. "My experience is, women in love aren't often unfaithful."

She twisted up and stared at him, propped on an elbow. "You do make things blunt, don't you?"

"What's more I doubt extremely if you love him."

"Again, Mr. Culpepper, may I ask why you're so sure?"

"My dear, I know it from every inch of your skin and your soul and your face."

Then later:

She sat up straight in bed, with a strange, wild, maidenly look—above all, maidenly—her head bent so that the chin almost touched her throat, and her knuckles pressing hard at the side of her breast. "I didn't know I'd be so aroused," she whispered. "I didn't know I'd be so shaken. I didn't know I'd feel so much emotion."

He watched her, nodding. She felt again the touch of his hand: warm, strong, positive.

"Does your heart hurt this way?" she asked him, puzzled and almost timid. "Hurt with a sweet pain, that goes all over your body, and then comes back again wandering to your heart?"

Again he nodded, and a look of the most extreme tenderness came into his eyes. She turned her head and now watched him. For a moment or two she kept staring at him. Then she was profoundly moved again, because she recognized the emotion welling into the eyes that still let hers look straight into him: not only tenderness, but gratitude.

"Darling, oh darling. I think I'd better go home now."

"No. Please. Sleep a while, and we'll have breakfast." And in five minutes he himself was sound asleep.

Then came that gay all-worked-out breakfast, and the wonderful rolls the hotel had, which almost exploded when you dented them, and a good, relaxed, curious exploration of their daylight worlds; then the rose-colored currant jelly, and the competently served crisp bacon, and the kiss on her forehead and slowly on her lids, then behind her ears and inside her elbows, and the decisive, admiring way he watched her.

He was certainly the most positive man who ever lived.

"You're not really beautiful," he said calmly. "Not conventionally beautiful. But you're wonderfully interesting and I don't think I've ever met anyone more attractive."

Then they dressed and Leslie wondered how she was going to get out of the hotel inconspicuously and there came that remark that she could never forget, that shocked her and made her angry and amused her too.

"Listen. You're a good girl. We can do anything you want, except one thing. Maybe I'll fall in love with you. But don't fall in love with me. I'm a bad risk."

It was shattering. He did not 'phone all that day, nor the next. A tremendous heap of red roses came, but without a card. She waited by the 'phone the whole of the third day. The hell with this, Leslie thought, the morning after. Maybe he was applying a well-known but nevertheless effective technique. Or perhaps something else had happened. Maybe he was ill, or perhaps he had had an accident. But when she finally did 'phone him, in nervous agony, it appeared that he had just been busy. He was doing a lot of things. He hadn't time.

"Yes, Leslie. I'll be clear by Monday. Yes. Meet me at the Rue Duphot Prunier's at eight o'clock. Thanks. So long."

Several days later she wired Hal that she was not returning to Berlin for a while, and she and Robin went to a chateau near the Loire lent him by a French industrialist. Every hour, every day, she continued to pinch her mind to know if this could possibly be true. How *was* it possible? How *had* it happened? They took long walks; they talked incessantly; they saw no one; they had great and robust laughter; for the first time in her life, at twenty-five, after four years of marriage, she really loved, she was in love. And Robin loved her too.

"Darling . . . oh, baby. Darling, oh baby, oh dear heart, baby, darling. Oh dear heart, oh murder, dear heart, oh baby darling." She was like a fountain, twisting, climbing. And then the little half-laugh, half-sob, of pure thanks and wonderment, the pure gasp at the miracle and wonderment, each time the miracle of consummation new again, the miracle unfailing, the absolute thanks and wonderment.

What did Robin like most? Tramping in the woods; power; mountains; all wines but mostly dry burgundies, though he drank very sparsely because it might interfere with all the work he did; any airplane going anywhere; Balzac; sonnets by Edna St. Vincent Millay; most dogs, particularly pointers; London; driving alone at night; orderliness; his jobs; almost all doctors, perhaps because he was the healthiest man alive; the Encyclopedia Britannica; *jambon de Bayonne*; old armagnac.

What did Robin dislike? Anything slipshod; bad weather; winter sports; people who feathered their nests in the name of principle; dull talk; most Roman Catholics; pipes and cats; experimental literature; Greenwich Village, café life and gossip columns; telephones that didn't answer promptly; almost all music, for which he had no ear; most movies; Berlin; timidity; birds to eat full of small bones; too much sleep; vulgarity and hypocrisy.

What was wrong with Robin? Well, several things. Not just the selfishness, the ruthlessness. But a peculiar kind of limitedness: an incomprehension of any world not his own. He was a buccaneer. A pirate. A tycoon. Then—it had not mattered to her so much at the time, but now, in Istanbul, it shocked her deeply—he *liked* the war. That was the only way she could express it. Actually, he liked it. Apparently he never gave an instant's thought to all the pain, the suffering. Somehow, none of that existed; it never entered his head, or he brushed it all away. Even though his sons, sixteen and fourteen, would of course be called up if it went on long enough. Robin thought of the war as a kind of gigantic game which gave full scope, full opportunity, to his own immense energies and talent. He practically thought of it as something marvelously dramatic which had been created so that he could do a perfect job.

"How *I'm* changing," Leslie thought, as she talked on to Gerald, with Gerald tensely listening . . .

Right at the beginning, Robin put it frankly on the table about his marriage. For hours, with the strange cruelty of the candid, he told Leslie about his wife, his house in Maryland, his two boys. He and Elsie had been, in effect, separated for years, but neither had ever wanted a divorce, and they maintained a friendly, casual relationship; he was flagrantly unfaithful, he was always being mixed up with women, but usually he spent week-ends home, or every other weekend. At this point Leslie found herself vigorously taking Elsie's side. Feminine solidarity or something of the sort. Good Lord! She loved this man to the marrow of the bone, but she resented it terribly that he should treat his wife so badly.

Robin looked at her. His smile was a burst of affectionate admiration. "You *are* a good girl, aren't you? You really *are* a nice person, Leslie darling."

What had happened to her was the *coup de foudre,* nothing more, nothing less. And that was something that, in the great majority of cases, occurred to a girl only once in her lifetime, when it got you in the knees, and stayed there. "Don't kid yourself, Butch," she said to herself roughly, "this is it."

Then a madly happy month or two. The chronology got lost, it was all confused. She went back to Berlin, and then

Robin followed her there. For a person truly in love, *any-thing* was excused, justified. It had nothing to do with character. It was chemistry. You did or you didn't. Then she managed to contrive another trip to Paris; she learned that a woman in love could contrive *anything*, and would take *any* risks. Hal simply didn't exist. She would scarcely have recognized him on the street. And he was drinking all the time. The war came. Robin had to catch a clipper and return to the United States. She went back to Berlin, and told Hal frankly that she couldn't help it, she had to leave him. She flew down to Genoa, and took an Italian boat home; Robin met her in New York, and a week later she was on a plane to Reno. Hal, who had always been on the generous side, turned cheap and mean. Returning east, she found a small apartment in the East Sixties, and from that time on she and Robin had part of every week together.

What was Robin's power over her? That he always made her feel at her best, and that he knew her for what she was.

What was it that disturbed her most? That they were so *married*, without being married.

What was it that she couldn't bear? That she knew nothing of his sons, she had never met his sons.

And what else? All the time, the terrible worry about getting pregnant, and wanting so terribly to have a child.

What else? The contempt she felt during the early days for the safe, smug, conventional world outside; and then a hatred of it; and then an envy of it.

What did she learn from Robin? Good heavens, every-thing!

She learned that you could measure love by what it cost, by its capacity to inflict pain, by how it hurt; she learned that after a year she could still catch her breath sharply when the 'phone rang, and have a wild lust to kiss a man in a crowded room; that she had to do things for him quite beyond ratiocination or will, even when she knew they were wrong things, because he had become she, and she he; that when he behaved badly she could not bear to punish him because

it was only punishing herself; that the knowledge acquired
in this love affair would, if she lost him, somehow help her
some day in another; and that no two people in the world,
no matter how they loved, could both be in love every
minute.

Also, she helped him with his work, enormously. He
worked better than he ever had . . . After Pearl Harbor
he had to be in Washington all the time. He was running
that whole vast agency now . . . She moved to Washington
to be close to him and because he insisted. At first he did
not want her to have a job of her own; he wanted her only
to help *him*, to be fresh and lovely for *him* in the evenings;
sometimes when he worked into the night hour after hour,
there was nothing left for her but a person out of whom a
hundred other persons had sucked every drop of vitality
during the long day. Their first quarrel came when he tried
to keep her from working too. Then he saw her point—his
selfishness was always interspersed with mad generosities—
and he found her the job in Lend Lease and they were very
happy. And he was willing to work less hard after a while
when he saw that she was worn out in the evenings too . . .

She always loved him most when they had week-ends in
the country, among friends, among happy people. And there
was that time near Roanoke when the cherry blossoms looked
like beautiful white popcorn. And she thought of the popcorn
man, her first friend, in the remote childhood in upper
New York State . . .

For months that became more months and more months
and yet more months they loved, so they thought, more than
anybody else had ever loved. And then, gradually, mount-
ingly, helplessly, they began to tear each other to bits, mostly
because of his insane demandingness, possessiveness. He
adored her violently; yet he would not leave his wife. He
would allow her to see no other human being; he went into
childlike frenzies of jealousy if she so much as had lunch
with an old friend; yet all the time he refused to counte-
nance the idea of divorce, he insisted on maintaining his

family relationship, his marriage. For himself, like a child, he wanted it roses all the time; he ignored her thorns. His dependence on her grew almost frighteningly; yet she would not have been surprised to know that he had perhaps dipped quickly once or twice into some other affair. And why did she endure it? How *could* she endure it? Because she loved him.

She realized, one gnarled winter day in Washington, that she would sooner or later have to give it up, because now he was taking advantage of *her* weakness, bullying her and trading on it. They had a fierce, sleety quarrel, she who hated quarrels, and she left him. She packed up, quit her job which she had come to love, and went home to her family. They could not have been more wonderful. Robin in a kind of immature way went crazy. Almost literally crazy. One day he telephoned her long-distance eleven times, until she thought she would go crazy too. One day on her doorstep in Juneville, delivered from florists forty miles away, came one hundred dozen tulips, her favorite flower. Then without warning he popped up at her home. Her father understood better than her mother. After a day she went back with him to Washington. But she knew finally, though for years they had talked about it off and on, that now he would never get a divorce.

At first his wife had refused; she considered that what Robin was going through was simply an infatuation. But now, though he denied it, he didn't *want* a divorce. She knew. Any man could get a divorce if he really wanted to. Any man. But he wanted them *both*. He liked Elsie, he was fond of her, he thought he ought to take care of her, he liked his home, he liked his life untouched by scandal or complication, he liked Sunday evenings with his growing sons. Elsie must be something like his mother, Leslie thought. And she learned the tremendous lesson that in the long run healthy people do what they want most to do.

One of those last days. She was wild, shaggy, biting. And then sadly it was almost as if they were living a scene from their own past . . . And then another of those last days. And they both felt a dreadful emptiness, as if all that they had gone through had sapped the love out of them.

Leslie said at the end, "Oh, darling, darling . . . never forget some of the happiness we've had . . ."

"Of course not." His voice had a kind of dogged grimness. "I love you . . . love you . . . love you."

She wondered if he could entirely read her face, as she, unseeing, read it: the ardor, the it-might-have-been tenderness, and—yes—the reproach.

But she said: "God bless you."

For weeks all that Leslie wanted to do was crawl blindly in the dark, like a broken animal. She thought physically that she could not live without him. Yet this must happen to many women, and some men; and somehow people did keep on living . . . Robin had a much bigger job now, really staggering, one of the half dozen most important civilian jobs in the United States. He worked fourteen, sixteen hours a day; and she read about him in the papers . . . They did not meet for long months. Then after more long months they had a quiet lunch and he arranged for her to go to Istanbul. She took the train to New York, the train past the factories burning with light all night and filled with his production; she sought to distill out of the shattered essence of her being some comfort, some consolation, some compensation. In the long run, the *very* long run, you always love yourself better than you love anybody else; so in time you will get over it. Nevertheless, no matter what, you never so long as you live get *all the way* over it. But because they had never been married it was better that they should stay apart. Leslie waited for her plane at La Guardia. She lifted her chin firmly and looked at the night sky boiling with confused stars.

IV

Gerald looked intensely sober and also immeasurably relieved. "And you broke up about a year ago?" She nodded.

That was what seemed to interest him most. Either from the point of view that she still felt such intense emotion about anything so long past, or with relief that it was not more recent. Can she get over it? his face said.

Leslie looked up. My goodness, I'm glad I've told it all! she breathed to herself. She felt that an immense, lifelong burden had been lifted; suddenly she felt more free of Robin than at any time since they had separated. And telling it altered sharply her feelings about Hugo. They cancelled each other out. Compared to Robin, Hugo was so absurd!

"Do you think you can forget him?" Gerald asked.

"I don't know," she answered slowly. "I hope so."

"You do *hope* so?"

"It's something that has to come from within . . ."

"You have your own happiness, your own life, to consider!"

"Yes. But all that was so bound up with him for so long."

Oh Christ, how I love this girl, Gerald thought. Now he understood her; now she was a complete human being at last and he loved her more. But his face darkened: "Do you want very much to go back to him?"

"Sometimes," Leslie said candidly. "I can't deny that. But less and less, as time goes on."

"Do you think he wants you to come back?"

Her face was sad. "I don't think I could have left him if I hadn't realized, somehow, that he wanted me to go."

"In that case . . ."

But she went on honestly, "If he should get sick, or need me badly, or something of that kind, I can't answer for what I'd do."

"Of course not." He hesitated. "But don't you think there's at least an outside chance you could become fond of me?"

She looked at him gratefully: "Perhaps . . . I think so. I don't quite know. I—"

"Well, I've declared myself," he cut in briskly. "I've declared myself, and I won't go back on it."

She thought of her names. Leslie Matthews . . . Leslie

Corcoran . . . she who might have been Leslie Culpepper. She
spelled out his name in her mind. G. e. r. a. l. d. H. e. a. t. h.
She tasted it, lingering on it.

He looked at his watch. "I say, I've got to catch a train.
Sorry, but I must go. Matter of duty. Now: I'll be back in
about a week, I think. Then we can have some time together, and we'll talk some more."

Again her look was grateful.

"And I might as well tell you something else. If necessary,
I'll wait twenty years for you!"

v

They hurried over to the Park, to pick up Gerald's bag;
she said she'd go with him to the ferry. He just had time
to catch the train; it would be the devil if he missed it. He
came down from his room and paid his bill; then as they
walked swiftly across the lobby they ran into Hugo Reichenau, coming in.

The German looked utterly dumfounded. He stared at
Leslie, as if dazed and stupefied; then he saw Gerald.

His face turned white; he stretched out an arm and
stopped Leslie as she was passing.

"So . . . *Aber* Leslie. I did not know—"

Gerald and Hugo had seen one another a hundred times,
but they had never spoken.

Gerald stopped. He said quickly and easily. "Reichenau,
I'm catching a train. Otherwise we'd have a talk."

"What?" Hugo still looked dazed. "We would talk?"

People in the lobby looked at them curiously; they were
directly in front of the big glass door, holding people up.

Impulsively Leslie grasped Hugo's arm. "Come," she commanded. She hooked her other hand under Gerald's elbow,
and propelled both men outside.

"I did not know it was for Mr. Heath you have broken
our engagement tonight," Hugo declared somberly, ignoring
Gerald.

"I would have told you."

"Reichenau, I want you to let Leslie alone."

"It is nothing of your business." He moved an inch forward in the courtyard.

"I don't want you to be seeing her hereafter."

"I will do as I most please," Hugo said.

The two men were facing one another.

"Listen, Reichenau, I won't have it." Gerald moved forward too.

"You may think—"

"Hugo . . . Gerald . . . I *won't* have anything silly. Now stop. Both of you. Please be grown up . . ."

Gerald jumped a mile in a second. "I say, old man, it's rather refreshing to be actually talking to you, at last."

Hugo was stiff as iron. "If there were more time . . ."

Gerald went on easily, almost airily. "Matter of fact I've always hoped we'd meet some day." He laughed. "Lots to talk about . . ."

Hugo was furious. "I will talk to you in my own good time."

Gerald was throwing his bag into a taxi.

"Come along, Leslie," he shouted.

"Hugo, this is nothing to be upset about. I'll explain."

"I need no explanations."

"So long, Reichenau," Gerald called.

Leslie saw Hugo's face as they drove off. Hurt pride and hatred were grinding out of it.

CHAPTER XIX

A Boating Party

I

PERHAPS it was because she loved so much being among happy, good people. She felt creamy, golden, foamy. It was another Sunday; they were picnicking, if that was the proper word, on the Ambassador's burnished cruiser.

All the great embassies had their yachts, their motorboats, their cruisers; it was the only way to get around. The Spauldings made up a party every Sunday, but this was the first time Leslie had been invited. Also, Yvonne had tactfully asked the Musifers; and on the dock Leslie greeted Dave Urquardt, Saxton the British journalist, the American consul general whom she had not met before, one of the military attachés, and the Ambassador's buzzing, abstracted secretary, Mr. Rummel. This was a different world; she was among her own kind. She felt far away from the clangor and tension of Taksim's or what Strangeways would do next or who was following whom.

Leslie wore her navy blue slacks, a white silk blouse, a light cashmere sweater, and the chamois-colored doeskin play shoes. Her hair was down, in a dark red snood.

That story about Robin. That scene between Hugo Reichenau and Gerald . . . No, put it all out of her mind. A man had asked her to marry him . . . Put that out of her mind too?

Etta clung to her. The little girl would not be separated from her for an instant or by an inch.

Etta had with her a picture book. She pointed out a photograph.

"That's a kind of duck I suppose," Leslie looked at the illustration seriously. Dr. Musifer translated.

"Oh!" Etta exclaimed, clasping the book close, "you wouldn't know anything about things like that." Her voice held the indignant scorn of a child who knows all. "Why, that's not a duck, that's a *flying* bird."

"Don't ducks fly?"

Etta was caught out. "Well, they don't fly very *much*. They like to lie on their tummies."

Mr. Spaulding sat in the prow, letting the sun catch his gaunt, creased face. He explained that they'd go up the Bosphorus for a while, and then circle back toward Prinkipo, and then cruise along the beach to Florya, where he would disembark briefly, he alone, because the Prime Minister had telephoned him, and asked him to drop in for a chat at the villa where he was week-ending. Then later if there were time they would fish around one of the small islands. The American military attaché was crazy to do a little fishing.

Mrs. Musifer was telling Mrs. Spaulding in a shocked but impressed voice about the evening Etta had climbed from bed and followed Leslie to Taksim's; the little girl watched them and sensed intuitively what they talked about.

"Why do I have to go to bed early?" her child's voice asked.

"Because you have to grow," Mrs. Musifer replied.

"Do *you* grow?"

"No."

"Why don't *you* grow?"

"Because I'm grown," Mrs. Musifer said.

"How long do people grow?"

"Till they're about twenty."

"No—till ninety."

And she shrieked with laughter.

Gravely then, through Dr. Musifer, she turned to Leslie: "How old is a baby the day a baby is born?" She could not believe that wonderful superior creatures like Leslie, or, in

a different category, her mother and father, had ever been
little like herself.

The Ambassador was thinking hard. He and his veteran
councilor and Mr. Rummel had been up most of the night
waiting for the last instruction to be decoded, and then
drafting the tentative reply. The Prime Minister must know
what was coming, what was in the offing. That was why
that sinewy, stubborn Turk had for the past few days been
so eager to see him, informally, alone. Even if Washington
hadn't come through, at last, with these instructions, Mr.
Spaulding would have taken a chance and gone ahead on
his own. The Turks were selfish and wily enough, God knew,
and they bluffed hard and well, but now Mr. Spaulding
thought he had them cornered, just where he wanted them.
And this seemed to be the perfect moment. He had been
hoarding up for this moment for a long time now. He would
have to be very tough. Mr. Spaulding hated to be very tough.
He wondered if he would be tough enough.

The boat cut sharply through the glittering current, and
reached the point where the water from the Black Sea and
the Sea of Marmora met angrily. They were midway now
between the continent of Europe and the continent of Asia;
rather, at the point where Asia, like a buffalo, ripped its
head to and fro and tossed forth the chunk of peninsula that
Europe was.

Here along the shore was spaced the line of massive, old-
time embassies. The Russian and the German were side by
side, as they were in Ankara too; the Russian stretched for
miles, so it seemed. The Italian, ornate and down at the
sills; the French, painted the color of dried blood; but mostly
they watched the German, with its swastika bluntly flying.
It seemed an affront, a super-embodied ugliness amid all this
beauty . . . The Nazi edifice was a pointed twin building
with red slate roofs; it looked like something out of Grimm.
Then Leslie turned. On their boat the American flag was
waving stiffly and corrugated. They shot down the channel,

as if their own beating flag at the stern, so proud, drove them on.

Now placidity again, placidity and repose . . . Now again the Golden Horn as they darted smoothly up the Sea of Marmora . . . Now, once more, and as always Leslie took breath, the most imperturbably glorious of all views known to this earth. The Seraglio held a lustrous glow, and the bland dome and minarets of Sultan Ahmed shone like white fire . . . "Look," the Ambassador pointed out. Again the world of the moment hit them in the face; a Nazi tanker was steaming past.

Mr. Spaulding mused aloud: "The conventional thing to say is that Germany must be disarmed, occupied, controlled." He brooded. "It won't be easy . . . far from easy . . ."

He began again. Some were listening. "No one can make peace by force alone. Surely that is one of the supreme lessons of this war. To maintain peace indefinitely by force alone is impossible.

"We can draw up a kind of logical structure. What we want is a peaceful Europe that will live. Without Germany, Europe cannot live. Therefore, the Germans must somehow be brought into a peaceable, stable European system . . . This will be impossible unless Germany is demilitarized and made democratic. Agreed. But can you forcibly *make* a people democratic if they persist in refusing to be democrats?

"We've got to have something better than Weimar. Much better. What? I don't know. But something much more positive and dynamic, effective and forward-looking . . .

"Fascism will be discredited. So, also, will be conventional democracy. Because Fascism came as a reaction against the failures of democracy; Fascism came because people were disillusioned, frustrated, outraged, by the *reductio ad absurdum* of the democratic process.

"That is, the failure of the democratic process in those countries not educated enough to understand it . . .

"Certainly it would be ridiculous to assume that we can simply return to the *status quo ante*. The world *moves*.

Nothing will ever be the same again. And we must think in terms of orderly development; we must learn to avoid intolerable situations out of which militancy and aggression are bound to arise. How? I don't know . . .

"Punishment . . . Control . . . Occupation . . . Education . . . Development?"

Mrs. Spaulding said, "Nations, like people, make mistakes. There would be no wars if people understood the simplest facts of life."

"Such as?" the Ambassador smiled awarely.

"The fact for instance that all children are good."

A most amazing and delightful buffet appeared; there was one silver thermos of martinis, and a bottle or two of Montrachet and beer and soda water. Then came American frankfurters, American mayonnaise, American pickles, and Vassily, the majordomo, made hamburgers on an electric grill. They had lettuce sandwiches, peanut butter sandwiches, olive sandwiches, bacon sandwiches, and chocolate ice cream that might have come from Sherry's.

Etta was having fun with numbers, and then with dates; she was scribbling numbers gleefully in her book. Leslie asked Dr. Musifer what she was saying. "The child is too fanciful," he replied. "Now she says it is 25 in the afternoon. And that on the 13th of autumn, it will be a sunny day."

Mr. Spaulding had an ironic thought. If things didn't work out the way he hoped, even with that telegram from Washington in his pocket, and if the Prime Minister called his bluff, which he might quite possibly do, then Urquardt and Leslie would be out of jobs, among much else.

Leslie handed the Ambassador a double martini and a sandwich. Again, she thought that he had all the humanity that Strangeways, for instance, lacked. Then she heard Urquardt say quietly:

"Yes . . . everything you say, Mr. Ambassador, jibes with a thought that sometimes wakes me up at night . . . All the turmoil and hardship and agony of readjustment and bitter violence that peace may bring. Has it ever occurred to you: the peace may be worse than the war."

II

They anchored off Florya, and Mr. Spaulding descended to the shore on a fragile skiff; they put on bathing suits and swam lazily from the boat; they had tea, talked, dozed, and gossiped.

Saxton was thinking:

"When the Russians reach the big rivers they'll be stopped a while. Those blighters certainly have got something. I wonder why I hate them so. I hate them worse than I hate the Nazis. My God! I shouldn't say things like that, even to myself."

Mr. Rummel was thinking:

"If Yvonne hadn't filled that inside straight, my two small pairs would have been good enough. If Kazîm hadn't bluffed me out of that first pat hand, I'd have raised him to the sky."

Dr. Musifer was thinking:

"We must stay out of the war till the extreme last moment . . . But we must calculate that moment with discriminating care . . . What we need above all is time, time . . . Territory? Imperialism in the Balkans? Nonsense. What all Turks should want is to beat malaria . . . Let's have more public schools. More teachers . . . Ah, what a great revolution we have already made! Yet what enormous difficulties remain to be overcome! We have reduced illiteracy by seventy per cent in fifteen years. We have abolished the sultan, the caliphate, the harem, the fez. We have Latinized our alphabet, so that it now has twenty-nine characters, instead of 482. We need . . . tractors, roads, breeding stations, better agricultural methods, more machines. We must raise the farmer's standard of living somehow. In the towns a workman gets seven cents an hour. We must see that he gets more . . . My country . . . Eliminate the greed, stimulate self-respect, pare the bureaucracy down, get people educated. War? What do we want of war!"

The military attaché was thinking:

"These Turks are a dumb lot of dumb clucks. By God, never think of a God-damned thing except playing us for a bunch of suckers."

Dave Urquardt was thinking:

"There ought to be another letter soon. Tonsillitis isn't anything to worry about, but sometimes it leaves after-effects. Heart, I think. Peter will go to camp, I suppose. Does that place in the Catskills take kids so young? I wish Hilda would write more often. Damn it all, why can't she write once a week? I wonder if that job she's got is really good for her. There's absolutely no reason why she shouldn't write oftener. Christ, why won't she write . . ."

Mrs. Musifer was thinking:

"When Atif becomes a minister, we shall have a villa in Ankara, and Etta can go to school in Switzerland."

The American consul general was thinking:

"Old man got something on his mind. Wonder what he's up to? Hell, did I forget my Lucky Strikes?"

Etta Musifer was thinking:

"Oh boat is a lovely boat. Oh day is a lovely day. Oh I want all the loveliness. Oh, oh."

Mrs. Spaulding, her hair a flashing yellow in the sun, called sharply:

"There's the Ambassador! He's walking up the quai. Vassily, we'll push off at once!"

III

Homeward now. They passed the island where, in former days, the Turks dumped all the stray dogs of Istanbul, and let them starve. You could see the bones along the jagged beach; no one ever got off on that island. They circled close to Prinkipo, glowing with mottled shadows, and then went round and round a blue-green islet, while the consul general and the military attaché took turns fishing. This was just the right time, they kept saying. This was when you got the big ones, in the metallic shadows just under the purple shifting water.

Mr. Spaulding had a tall Scotch and soda, and sat with Mr. Rommel in the stern, talking in an undertone. He looked satisfied and secretive. Yvonne came up, and asked if she were interrupting. He shook his head, and she sat close to his knee, lightly touching him. He had another drink, and then seemed tired.

"Has it turned out as you hoped?"

"I think so."

But the Ambassador had not even told his wife what he had seen the Prime Minister about.

"Say!"

The military attaché, Colonel Gorman, yanked in his line. "Well, I'll be damned!"

Everybody was standing up. "Oh, don't look!" Yvonne Spaulding cried.

The hook had caught on a piece of uniform, the shoulder, and as Colonel Gorman sharply reeled in, parts of a body with a white bone sticking out plunged back into the calm, darkish water.

They looked at the soaked shoulder with its insignia stained and swollen. "German," Colonel Gorman snapped. "Sneaking troops from the Russian front through the Dardanelles, on those tankers."

"What killed him?"

"Who knows? Fell overboard, maybe."

"Poor devil," Saxton said.

IV

"My own idea would be, one less Hun to have to shoot," Colonel Gorman said.

"Germans like so much to be buried in small neat grave-yards," Mrs. Spaulding said.

They fished no more. They got back to the Embassy at about nine, and there a casual, comfortable Sunday supper was awaiting them.

Leslie helped herself to crabmeat from a chafing dish. And she wondered what she was going to say to Hugo the next time they met; and what to Gerald.

CHAPTER XX

At the Mines . . .

I

GERALD got off the train feeling very good. He went straight to his office and started work. Nothing of any importance had happened in his absence. He was relieved . . .

A month ago, he wouldn't have believed that this job could have turned out to be such sound and productive fun. He had put into operation several new ideas. For instance he baffled and infuriated Aschentoller by new-type delays and breakdowns in delivery of the German chrome. He had told himself to pay less attention to the plant managers and engineers. Instead Gerald began to cultivate the little people, the straw bosses, the actual workmen, and he had produced a wave of strangely effective and almost undetectable sabotage. The men simply worked more slowly; they worked less well. Yet nobody could prove negligence or actual interference; nowhere in Asia or Eastern Europe could anybody draw precisely the line between what seemed to be natural inefficiency and deliberate sabotage.

He checked his mail and found a long cipher message from Strangeways. The enemy, it seemed, was suspicious just now and full of nerves; for the next few days he should take special precautions that everything go smoothly. "Righto," Gerald said to himself.

He certainly wanted things to go smoothly too. Because, now, he was above all in a hurry. He wanted to get this chrome business cleaned up for good and all, and on a solid footing for someone else to take care of, so that he himself could get away within the week.

"Why do I feel so much better about my work?" he wondered. It was not merely that Florian had been here; it was something deeper and more permanent than that. Why had he become so much stronger, better integrated, more composed, without any of the former self-doubt, self-division? Surely his emotion for Leslie must have a lot to do with it. For the first time in years he had awakened to a sharp, positive interest in life, an interest that he knew was *right* for him. And this positiveness wiped out other dubieties. Everything else was solid too.

He looked out of the window. The twisted lines of pipe, the brown funnels like those on a boat, the cranes and catwalks, the triangular cars filled with ore, the water tank and all the smudge, the smoke. All of it so ugly. But happiness, beauty, beat in his heart.

"I say, Neale."

"Yes, sir?"

"It's a wonderful day, isn't it."

"What, sir?"

"It looks like a wonderful day outside."

Neale was a man of fifty, an engineer, formerly a sergeant.

"What do you want most in life, Neale?"

"To see the owld woman at 'ome, sir."

"Yes, but beyond that."

"Well, sir, there's always a spot of work to do."

To love; to be loved; to have good work to do . . . These were the values of a proper life . . .

"I 'aven't been 'ome for a matter of three years, sir. It's a round long time."

That morning, waking up in the train, Gerald felt tangibly that Leslie was with him. She was so close that she was with him. Now, every minute, he saw her face; it floated, tangibly, between the lines of the report he was reading. He felt hollow inside; he wanted to breathe deeply; something in him physically ached; he wanted to stand up, then sit down, then pace the room.

Hugo?

He felt sure that that was not the problem.

Robin?

The point was how to *win* her. To win a woman—the most exciting, rewarding, and sometimes harrowing occupation known to man.

And it might be terribly difficult, too.

How was he going to win her?

He had said he'd telephone her every evening, no matter what the obstacles; he must wait till six. What a pleasant voice she had, on the low side, clear and quietly modulated, with alto tones. And she had promised to write him. And he would write her too, at once, a letter both gay and earnest, well-thought-out and easy. He was tremendously curious to know what she would write. He had never even seen her handwriting; probably it would be very round, smooth-flowing, and above all clear. He wondered how intimate she, a private and non-effusive person, would allow herself to be. He hoped fervently a letter would come to-morrow. There was nothing like the written word . . .

Gerald walked that evening from the office to the station. He had a drink, and then wandered toward the river gardens. He had another drink, and started to saunter back to the hotel.

For a moment he was lost in the glowing clouds. What was real, what was unreal, Gerald smiled.

. . . They would be proffered a state ball at the Élysée, after he and Leslie came back from Africa. He had saved Morocco for civilization after the disastrous uprising of 1962. She would be wearing a long white dress, she'd be stately but graceful, too, exquisite and charming. He would explain with careful ease how, as British plenipotentiary, he had negotiated with the rebellious tribes; how, however, in the interests of peace and the newly underlined interests of the common man, Morocco was promptly to be given its full independence. The President of France looked dubious at first. Gerald would be tolerant in manner but implacable in his convictions. Then gradually the President, with his Minister of Foreign Affairs glumly acquiescing, would concede the argument. *"Vous avez raison, votre excellence."* Meantime two or three of the Ambassadors were hovering close to Leslie, flattering her, lifting their glasses in toasts to her . . .

Oh, balls, Gerald laughed. But like many modest men he had his secret megalomanias.

. . . His first symphony would, of course, be performed at Carnegie Hall, on an October evening for which the whole world of art impatiently waited. His force and integrity of character burned defiantly, but not too defiantly, through the score of what even unfriendly critics conceded to be a work, not merely of talent, but of authentic genius . . . From an upper box, Leslie would of course watch him conduct. For weeks, for months, she had helped him with a devotion both blindly patient and inspiring. She would be a little gray now; she was even more beautiful with that slight touch of gray above the temple. And for long they had been very poor . . .

What was real, what unreal?

Gerald was feeling wonderful.

He saw a motorcar turn sharply from a narrow side road, going fast. Now it was slowing down and coming close to him as he sauntered under the trees. Who would be in that car, Gerald wondered. He did not recognize it in the dusk, though he thought he knew every vehicle in town. It might be the Prime Minister come to greet him. It might be a deputation from Aleppo, where he had been born. It might be a gang of assassins sent to kidnap him. First, steel-witted, he would argue. Second, argument hopeless, he would put up stiff resistance. Third, cleverly, as he was captured—

Gerald saw a dark face, and then an arm extended. He dropped fast, but not fast enough. The car bent around him, and what he saw, in a blinding instant, was a twin-focused roar of exploding light.

Then two more shots, and the car was gone.

Gerald tried to sit up. Must get up. *Must* get up.

He tried to scream, but could only gasp.

CHAPTER XXI

"The Teeth of Tomorrow"

I

LESLIE straightened the papers on her desk, and closed and locked it. The day was warm and sticky; she opened the heavy casement window. The noise of the traffic rose upward; it sounded like a million rats on roller skates.

This was Wednesday. She hadn't heard from Hugo since last week. She had thought surely that he would call Monday after the boating party. But not a word. He must be furious still that she had broken that engagement and gone out with Gerald. Or perhaps, artful and proud, he was waiting for her to call him. Perhaps, confused, he didn't know what to do . . . Leslie felt upset. It was on her conscience that she had stood him up. Anyway she hated loose ends like this; they were untidy, frustrating. If they were to break everything off let them break it clean. And she felt so terribly *sorry* for him; how he would hate it that anybody should pity him, she reflected. That would be one thing his Germanness could not endure . . .

Also, she couldn't help it, she *wanted* to see him, if only for one last talk. I'm a poor weak creature, Leslie thought.

Miss Hanun and Giji popped their heads into her office, and suggested lunch. But today she preferred to eat alone.

The 'phone buzzed. There he was.

She had never heard a more arrogant voice.

"Dine with me tonight."

But such arrogance must conceal panic.

"All right," she said.

"Meet me at the little cafe."

He rang off.

The thing to do now was put him out of her mind till evening. She left the building and walked to the corner. Tonight would be decisive. Either he would; or he wouldn't. Probably this was the last time they would ever be together. And perhaps it was just as well. But oh—she was so *sorry* . . .

Keep it out of her mind. Crisply she walked to the Grande Rue, pausing at a kiosk. Might as well pick up something new to read. About half of the magazines looked like *Life*; she saw *Signal*, *Tempo*, *Images*, *Parade*, *Ülkü*. Inside she bought a *Journal de Genève,* a London *Times,* a Moscow *Daily News*, and a *Völkischer Beobachter*. It always gave her a peculiar sensation to see the Russian and German papers side by side.

After lunch she dropped in at Hayîm's, the great art shop. This was not like the bazaar; there was no junk here. The rugs hung on the wall were floating panels of cream, rose, blue the color of cornflowers; in the cases she saw a set of jeweled chessmen like pieces of candy showered with sparkling dust; ropes of pearls from Bahrein and gold and enamel ornaments from India; two or three wildly ornate Turkish bracelets, and a cold, sinister-looking necklace that had once belonged to a czarina.

But what she always looked at most closely was the tile, framed reverently on the best wall of the shop. She could not tell why this luminous sixteenth century rectangle so fascinated her. Perhaps it told her something of what Byzantium was, and what Islam was, and something about herself. The design was of tulips, intertwined with carnation leaves; the colors were a subtle red between tomato and vermilion, with lucent touches of green and yellow; all on a glazed background of smooth blue-white. The movement was flowing, yet perfectly arrested at the borders; the harmony had a note of the mysterious. It was aged, but fresh as new grass.

She walked back to the office slowly. She would like to

be like that tile, she thought. Composed, yet vital; immaculately balanced, yet warm; exquisite in shape and color; simple on the surface and smooth to touch, but profound. "I'm losing my mind, I guess," she laughed oddly.

Not much work to do this afternoon. She thumbed through the *Völkischer Beobachter*. It seemed to her almost inexplicably strange that the official Nazi newspaper still printed with fair completeness the proceedings of the New York Stock Exchange. She saw that "Amer. Lokom." was 12⅜, "Dup. de Nem." 144.75, "Int. Teleph A ausl. Zert" 14.50, and "Mongomery" 45. One of Robin's companies seemed to be way up if she was remembering the old quotations correctly. They always would be up.

The 'phone rang; Strangeways' voice, weighted heavily. "Got some news for you. Gerald's just been shot."

II

Late that afternoon he came to see her. He was rigid like a man on a hunt.

"Might have been much worse. They pinked him in the shoulder. And a broken shinbone. Painful. Damned painful. A narrow squeak. But he'll recover."

"How did it happen?" This was awful. *Shooting* people. *Her* friends. Her special friends.

Strangeways explained as well as he knew.

"Why did they do it?" She was trembling.

"Lots of reasons. Their chap up there, he hated Gerald. And Gerald was doing damned well on the chrome."

"But Gerald will get better?" she asked anxiously.

"Oh yes. In time. He'll be in hospital a bit."

A wave of relief swept through her. But what did Strangeways mean by "in time"? Again she felt terribly anxious. "Is he *badly* hurt?"

"No. Just something that'll lay him up a while."

"You're sure it isn't really dangerous?"

"Quite sure."

Leslie thought of that last glimpse of Hugo's tortured face. Could Hugo have had anything to do with this? Oh, no! Really—how she hoped—oh, but *no*!

She ought to know by this time what kind of things the Gestapo did. But surely *Hugo* would not have had anything to do with an affair like this. Oh, Hugo, she thought despairingly.

Why was she being so naïve. Hugo couldn't get away from what he represented. And this kind of shock and grief must come to anyone who did not differentiate enough among enemies.

III

"Now, got something else to tell you," Strangeways went on triumphantly. His voice was cold and anticipatory. "Rather, show you. I'll read you parts of it. You'll be interested."

He took out what seemed to be a series of cards.

"Some pages from your friend Hugo's notebook," the Englishman said.

"Suppose we start back here. Some of it we can't make out. In a peculiar German shorthand. But we have enough. Germans certainly like to write things down. That's the way we always get 'em; they *will* be orderly and write things down. Regular diarist, your Hugo. Quite a style. And thorough. At the beginning, he's very bored and lonely. But lots of things on his mind, apparently. Girls . . . Sees a bit of someone initialed Y. Little marks and crosses after her name. What do you suppose they mean, eh? Then some stuff on F. Not so many marks and crosses. Maybe Florian not giving him so much, what! Political worries, too. What should good German think of Badoglio surrender, French underground, Rommel debacle. Goes quite a way back. We owe unfaltering loyalty to Führer. But what about catastrophe eastern front? What a German! Has to write it all down. For the record. Ha! Now we get to you. When he started chasing you. Here's an item. 'Making good progress with L.C.' How do you like that? Very cute, Hugo. Then a nice little line on me. 'S. hovers around like watchdog.' Me a watchdog? Now what do you think of that? Fancy! 'L. very intelligent, but doesn't know her own mind. Can get her.' Now listen. 'Conference D. Orders given, stop G. H. all costs.'"

Leslie took breath.

"How did you get it?"

"Simple."

"Won't he miss it, know you have it?"

"Don't be a damned fool. We took it, photographed it, put it back. He doesn't know we have it."

"You don't seem to have much trouble visiting him."

Strangeways grinned. "Naturally not. Always did it when he was going out with you."

"You son of a bitch," Leslie said.

She went over the pages slowly, line by line. She wanted to defend Hugo now, before this Englishman. Later it would be different.

"As a matter of fact there's nothing terribly incriminating in any of this," she considered slowly. "Hugo *was* going through a crisis. I suppose I started it. After all what would be more natural than his writing that he was making progress with me? I don't like it, but I can imagine that was exactly what he felt."

Strangeways lit a cigarette, and watched her.

"If there's anything you haven't shown me, anything that says he and I were intimate, it isn't true," Leslie averred.

He kept on watching her. The smoke came out of his nostrils slowly.

"But if you think this proves that Hugo was actually a party to shooting Gerald, then I'll never see him again."

Blood on his hands, Leslie thought. Maybe he's innocent himself. But it's blood on his hands just the same. You can't separate it out.

Strangeways snapped drily: "Depends on definition."

She had to grasp toward something else: "You're the most laconic man I've ever met."

"Dear me, nothing to get loquacious about."

Slowly she considered again and went on, "All it says is, Dortmund issued orders to somebody, most likely somebody at the mines, I should think, that Gerald was to be stopped. It doesn't mention murder. It's the kind of thing you folks do, on our side, all the time. You know perfectly well that you do it too. It doesn't incriminate Hugo except as an . . . an observer. It doesn't directly incriminate him, not at all!"

"That's a way to put it," Strangeways said.

IV

After he left Leslie thought a while and walked to the telephone and called Hugo at the Park.

She said into the 'phone, sadly, "Hugo, did you have anything to do with shooting Gerald Heath?"

"No," he lied. "Certainly not. *Nein!*"

"You'll have to prove it," she answered, and bumped the receiver back on its hook.

CHAPTER XXII

Gerald

I

GERALD was fairly comfortable now, though it would be at least a month before he could budge from bed. The Turks let the British military attaché send down for him in one of the hush-hush R.A.F. planes. Later there would probably have to be an operation to reset the tibia near the knee, since that had been a crude job done by the Turkish doctor at the mines. The puncture in the deltoid muscle was a serious but not dangerous wound; a rib deflected the bullet from the lung, and smashing out through the armpit it had missed the big veins. Nothing to worry about if it did not infect.

With the hand he could use he turned the knob on the small radio near his pillow. The Ankara station was playing the Number Five Beethoven piano concerto, from records. He listened hard and then dozed awhile. When he woke up he could not tell whether it was the H.M.V. recording by Schnabel and the London Philharmonic, or that of Gieseking and Bruno Walter. The second movement sounded like Schnabel, but not the rest. But he was too tired to think.

There came a light rap on the door. Strangeways had been in to see him earlier and Florian had sent a message that she would call tomorrow. He was half-asleep but he knew who it would be.

"Hello," Leslie said, smiling.

"Hi," Gerald said.

"I'm awfully glad to see you," Leslie said.

She walked to the bed and kissed him on the forehead with

soft, warm lips. He pulled her down on his chest for a second with his good arm.

"Well," Gerald said. He gazed at her, and also inwardly at himself, as if he were surveying, appraising, the impression they made together. His eyes were wan, they were filmy with morphine; yet there was something resolute in the way he looked.

"Well . . . nothing like having a couple of bullets pumped into you to clear the mind," he tried to laugh but the laughter hurt. He switched the radio off.

"Did you need to have your mind cleared? A rather drastic treatment, I must say!" she smiled.

Dr. Pastor came in and told Leslie that she could stay as long as she liked, but that Gerald shouldn't talk too much. Then she was surprised because her emotion was not simply that of a woman solicitously visiting a sick and wounded man; rather it was that she yearned for succor, sustenance, from him, even though he lay broken on a narrow bed.

"Let's put the radio on again," Gerald said.

"Yes . . . please."

The windows began to fill with blue dusk. The music was Bach or Vivaldi.

"You're not very musical, are you?" he asked.

"Not very."

"What a pity. You know the way that stuff makes me feel? It makes me realize what a fine and wonderful place the world is in spite of everything. It makes me want to *do* things!"

"Shhh. You mustn't talk." She tiptoed with her voice.

"I'm quite all right."

"Is there much pain?" Leslie asked.

"A bit. And I'm sleepy from this dope they give me."

"I'll go now," she volunteered.

"No. Please stay. I'd like you to stay because you're so nice to look at."

She was pleased. "All right."

The records changed to the Kreutzer Sonata. "You know

what that is?" Gerald murmured. "It's a kind of love affair between a piano and a violin."

Then his eyes were closed; the room was almost dark; he reached over and put his fingers around her forearm, just above the wrist. She felt his fingers, cool and strong; she did not dare move her hand and the fingers stayed there on her wrist, till they relaxed and she knew he was asleep. She sat for a long time, until the room was completely dark. Her hand got stiff, but she didn't want to move.

"Hello," he smiled, half-waking.

"Hello," she said.

"You have a nice voice, too."

"I'm glad."

"I love you," Gerald said.

A moment later she disengaged his fingers and slipped quietly from the room.

II

Hugo had been 'phoning her off and on all day. His voice was desperate.

"But I don't *want* to see you!" she kept repeating into the 'phone.

"Just because a man is shot . . . something with which I had nothing whatever to do . . ."

"I don't believe you, Hugo." Her revulsion was complete and final now.

"I must once more implore you, give me but one chance to explain."

"You knew that Gerald was going to be shot, didn't you?"

"I knew only in the vaguest way. Anyway this is not something to discuss by way of telephone."

"I can't help it, Hugo. I just don't *want* to see you."

"But in a day or two you will be friendly again."

"It isn't a question of friendship. I thought it all over and something closed up in me, that's all."

"I will do anything you say. *Anything*."

"I doubt that, Hugo," she said coolly.

"Give me a chance. One more chance." He sounded hysterical.

"I can't help it. I'm sorry."

"You cannot be so brutal. You are the most brutal woman I ever heard of."

"I'm sorry, Hugo."

She hung by the 'phone a second, pressing her thumb knuckles into her eyes till they ached.

III

Gerald was much better after a day or two. The hospital, a low stucco building, stood on a hill a few blocks from the Musifer apartment, and she walked over almost every afternoon.

One day he told her a story. They had been discussing what people and events most influenced them, how the skeletons of their characters were formed, and Gerald mentioned the school he had gone to before Oxford.

"Something happened there that marked and scarred me for quite a time," he began casually. "Beastly little school it was. And a beastly set of odious boys. Perhaps I was as odious as the rest . . . Don't know. We had one bully, a big chap, only thirteen but five feet ten or eleven, a malformed kind of chap. Well, one evening, just as we were getting ready for bed, what should he do but pull out a pistol. He said 'Get down on your knees, Heath, I'm going to kill you.' I was frightened. I was stunned with terror. But I hated the idea of getting down on my knees. He pressed the pistol against my forehead, and repeated, 'Down on your knees, Heath, and pray to God, before I kill you.' So I got down on my knees, and I could feel the pistol make a cold ring against my forehead. 'Now pray,' he commanded. I hadn't had much experience of prayer and I didn't know what to say. 'I won't pray,' I cried. 'Pray,' he repeated. 'I can't pray,' I said. So he pulled the trigger and there was a hell of an explosion. Bang! I thought I was dead. And I suppose I fainted. But I wasn't hurt. He had put a blank cartridge in the gun, not an actual bullet. But what a noise it made! For months and years afterward, I could hear that noise, the noise of my own death."

"What did the boy do it for?" She was horrified.

"Oh, just for fun. Practical joke, you know."

"A boy like that ought to have been shot himself," she asserted. In an electric instant she thought, "When I said that it sounded like my mother's voice."

"I wonder what ever happened to him," Gerald meditated. "You can't always tell about kids. Maybe he grew up to be a useful citizen. One of those big chaps who go around making big decisions . . ." he grinned.

"Don't you hate him?"

"Hate him? Hardly."

"Gerald, sometimes I think you're *too* tolerant," Leslie said; her voice had a warm snap. "Don't you think that *any*thing is evil?"

He did not answer directly. "All those years that that gun fired and it was a blank cartridge . . . Now, by heaven, someone *has* really shot me, someone *did* actually try to kill me. And in an odd way I feel all right about it. Perhaps because I *was* really shot. I suppose I had been waiting to be shot for years. That second, that unending second, while I was on my knees . . . And now the whole nightmare is wiped out, liquidated. I don't need to think about it any more. I don't have to wait to find myself still alive."

"What you're saying is that there may be compensation for tragedies, but that doesn't mean evil things aren't evil just the same."

He thought a moment. "The secret of life is to forgive and forget. To be happy is to overcome the past." He laughed. "Time, as they say, cures all."

IV

Another day. She watched him, happy. He was bright and full of ideas about himself and talkatively introspective, but sometimes his eyes were closed, and his lashes lay on the cheeks like apples. There was something stirring in her, very deep.

"One mustn't be too glib. It's so easy to rationalize after the event. One could say that all my inadequacies, my frailties and failures, have been the result of that incident at school, the phobias it produced. But that's too facile an explanation. One could say that I began to feel better about my work and my relation to the world after . . ." he hesitated but without embarrassment . . . "after Florian came out to the mines. But that's far too simple too . . . As a matter of fact there are quite a number of varying explanations and determinants for almost any given event. The main thing to say is that the right kind of people *do* change. And grow. But maybe," he laughed, "that's too simple an explanation too . . ."

My God, Leslie thought, I do *like* this man. His mind worked exactly as hers did; talking to him was not only satisfying but effortless. Every time she left him after an hour, the hour had been two minutes. She felt completely at ease with him, completely secure and comfortable. It was almost as if she were alone with herself in a good mood . . .

"I don't believe in things very easily." He paused. "And the things I'd *like* to believe in seem so distant, so chimerical. I'd *like* to believe in a world state for instance. Yet it's so difficult to square one's beliefs, one's hopes, with concrete reality. Of course," he proceeded, "I've had a lot of belief knocked out of me. A lot of *faith* knocked out of me."

Fleetingly, he thought of Rose, who had been his wife; he remembered all the ornate dreams and aspirations of his youth. But now his only emotion about her was a kind of puzzled wonder that she, who had once meant so much, could mean so little. She meant absolutely nothing. It was precisely as if she had never existed, never even lived.

Leslie wanted intensely to contribute something to this; she wanted to be intelligent and useful. She felt an idea forming. "Of course it's nonsense to say that you don't believe in anything."

"What do you mean?"

"Well, maybe it's just a fancy paradox, but couldn't you say that you *do* believe in doubt?"

"Well . . ." he laughed. "At that, it wouldn't be a bad thing to believe in. After all, most intellectual progress is due to doubt. The origin of science, the scientific method, is the will to doubt. In a way what we're fighting for is the right to doubt!"

"I should think the point ought to be," she replied tentatively, "that the doubter should have a good healthy doubt about *things*, but faith in himself."

"Yes. It all comes back to the personal equation. To character. The only thing that counts is character." That was what *she* had been brought up to believe, she reflected.

He fumbled trying to light a cigarette. She reached over, lit it, and put it in his mouth. She felt a quick excited emotion. The way he rolled it on his lip, the way his lower cheeks got sucked in, as he drew on it, the way after a second his mouth opened slightly, and the smoke came out, in a little puff.

"Look at Darwin . . . Pasteur. Kelvin. Freud. They were all doubters. That is, they refused to accept what people told them. They insisted on investigating for themselves."

"But they certainly had a tremendous quality of belief too. They believed in themselves, or they wouldn't have had the energy, the stamina, the faith for all the work they did."

"They believed in the only thing modern science justifiably believes in, the demonstrable fact."

"No. They believed in *themselves*." She was watching the cigarette still. She felt pin-pricks along her skin.

He laughed, but appreciatively, and quoted a jingle from I. A. Richards:

> "If the sun and moon should doubt,
> They'd immediately go out."

Leslie had a new idea. "If doubt is the origin of science, then I suppose affirmation is the origin of art."

She thought of the piece of tile at Hayîm's. Urgently, she wanted to show Gerald that tile, and have him love it too.

"This is getting very advanced," he chuckled. "When you get into art, that's really my field, and we'll talk about it another day. Now let's have some tea."

"Let's." Her face shone alive. "Oh! I'm enjoying this so much!"

"That's because you know I love you," Gerald said.

Later he asked her about Robin; when she talked he could see a struggle in her face; it looked split apart, the eyes and mouth not matching.

Gerald grasped suddenly that the worst thing of all would be to press her; it would be the best tactic not even to ask about him. Just let her grow, let things develop. But how to win her—*how*? He knew again how difficult this was going to be; he knew that facing him was the biggest intellectual problem of his life.

v

She ran into Strangeways in the hall the next day. He was leaving Gerald's room. "Glad you're taking care of my young man. At last."

"I'm taking care of myself too," Leslie smiled.

"Eh? It seems I may be going away for a couple weeks," Strangeways said. "Keep an eye on him while I'm gone. You know Gerald was going to do a job for me. Blasted Nazis, they've knocked him out. So think I'll take it on myself."

So Strangeways would be doing that dangerous Aegean show. It must have something to do with invading Greece, she thought. She hoped he'd be all right.

"Remember what we were saying yesterday?" Gerald greeted her. "Look at Alec now. How can anybody try to maintain any . . . any idealism as against folk like Strangeways? Their cynicism—they call it realism—is so revolting. But also it's effective and damned convincing at times. You know what Alec thinks about most nowadays? In fact it's the only thing he *really* thinks about. How to make England strong for World War III."

"It's sensible enough if you're a patriotic Englishman and think that World War III *is* coming. I hate it. I loathe it. But I can understand how a man can feel that way."

"Leslie, dear!" He had never called her that before, in that tone. "Now it's you who're being too tolerant! Get enough people thinking in those terms, and you'll condition everybody toward making World War III inevitable!"

"I suppose you mean a war with Russia." She thought of that Soviet consul general and how impressive he was just to look at.

"Of course. Or with anybody who becomes the strongest power in Europe, to prevent any single power from dominating it."

"I hate it!" Leslie snapped. "The whole idea is intolerable."

"I agree. But it might happen, if enough stupid and prejudiced people are in charge."

"I haven't any overwhelming brief for the Russians, though I admire them in general and I appreciate tremendously the way they're fighting. But please don't ever drag us into a war against them! It's the one thing that would make me an isolationist."

She talked to him about her work, which was fascinating her more day by day. She sketched Urquardt's theories about Lend Lease and told him all the office gossip and described how she went through her routine and what she thought about it.

"What are you, anyway?" he laughed, but lightly, "the voice of the United States growing up and becoming conscious of the rest of the world?"

She shook her head. "I think a lot about the future. Our generation has done a lot of suffering and I think we have a responsibility to watch carefully so there's no catastrophe again."

He still laughed. "You're the new America."

She was stubborn. "It's our turn now. And we've earned it. I want to march with the times. I want to believe in a good tomorrow."

Suddenly Gerald thought of Robin. His face became intently serious. He had an idea.

VI

Leslie pondered. She shook out the white dirndl-like pique. Damn. If only she had brought along a small electric iron. Gerald now. All she felt about Gerald was hardly sufficient explanation for this mysterious emotion she was undergoing, not merely happiness, but a sense of confidence about herself. She felt a strange, a poignant, an exquisite change within the walls of her own nature, her own being. For the first time since she and Robin left one another, for the first time in a whole year, she felt that the parting was not her fault. No longer did she feel that she had lost Robin because of some deep failure in *her*, some profound and inexplicable factor in which she had been found wanting. Perhaps it was because she so warmly wanted Gerald to be surer of *him*self; perhaps because she had such confidence that she could take care of Gerald, and she knew he needed care.

Propped up in bed, restless, happy, and impatient for her to come, Gerald scanned thoughtfully the contours of the present. Leslie now. He glanced at his watch; he turned off the radio; she would be coming soon. He felt still that there was something mysterious about her, something that eluded him. "I know what it is," he said to himself, "I think I've got it. She puts up a pretty slick front and all that, but basically, she's a hand-full, and what she needs is someone to take care of her."

Leslie slipped off her suit quickly, and put on the dirndl, though it did need pressing slightly; then she let her hair down, and combed it out. She groped in a drawer for the pair of pale green roses, and stuck them gaily in the fine, lustrous, walnut-table-colored hair. Gerald had never seen her with her hair down. The ends curled glistening.

Gerald flipped with one hand through the afternoon papers, the *Journal d'Orient* and *Cumhuriyet*, and wondered how long it would be before he was well. The doctor had been quite encouraging this morning; he might not have to have an operation after all. Anyway they'd take the cast off after a while and soon he'd be in a wheelchair, when the shoulder healed a little more. Jove, to be on his feet again!

There came the firm, gentle knock.

"Hi," Gerald said.

"Hello," Leslie said.

His eyes got large; they expanded. "My God, what have you done to yourself? You're too marvelous. Aren't you *lovely*?"

And this afternoon each felt a new and particular closeness of emotion: a mounting tenderness. They ordered drinks; they chatted; but there was a difference. He could not take his eyes away; something had been shaken loose, in her, or him. She began to think: Maybe a firm, fond friendship is a better basis for a lasting relationship than a fervent love affair.

He must be a mind reader. Because he was saying, with all that directness, charm, and curious innocence combined, "You know there are lots of girls who like to be torn to pieces. They're not for me. Thank God, girls like that *bore* me!"

But each, though secretly understanding the feeling in the other, kept most of the conversation personal-impersonal. They talked about Stravinsky, where the big invasion would hit first, whether or not the Turks would come into the war, the Spauldings, why learning a new language was like having a new room in the house, short stories by A. E. Coppard, the color purple, was so-and-so a fairy, what H. G. Wells would be like to meet, and what was the best restaurant in Paris for hors d'oeuvres.

He thought: "We'll marry in about six months."

He said: "Leslie darling, pass that ashtray, will you?"

She thought: "Robin once said that only love can kill love."
She said: "I've got to run now. But I'll drop in tomorrow."

VII

The rap on the door was vigorous. "Come in," they both
said. And there was Florian.

Leslie blinked. It was practically the most oo-la-la costume
she had ever seen on a girl: an enormous magenta hat, with
feathers and a veil; a magenta dress that matched almost
achingly, cut excessively low and with a fancy drape; dark
purple cut-out shoes; a large cerise handbag; and—Leslie
passed an imaginary hand over her forehead—long white kid
gloves. And she was doused with something that was probably Ciro's *Danger*.

Florian bent to kiss Gerald's cheek. The hat covered him
like a tent. Gerald looked oddly, vaguely, troubled.

"Hello!"

"Hello, *Liebschen*."

"Hello!"

"Leslie, hello."

Was this the girl who had been so athletic and *gamine* at
the Klub Lido? Ye gods. Yet in five minutes Leslie felt a
greater camaraderie for her than ever before.

"You have not been yet to Taksim's," Florian whirled on
her accusingly. "You have not seen me since my return in
two new numbers. Gerald, what nasty business people do;
think, if I had stayed longer, they would not have dared to
shoot! *Liebling*, when I heard, I came near to collapse, then
I began to laugh because . . . I don't know why . . . I thought
it was so funny . . . how very angry and *böse* they would be
that they had missed! Leslie, oh, when do you take me to
United States with you?" She glanced at her wickedly.
"Gerald, I can stay no more than five minutes, please for
beautiful Florian to have a drink!"

After she left they were silent a while. And Leslie knew
from his face, not hers, that Florian was in love with him.

VIII

In violent contrast the next two days were among the unhappiest of Leslie's life.

In the hospital corridor she ran into the Spauldings, surrounded by a moving skein of doctors, military attachés in mufti, and almost all the journalists. Seven American boys who had bombed the oil wells in Rumania had been picked up on a Turkish beach. Two were only slightly hurt; but one had his kneecap cut off sharply as by a cleaver, and another had concussion, a broken arm, and a terrible wound in the chest; one had an eye ripped out and the bridge of the nose shot off, and another had just had a leg amputated at the thigh. All seven had lain on the beach for hour after hour, beginning at dawn the day before, while ignorant and frightened villagers watched them, not knowing what to do.

Mrs. Spaulding exclaimed firmly: "It'll do them good to see a pretty American girl. Come!"

Why, the two boys who were only slightly injured looked like high school sophomores. Why, they looked like kids playing hooky after a game of basketball. Why, they looked just like her brother Fleming!

One had an eager nose, a southern drawl, and a stiff pompadour of ginger hair; he was dazed, friendly, and respectful. "Why yes, ma'am," he kept saying. The other sat with his body bent so that his head seemed almost in his lap, and when he looked up his eyes were red with swollen tears.

They went into the ward. Mrs. Spaulding led Leslie to the boy with the eye and nose gone; only a patch of his face was visible in the stiff, unmoving whiteness of bandage, sheet, and pillow. But this part of his face was the mouth. The lips were cracked and black and drawn over the teeth so that they were rigidly exposed, and the panting snarl was that of an animal.

The boy with the kneecap sliced away was not critically injured; but he seemed dumb with shock and pain. Mrs. Spaulding put her hand on his shoulder, and Leslie tried to say something cheerful. The boy was murmuring, but the words made no sense. Then he began to shiver spasmodically, to shake violently and shiver, as if some hideous gooseflesh of the soul had extended itself to all his skin.

Then from a room across the hall they heard screams, then a choked moaning, then screams again that tore through the building. A doctor came out dappled with sweat and dead white. "Jesus, oh Jesus," the doctor said. Leslie tried to control herself. She grasped Yvonne's taut arm, and closed her eyes. But she remembered what Yvonne had said once; she must fix it in her mind, she must always keep it there. *War, war itself, was the real atrocity.*

She kept thinking, "Oh, let's win it, let's get it over with. Let's win it, win it soon, and make it so there'll never be another. Then we can all lead decent lives again."

What would Gerald say? He might say, Forgive them, the enemy, for they know not what they do. No: that was too glib and pat; it was too Mr. Britlingish; it was far too easy.

End it, end it quick, Leslie thought; make it the last one ever. World War III? She would die first. Make it the last one, forever.

IX

That night she had a dream, a nightmare. Fleming's birthday. But was it actually his birthday? No, it couldn't be; this was May, and Fleming had been born, like herself, in October. But in the dream, the nightmare, it *was* his birthday; or wasn't it? His birthday or some other kind of day. Deathday? *Death*day? First Leslie saw dark slanting shadows, then a road twisting under heavy trees, then a meeting with her mother (was it her mother?) at a railway station, where everybody was tramping backwards; and then the twisting underpart of some big building, with pipes laid along the basement ceiling. A swift change then to brilliant mountain scenery. And Fleming skiing. Or was it Fleming? Could it be Hugo? Then, infinitely sharp and painful, so that her whole soul closed in on itself, icy, the knowledge came that Fleming had been killed, that he was dead. A mournful procession wound down rutted streets; then her mother's face shone through a calendar, grave and sweet. Abruptly came a vision of another calendar, in Russian script, and a Russian word, a place name, Kursk. Now what could that have to do with Fleming? Fleming was flying in the South Pacific. Then the word Kursk became the word Curse and a violently agitated procession bearing the body of the dead closed in on her. Armies poured through cracks in fences, like mice. It was not a birthday, it was a deathday. The Nazis and Japs were killing everybody. Fleming's dead face hung over her. Leslie woke up.

All the next day at the office she felt nervous and shaky; she was terrified that the dream portended something true. It was silly to give way to such premonitions, but she could not help it. She had a clairvoyant certainty that she would get some word from America today. At noon, while she was taking instructions from Urquardt, a telegram did indeed come, delivered from the Embassy. She held onto the desk top. It was for Urquardt; it concerned some routine matter. But she thought she would faint. She was certain, absolutely certain, that sometime today she would get a telegram, and that it would tell her that Fleming had been killed. Leslie had lunch with Miss Hanun and Giji; but she could scarcely talk to them. Urquardt asked her if she were ill, early in the afternoon, and she said that she must have eaten something that upset her. He urged her to go home. She thought first that she would telephone Gerald and omit her visit to the hospital, but she hated to disappoint him, and she dragged herself over there, quivering.

x

She had promised to dine with Strangeways and they met at the Turquoise, spelled Turkwas. She could not hear a word that he was saying; she thought she'd have to leave. She *knew* that when she arrived home at the Musifers' a telegram, forward from the Embassy, would be awaiting her. There was no longer any possible doubt; she *knew*. Nothing could prevent its being there; a bony fate had stretched out a claw in her direction, and would not let go. Nothing could bring Fleming back now. He was dead.

"Having good time with Gerald?"

"What?" She had not listened.

"You're a bit preoccupied tonight."

"I'm sorry. Those boys at the hospital upset me."

"Gerald's getting along very well."

"Yes."

"Lucky we got him here so fast."

"Yes."

She tried to tear herself away from her obsession. She said during coffee, "I wish you'd promise me something. If there's trouble of any kind, and you're not here, I wish you'd see that someone watches out for Florian."

"What a strange girl you are. Why should you bother about Florian?"

"I like her. She did you a good turn and Gerald too. And I have a feeling she's going to face an unhappy period."

"Gerald's not in love with her any more."

"I know."

"Nothing like a bit of propinquity," Strangeways said, "to terminate a love affair."

"Not all love affairs," Leslie said.

This man *is* too heartless, she couldn't help thinking. And she wondered what could be the basic reason for his inhumanity. Had he some secret? Had he, perhaps, some hidden, esoteric responsibility to someone quick, or someone dead?

He watched her narrowly. He misread her face. "Maybe she's going to fall in love with Gerald," he said to himself.

XI

She asked to be excused early, and he took her home at half past ten. She went up in the elevator quaking with terror.

Yes. She was right. She shuddered to the bone. On her bed-table was a telegram.

She sat down weakly on the bed. Then she tore it open, and started to cry silently. It read:

HAVE ASKED ELSE FOR DVORCE SHE GOING RXNO NEXT WEEK. WILL YOU COME BACK MARY ME.

ROBIN CULPEPPER.

CHAPTER XXIII

The Last Night at Taksim's

I

DR. MAX DORTMUND leaned over the table, panted heavily, and glared at Hugo. "And how proceeds your flirtation with the *chic* American?" It was late afternoon.

"*Herr Doktor*, I have not seen her for some days."

"So . . . So . . ." Dr. Dortmund's notched, corrugated lips advanced into a pout. "She will have nothing of you and so our darling Hugo is frustrated and unhappy."

He could kill this man, Hugo thought.

When Mr. Poppa had told Dortmund that Hugo and Leslie were seeing one another, Dortmund had first rebuked Hugo and then excused him on the supposition that he might pick up something useful.

"So . . . So . . . And in all the time you have played with her, you obtained nothing, you benefited the Fatherland with absolutely nothing, *nichts*."

"I did not see her for that purpose," Hugo said coldly.

"You are the emancipated young man, so seemingly sure of himself, who consorts with the enemy while crisis mounts. Bah!"

The dead know that I shall die, Hugo thought suddenly. The waiting dead know that I shall die.

"Perhaps you will have the goodness now to devote some of your time and energy and so-called talents to business that engages us," Dr. Dortmund said. "Hugo darling."

"*Jawohl, Herr Doktor*." I could kill him easily, Hugo thought.

"Bunglers, bunglers," the Doctor spat out. "The Ambassador himself is deeply concerned that everything, like the attack on the Heath, is so miserable and disgusting a failure."

"Not my fault, *Herr Doktor*."

"We must put our heads together."

"If you so wish, *Herr Doktor*."

"Sit down. We have it now on our best authority, the authority in the Spanish Embassy, that the Strangeways is to replace the Heath on the Aegean mission. Ha! They think *they* know all! They think *they* have accurate information. Our intelligence is still the most superbly efficient in the world!"

Hugo listened to the former dentist pant.

"I would like it much, very much, that the Strangeways does not get immediately to the Aegean. If he could be delayed even a few days, it would be valuable!"

"What do you propose, *Herr Doktor*?"

Dortmund seemed to be groping. Kidnap him? Not quite satisfactory. Murder him? Not quite practicable. He heavily swept around for an idea.

"Think, you dumb fool!" he roared, sloping over the desk toward Hugo. "Have you nothing in your head but thoughts of women?"

"I do not know what to suggest, *Herr Doktor*."

Dr. Dortmund's eyes suddenly ignited. "Of course we could use the old baby trick. Now that is not a bad idea; we could use the baby trick. Yes! Of course! We have not used that trick for some time. Throw some baby under Strangeways' car! That will delay him here! Have Numini come to see me. Get Numini at once." Numini was the depraved little Italian gunman whom they occasionally employed.

Hugo carefully lit a cigarette.

"It might be dangerous, *Herr Doktor*."

"Dangerous? Have you become a coward as well as a fool? Now let us see. Hugo darling. We must have a baby. Yes. A baby." The lips fell open with satisfaction. "Ha! We could kill the baby of the Turkish journalist, Musifer. The child I saw the other night . . . She is a little too old, perhaps. But she will do. Of course!" He closed his lips. "Never mind Numini. You could handle the affair yourself. Of course. It is natural. You know something of the child's movements. You could arrange it late in the day when the American visits the hospital. Strangeways, too, is often in that neighborhood. It will take some ingenuity. But I have every confidence that you can manage it!"

"I have never done that sort of thing," said Hugo narrowly.

"So?" Dr. Dortmund watched him.

"It is not part of my job," Hugo protested.

"You will nevertheless do it. *Schluss!*"

"I beg to state, *Herr Doktor*, it is not something I can do."

"You disobey orders? You disobey *me*?" Then Dortmund's face changed. He beamed. "Dolt! You think I am serious? You think any such scatterbrained scheme could succeed? Dolt! I tell you this to observe your reactions, only to test you. Dear little Hugo."

Dortmund laughed harshly. A moment or two later Hugo left his office. He was not so sure.

II

The Ambassador leaned back; he was smiling enigmatically, and he tapped the table gently. He had called in Strangeways and his opposite number, the American secret service man. The American was an underconfident young man who had been an insurance broker and who had a sick wife and a brother-in-law he hated in a suburb on Long Island, and who was not seen around town very much.

"Well . . ." the Ambassador picked up a sheet of paper. "I have some news for you, I think . . . It'll be announced publicly in a day or two. But I think I'd better tell you in advance. I've already communicated with your Ambassador," he nodded to Strangeways. "The Prime Minister has just informed me . . ." he consulted the sheet of paper with part of his eyes . . . "has just informed me that the Turkish government has, in view of the exigencies of the international situation, decided forthwith to terminate all exports of chrome to Germany." Mr. Spaulding looked up. "So you can call off your boys at the mines."

The Ambassador could not resist a distant grin. Who said that the old type of diplomacy wasn't effective any more? Who said that the veteran diplomats couldn't do just as good a job as the cloak-and-dagger lads?

"I'd like to ask you how you did it, Mr. Ambassador," the American secret service man spoke respectfully.

"Oh, quite simple. But I don't think I'd better tell you. Security, you know."

Really it did seem obvious now. All he had done was threaten to cut off Lend Lease if Turkey didn't stop the chrome.

The Ambassador rose. "Have a cigarette?" he smiled.

III

Gerald lay flat on his back, aching with pain; not pain from the stiff shoulder or the bone under the plaster swarming with itches, but the pain of having to be inactive, immobile, just at this moment of his life when, to win Leslie, he wanted to be active most. To think that he might lose her made him groan aloud . . . "I *can't* lose her!" he muttered to himself.

Swiftly he calculated back; she and Robin must have been together about four years. That was a very long time in the life of a young woman. How could he batter his way through such an obstacle?

He was a man in love; he tried to think out every possible gambit he might legitimately attempt. How could he influence her, penetrate her love for Robin, break her down? If only he could walk on his two good legs again! Yet this was not going to be decided by anything in the realm of the physical.

Once he was well, Gerald felt that he could compete with any man.

Yesterday when she came in she seemed tense in the extreme, more upset than he had ever seen her . . . And she had talked about Robin more than at any time since that dinner, mostly in regard to politics and things he believed in. Robin had been pretty much of an isolationist until the fall of France, Leslie told him. Then he woke up. But he still had that curious lack of understanding of any politics beyond his own immediate touch.

All this Gerald rotated in his mind today. Not only must he try every possible gambit; he must take any kind of outside chance . . . First he had talked about Robin's point of view while being careful not to criticize him; then he outlined, as cheerfully as he could, a lot of the things he himself felt strongly about. Did Robin understand what *kind* of a war it was, Gerald asked.

At noon Leslie dropped in. The "hello" stopped in his mouth when he saw her face. She was white; her eyes looked as if she hadn't slept.

"Leslie . . . what's the matter?"

She sat down, as if lost; she drew thumb and fingers across her brows, and then squeezed her closed eyes. Not looking at him she opened her bag, with her fingers taut, and pulled out a telegram. "It came last night," she said weakly.

Gerald read it. "Oh . . ."

"I don't know what to do," Leslie said.

She could see him attempt to rise physically from the bed; his whole body shook with strain so that the bed shook too; every nerve in his body quivered, each muscle in his face became tense; he lifted his good arm straight out, as if to make it an inch longer than it had ever been before; the fingers trembled, and his voice emerged as if out of a deep recess; he said with intense, biting clarity:

"No! I won't *let* you go back to him!"

IV

Etta Musifer burst out of the house, glowing, happy. She had her allowance for the week, and she was going to buy a paper doll at the stationery shop near the Waytaus. She hiked up her skirts, crossing a vacant lot full of rubbish, and then stood pigeon-toed, bent at the waist, as she inspected with rapt attention some rocks underfoot. Oooh, ooh, Etta thought.

She raced down the street, skipping part of the way. Her hair floated behind her; the great olive eyes were shining. Missis Korkor would be home at six, Etta thought. She would have the doll to give Missis Korkor then. Oooh, oooh, she hummed to herself. In the shop she tiptoed up to the counter and craned upward and bought the doll. Now she was on the way home again.

Traffic was thick at the Waytaus corner, and several heavy automobiles were swinging past. Prudently, dutifully, Etta waited until it was safe to cross.

V

The Spauldings were having a big informal party at Taksim's, and Leslie hurried home to change. They had been rushed, very rushed and busy, at the Lend Lease office, making up the pouch. She thought she'd wear the black wool; she hadn't had it on since that first evening at Taksim's, six weeks or so ago. Pity she hadn't time to go to the hairdresser; she'd wear her pearls too; Lord, she'd be late.

The 'phone rang just as she got inside the door.

"Yes, Hugo." She hardened.

"You will be interested, I have now decided." He seemed steely; he seemed far away.

"Oh, Hugo." Now she could tell. She didn't know quite what to say. She gripped herself.

"It is reckless to talk this way over the 'phone. But what do I care now?"

"Tell me."

"I do what you request. I come over to your side. I sell out. It is all over for me now." Yet he would be free.

"Hugo, I'm so glad! We could meet tonight, but I'm going to a party given by the Ambassador. You understand? Oh, Hugo, I'm so *happy*!"

"I see you tomorrow, then?"

"Yes, of course." But she felt a stab of uncertainty. Gerald?

His voice sounded very grave now. "You can realize what this means to me?"

"Oh, yes, Hugo!"

"We meet and then you do with me what you will, what you decide."

"Pick me up at the Lend Lease office."

"All right. *Ja.*"

"Twelve-thirty, say. And we'll have lunch and then go to see Strangeways right away."

"All right. *Ich liebe dich.*"

"Hugo, darling, I'm so glad." But she oughtn't to call him darling. She oughtn't to encourage him.

Neither wanted to hang up. The current between them held. Then Hugo said,

"One thing I did not mention that first day. I did not like it in your country that there were no receipts when you sent telegrams. It seemed disorderly and unsafe."

Had he gone out of his mind? "Hugo . . ." Such a German. He couldn't let anything alone. He had to have an advantage over her in *some*thing.

"It occurred to me the other day. I have just wanted to mention it," he added with complete dignity. "Always there should be a receipt for a telegram."

"We'll talk tomorrow. I've got to run now, Hugo darling!"

"You go to Taksim's?"

"We're meeting for cocktails at the Embassy."

"Good night, Leslie. *Ich liebe dich.*"

"Good night. I'm so glad."

VI

She dressed hurriedly, flung a kiss at Etta, paused to inspect a paper doll the child had bought her, and picked up a taxi to the Spauldings'. What?

Hugo was standing there, half-hidden in a niche near the courtyard gates. The old White Russian doorman, poking his head from a booth, watched him with aware attention. Hugo's hat was slanting low on his forehead like one in a gangster film; he walked out to greet her, and her heart contracted.

"Hugo . . . you shouldn't be here."

"I had to see you. Once more, I had to *see* you."

She fumbled for change and paid the taxi.

Whispering, he took both her hands. The doorman kept on watching.

"Oh, you are lovely. Also, there was something I could *not* say on the 'phone . . ."

Other guests were arriving, and within the Embassy lights glittered. As another taxi whipped up she could see Dave Urquardt inside. Hugo pulled her softly into the darkness.

"Be sure, tomorrow, be absolutely sure that the Musifer child stays indoors."

He still held both her hands. She could feel them grow icy. "Etta? Why?"

"I will explain. But it is difficult to talk now. Keep the Musifer child indoors and not alone."

"Good Lord, Hugo, what do you mean?"

His face was not an inch from hers. His eyes were wide open, bulging from black shadows. She would never forget his face as it was now: drawn by some hideous pain, ravaged and torn by conflict, distorted with his lips apart.

Then he stuck his hand in a pocket and pulled out the brooch they had bought that day. He squeezed it in her hand, so that the sharp edges hurt. "Oh . . . how sweet. Thanks, Hugo." Sharply she remembered the ballet dancer clip, which Robin had given her but which she had decided to let Etta keep.

"The child is perfectly safe, but tomorrow until you see me she should stay indoors."

"All right."

"Go now."

He fumbled to clutch her in his arms, and she touched his mouth with a quick kiss.

VII

Hugo watched the Embassy lights for a moment, enviously, and he thought he could see Leslie, or her shadow, climb the stair . . . He turned back toward the Park. So he had not had the courage. He was a coward. But tomorrow he would tell her, beyond doubt, beyond question. Tomorrow he would most certainly tell her all. *Bestimmt!*

To lie was the worst thing, Hugo thought. Remotely he remembered his youth in Fröbelstein, before the Nazis got him, before all moral values became distorted. It was very wicked to lie, Hugo thought. But he would confess all to Leslie at lunch tomorrow. And he thought that Leslie would understand and forgive him. He could visualize how he would surround her with his love . . .

When Dortmund first ordered that young Heath should be stopped somehow at the mines, he, Hugo, had protested; actually, he had dared to protest. And from that moment, Dortmund had distrusted him. But then came that terrible, twisted night when he met Gerald and Leslie at the hotel and Gerald had laughed at him and it seemed that Leslie was betraying him . . . that night he became insane . . . Such a simple matter to telephone Aschentoller at the mines, hint at new instructions, snap at him that *anything* they did to Heath would be all right . . . Hugo momentarily forgot his intention to be reborn.

Then that lie to Leslie over the 'phone. And then Dortmund's proposal to murder Leslie's friend, the little girl. It was not merely that this proposal had been too much; there was a point in every Nazi where he couldn't stand it any more, but this was not his only motive for giving himself up to Leslie now. By giving himself up he was somehow making up for that awful lie . . .

Tonight she had not even asked him about Gerald; perhaps she had already forgotten. *Should* he tell her tomorrow, Hugo began to wonder sharply. Maybe there was no point in telling her . . . now. Maybe it would only mix things up. *Should* he tell her, after all, Hugo wondered . . .

VIII

The floor show seemed alive again, now that Florian was back. All of Taksim's seemed alive again, with Florian back.

They sat, fourteen or fifteen, in the biggest private loge; the establishment was crowded, and it bounced with business-like excitement. Mr. Poppa was vastly happy at the honor of having His Excellency the Ambassador of the United States of America present with a large party, and he outdid himself with the olives, the lobster, the shashlik, the Kavaklidere wine. Leslie sat between an elderly French naval officer, and the American commercial attaché, a man named Macready. She found it very difficult to concentrate on their conversation. She was unable to get a word alone with Strangeways until the table broke up and people started to dance. She found his eye and then he moved next to her.

"André," Strangeways said, "another coffee. Hello, Leslie. Something going on tonight. Noticed? Place full of Turkish cops."

The Greek waiter brought the coffee and then fetched sugar from down the table. "I've got some news for you," Leslie said briefly. "Hugo is going to give."

"What? You don't say." His face turned rigid. "This is quite a thing."

She didn't notice that André was still standing there. He slid around the end of the table, bringing her a fresh spoon.

"You told me once you'd pay a lot for him," Leslie said. But she did not feel any elation or jubilance now. Her voice was sober, almost sad, and the red balloon of a mouth seemed deflated.

"You look miserable. Don't be worried. We'll give him complete immunity, of course."

"I think I want a drink."

"André, two cognacs, please."

They danced a moment and then walked into the small bar; while they talked they waved occasionally to the rest of the party, to keep in tune with it. In a low voice, quickly, she told him what had happened from the beginning.

"Well, I guessed most of it." He nodded as if to himself. "Very useful bit of work. My warm congratulations."

She felt tears grow in her eyes. "What happens next?"

"Well, we question him. Then I imagine send him somewhere safe. Don't worry. He'll be all right." He looked at her keenly. "I suppose you'd like to have some time with him?"

"No. Not necessarily."

"What are you so upset about, then?"

"I don't think you'd understand."

IX

Florian sang some ballads Leslie had heard a long time before in New York, and as her second number, in a black-and-red gypsy costume which made her look more beautiful than she had ever seen her, danced a cachucha. The Ambassador, who almost never went to night clubs, had never met her; when he found out that Leslie knew her, he suggested that they invite her over. By André, who seemed in a tense mood tonight, Leslie sent her a note. And after changing into street clothes Florian joined them. It made Leslie very proud that she was introducing her to the Spauldings, and Florian was duly flattered.

"How's that young man who was wounded at the mines? Is he getting along properly?" Yvonne asked Leslie.

"Yes. He's fine." Leslie glanced at her watch. It was just midnight.

Mr. Spaulding was having a splendid time buying Florian champagne and letting her make eyes at him. Then as she talked about Gerald to Yvonne Florian smiled at her.

Again, always, the irresistible obtrusion of the personal. Was it this way with people all their lives? Didn't anybody *ever* get over conflicts? Florian who had never been in love was now in love with Gerald. What ought *she* to do? Because she knew that she herself was close to being in love with him. Gerald, so acute and imaginative and sympathetic, so humane and wise.

Yet so far, close as they were, closer as they got every time they met, something blocked her. Was it jealousy of Florian? Was it that she could not but resent how recently Gerald and Florian had been together?

And Robin? What about Robin? What was she going to wire to Robin?

Someone new to Taksim's, an American said to be an important radio commentator who had just arrived in Istanbul, a tall man with a harried look and a stoop, kept watching Florian from the bar. He couldn't keep his eyes away; he started to flirt violently. He did not know anything about her but he could not keep from watching her.

"I go now," Florian said. "Good night, Leslie."

"Good night. Will you have tea with me later in the week?"

Florian nodded, and said good night to the Spauldings. The American saw that she was about to leave the table and would pass near where he stood; he moved away from the bar and started to intercept her and smile toward her, flirting.

Florian did not so much as bother to look at him. Walking past him she said No contemptuously with her hips.

CHAPTER XXIV

Several Endings

I

NOBODY ever found Hugo's body.

Perhaps the fish had it, the sleek, slowly wriggling fish near Prinkipo; perhaps it lay shriveled at the bottom of the Bosphorus, weighted; perhaps it was a lump of ash in the basement of the German Embassy, that looked built by Grimm; perhaps it was bent double in a mail sack addressed to the Gestapo in Sofia, Budapest, Munich, or Berlin.

"The poor son of a bitch," Gerald said.

It was Strangeways who explained, more or less, what happened.

"André did it," the Englishman snapped. "All André's job. He heard Leslie tell me Hugo was going to give. Well, was that Greek going to let Hugo Reichenau get away with giving? Not by a long shot! Let him live out the war in comfortable immunity in Kenya? Not on your life! What did André care about how valuable Hugo might have been? That Greek didn't think about things like that at all. So what did the little beggar do? Dash it, most extraordinary. He didn't call any of our people. He called old Dortmund! André, one of *our* men, quietly picks up the 'phone in Taksim's lobby, and tells the head of the Gestapo that his own Hugo's going to sell out! So of course Dortmund has him shot. They sent one of their little murderer-chaps after him at about 2 A.M. By God, you should have seen his room. They blew his head right off. Most of it stuck there against

279

the wall." Strangeways lit a cigarette. "Naughty of that Greek. Very naughty. We'll have to discipline him a bit."

Strangeways opened his wallet.

"Here's just a line from the diary Hugo kept on posting. Silly creature. 'May not see L. till after the war. Hope she won't . . .' Rest is indecipherable."

"The poor devil," Gerald repeated. "The poor dumb son of a bitch."

"Dumb?" Strangeways put his notes away. "It's the way the end will come everywhere. They'll all kill themselves off at the end. Internecine. May be bloodiest thing anybody ever saw. Like that business in 1934, only worse. You watch. They'll kill each other off. Try to kill Europe, too."

II

Oh, oh, Leslie cried stormingly to herself, oh, I can't bear it, I've killed a man. *Killed* a man! Indirectly. But the brutal fact was a fact. I've caused a man who loved me to get *killed*.

Nonsense. Exaggerated nonsense. That was what Gerald had said, trying to calm her. Gerald said, How do you know that it wasn't something else that made him decide to give? For all you know he may have been thinking of turning himself in for months. Strangeways always thought he would, and you know how smart Alec is. Maybe Hugo simply decided that the game was up and the war lost and all that. Besides, what about the way he talked about Etta Musifer? He never told you what he meant. But obviously he thought the child was in some kind of danger. Maybe something in that connection forced him to give himself up.

No, no, Leslie rocked her shoulders back and forth, eyes tight shut. She felt she could go out and kill herself. I'm so glad I called him Darling once. Oh, how she would like to have *seen* him once more, to tell him warmly, gratefully how glad she was, to let him hear her appreciate him, be fond of him. She had never even really kissed him. She had been so cold, so harsh. If only I had given him *some*thing. If only he had known a little of what I really *was*. No, no, she told Gerald, I wasn't in love with him. Not really. No, that's what makes it worse. If I had had any big or genuine emotion, then I would feel less guilty. But this way: it just seems death for life, a cold ugly death because I was playing with life without heart. I feel dirty. I feel cheap.

When Gerald tried again to reassure her, to calm her, he had said, But please be reasonable, be sensible, please. After all, Hugo was a dangerous and important enemy. After all, getting rid of him was, to be blunt, a kind of service.

Leslie looked at him. She felt that she could go out and bash her head against the stones. Have you ever killed a man?

III

Yvonne Spaulding sat by the chair where she was hunched, crying bitterly. They had been talking for what seemed hours and hours. She had told Yvonne everything. Yvonne was a rock, an anchor.

Then her face was altogether expressionless, altogether stony. She said to herself, coldly and accusingly, "Mostly I think I feel such a sense of guilt because I didn't love him. If only I had let him *have* something of me!"

Yvonne was coiled like a small blonde spring. She would let her talk. It was the best thing for her to talk. And Yvonne knew that full maturity came to character in strange ways. That was all that mattered, maturity and character.

"I thought I was quite a girl, quite a woman. I was quite a superior person, so I thought . . . Isn't it too awful? And now I'm nothing. I'm less than nothing . . . I don't know what values are." She twisted her head forward. "Why, when I arrived here, and Strangeways and Gerald talked to me at Taksim's, and I met all of you, and began to feel something of the atmosphere, why, I thought I'd be a *useful* person. I wanted to *do* something for the war; I wanted to contribute something. I was tired of being a kind of ornament. I thought it would be useful, and important, and a feather in my cap, and fun, yes, that's the really awful thing, I thought it would be *fun,* to keep my own council and play my own hand, and show all those experienced men what an American *girl* could do, just a girl who happened to be in town . . . I thought it would be daring, and adventurous, and fun! To catch a Nazi spy. Think! How unutterably awful! I feel that every prop beneath me has been splintered and broken, that everything is gone. I feel that I've lost all that counted. I've lost my own humanity . . ."

"You have completely neglected to take into account one aspect of this," Yvonne said.

"What, please?"

"Your own life in Germany."

"What do you mean?"

"You lost a child there. I don't mean anything so vulgar as that you were motivated by any subconscious thought of revenge. But I feel that perhaps you have come full circle, and that all the suffering you endured in Germany worked itself out while you were seeing Hugo, and now the agony is past."

Leslie blinked, and then stared at her.

IV

Gerald helped too.

"I don't quite understand about André," Leslie said dully the next afternoon.

"Well, let me explain. I know that Greek fairly well. In fact I picked him up for Strangeways, when I did a little job in the Dodecanese last autumn."

He went on: "André worked for Strangeways, but I don't think he liked him much. In fact, he probably hates him, hates him almost as much as he hated Hugo. Why? Well, to Strangeways and Dortmund all of this business here was a kind of a game between professionals. But to André it was not a game at all; it was life or death. To Strangeways and

Dortmund—poor Hugo was just a kind of pawn—everything here was a battle, yes. But to André it was not a battle; it was a *war*; and a war for keeps, with death the stakes. Don't you see?"

"Yes."

"Another thing." Gerald's voice was steady. "I suppose something else is indicated. Hugo wanted to change sides and forget. But that Greek waiter proves that nobody can be permitted to forget. Nothing that's happened in this war can be forgiven or forgotten. That's not my point of view necessarily; but it's certainly André's point of view; probably too the point of view of all the submerged peoples. Hugo thought he could get away with selling out. But André proves that the good and half-good will get punished with the bad. Hugo's had to pay for all the crimes of his kind, his generation. As all Germans will probably have to pay!"

He saw that she was still disturbed.

"There's another point," Gerald continued a shade tartly, but with good humor. "You might take into consideration the fact that Hugo was almost certainly implicated in shooting me!"

But he knew that if he ever won Leslie, having been shot was the luckiest thing that ever happened.

v

For the next day or two Leslie did not visit the hospital. She finished work one afternoon, and Urquardt saw how seriously clamped her lips were as she left the office. She took a crowded bus over the bridge into Stamboul, stayed a moment in the Blue Mosque, and wandered alone in the Seraglio gardens. She sat down on a stone bench near the water. Again the ineffable view fanned out before her; again she saw the silken glow of the Asia shore, and the water looking raked where the current shifted.

Should she go back to Robin?

The night she had received his telegram she fell asleep

hard but unnaturally, as if doped; then she awoke after an hour and couldn't sleep again till dawn. At breakfast Leslie decided to return to New York at once. Dear God—this man had been the burning core of her life for years. And now he wanted her. At last he made the gesture she had so long awaited. Now Robin had really said Yes in his close-woven heart. And she felt that she couldn't bear to live alone another moment. After a solid year without him, without anybody. All the dreadful *waste* . . . Grimly she pushed a fist under her jaw.

She'd dutifully give Urquardt her resignation, and Strangeways would get her a place on the British plane from Adana. Or she could take the Taurus; it might be fun to puff ruggedly over those mountains . . . Then two or three days at Shepheard's. They might keep her kicking around a while waiting for priority. But no. Had she forgotten what Robin was? Robin would stretch out a mighty hand from Washington; she'd be on an express plane in twenty minutes. Then that wonderful flight across Africa again. But this time she would be returning to his arms, not leaving him. The stockade at the airport in the jungle, where she'd seen a leopard, the midnight snacks at the emergency fields across the Sudan, and never a ladies' room; the efficient bustle, the casual sense of a new world being charted, at Accra and Ascension and Natal. Then home. And Robin would of course meet her at Miami. A divorce took six weeks. They could be married in July or August.

But what about Elsie? Well, that was just something painful they would both have to forget. Yet, her eyes filmed. She had even had moments of loving *her*, because she loved Robin too.

What about Gerald? What should she say to Gerald, and what would he say? How could she hurt him so?

This afternoon at Seraglio Point Leslie walked to the harbor and then moodily prodded around till dusk. It had all seemed clear and simple enough until Gerald half-rose from his bed and told her that he would not allow her to return.

Since then, since the evening at Taksim's that followed, she had been violently confused and uncertain. Frankly, she had become that most unattractive of creatures, a woman who could not make up her mind. Still, this was the supreme decision of her life; she couldn't be blamed if she took a day or two to think it out, to suck the truth out of her inmost soul. Would Gerald really love her always, forever, for keeps? Yes, she was sure of that. But what would the rest of her life be without Robin? Rather, what would it be like *with* him? Which of them did she *want*?

Strangely, a conversation between Gerald and Robin became projected in her mind:

ROBIN: Glad to meet you, Mr. Heath. Leslie's told me a lot about you.

GERALD: Glad to meet you, sir. (The "sir" would kill Robin. How he hated to be thought old. By working so hard he persuaded himself that he was still young.)

ROBIN (dogmatic, masterful, friendly): What's all this stuff you've been filling Leslie with? What's all this talk about how she'll need you in the future?

GERALD: The future interests me very much, Mr. Culpepper: her future and *the* future.

ROBIN (cheerfully): Me too. How do you see it, Mr. Heath?

GERALD: I think it's apt to be pretty grim. Collectivism almost everywhere. Discipline and rigid state controls. The end of free enterprise and the bourgeois world. I don't say that I'm going to like it; I'm just saying what it's going to be like. But it's my future and I'm going to have to live with it and I want to make as good terms with it as I can.

ROBIN (confident): Are you a socialist?

GERALD: Good Lord, no. I'm a musician.

ROBIN: The two aren't incompatible, are they?

GERALD: All Englishmen are socialists in part. I'm a kind of liberal. I believe in progress and change.

ROBIN: I'm a conservative. I believe in conserving things. (Amiably) But don't think I'm a reactionary. I understand all about your paternalism and all that! (So attractive) But tell me more about what your new world is going to be like.

GERALD: I could tell you better if I knew what things you wanted to conserve.

ROBIN (briskly): Standards, for one thing.

GERALD (amused—with perfect good humor): Does that include three dollar beefsteaks, yachts and circuses, monogrammed shirts, dancing at cocktail time, and luminous parties on soft lawns in Westchester?

ROBIN: Come now. (Irritated). You probably like those things as much as I do.

GERALD: I'm facing facts. I don't think the new world will give much chance to private manipulators gaining control of vast public agencies of production. After the war I think the great bulk of people everywhere are going to demand economic as well as political power and freedom. I don't think there'll be much room for wanton individualism.

ROBIN (as always bored by anything abstract): Let's be more personal. (Rather proprietary) You seem to know Leslie very well. And obviously she's quite fond of you. Why is she thinking of not coming back to me?

GERALD (with the unknowing cruelty of youth): She hasn't made up her mind yet. But if she doesn't go back I think it will be mostly because you're out of date.

Leslie impatiently looked for a taxi near the bridge, and lost her temper when the driver misunderstood her address. Back at the Musifers' she found messages that Gerald had called twice. She didn't call him back for the moment. She wanted to be sure, absolutely sure. But when she picked up the 'phone after dinner her voice was happy and composed.

VI

She had tea with Florian the next day at Florian's apartment. A dark room. Biedermeier furniture. The curtains draped heavily.

Florian now. Maybe she had been wrong about Florian. She had thought there must have been some great childhood hurt, some break, some twist in the limbs of her soul, when at the beginning she seemed so feckless, so inert. But probably she had just been born that way, magnificently sinless, generous, with no great reservoirs of emotional capability. You didn't have to grope for explanations always. People were the way they were. And let them be.

But Leslie felt acutely troubled as she walked in. By every criterion, she knew how much Florian liked her. And somehow, perhaps because of Hugo's death, she felt that, in a curious way, she must cleanse herself, purify herself, before Florian. Ought she not *do* something for this girl? Especially if she did return to Robin, after all? Should she not offer to give Gerald up? She remembered how she had once made a gesture of renouncement about Hugo. *Could* she do the same thing again? It was too childish. But—?

Florian settled it for her in two seconds, and Leslie felt that she had been slapped, but nicely, between the eyes.

"Leslie, I love you very much. Perhaps you have thought about me and Gerald. All that is past with me." She had that *gamine* grin. "I give him up to you!"

Seldom had one short passage of speech dispelled so much uncertainty, Leslie thought. She felt she wouldn't have any feeling of constraint toward Gerald any more.

They sipped a vermouth steadily and talked about when the war would be over and each avoided mentioning Hugo's name for a while and then Leslie leaned back and asked her what she was going to do if she left Taksim's.

Florian's fabulous topaz eyes were both confident and sulky.

"I will not stay here longer. But I do not want much to go back to Budapest. For Florian that would be such a retreat, *nicht wahr*? What I will do is go elsewhere. I have friends who can arrange. I think I proceed eastward. I go on to Teheran for a time. And then I think to Moscow. Who can tell? Moscow may be very nice!"

It may be the capital of Europe, Leslie thought. Had Florian ever met the blond Russian consul general? Was that Russian consul general arranging all of this?

Leslie prepared to go; she powdered her nose and saw a small photograph of Hugo on the boudoir table. "Poor Hugo," Florian said. Her eyes misted. And Leslie felt strongly that if he had not been killed, Hugo would have gone back to her, and that it would have been a proper ending.

But Moscow? Florian in Moscow! It was certainly an idea. Gerald had told her how as the Hungarian girls grew older, they got pushed and squeezed out of jobs, and always they went progressively to drabber and more miserable towns. They went Istanbul—Ismir—Beirut—Bagdad. Or Cairo—Khartoum—Port Sudan—Zanzibar. At each new stop, they became poorer, tawdrier. In the end they married, got sick, or became exhausted whores. My God; a whore in Basra! But Florian would never be a whore. Not with reasonable luck. Who could tell what might not happen. She might easily become a duchess. Or she might marry an Egyptian millionaire or an American G. I., or be the mistress of a Russian commissar.

VII

The next morning Urquardt smiled benevolently, and rapped on his desk with a pencil.

"What's up, Dave?"

"I've got to go to Beirut for about a week. Big confab there."

"Well . . . How will you manage about this office?"

"You're going to run it."

"Why—"

"I may be away longer. You're in charge."

She felt dumfounded with the responsibility, and very scared and pleased.

CHAPTER XXV

"My Country Is Not Yesterday"

I

GERALD was out in the hospital garden in a wheelchair, and Leslie sat near him. Strangeways came in to say good-by; he was leaving that evening on the Aegean mission.

"Heard the news?" he inquired cheerfully. "World's come to an end. The police have raided Taksim's, and Florian's got malaria." He sat down amiably. "Old Poppa's wailing and groaning at the Ministry of the Interior; you can hear him bleat as far as the Sublime Porte. Why'd the police crack down? Too many of us around, I daresay. Think it's a nest of trouble. Besides, all the good customers get shot. First Gerald, then Hugo. Ha! Such an angry tone, Gerald. All right, I'll shut up. Florian? Nothing serious; she'll be all right."

Strangeways looked terribly worn, Leslie thought. His behavior was clipped as always, but his eyes were taut and bloodshot; he seemed stretched to the uttermost. Perhaps Strangeways was going to get killed, Leslie thought. Perhaps he would not survive what he called his little expedition.

Oh, win the war, win it quick. Win it, end it, get this wretched war finished, done with!

"Something more important. Announcement'll be made to-night, formal announcement finally, about the chrome."

Gerald was far away; he was thinking of something else, something he wanted to say to Leslie. Then abruptly, as if a spear of lightning had penetrated and split some hovering clouds, he seized on what Strangeways had just told them.

Lightning. Like an explosion. In a second, all at once, a totally forgotten episode burst back into his mind. That T.N.T.—the T.N.T. the Germans had been bringing into the mines.

His warning memory came too late. Strangeways instantly got in touch with their men, but it was not soon enough. The Germans blew up the mines that afternoon; they blew them up with great efficiency and thoroughness, it became clear later. They made a fine minor holocaust.

Strangeways ground his fist into a palm. So eminently German! And so pointless. Because the Allies could get chrome from other places. Suicidal. Cut off nose to spite face. No, face gone; cut nose off anyway. *Götterdämmerung*! Then he remembered an incidental point, that the mines were owned by British capital. Blasted Nazis, Strangeways thought. Blast them!

II

A month later. Summer now. A calm and brilliant summer now. Fast scudding clouds in a high sky at night and hard-etched, hazeless days. The rhythms of the world outside beat sternly against Turkey now. That June morning they had all been praying for had come; the invasion of the Norman coast began and got splendidly under way; and at about the time Cherbourg was taken Turkey broke relations with the Axis.

The Spauldings held a discreetly imposing party at the Embassy to celebrate; even the President of the Republic came. Every Turk, every neutral, knew now on what side his bread was buttered. Mr. Spaulding and Puffin, the British Ambassador, talked together on the terrace; they had won a victory, but they did not gloat. Yvonne, marching pertly through the drawing room, drawing her guests together as with a net, looked happy that news of the invasion, liberating *her* country, continued to be so good.

Leslie thought of all the talks they had had; she and Mrs. Spaulding had become inseparably good friends.

Love of country. What did it amount to, anyway? What had love of country done for poor Hugo? What had it brought Strangeways, whom quite possibly they might never see again? The main thing to say, surely, was that love of country *was not enough*. It was all right so far as it went. But it didn't go far enough. A healthy nationalism was all right, provided it was peaceful; but nationalism *alone* was not enough. Love of country aggressively applied always, in the end, led to war, that is, to the mutilation and possible destruction of what you loved. And that was pretty silly, Leslie thought. The United States itself would be a better country, more worthy of being loved, when it was a force making for peace and security in the *world*, no matter at what cost to sovereignty. Love of country wasn't necessarily antipathetical to love of other countries. The thing to do was to make the whole *world* a community.

Yvonne snapped, blowing cigarette smoke swiftly through her nostrils, "Have you made up your mind, Leslie? Are you going to marry that young man?" For some reason she always called Gerald that young man. But she liked him. And Leslie didn't mind.

"I'm not sure."

"It could be a contribution. I approve of marriages across frontiers. Look at mine," she spoke proudly. "You'd have Anglo-American children and I can't imagine a more useful political achievement."

Leslie laughed.

III

With Mrs. Musifer she took a walk with Etta. The child swung between them on their extended hands.

"My shadow is longer than I am," Mrs. Musifer translated for Etta, as they crossed the street in the sun.

"Much longer," she repeated. "Will I ever be as long as my own shadow?"

Leslie had brought her a real doll, in exchange for the paper one.

"It's time for my dolly's supper," Etta said. "Dolly is *my* little girl."

IV

She got to the hospital quite late. They had had a wearying and difficult day at the office; she scarcely had time to pat her hair smooth. She said hello cheerfully, felt how good-looking he was, kissed his cheek, emptied an ashtray, and closed the Venetian blinds. But he could tell that she was under a certain strain. My God, so was he! How he wanted to get well again, how he wanted to be able to do something positive and concrete.

"Come here," Gerald said.

She sat on the edge of the bed. "Yes."

"I fall more madly in love with you every minute. And not with your mind, either."

His arm went around her, bending her strongly across his breast; then his hand went down her back, gently, closely, squeezing along her spine. She put one hand on his hair, and leaned her temple against his cheek, relaxing; then the other hand reached around under him, tight. For a moment he just held her back. Always when her back was held that way it was like a bursting sunset. Through her dress, he caressed the supple flesh along her backbone; through the bedclothes, she felt his health, his warmth. She was drowsy all in a minute; her eyes closed slowly . . .

Never in his life had Gerald known anything like her kiss. The warm lips, solid but very soft, for the first moment restful; he felt his own lips press and sink into them, restfully, as if they were soft red pillows; then they were warmer, and he could feel the moistness; then they were moving pillows, so soft, solid, and warm; her lips were parted now and they became very moist and naked, as if skinned; then their mouths were one.

She gave a strong gasp; quivering she shook free and hid her face against his throat; then she was tasting him, happy, tasting herself.

"So that's the way it is." She asked herself dreamily: "What did I mean by that?"

He didn't answer. He murmured, "I don't see why I don't ask you. Do you really love me?"

"Let's not talk." She wanted terribly to be able to touch his other leg, through the heavy cast.

He kissed her again. What did it matter that she was the most reticent woman who ever lived, if she could kiss like that?

v

He could walk now, with a crutch. They paused at the bench in the garden; she lit him a cigarette. She looked glorious, Gerald thought: the open, honest face; her hair down soft and fine; the coffee-colored eyes which were perhaps not quite so brilliant now; the lovely downless arms, the lovely healthy hands.

"You'll be able to smoke yourself pretty soon," he smiled. The Americans were on the road to Paris. "It won't be much longer now."

Calmly, securely, she remembered Paris. "I wired Robin again last night. I'm not going back to him."

The tremendousness of what she said made his face explode. Then he caught something in her eyes. "Are you going to marry *me*?" For weeks it seemed he had been asking her that every minute.

"I don't know . . . I can't promise yet."

"Why not, if you're through with Robin?" His smile was alert, but a shade uneasy.

She hesitated. "Gerald, darling, I'm not going back—but I'm still so tied up inside—you must know how I adore you —but can't we wait a while, just wait a little while, and see how things drift?"

"You've never been much of a drifter."

"A person ought to be awfully sure about a second marriage. They're so much more important than first marriages," Leslie said.

"Yes. But by and large they have a fair chance to be happier than first marriages, because people profit by their mistakes."

Her voice was threading a needle. "I've always heard it's the rarest thing on earth for anybody to learn from experience."

He laughed cheerfully. "Well, anyway, you're not going back. That's the main thing after all."

"Yes." But her voice was sad.

"How does Robin take it?"

"Why . . ." Leslie looked helpless. "He keeps cabling me all the time . . . Urging me to reconsider."

"Oh Lord," Gerald said impatiently.

Why had she decided not to go back? Because she didn't think he was indispensable any more. Because in a way she seriously doubted that they could really pick it up again. Because she would be thirty soon and she was tired of all the wear and tear.

Beyond this there was that other vague something. The world was never going to be the same again; and Robin, vital though he was, seemed to represent the past rather than the future. In a curious way he resembled Strangeways. And she wanted to expand with the times; *she* wanted to learn and grow. Of course, in this last year, Robin might have changed. And Strangeways, at the end, might find humanity among the Greeks, the fountain-head of humanity in Europe —if he came back alive.

In that dialogue Gerald might well have asked Robin why he had awakened too late to the reality of *her* problem, why he had offered marriage a year too late. She wondered why her intuition was seemingly so strong that Gerald would fit into the future better than Robin, why he would be a more knowledgeable and satisfactory companion. Perhaps because he, unlike Robin, had truly suffered; therefore he could never be insensitive to human problems, that is to *her*.

Her thoughts broke off.

All right.

But—oh, Robin, Robin! . . .

Always she would remember all the good things. She could never forget all those things that were still so very good. Robin had been part of her in a way no other person could ever become part of her. She thought of moments—now past—when she would have gone back to him on any terms: because he was herself. But from that point of view she wasn't really losing him. She would miss him terribly; there might be an intermittent nostalgia for years. A whole life was behind her. But—the past was the past. A whole life was before her too.

How would *he* get along? Her lips trembled.

Patiently, with pleasant persistence, Gerald was asking her to marry him again. To marry is to *give*, she thought. And in the last days of the war and the terrible peace to come and its dreadful responsibilities they could have the strength of each other. But just the same . . .

VI

Then there was another thing—her job. Urquardt had returned; the few weeks she had been in charge had been fascinating. An intent conviction told her that she must see this job through. It was not only that her work continued to absorb her. But there was a war going on and it seemed that she filled a small niche adequately and it was her duty not to quit. Besides, she didn't *want* to leave Istanbul. She was *part* of something here. And the community had become part of her.

VII

"It's certainly hell on a man to be on crutches during a courtship," Gerald was saying cheerfully. "Now if I could chase you around and maul you a little bit . . . By God!" But his voice was easy. "Won't I give you a run for your money when I have two legs again."

But it might be quite a long time before he had two legs,

they both knew. The bone specialist said now that an operation would almost certainly be necessary. She put her cheek against his face, the way he loved it so much to be.

"When I want a woman I want her to want me. It's a natural enough attitude, I suppose." They were walking slowly. "Of course I'm playing it all wrong. You're far too sure of me. I ought to make you wonder a little, disappoint you and stand you up. You'll get bored by my devotion."

"No. I don't think that would ever happen."

"Of course," he declared, "I'd never dream of marrying you, never dream of it, unless I was sure you really loved me, unless I was sure I had your *whole* heart."

She felt a little flash. Then her smile was both warm and troubled. "That's just the point. That's why I think we ought to wait a little. It would be so frightfully unfair unless my heart *is* whole."

He looked restless. "Well, anyway, there's no hurry, until I can walk again."

"It takes time to get over things. Let's go in now," she said quietly.

"All right, sweet."

She helped him through the door; they ordered tea and smiled at one another. "I want to live with this woman every minute of my life," Gerald thought. But he steeled himself to an inner feeling that it might not turn out that way.

VIII

Leslie got home at about six, three days later. She reached to open the outside door, and then heard a loud "Hi!" She turned; a medium-tall man, squarely built, whose shoulders arched forward sharply, whose brisk walk seemed to say that he was always in a hurry—a man whom anybody would have known to be an American a hundred yards away—waved vigorously from the corner, called "Hi!" again, and started to run toward her, his hat high in his hand.

Something very large stuck in her throat; she crumpled

backward against the door, her knees broken and sagging. She felt transfixed; she thought she might choke. Then an enormous sunbeam burst through her heart.

"Robin! Oh, it can't be! It can't possibly be! Robin, *darling* . . . !"

It was as if they had not been apart for longer than a day. "You never thought I'd accept your No, did you?"

"Oh, darling . . ."

Then there was acute solicitude and worry on his face. "You live here? Let's go up."

In her room with the day bed she was sobbing violently and touching his cheek with her hands, clutching him and covering his mouth with quick, small, hungry kisses.

As always he read her mind instantly. He answered everything that she had thought about him for a year by saying, "*I grow too!*"

She felt telling him quickly about all that had happened that none of it had really happened; all of it now achieved reality for the first time because she was communicating it to *him*. Her voice held a ravishing tenderness. She murmured, "You'll have to help me get out of things . . . explain some things . . ." But with the terrible ruthlessness of one who really loves, she would feel little compunction. Everything was utterly obliterated. Nothing could touch her, armored with Robin's love.

"Oh, *darling!*" she sobbed again.

"It's been hell for me too," Robin said.

"I've learned such a tremendous lot," Leslie said.

"So have I!"

To fall in love, to be violently attracted to someone, to have a crush, that was easy, that was easy as could be, and it happened fairly often; but to love, really to *love*, that was a quite different matter; to *love*, that was very rare, splendid and difficult and rare; it didn't happen often in a person's life, and oh, it was wonderful, so importantly wonderful, when you had it.

Gerald? She had a strong sense that he would get over

the heartbreak, he would forgive her and understand. He was the nicest man she had ever met in her life; and he would understand. And even if he had lost her, he had gained himself.

Her job? Well, there would be a job back home, too.

"We must be very sober now," Leslie said.

The way he could hold her as no other human being could ever hold her; the way they matched, the way they fit . . .

"We'll be all right, honey," Robin said.

All the dubieties, the confusions, the hesitancies, were wiped out. And she felt that they *could* have a good life together, her whole life long. Because life itself always helped, if you made the right choice.

But what was beyond them—what shadows, what obstacles, what manner of unpredictable encounter in the world ripped asunder and soon to be built anew—that they could not be sure of, that they could only grope for in the twisting harmony of hope, that they could not know.

Set in Linotype Old Style No. 1
Format by A. W. Rushmore
Manufactured by The Haddon Craftsmen
Published by HARPER & BROTHERS
New York and London